# Scottish

# Werebear

## COMPLETE COLLECTION

◆

### LORELEI MOONE

# eXplicitTales

# CONTENTS

———•———

# Scottish Werebear

## AN UNEXPECTED AFFAIR

# CHAPTER ONE

———◆———

Throughout her flight into Inverness, Scotland, Clarice found herself repeatedly going over the printout she'd taken of her destination: Moss Cottage on the Isle of Skye. It promised unspoiled vistas, a homely atmosphere and most importantly of all: a quiet getaway from the hustle and bustle of modern life.

That's what she needed most: to get away. Away from the distractions of life in London, away from the constant buzz of her phone, notifying her of incoming emails or tweets. Away from all reminders of the life she used to share with Alan before she caught him cheating on her.

Upon her arrival at the cottage, she would send a message to Lily, her best friend, who had also been the one to suggest the Isle of Skye as a destination to begin with, and that was it. Clarice had promised herself to switch everything off. From nine to five daily, she would be *unplugged*, allowing her to focus on the task at hand.

After stealing a glance out the window - they were still descending through thick cloud cover - she flipped the page over, reading the backside again. *Local attractions include wildlife walks, beach walks, hill trails.* Walks, basically, all you could do on the Isle of Skye according to this text was go for a quiet walk.

*It is going to have electricity, though, won't it?* Clarice read the other side again and studied the accompanying pictures. There was a table lamp in one of the shots, which suggested that electricity was indeed going to be supplied... As long as her laptop had power, everything was going to be all right.

As the small plane landed bumpily on the runway, she felt a surge of excitement as well as nerves build within her chest. Soon, a mere three-hour drive away, she was going to arrive at her destination.

"Please remain seated until the fasten seatbelt sign is switched off," said the captain's almost robotic voice over the intercom.

Clarice smiled to herself. *No way that's going to happen.* Half these people would be up, carry-on luggage and phone in hand, before the plane came to a halt.

She leaned over to get a better look out the window. The views throughout most of the flight had been obstructed by a thick layer of clouds, far below the altitude of the plane. Now, the outside world looked as one would expect Scotland to look in early autumn: grey and damp.

*How does it matter, it's not like I'll leave the house, much.* Clarice took a deep breath, holding it in an attempt to calm her nerves. She had never done anything like this. Leave it all behind for a few weeks of solitude.

But this time, it was necessary. Early attempts to figure out if there was any flexibility in the deadline for her latest book had only resulted in her editor breathing down her neck harder. Apparently anything short of a deadly illness wasn't cause enough to postpone a release. A messy breakup and resulting existential crisis didn't count. That was why Clarice had been forced to resort to drastic measures to finish the manuscript on time.

Finally, the fasten seatbelt signs switched off with the customary ding, and soon after, the doors of the plane opened. Clarice smiled a final goodbye to the quiet old man seated next to her. The flight was relatively short, as far as flights go, but she was still surprised that he hadn't said a word throughout. He nodded, then joined the throng of impatient passengers heading for the door.

It was a small airport, meaning you didn't get one of those fancy walkways leading from the plane straight to the door. Instead, all the passengers were let off via a mobile staircase, and then they walked along demarcated pathways painted on the concrete taxiway, towards the modest looking terminal building to collect their bags.

The bags arrived in a similarly low-tech manner: on trolleys in plain view of the waiting passengers. Clarice found her suitcase and started walking, aimlessly at first, until she spied the car rental sign.

Alan used to take care of all of these things during their holidays together, but now it was all up to her. *How hard can it be?*

As it turned out, picking up a pre-booked rental car wasn't very difficult at all. However, Clarice was still battling residual nerves by the time she made it into the driver's seat and started leafing through the various printouts of the route to the Isle of Skye. It looked easy enough, there weren't very many roads to choose from. The maps on Clarice's phone concurred.

A deep breath later, she turned the key. So far so good, now it was time for the home stretch.

———◆———

As pretty as the drive towards the Isle of Skye was, it did nothing to prepare her for the beauty ahead. Stark black cliffs stood out against the dramatic clouds overhead. There wasn't much vegetation, just grasses and mosses with the occasional small grouping of trees that had managed to battle the elements for survival.

Though the road snaked through the landscape up ahead, Clarice still felt like an explorer, discovering this mysterious land for the first time. At every bend, she instinctively slowed, both to cater for oncoming vehicles - which were few and far between - as well as to admire the views.

She passed through a few small towns on the way, but for the most part, the island seemed unspoiled and almost barren. The road narrowed more and more as she reluctantly drove on. Every map she'd printed out, even the satellite navigation on her phone confirmed she was on the right track, yet the road ahead looked too small to lead anywhere.

Finally, she made it to a small settlement that according to Google was a mere twenty minutes away from her destination. *Village* would be too big a word for the cluster of houses she found. Luckily one of the buildings housed a small daily needs shop. Clarice parked right outside, eager to stock up on some essentials so she wouldn't have to leave the cottage at least for the next couple of days.

"Hello?" she called out through the open door.

No answer.

She stuck her head inside, looking around the dimly lit interior of the store. It looked like somebody's living room, with a few racks of groceries, as well as firewood and some camping supplies stacked up inside.

"Excuse me?" she asked again.

Finally, an old man appeared through the door at the far end of the room.

"Ah, a customer!" He shot her a smile that seemed to wrinkle up every inch of his face all at once. "How can I help?"

"I just wanted to buy a few things," Clarice explained, smiling nervously while eyeing the shelf of cookies nearer the wall.

"Aye, of course. Please take a look around. If you're

after anything specific, we may need to order it in."

Clarice nodded and gathered up some packets of digestives. It was a bad habit, snacking while writing, especially when writing was your main job and you spend a lot of time doing it. With the deadline hanging over her head, she didn't know how else to cope.

She rounded off her selection with some bread, eggs, and other daily essentials, then made her way towards the counter where the old man was waiting. He didn't even have a till. Instead he listed up everything on a notepad and totaled it in his head.

"Where are you staying, if I may ask?" He handed her the torn off sheet of paper, with the total, £20.78 written in shaky pencil.

Clarice paused for a moment, wondering if it was wise to answer. *What the hell, this place is so small, he would probably find out anyway. You're not in London anymore!*

"Moss Cottage. That's just up the road I suppose?"

"Ah yes. The old McMillan farm. Lovely place, very quiet. Just-" He leaned forward, raising his hand gravely. "Take care of the bear."

"Thanks. Umm, wait, what bear?" Clarice asked.

"Up in the hills around the farm. Keep your eyes open if you go wandering out by yourself. Especially in the evenings."

Clarice scrutinized the old man's face, looking for any sign that he was just pulling her leg, but his expression remained completely serious.

"I wasn't aware that there were bears in Scotland?"

The old man let out a chuckle. "Well, according to the authorities, there aren't any, but we've all seen him. A big fella too, could tear you in half, he could." By the end of his sentence, again the old man's expression turned deadly serious.

"But enough of that, you seem like a sensible lass, you'll be careful. Enjoy your vacation." He smiled again, his weathered skin folding into a million little creases.

"Uhh, thanks."

"Bye now!"

Back at the car, Clarice tried to shake off her unease at the preceding conversation. *A bear. Here? That's ridiculous, right?* As far as she knew, bears had been extinct in Britain for pretty much forever. Unless it was some kind of zoo escapee.

*No, perhaps the old man had been enjoying his Scotch a bit too much. That must be it.*

# CHAPTER TWO

McMillan Farm had been in Derek's family for generations. He was born there, grew up there, and was likely going to die there if he had his way. Ever since his parents' passing many years ago, the farm had been mostly Derek's responsibility. Sure, he had an older brother, but Aidan preferred to travel the world rather than stay home and tend the land, and as such only came by a few times a year.

Derek's farm was the perfect place for a bear, actually, that's why his ancestors moved here two centuries ago, and why he was never tempted to leave like his brother. The vast countryside gave him plenty of space to roam. The rivulet carving its way through his property provided ample opportunity to fish when the season was right, and the best part was, there weren't many people around.

The only people that did turn up were paying guests: mostly middle-aged or older couples, or the occasional young family that was trying to teach their children about nature. Avoiding them when the urge to shift took over was quite easy. He'd never been caught, which was fortunate, because all bears lived by the code of secrecy.

The holiday cottages were set away from the main farmhouse by a safe distance, and visitors were mostly self-sufficient. All Derek did was make sure everything was in working condition and provide some basic supplies. Although it wasn't ideal, inviting strangers into his territory, it was his way of earning a little extra money from his land without much effort.

This month's visitor was probably going to be the

same. Clarice Adler from London.

The name had conjured up images of white permed hair and floral dresses in Derek's mind. A posh old lady, no doubt, who he imagined used to spend her younger days riding horses in the English countryside before moving to London. Her insistence in the comment box of the booking form that her stay should be as quiet and undisturbed as possible only supported his assumptions. This was going to be someone who had grown up in the country, who was now yearning to get back to a simpler life for two weeks.

When her grey rented hatchback slowly crawled through his main gate, he didn't need to sneak a peek to know what she'd look like. After fifteen years in the tourism business, his instincts were always right, so he kept on mowing the lawn as if he hadn't noticed the new arrival.

The car came to a halt a little way up the drive, and then it turned left, following the signs he had put up last winter, leading to the cottages. Derek had already prepared Moss Cottage for its latest guest. The bed was made, the pantry was stocked, and the key was in the front door.

Although he did often check in with visitors on the first day, just to see to it that they were comfortable, he preferred to play as small a role as possible in their visit. It wasn't that Derek disliked the tourists, he was just a very private person.

When he was done with the lawn in front of the house, he prepared himself for his regular evening routine: check on the bees as well as the other animals, take a round of the kitchen garden to harvest the last of the summer crops to add to his winter stash, perhaps say hello to the visitor before retreating to the farm house to prepare a nice cut of meat for dinner.

"Hello? Is anybody here?" a clear female voice called

out to Derek from outside the barn where he had just parked the lawn mower.

He wiped his hands clean on his overalls, then marched out to greet what he assumed must have been the old lady staying at Moss Cottage. Nothing could prepare him for what he saw waiting for him outside, though.

The shapely woman with brunette hair standing in front of him couldn't have been older than thirty at the most. Her amber eyes flitted back and forth skittishly between him and the surrounding trees as she waited for him to reach her.

It took a lot of focus for him to remember the usual niceties city folk expected.

"Derek McMillan. Nice to meet you," Derek said, sticking out his hand to greet his guest.

Though he tried not to stare, her feminine curves invited a closer look. Instead of acting rude, he tried to focus on her face. High cheek bones, full lips, almond-shaped, kind eyes. Perfection.

"Oh. Clarice. Just call me Clarice." She hesitated for a moment with her arms hanging down her sides but finally took his much larger hand anyway.

It was as if an electric current passed between the two when their fingers first touched, but she barely reacted - at least not favorably. In fact, she pulled her almost fragile little hand back almost possessively after the shortest of greetings. That proved it; the attraction was definitely not mutual.

"Is there anything I can help you with? Did you find the cottage to your liking?" Derek asked.

Her eyes met his for a split second, but then she looked away again. Her demeanor reminded him of prey, painfully aware of the danger it was in. And her scent was more enticing, lovelier than a summer meadow in full bloom.

There was something about her that he couldn't put his finger on. Something tempting that made the most primal part of his being want to own her.

"I..." she began, but then fell silent again.

In all his years running the cottages, he'd never found himself in an awkward position like this. Sure, he'd had as many female guests as male ones over the years, but never one who affected him so. Humans didn't hold much interest for him - not until right this moment - neither did most of his own kind for that matter. He had always been happily solitary: a bachelor by choice as well as circumstance.

Bears didn't live in large packs like wolves did, and they favored vast territories all to themselves. That was one of the reasons his kind was dwindling; they simply didn't get the opportunity to pair up often enough.

"Yes?" he asked.

His reaction to her was visceral, involuntary, and completely undesirable. The longer he stood in front of her, the more difficult was it for him to suppress his instincts and remain civil. All he wanted to do was pounce. Take her into his arms and make her his.

He didn't understand it, how a human could have this effect on him. Everything he felt, how the bear in him threatened to take over with every breath he took, made the hair on his forearms stand up. It felt like something he'd heard about a long time ago. But that kind of behavior was limited to bears and their mates. It didn't apply to human women, did it? Perhaps he had kept himself isolated for too long, and his instincts were rusty...

For once he wished Aidan was around. Since his brother was much more well-traveled, he might have had advice for Derek, but it was up to him alone to sort out this mess.

# SCOTTISH WEREBEAR: AN UNEXPECTED AFFAIR

The next couple of weeks were going to be difficult, if not impossible.

"I just wanted to say hello. And to thank your wife... for the cake you left on the dining table. A lovely gesture."

He was about to interject that he wasn't married, but restrained himself, his hand instinctively reaching for a non-existent itch on his chin instead. So what if she mistakenly assumed another female presence had baked that cake to welcome her? Even though it pained him to let her think that there was someone else in his life, at least it would provide him with excuses to keep even more of a distance than he usually did with visitors.

"You're welcome. Now I'd best get back to work."

"Of course. Don't let me keep you. Thanks again."

He nodded at her and almost fled back into the barn. In fifteen years, he'd never been wrong at sizing up his guests from names and booking information alone. Had he had any indication that she would affect him like this, he would have canceled the reservation in a heartbeat.

In one afternoon, everything he had previously known to be true about himself had changed. No longer was he the stoic, practical bear he thought he was. She had awoken something in him that he never knew existed. A dangerous urge he'd heard spoken of in stories his parents used to tell when he was only a cub.

He regretted not being able to ask them for an explanation either, for advice on how to handle the situation. But they died a long time ago, and Aidan was God knows where.

Either way, Clarice Adler was here to stay, at least for the next couple of weeks. Derek couldn't yet guess just how much of an effect Clarice's presence at McMillan Farm would have on his life going forward.

# CHAPTER THREE

———— ◆ ————

Clarice was still reeling with the after effects of her meeting with Derek as she wandered back up the gravel path towards her cottage. The short exchange with the bearded stranger had left her completely off kilter. He was a handsome man, in a raw, extremely masculine sort of way. Broad, no doubt strong after years of physical work on the farm. Big hands, bigger arms. His wife must be one lucky woman.

She chided herself for objectifying the man. If someone ever admitted to thinking about her that way, she'd be offended - not that anyone did think of her that way. And yet, her thoughts couldn't help but return to the gutter even as she locked herself inside the cottage, closing the curtains in an attempt to isolate herself. Yet that dirty part of her brain, which insisted on feeding her speculations of how Derek McMillan might be in the sack, refused to switch off completely.

It had been a while, sure. Even before kicking Alan to the curb just after Valentine's Day, they hadn't shared a bed for at least a month as things had cooled off between them. While she was quite sure that things were pretty much over before he stepped out on her, part of her had kept wondering if it was all her fault. Perhaps she should have tried harder to keep the magic alive?

*Stop it, that's the kind of thinking that makes a girl desperate.*

Desperation was indeed pretty close to how Clarice felt now. Giddy like a school girl coming face-to-face with an unrequited crush. Her heart was still racing when she remembered the one thing she had gone to ask Derek about: cell phone reception. *Damn.*

The slightly stand-offish manner in which he'd interacted with her, plus her confused desires discouraged Clarice from going back and talking to Derek again. Plus, knowing her luck, she would probably find herself tongue-tied and swooning over the man, with a jealous wife looking on from inside the farmhouse. That sort of thing was bound to make her two-week stay even more awkward. *No thanks.*

Clarice decided to make herself a cup of tea and enjoy a slice of the still warm, slightly sticky lemon and honey cake along with it. Once revitalized, and slightly more in control of herself and her impulses, she decided to go out for a walk. Perhaps if she backtracked the way to the village on foot, she could find a spot where her phone worked long enough to make a quick call to Lily.

The lack of network around the cottage wasn't such a bad thing. A blessing in disguise, Clarice thought, as she turned onto the main road outside the gate. There was no way she would be tempted to check her phone during working hours if she didn't have any signal in the first place.

Still, until she could get in touch with Lily to let her know she'd arrived safely, it was a bit of a nuisance. The village wasn't far, at least it hadn't seemed far in the car. But now that she was walking on the narrow road, through the little wooded patch outside the farm boundary, she felt as though she was completely cut off.

Unlike where she lived in London, here, a car was an absolute must, she could see that now. But she was determined to soldier on a bit further down the road to see if she couldn't find a connection at least for a short while. Even if it was just one bar on her phone, that would be enough to send a quick text message, right?

In her eagerness to get word out, she started typing it already while walking, not paying much attention to the road surface underfoot, or the views around her.

*Dear Lily, I'm here but have crap network so am doing this real quick by text. Don't worry about me. The place is lovely, and I'll get loads done here. Love, C.*

Send.

Clarice kept staring at the screen as the phone attempted to send the message without any signal. She continued along the winding road for another five minutes, almost stumbling into a pothole on the way. Then the tree cover opened up. The view stretched out ahead of her, revealing grasslands and even a bit of dramatic coastline in the distance.

Her phone also seemed able to 'see' much better from here, despite the thick gray clouds overhead, and the message finally went through.

*What a relief.*

Clarice put the phone in her handbag and looked around properly now. It really was a beautiful place, this island. The fact that there was not a soul around was eerie and enchanting in equal measures. As she kept standing there in the same spot for another few minutes, a chill seemed to pass over the landscape, signaling the arrival of dusk. It wasn't very late yet, but the clouds made it seem much darker than it should have been, and the wind had picked up slightly as well.

Time to head back.

Clarice turned, when from the corner of her eye she thought she could see movement in the trees. She didn't manage to see it properly, but it looked big. Much bigger than a person. Startled, she clutched her handbag tightly to her chest and just tried to remain calm. *Deep breaths. It's probably nothing.*

But her instincts, however frazzled, insisted that it *was* something. She could practically hear the old man from the village store warn her about that bear all over again. What if he was right? What if on her first evening here, she came face to face with a fierce beast that would eat her alive? With her car parked outside the cottage, Derek or his wife would just assume she was still inside. There was no telling when - *if* - her body would be found!

She stood deadly still for another minute or so, scanning the trees around the road she'd just come from. Although they were only medium sized trees, and not very densely planted, the gaps between them were quite dark already. As if night had fallen early. All around her seemed quiet, though. Her frantic heartbeat slowed slightly.

Perhaps she had just imagined it. She took another deep breath and tried to banish all remaining thoughts of bears and danger from her mind. She had to get back before it got really dark.

Step by step, reluctantly at first, she walked back into the woods, careful to avoid fallen twigs and other debris on the road that would make noise if she stepped on them. As she grew more confident that she was alone, she sped up, eager to return to the safety of the farm. She had just imagined it. There was nothing in these woods! She was just being ridiculous. The over-active imagination that made her a good writer could be a curse at times like these.

The road wound left to right and back again, never revealing more of what lay ahead of the next turn. She didn't recognize it really, but then how could she? Things looked different in this light, and she hadn't paid much attention while walking earlier, because she was trying to type out that message to Lily.

She continued on for five, six minutes, growing more and more worried that perhaps she'd gotten lost somehow. Finally, she spied a sign up ahead. McMillan Farm. *Thank God.*

As she passed through the gates that lay just beyond the next bend, she turned back one last time. Through the dark passage among the trees, a distant roar sent shivers down her spine. It made way for more silence so soon after that she doubted she'd actually heard it. Her mind was playing tricks on her.

She rushed up the drive, over to the left, along the bumpy gravel track leading to her cottage, almost running by the time she got near it. Then she turned the key in a rush, opened the creaky door and slammed it shut behind her, dead bolting it for extra security.

The thing with Alan had driven her a bit nuts; she already knew that. And this being her first solo trip in a very long time, possibly forever, had also affected her. But this was crazy, hardly enough cause to start hallucinating!

Back inside the cozy cottage, the entire experience seemed almost comical to her. She let out a nervous chuckle as she put her handbag down on the side table and unbuttoned her coat. Maybe it had been just the stress.

She double-checked all the curtains and switched on every lamp she could find. It wasn't very cold yet, or she would have been tempted to light the fireplace as well.

*Now what?* Perhaps she should have not been such a coward and actually waited at the edge of the woods to call Lily up properly. It would have been nice to tell her about the lengthy drive across the Scottish Highlands, and of course about Derek. None of that was an option anymore now, not until she headed out towards the village again.

There was no TV in the cottage, just an old HiFi system, the type with an LP player on top. The bookcase that stood beside contained a selection of old records. Clarice read the spines of a random few and selected the first thing she recognized: The Beatles, and placed it on top of the deck with trembling fingers. As the first guitar chords started to play, she felt herself relax.

Too bad she hadn't picked up a bottle of wine from that little shop. Perhaps she would drive back there in the morning...

Exhausted after her eventful first day in Scotland, she settled into the large armchair facing the empty fireplace and closed her eyes. The music did its best to soothe her. She wasn't hungry after eating the cake earlier, and neither did she have the will or energy to get up and prepare dinner.

Tomorrow was going to be another day, and she had to be ready to make the most of it. Four-thousand words at least, if not more. This was a sprint as well as a marathon; that's why she was here. She had two weeks to finish her book, or her publisher would drop her, and she couldn't afford for that to happen.

She didn't have time for crazy shadows in the woods, or stories of bear sightings in places where bears shouldn't even exist.

It didn't take long for sleep to overwhelm her, as she sat in that comfortable chair. Even after the LP had stopped playing, and the music had made way for complete silence, she still didn't stir.

That's where she stayed until the morning.

# CHAPTER FOUR

———— ◆ ————

That had been a very close call, Derek thought to himself. He couldn't shake the emotional confusion he'd felt after coming face-to-face with Clarice for the first time, so after finishing up in the barn, he'd decided to go for a quick walk.

He had to release tension, to blow off steam. There was no better way to do that than to shift and let his animal side take over for a while. In order to ensure her safety, he made sure that he was well away from the farm before taking off his clothes and hiding them in some fallen leaves in among the trees. Then he closed his eyes and focused.

It didn't take much. Shape-shifting was easier when you were already riled up about something. He felt a tickle pass over his spine, which then traveled down his arms and legs. He watched as his formerly relatively smooth limbs sprouted thick brown fur.

Shifting always started from the core outward. His torso would change first, and then a split second later his head, arms and legs would follow until he had transformed completely into a brown bear.

Derek planned to go for a bit of an outing, head towards his favorite stream for an evening snack of raw fish perhaps. What he wanted the most was to get away from the farm for a while, so that there was no risk of picking up Clarice's tempting scent, which he knew would whip his hormones into even more of a frenzy.

Only, things didn't turn out quite how he had planned.

Once he had shifted and started running towards the

stream that lay about halfway between the farmhouse and the nearby village, he couldn't clear his mind of all the thoughts and urges Clarice had stirred up. In bear form, he was even more susceptible to the attraction he'd felt toward her.

The sights and smells of the woods did nothing to distract him. He could even still pick up her perfume, despite being almost a mile away from the farm.

Once at the stream, all he could do was listlessly watch the fish as they struggled to jump up the fast currents. He didn't feel like reaching out and catching one. He didn't even want to cool his paws in the icy waters as he normally would have.

None of it held much interest for him. Instead, Clarice's scent kept making its way into his nostrils, beckoning him to turn around and seek her out.

He left the stream and didn't walk as much as drag his paws on the way back to the farm. His entire being was spurring him on to run to her, but he did his best to resist. He thoughtlessly wandered on, carving a path through the empty landscape that ran parallel to the road.

For the first time in all the years he'd spent on his own, he wished for someone to talk to. He had to figure out why he was so affected by a human, of all things. He'd read of bears who had gotten so used to their animal form that they'd sought out the company of actual bears over their own kind, but never did he hear of anyone mating outside their species.

To take a human mate was wrong, wasn't it? How would it even work, when the bears' code of secrecy insisted that humans should never find out about their existence? If she found out the truth about him, it would endanger his entire kind. Humans were afraid of what they didn't understand. If he tried to pursue her without telling her the truth, that would be equally wrong.

And yet, he couldn't help how he felt about her.

His brooding thoughts were interrupted by a fresh waft of her scent accompanied by footsteps against gravel. *Clarice.*

Across his entire body, his fur stood up to attention, as if he was readying for a fight. He paused and got up on his hind legs, standing as still as he possibly could while observing her.

*What was she doing here?*

He watched as she walked along the road, clumsily stumbling over a particularly rough patch of gravel, until she recovered herself, phone in hand.

When she reached the edge of the woods, she paused and looked around, raising her phone into the air and waving it around ahead of her. Finally, she let out a triumphant 'Aha!' and smiled, placing the phone back into her purse.

Derek didn't have a cell phone, only a land line, which nobody ever called except telemarketers and tourists hoping to book a vacation. Still, he'd heard visitors say that most mobile providers didn't cover his farm. Most tourists didn't mind, but it seemed Clarice had had a pressing need to contact someone. A boyfriend perhaps?

The thought angered him.

His jaw tensed, and his upper lip curled instinctively into a snarl.

He decided to turn around and leave before he was spotted, though just as he got down on all fours again, Clarice turned as well and let out a fearful gasp. He hadn't been able to pick up on her physiology before, she was too far away, but now that she was startled, her bodily responses were loud enough for his sensitive hearing to pick up. Her heartbeat had sped up into a frantic pace.

# SCOTTISH WEREBEAR: AN UNEXPECTED AFFAIR

*Shit. She had spotted him.*

Both froze, Clarice with her arms wrapped around herself, and Derek partially hidden behind one of the thicker trees in this part of the woods. Seconds passed as she continued to look in his direction, and then her breaths as well as her heartbeat relaxed, and she started to walk back to where she had come from before: the farm.

He breathed a sigh of relief as well, then made his way deeper into the woods, taking care to only walk on those extra mossy patches on the ground so that he didn't make any noise. Once again, a very close call.

That was it. He had to resort to desperate measures if he was going to remain sane throughout her stay. He left her to walk back to her cottage on her own and ran.

As fast as his paws could carry him, he pushed on until he had made it to the edge of his territory. There he let out an almighty roar, calling out for whoever was listening. Bears were territorial, so his call was bound to be noticed.

———◆———

"Derek," a calm, if slightly cold female voice called out to him, almost an hour after he had reached the no-man's-land that lay between his and his closest neighbors' lands. Elise - his older cousin from his mother's side - had come to answer his call.

He nodded and waited patiently as the female approached. The light brown bear that emerged from the shrubbery surrounding his meeting place of choice eyed him suspiciously.

"What brings you here?" Elise asked.

"This is going to be awkward, but I was hoping for some insights." Derek straightened himself in an attempt to appear rather more confident than he felt. It was a massive hit to his pride, coming here for advice, but even though they hadn't been close ever since he'd taken over the farm, Elise was still family. He didn't know who else to turn to. "As you know, other bears are hard to find nowadays. I was wondering if you could share some information, for old times' sake."

"What about?" Elise asked.

"Uhh... it's rather delicate."

"Just spit it out, Derek."

"When you and Jack got together, it was fate, wasn't it?"

The female bear cocked her head to the side and simply stared at him.

"Was it?" Derek pushed again.

"I wouldn't say *fate,* but I knew immediately what was going on."

"I don't understand, the way Mum used to talk about what happened between Dad and her, she said it was their destiny to pair up."

"Your mother always was the romantic sort. No, I'm convinced it's biology, pure and simple. We pick our mates according to who is most compatible biologically. It's nature at work; that's all."

"But it only happens once in a lifetime?" Derek asked.

"Again, it's in our best interests to mate for life, to ensure the survival of our cubs. Once we pair up, our brains release certain hormones to ensure we remain faithful to that one significant other."

"Right." Derek paused for a moment, uncertain about how to ask the most pressing question on his mind. "So it's all to do with producing healthy offspring, correct? Which means this sort of thing could only happen with another bear..."

"What are you suggesting? You've developed a crush

on a wolf or something?" Elise curled her lips, revealing a row of perfectly white sharp teeth in something somewhere between a smile and a sneer. The rivalry between wolves and bears ran deep, so it wasn't surprising for her to tease him like that.

"Not exactly."

Elise observed him in silence, which made him even more uneasy.

"Have you ever heard of a bear choosing a human mate?" he asked at last. As awkward as the situation was, he really did need to know. And there wasn't another bear to ask for many miles.

"A human..." Elise sat down in the damp heather, seemingly lost in thought. "Apparently in the cities, inter-species dating is a lot more common than it used to be. The challenges are many, though. It only works for those who have chosen to live fully in the human world and lost their bear side. However, now I'm reminded of another story from a long time ago - it's more of a myth than anything else. Did your mother ever tell you of Bhaltair and Aileen?"

She looked up, her eyes locking with Derek's, and her expression once again grave and serious after the werewolf remark, which had been partially in jest.

He slowly shook his head, the names did seem familiar, but he did not recall the story at all.

"In the olden days," Elise began, "back when we lived openly among humans, once every few generations, a bear would discover his true mate in a human. My speculation is, it's to do with revitalizing the bloodline. As the story goes, Bhaltair was the leader of his clan, a bachelor well into adulthood, who despite being surrounded by women of his kind never bonded with any of them. One day upon visiting a nearby village, he came across a human girl,

Aileen, and it was as if lightning struck. His inner bear knew, he knew, he had to take her as his mate. Of course, Bhaltair, being a clan leader and accustomed to being in charge wasn't subtle about the matter, and some say that there had been hostilities between his clan and the humans already. It was more of an abduction than a love story in the end..."

"Oh?" Derek could barely hide his shock at hearing Elise describe pretty much what he'd felt when he first saw Clarice. *Lightning.*

"When Aileen's father, Lord Domnall, found out where she'd been taken, he collected as many men as he could, calling them in from the surrounding villages. It inspired one of the greatest genocides in our history. You will have heard of the *Sons of Domnall...* It is said they evolved from that very first group of soldiers, who vowed to hunt us to extinction."

"And that's why we keep our existence a secret," Derek remarked, finally remembering bits and pieces of a similar story his mother had told him a very long time ago.

"Perhaps. Or perhaps it's just a bedtime story we tell our cubs. A morality tale aimed to illustrate why the code of secrecy is so important. Any particular reason you're coming to me with all this?" Elise asked.

"I was just curious, didn't know who else to ask... As you know, Aidan's turned into quite the globetrotter, so you're the only family around." Derek brushed away her question.

"I see. Well then, glad to be of help."

Derek nodded at Elise, who understood that this signaled the end of their little chat. She turned back one last time, no doubt wondering what he had gotten himself into, then ran off North, where undoubtedly Jack would be waiting for her at home.

# SCOTTISH WEREBEAR: AN UNEXPECTED AFFAIR

It wasn't what he had wanted to hear, especially her mention of the *Sons of Domnall* was very worrying, but at least he now knew his situation wasn't unique.

Although his mother had been a firm believer in following your destiny - especially when it came to mates - Derek was a lot more practical. He wasn't about to leave his reality in favor of a human existence. His inner bear wouldn't allow it anyway, it practically tried to claw its way to the surface every time he got near Clarice. No, he refused to jump head first to his doom.

Elise's story suggested that Aileen hadn't felt the same connection with Bhaltair. Humans must be incapable of sensing these things as bears do. Chances were, his own lightning strike with Clarice was equally one-sided.

Then there was the code of secrecy to consider. It existed for a reason, and not just to hide from the mythical bear assassin squad, the *Sons of Domnall*. Those guys were probably a figment of bear imagination, but that didn't detract from the fact that people were scared of what they didn't understand, and scared people were dangerous. Even if Clarice did feel an attraction for him, he couldn't trust her with the secret of his species.

He was going to fight this thing tooth and nail. It was only two weeks, for God's sake. Surely he could resist his urges long enough to watch Clarice drive off in that rented hatchback of hers, never to return...

# CHAPTER FIVE

———◆———

Indeed, the next morning brought a brand new day for Clarice. She was up bright and early by seven, made herself a hearty breakfast and settled down on the comfortable armchair by the fireplace with her laptop. It wasn't ideal, writing in an armchair, but she couldn't resist its inviting plushness and the feel of its velvety material against her skin.

Before everything went south with Alan, Clarice had already prepared an outline for her latest novel and written the first three chapters. Everything from the fourth chapter on though was as good as useless. The moment she'd caught Alan red-handed, she couldn't get into the mood to write the sweet historical romance she had set out to write, and instead found that her characters grew minds of their own.

Chapter after chapter consisted of the hero and heroine arguing, their antics escalating drastically with each sentence. By the end, she was in a good mood to kill off both of them.

*That's not a romance,* Clarice said to herself while re-reading it all. She might as well have missed her deadline entirely if she was going to submit something this inappropriate.

With a few clicks on her touchpad, she got rid of all of the offending words and was once again faced with a blank page at chapter four.

*Think happy, romantic thoughts.*

Instead of the blond well-polished and svelte hero of her outline, she kept thinking back to Derek's imposing physique. The face of her romantic fantasies wasn't clean-shaven as she originally imagined but featured a scruffy, extremely masculine beard and brown hair.

*Screw it.*

Clarice picked up her notebook, the one she was accustomed to recording early thoughts and book ideas in, flipped it open and started to brainstorm. After writing frantically for the better part of an hour, she had a new character profile and plot outline ready.

Her heroine, Lady Adlington wasn't going to fall head over heels in love with the Duke of Harringate as initially imagined. No, she would have an illicit affair with the brusque stable hand in the Duke's employ. When the relationship inevitably came to light, it created a huge scandal. It caused the two lovers to go on the run, to find a place where they could live their lives undisturbed, away from the strict class divide of Victorian England that sought to end their romance. Perfect.

She put the notes down and picked up the laptop again, going through the first three chapters to make the necessary changes. Most of it still fit. After adding in the odd hint here and there, as well as a scene when Lady Adlington first laid eyes on the handsome man of her dreams, Clarice's fingers seemed to fly over the keys at an incredible speed.

This place had worked out amazingly well for Clarice. Gone was the anguish over her failed relationship that had stood in her way back home. No longer did everything feel hopeless, because in her heart Clarice had felt all love was doomed to fail.

She had found her inspiration again. Her muse came in the unlikely form of a married farmer with rough, strong hands and broad shoulders. A man who probably had never opened up a romance novel or thought much about emotions in general. A man so unavailable, Clarice couldn't help but be attracted to him like a moth to a flame.

———— ♦ ————

It was already dark by the time Clarice put down the laptop. She'd forgotten to eat or drink anything. She'd even failed to get up and stretch at regular intervals, and as such her day of laser focused writing had taken a toll on her.

After a cup of tea, she felt some of her senses return to her, but her body was still tied up in knots. A walk, that's what she needed.

She stretched her arms, her legs, even tried to untangle her spine, and picked up her coat to head outside. As she opened the front door, she noticed a parcel wrapped in newspaper waiting for her on top of the welcome mat outside.

After picking it up, she weighed it in her hands. It was heavy, despite its rather small size.

Back indoors, she placed it on the small round dining table and started unwrapping the various layers of paper. Inside she found a plain piece of paper with a note, resting on top of what looked like a big fish fillet covered in cling film.

*Freshly caught this morning. Don't leave it too long.*

The note wasn't signed, but it was obvious that it had come from the farmer and his wife. Probably more from his wife, Derek himself didn't seem like the sort of guy who went around randomly gifting people food. Still, the gesture made her smile, and immediately her stomach rumbled to remind her that indeed, she hadn't eaten all day.

# SCOTTISH WEREBEAR: AN UNEXPECTED AFFAIR

If only she knew how to cook, or at least had a connection on her phone which would allow her to consult Google for instructions.

Flipping the note over, she saw that there was yet more writing on the back. A recipe. *How thoughtful.*

After leaving the parcel in the modest fridge underneath the counter, she once again stepped out of the cottage for a short wander around the farm. No way was she going to risk her sanity as well as safety by leaving the property in the dark. She had thoroughly learned her lesson the previous evening.

She wandered down the gravel track towards the driveway leading up to the main house and for the first time since arriving on McMillan Farm, she allowed herself a good look at the building. It looked old, at least 100 years, if not more. The pitched roof suggested the farmhouse was very spacious inside, which seemed unusual for a utilitarian building of that age.

The barns surrounding the house stood in a grouping of three, around a main courtyard facing towards the other side of the driveway. There was a stable set further back, but no sign of any animals, perhaps they were still out grazing.

She walked along the side of the house, taking care that nobody was watching her. Although she didn't want to seem sneaky, she really didn't want to be forced into any polite conversations with anyone, least of all Derek, the sexy farmer.

The net curtains on towards the left of the building barely concealed the dim lighting inside. Perhaps they were just sitting down for dinner, the man and his wife.

Clarice walked on along the path through the partially wilted summer flowerbeds planted along the main wall either side of the large front door. Once she'd reached the corner, she noticed that this side of the house featured a well-manicured kitchen garden, with vines climbing neatly erected poles. She wasn't sure what they were growing there; she'd never had much of a green thumb herself, but it sure looked pretty as well as useful.

Further along the side of the house was a small fenced off area containing a few chickens that were surprisingly quiet. Perhaps they had already fallen asleep in their coop for the night.

Before she had much of a chance to explore further, did a light switch on inside the room looking out over the kitchen garden. This window didn't have any curtains, allowing her a clear peek inside. She could see Derek's silhouette walk into the room that turned out to contain a dining area, carrying a large tray. Yep, they were getting ready to eat.

Outside in the darkness, Clarice was reasonably certain she wouldn't be seen, at least not as long as the light was on indoors, but she didn't want to take any unnecessary risks.

After observing the man as he sat down at the rustic wooden table in the center of the room, and waiting for a moment to see if his wife would follow - she was nowhere to be seen - Clarice quietly traced her steps back to where she'd come from. Around the side of the house, crossing the lawn in front of the main facade back to the driveway that led to the gravel track. She took care to step only on the grass, not on the gravel so that her footsteps wouldn't make much noise.

It occurred to her that there was something odd about this farm, something missing. Not only was it weird that she'd never once seen the farmer's wife, that wasn't all that piqued her suspicion: they didn't have a dog. Didn't almost everyone in the country keep at least one watch dog?

# SCOTTISH WEREBEAR: AN UNEXPECTED AFFAIR

*Weird.*

How would they know if anyone intruded onto their land? Cameras? No, the farmer didn't seem like the techy kind. She shrugged to herself and tried to stop her imagination from running away with her again. Perhaps they just didn't like dogs...

Clarice took one last breath of the earthy, cool air outside her cottage, then stepped back indoors and undid her coat. Time to tackle that fish, for better or for worse. She didn't have anything else to eat besides bread and eggs, and those could get tedious after a while.

———— ◆ ————

Day after day passed in largely the same fashion. She got up early to do her work, and her focus was never broken until hours later when she felt her body revolt to the crazy work ethic she'd developed.

Her novel was progressing nicely, and the story turned out to be much more captivating than that first outline she'd prepared months ago. She was certain her editor was going to love it. The drama was intense, the romance palpable, and the characters seemed so real to her that they could very well just walk off the page as actual people. It was magical, how she'd found joy in writing again, when previous attempts the last months had felt more like pulling teeth.

Life at Moss Cottage seemed easy otherwise also. Every day a new treat ended up on her welcome mat, which she gratefully accepted. Often it was something sweet, but occasionally it was a piece of meat or fish, as well as fresh vegetables that undoubtedly had been grown in the kitchen garden. In case of the latter, there was always a brief note attached with a recipe on the back.

She made it a point to thank Derek - and pass on the message to his wife - whenever she had the opportunity to speak with him, which wasn't often. He seemed to be a very industrious man, always busy, always working.

Although she'd tried to put a stop to her wandering thoughts, every time she saw him, whether close enough to talk to, or hard at work further away from her cottage, her desire for him grew.

Every time she actually saw Derek during the day, she couldn't shake the feeling that they'd formed some kind of connection, a magnetic bond of some sort. Of course she knew that it was all one-sided, that desperation and perhaps loneliness had colored her perception.

The more she yearned for Derek's attention, the better the progress on her novel.

He visited her in her dreams in the mornings, before she was properly awake. It was during those hours that he whispered the words into her ear that the hero of her novel - Lady Adlington's unexpected lover - would say to melt her heart.

Meanwhile, the man himself had shown no indication whatsoever that he felt any attraction towards her. His routine never wavered. Even when he was doing chores around the cottages, repairing a fence, or trimming the hedges, he showed no interest in what she was up to. He never came by for a chat, and the occasional exchanges between the two seemed to irritate him rather than give him enjoyment.

In the evenings, when Derek had retreated inside the main house, Clarice continued her short walks around the farm. Although she'd tried to be stealthy - though not in a creepy stalker sort of way - she did at times feel like she was being watched. Either way, her walks were the only thing keeping her back from locking up after largely sedentary days, so she wasn't going to give them up no matter what. And part of her kept hoping she could catch a glimpse of Derek's wife.

She wasn't sure what she was hoping to see. Worthy competition? A confirmation that she stood no chance at all? Perhaps she wished most of all to see Derek's wife as a kind person deserving of his loyalty so that finally she could stop obsessing about the man. But his wife never left the house as far as she could tell.

Clarice never once laid eyes on her.

# CHAPTER SIX

———◆———

One afternoon, a week after her first arrival at McMillan Farm, Clarice was already coming up to the final climax of the novel. It was crazy to think that she'd achieved so much in so little time, but she knew the work had taken its toll on her.

She decided to take a break while it was still light out. A chance to let her sore muscles relax, while drinking in the beautiful surroundings of her rural retreat. Once she put her head down and started to write, she might not be able to resurface until the resolution to her fictional couple's troubles had presented itself, and by then it would be too late to head out.

Plus, she'd run out of cookies and eggs, necessitating a trip to restock. The skies overhead were grey as ever when she stepped out of the cottage, and the wind rustled against the remaining leaves on the trees all round.

Fortunately, because Clarice had access to her rental car, the weather did not worry her. Walking might have been healthier, but the village with its tiny store was so far off, it would be less of a walk and more of a hike to get there and back.

She was slightly disappointed that she didn't see Derek anywhere on her way out the main gates, but then just focused on the drive ahead. Her car whirled up fallen leaves from the road. The trees had turned color completely during the short stay at McMillan Farm. Clarice took note of the shades of red and orange she saw, determined to embellish some of the descriptions in her novel with details of the same.

# SCOTTISH WEREBEAR: AN UNEXPECTED AFFAIR

Clarice even wound down the window to allow the brisk, damp autumn air into the car. It smelled earthy, rich, and it was cold enough to prickle against her skin. By all accounts, it was a beautiful day in its own right, despite the sun not being anywhere in sight.

As she came up to the turn that headed out of the wooded patch around the farm, she remembered how about a week ago, this was where she had come to send that message to Lily. She ought to phone her from the village just to give her an update on what was going on. Should she mention Derek? Why the hell not? Perhaps Lily could talk some sense into her.

The road wound on through the heather covered landscape. Over smaller as well as bigger hillocks, over the occasional cattle grill dividing up the asphalt. She passed by fields with grazing sheep, which were one of the few reminders that this place was actually inhabited.

Clarice told herself that as soon as she'd finish her book, she would take a day or so to explore the island some more. Perhaps with the help of her satellite navigation, she would be able to find a road leading directly to the coast. If the distant views were anything to go by, a close-up of the shoreline should be breathtaking.

Darker clouds rolled in over the taller hills in the distance, but before the weather turned for the worse, Clarice could see the first houses at the edge of the village up ahead. She was almost there.

Minutes later, she parked up beside the house with the daily needs shop. The door was open just like last time. She set off an automatic bell as she entered.

"Afternoon," the old man's voice greeted Clarice from across the room, where he sat at his table with a newspaper.

"Hello!" She smiled widely at him, glad for the

interaction, however short. "Just hoping to restock on a few things."

"Of course. Please help yourself."

Clarice walked through the aisles, picking up mostly the same items she'd bought only a week earlier. Cookies, eggs, bread, as well as the only bottle of red wine she could find in the entire store. She would use the latter as a reward for when she finished the book.

Coming up closer to the table where the old man waited, she spied a rack of greeting cards, where she paused for a moment. A souvenir of this place would be nice indeed. She picked out a particularly scenic shot of the rugged cliffs that rose up from the center of the Isle of Skye. Once she got her hands on a first copy of this novel she'd been working on, she planned to keep the card inside it, as a reminder of her time here.

A better reminder, of course, would be a picture of Derek, her main inspiration, but she didn't think she could muster the courage to ask him if she could take one.

"Are you able to find everything you need?" asked the old man while looking up from his newspaper.

"Yes. All done." Clarice wandered over towards him, placing her various purchases on the table. She waited while he added everything up on his little notepad, just like he'd done the last time she was here. If she didn't start a conversation soon, she would lose the opportunity. Yet she wasn't sure how to begin, nervous that he would see right through her and guess her intentions.

"So... The weather seems to be taking a turn for the worse today," Clarice began.

The old man nodded. "A storm's coming in from the East; looks to be a bad'un." He handed her the note after finishing his calculations. "So how have you been enjoying your stay at the cottage?"

"It's very nice. A real quiet getaway. Just what the doctor ordered," Clarice said. This was her chance.

"And what lovely people. Baking cakes, and whatnot leaving it outside my door.

The old man cocked his head to the side, his grayish-blue eyes fixed on Clarice's face.

"Derek McMillan does take pride in his produce," he remarked.

"Mhmm," Clarice agreed.

"What *people* do you refer to? Has his brother, Aidan turned up? I haven't seen him about in a while," the man remarked.

"You mean, it's just him living there? I assumed..." Clarice couldn't hide her shock. "The cakes and everything..."

There was an awkward silence between the two.

"You thought he was married," he said finally.

"Well... Yes!"

The old man let out a laugh. "He doesn't seem like the baking type, true, but I've been lucky enough to taste some of his creations at the annual village fete. McMillan has hidden talents."

Clarice remained quiet. What a strange man, to never correct her once when she mentioned his non-existent wife. It hurt because it clearly signaled that he'd preferred keep up with her mistaken assumption, if it made him seem unavailable. He must really dislike her.

She picked up the paper bag of groceries and forced a smile while avoiding eye contact.

"Well, I'd better be off then, before the storm hits."

"That would be wise," the shopkeeper said. "Bye now. Drive safe."

"Bye." She turned, just a little too eagerly, her eyes glazing over slightly despite her best efforts to keep her emotions in check.

*Shit.* She knew most guys wouldn't consider her a catch. She wasn't skinny, glamorous, or even particularly exciting company due to her introverted nature. But to find out that someone found her so repulsive that he wouldn't even correct her about the whole wife assumption, in an attempt to keep his distance from her? That was a new low.

It was the icing on the poisoned cake. A new blow to her self-worth that almost stung worse than Alan's unfaithfulness. She had been mostly indifferent about Alan up to that point. She was far from indifferent when it came to Derek.

She carelessly dumped the groceries onto the passenger seat of the car and took her place behind the wheel. What a mess. She had to get away from here, to get out of the village, and far away from potentially prying eyes before the waterworks began.

Still shocked, she turned the car around and slammed her foot down, speeding back up the road where she had just come from. Tears clouded her vision as she navigated largely on autopilot. Around the blind bends, over the cattle grill, which made a hell of a noise underneath her tires. The only thing louder was the rumble of thunder overhead.

The sky might as well been falling. Her headlights turned on automatically as the dark clouds gathered above the car. The weather was a perfect reflection of her mood. She felt humiliated and deeply hurt in what little remained of her pride. She wanted to scream. Instead she hit the steering with her fists a few times, then cried at the hopelessness of it all.

The worst part was, the whole thing with Derek, whatever she felt, it was just a stupid infatuation. She didn't even know the man. All she knew was that he was tall, broad, and had a certain rugged, masculine charm that had drawn her to him involuntarily.

She didn't know the first thing going on in his head - if anything actually did happen in there - except that he clearly had developed some kind of instinctive dislike for her. There was no other explanation.

The winds started lashing against the car, making it feel slightly imbalanced. She felt more pressure on the steering, forcing her to correct against the stormy gusts aiming to push her off the road.

She didn't need this. After all the shit with Alan that threatened to ruin her career as a writer, as well as her sanity as a person, she really didn't deserve to be kicked back down when she'd finally found her bearings again. How was she going to finish the book now? How was she going to find a resolution for her imaginary couple, when her muse had all but betrayed her?

Although she wasn't sure how she would react if she saw Derek now, she had nowhere else to go but back to the cottage. Chances were, he wouldn't be around anyway. He rarely was at this time of day.

Tears were streaming down her face now, silently. She'd stopped sobbing.

The landscape that had looked so pretty in the misty conditions from before now seemed hostile as well as bleak. She was relieved to see the woods up ahead. Soon she'd be back, and she'd lock herself inside the cottage and perhaps open that bottle of wine a few days earlier than planned. Or she would make some tea, better yet, she'd make a hot chocolate using the cocoa powder she'd found in one of the kitchen cupboards.

Only, the weather had other ideas for her. As soon as she made it into the dark wooded patch surrounding the farm, a bright flash of lighting followed instantly by a loud thunder crack startled her, making her jerk the steering. The car skidded onto a patch of wet leaves. A split second later, one of the trees that had stood proud and healthy moments before, split and started to lean over dangerously across the road ahead.

She had no way of stopping, no opportunity to avoid it. The charred trunk was falling too close to the front of the car, and she was going too fast to be able to react. A jarring crash later, did both the car and the felled tree come to an abrupt halt together.

Her vision blurred, details of trees and brown, wet leaves making way for nothing but a bright, loud white. Then the darkness took over.

# CHAPTER SEVEN

Although it pained him, Derek knew that his efforts to stay far away from Clarice were in both their best interests. Every day he had tried to limit his activities near the cottage to times when he knew she'd be working inside, and he wouldn't risk running into her.

The thing about running a farm alone was that there was always something to do. The work never finished, so he could keep himself occupied as far away from her as possible whenever the need arose.

The one thing he hadn't been able to stop himself from doing was leaving her treats.

His evenings at the house consisted of stockpiling supplies to prepare for winter. He was doing his best to harvest all he could before the kitchen garden would inevitably stop producing. Whatever he didn't eat straightaway, he preserved.

Still, he couldn't resist using some of his existing supplies - especially sweet ones - to produce the occasional cake or other treat. Not for himself, though he had always had a sweet tooth, but for her.

His keen sense of smell told him that without his intervention, the woman ate eggs for dinner every day, which was something he could not accept. Whenever he went fishing, he caught a little extra for her, when he planned to eat lamb for dinner, he shared his ingredients with her.

She always thanked him profusely, or rather, thanked his imaginary wife - same thing - so he was certain that she did appreciate the gifts.

And she didn't seem like one of those neurotic diet nuts, the ones who read the labels of whatever they eat, and seemed to revel in denying themselves any pleasure from food. No, Clarice was more of a hedonist, someone who allowed themselves to smell the roses - or eat the chocolate in this case. He appreciated that about her.

But despite his best efforts, things had changed over the past week. No longer was his attraction towards her largely shallow, inspired by the odd glimpse or scent. Even when he had his back turned towards her, it was as if he could see her more clearly than when he was actually looking at her.

Derek couldn't explain it without making comparisons to the stories his mother used to tell him. When bears found their mate, the one that fate - or biology, as Elise had put it - had in mind for them, they connected on a deep, subconscious level. They started to share a kind of understanding that didn't require words to communicate.

Empathy as a term didn't quite cover what happened to bears and their soul mates. And if this wasn't happening to him now, he would have never even believed it was possible for a bond to run so deeply.

When he walked past Moss Cottage, he could sense what Clarice was up to. If her work was going well or if she was pondering something. It wasn't clear, he wasn't a mind reader, but he always had some idea of her mood. In the evenings when she went for her short walks, he knew where she was without fail. He could pinpoint her position accurately, without even looking out the window.

In the old stories, these strange feelings and bonds were always mutual, but in his case, they couldn't be. She was human. There was no way that she could sense things as keenly as he did. The story Elise had told him confirmed this, plus Clarice hadn't acted like she felt anything but unease for him.

He tried to keep his thoughts about her to a minimum, to stay away from what-ifs and speculations on what might have been if she'd also been a bear and not a human. Instead, he'd marked the date of her departure in his calendar in bright red, and counted the days leading up to it with keen anticipation as well as dread.

Today, they had crossed the half-way point between her arrival and impending departure. It was a relief that he'd gotten this far without doing anything stupid, but also a worry that in just a week, he'd connected so deeply with her. There was no way of predicting how much stronger her pull on him would get before she left.

She'd worked as usual for most of the morning, then abruptly taken a break and gone out. He could hear her car start, and the crunch of gravel under her tires while he tidied up the raised beds in the kitchen garden. She was happy, almost triumphant as she left, and Derek caught himself whistling as he worked as a result.

Only when she was gone, did he realize how distracting her presence on the farm had been. He hadn't even noticed the dark clouds and the electricity building in the air. Bad weather was coming, and it had completely caught him by surprise.

He scanned the darkening skies, then hurriedly put away his tools and headed indoors. The radio confirmed his suspicions; the weather was going to deteriorate quite a bit, and the Met Office had even put out an amber alert.

Hopefully, Clarice would be back by the time the storm hit. Weather could get dangerous on the island, and they were predicting gusts strong enough to cause quite a bit of damage.

As he waited, he reorganized the stack of wood beside the fireplace. If the predictions were accurate, temperatures would plummet. Once he'd finished that, he headed into the kitchen to put on a pot of stew.

If he wanted to stay alert, he had to make sure there'd be plenty of warmth and nourishment available to him, or the urge to hibernate would threaten to overwhelm his senses. Hibernation was something he wasn't willing to risk with a visitor on the farm.

Just as the large pot started to simmer on the stove, and Derek had the chance to sit on one of the heavy dining chairs, did a feeling of unease start to pluck at his thoughts. The rain started to lash down against the windows, and the winds were whistling in the trees surrounding the farmhouse.

Surely, she couldn't have gone far? She would have just driven to the village, probably to visit the modest shop there. But he didn't sense her anywhere nearby yet, so she was still out of his range.

His discomfort grew until his instincts were almost screaming at him that something was going terribly wrong. Finally, he could no longer fight it. He put on a warm, waterproof coat and left the house to investigate.

For a moment, he paused near in front of the barn containing his trusty old Landrover. No, the route through the forest would be quicker, as well as more sheltered from the elements. His feet carried him forward almost involuntarily, and by the time he made it through the farm gates, he was sprinting.

He'd barely crossed the first tree-covered hill that lay between him and the open heathland nearer the village when a sharp pain pierced his chest. This was no longer a merely hypothetical worry that had inspired him to leave the house and brave the storm. He could feel the danger, the pain Clarice was in with as much clarity as he could feel the rain hitting his face.

# SCOTTISH WEREBEAR: AN UNEXPECTED AFFAIR

Despite being fully clothed, he didn't stop to undress but shifted instantly. The winds were battering against the trees with so much intensity, it drowned out the sound of ripping fabric as his once smooth human torso sprouted thick brown fur and ripped its way through the much too small jacket. Everything he had worn only moments earlier was left in tatters on the wet, moss-covered ground underneath.

Up ahead, dim lights filtered through the trees and dense rainfall. As he approached the scene, he could see that it was indeed Clarice's gray hatchback. One of the first things he noticed was the smell of burnt wood, originating from a tree that had split in two across the base, causing the top end of it to fall into the road. The second thing was... blood.

His heart sank. There were no cries of pain, no noises at all coming from the car itself, just the incessant drum rolls of heavy rain, hitting the roof. Inside, Clarice slumped forward, her head resting on a blood-stained airbag. Of course, he feared the worst. She wasn't moving, and he couldn't hear her vital signs through the howling winds surrounding them.

He grabbed at the handle, but the car door wouldn't budge, so he rushed to the passenger side of the car and broke the window with a powerful blow from his paw. The glass shattered into a million little pieces, covering the seat inside, some of it landing in Clarice's hair. He grabbed at the rim of the door, and a strong tug later, threw the twisted remnants of it into the shrubbery behind him.

It didn't matter to him anymore that he risked discovery, that if Clarice was, in fact, fine, she could open her eyes at any moment and come face-to-face with a huge brown bear. He couldn't just leave her here, stuck inside this tin box. The road to McMillan Farm was secluded and lonely at the best of times. The nearest help was the voluntary fire brigade based in Portree, forty minutes away, and during a storm like this, there was no chance of them arriving anytime soon.

Whatever had to be done was up to Derek, and Derek alone.

He climbed into the car, his massive weight causing the suspension to creak dangerously. Although he could reach Clarice with his snout, he was too big to fit in far enough to get her out. At least from here he could hear her heartbeat. She was alive, but who knew for how long if she stayed here.

With one surprisingly accurate tap of his claw, he managed to undo the buckle of her seatbelt. He reached out and gently pushed her back into her seat, and then aimed the next blow at the airbag, tearing it free from the steering wheel to give him more of a view of what was going on.

She seemed to be in one piece though there was an ugly gash on her forehead with blood dripping from it. Her breaths were slow, calm, but not weak. Despite everything, she was still the most beautiful woman he'd ever seen.

Still, she wasn't conscious, so there was no way of finding out if that bump on her head was her only injury.

With so many unknowns, and the bad weather continuing, Derek didn't have time to carefully deliberate his next move. He closed his eyes and focused on his human form, feeling his limbs contract back to their original shape.

Taking advantage of his much more dexterous fingers, he freed Clarice of the seatbelt completely, then checked that both her legs were free underneath the steering wheel. He carefully levered her out of her seat, over the gear knob and into the passenger seat. Then he got out of the car completely, and with one arm supporting her shoulders, the other running through the crook of her knees, he lifted her up towards freedom.

She was still limp, completely out of it, which was just as well because the situation looked bad. His clothes were lying in tatters somewhere in the woods, and he preferred not to have to explain his current nudity to her.

There was no doctor nearby, and the storm was far from over. The cold rain started to chill his naked skin, and Clarice didn't have much warmth in her either. The nearest clinic was halfway across the island, and if the storm didn't get them on the way, the cold temperatures surely would. There was nothing else he could do but carry her home and hope that she'd wake up on her own. He had to trust that she would be fine without immediate medical attention.

He started walking back up the same way through the trees as he had come earlier. But in his human form, without the protective thick fur, the cold significantly slowed his progress. Derek could feel his muscles tighten and lethargy wash over him.

He looked down at Clarice's face. She was completely still, even as the heavy droplets hit her ivory skin. It took all the energy he had left to transform yet again, taking the utmost care that the claws his hands sprouted didn't hurt her. Once again covered in warm fur, he started on the walk home.

Running on all fours would have been quicker and more comfortable for him, but as long as Clarice was protected against the elements in his strong arms, slow and steady would have to do. He kept going, zig-zagging through the woods while hunching over just enough to keep her dry.

By the time they got back to the farmhouse together,

her cheeks had even warmed to a rosy pink. If he didn't know any better, he might have thought she was sleeping.

# CHAPTER EIGHT

————◆————

Clarice had the strangest dream.

After crashing her car into the tree - or having the tree crash into her, she wasn't certain how it had happened exactly, she'd been trapped in a world of white noise. She couldn't move, couldn't scream, couldn't even feel her body.

Somehow, she had made it out of the wreck and back to the cottage, though. She had been aware of her movements, somewhat, as well as the noises around her, but she hadn't been able to see much of what had occurred. The one thing that stood out to her was Derek's voice. He'd asked if she was okay, and if she was in pain. He'd hoped out loud that she hadn't been badly hurt.

Clarice had wanted to tell him that it was fine, that he didn't need to worry himself, but couldn't open her mouth to form the words. She had caught a glimpse of his face looking down at her, before the overwhelming urge to sleep on had dragged her back into the white. Or perhaps all that had also been part of her dream, and it wasn't Derek who had rescued her.

Somewhere between the car wreck and the farmhouse, she was certain that there had been another presence as well.

She had crashed near the spot where she'd first seen that shadow in the woods and was now certain it had been the bear. Throughout her mysterious rescue, the bear had been watching all along, she could feel his eyes on her. At one point, when her eyes refused to open, she thought she could even feel fur, brushing against her cheek.

The strange thing was, even though she knew the bear was there, close to her, she didn't feel like she was in danger at all. She felt completely safe, cared for even.

The feeling still lingered when she finally did open her eyes.

While she was in the white world, time seemed to hold no importance. Upon waking, and struggling with her vision as her eyes adjusted to the light in the strange room she found herself in, Clarice had no way of figuring out how long she'd been unconscious.

There was a flicker of a candle on the heavy wooden dresser in the corner. She tried to lift her head to get a better view of the rest of the room, but a thumping headache prevented her from moving too much. The bed was comfortable and smelled of clean cotton.

Clarice reached upwards, carefully exploring the painful welt on her forehead with her fingertips, before letting her arm drop beside her body, back onto the soft, bouncy mattress. After staring at the black wooden beams holding up the ceiling for a moment, she turned onto her side.

She was definitely sore, and not just on her head, though there didn't seem to be anything else wrong with her that she could tell. The dresser, the huge wardrobe and the equally solid looking door looked very similar to the furniture and decor of Moss Cottage. But this wasn't her bedroom.

After taking a deep breath, and closing her eyes to focus, she lifted herself, bringing her back closer to the headboard of the bed. It was only then that she realized she was not alone. Towards the other side of the bed, in the corner, a figure slept in a wicker armchair.

Although the candle light did not brighten up that part of the room much, she would recognize him anywhere. Derek.

# SCOTTISH WEREBEAR: AN UNEXPECTED AFFAIR

So it hadn't just been a dream. He had rescued her from the car wreck and carried her all the way back to the farm, just like she'd thought. She wondered what else from her dream was true. The bear? It couldn't be, could it?

Her heart was hammering in her chest as she continued to watch him sleep. Was this his bedroom? Perhaps it was one of the other cottages, surely Derek - who as far as she could tell didn't even like her - wouldn't have brought her into his home?

He stirred slightly, readjusting himself against the side of the large chair. Clarice held her breath in an attempt not to make any sound, but next thing she knew, he had opened his eyes. She shouldn't have seen it, considering how little light there was, and yet there they were: two burning amber orbs, looking right at her.

"Uhm," Clarice started, too nervous to formulate proper words.

"How are you feeling?" Derek's deep voice attempted to soothe her, when Clarice remembered why she'd been upset earlier, before the crash.

"How long was I unconscious for?" she asked coolly. She felt torn. Although she realized how ridiculous it was of her to feel so betrayed over what was essentially a detail - one that isn't even any of her business - still, emotions threatened to well up again. Then again, he did rescue her, she should be thankful for that.

Derek sat up straight, his eyes still burning brightly at her. *Weird.*

"It's dark," Clarice mumbled.

"Power's out," Derek explained. He got up and moved in closer to Clarice's bed, keeping his eyes fixed on her. His movements were deliberate, purposeful. He looked like a man on a mission.

Clarice held her breath, but her heartbeat sped up

anyway. As he moved into the candlelight, she could finally see his expression. His eyes looked her over, lingering on her forehead - Clarice wondered if it looked as bad as it felt - then traveled downward, pausing on her lips. He seemed tense, with his lips pressed together tightly, disguising how sensual and full she'd remembered them to be.

Should she say something?

Derek sat on the edge of the mattress beside her and leaned over, gently brushing a lock of her hair out of the way and carefully inspected her injury.

"That was a close call," he mumbled.

His breath tickled her face as he spoke, and Clarice instinctively closed her eyes for just a moment too long. Having Derek this close to her now overloaded her senses. She wanted nothing more but to lean in, just to get a little taste of him. Despite her earlier assumptions, it did seem as though he cared for her. However, she couldn't be sure he cared for her *like that*.

All she could do to stay civil was to focus on her breathing, in and out, to force her body to slow down, when all it wanted was to spin out of control. She opened her eyes again and noted that he was still there right in front of her.

"That tree, it was too close. I couldn't avoid it," Clarice explained though the words seemed unimportant.

"I know."

"You carried me all the way." Although she'd intended for it to be a question, the sentence came out as a statement. Her memories, however muddled, already told her that he had, in fact, done so. He looked strong, with his broad shoulders and thick biceps that ever so slightly fought against the fabric of his shirt, but she'd crashed quite a long way away, and it wouldn't have been easy to carry her for such a distance. How had he managed that?

A hint of a smile played on Derek's lips, and he nodded.

"I couldn't very well leave you there, could I?"

"I suppose not."

This was the most they'd spoken in the entire week that she'd been at McMillan Farm. The familiarity in Derek's expression made Clarice feel like they knew each other a lot better than they did.

"You're not married," Clarice spoke in a whisper, more to herself than to him.

He shook his head, looking away at the crisp white bed sheet.

"Why didn't you say something?" Clarice wondered out loud. The whole situation was bizarre and confusing.

"I didn't think it made a difference. In another week, you'll go home..." Derek left the rest of his thought for Clarice to fill in for herself. So he did like her? He'd only kept the misunderstanding alive to avoid awkwardness when she left?

Her heart beat even faster, and an awkward silence spread through the room. Clarice had a million and one things she wanted to say and not say at the same time. She wanted to wrap her arms around Derek's shoulders and kiss him, to show him somehow that she wouldn't have just packed up and left if he indeed did have feelings for her.

Bizarrely, she could no longer believe that the attraction she felt towards him was just a childish infatuation. She'd had those before, but this... it ran deeper somehow. Not that she had an explanation for it at all.

Only, she didn't get the chance to do any of it, because the unusually large bedroom door flung open without warning, and there he was: the big brown bear she thought she had seen in the woods on her first day. The one that had wormed its way into her confused dream while she was passed out. She let out a shriek, and in a panic crawled backward against the headboard until she could crawl no further.

"What the!" Derek's voice boomed around the room, distracting the bear, whose gaze darted back and forth between Clarice and the edge of the mattress where Derek had just sat.

She looked over at Derek, hoping desperately that this was indeed his bedroom in the main house, and he had stashed a hunting rifle nearby, or at least something - anything - to protect the two of them against the wild animal that had just entered. But he wasn't sitting beside her anymore. Instead, his already imposing form had made way for an even more impressive one. Another bear, standing squarely in the middle of the room, mere feet away from the intruder.

Clarice didn't know what to do, whether to scream or cry, close her eyes and wish the two scary intruders away. Maybe she had never woken up. Maybe this - as well as the preceding conversation with Derek - was all still part of a crazy dream conjured up by her subconscious. A crazy dream turned terrible nightmare.

She started to feel faint, but the overwhelming sense of panic didn't let her consciousness wane again. Faced now with two bears instead of just one, it was only a matter of time before they'd pounce on her, ripping her to shreds with their huge, sharp teeth.

"Aidan. Bad timing," a voice that sounded more like a growl spoke from Derek's direction.

"Well... This is awkward," the other bear seemed to say, with an equally rough, deep voice.

Clarice felt herself calm down a little bit. There was a

voice in the back of her mind, Derek's voice, which told her she was safe. She believed it without question. Now that she was faced with two *talking* bears, it was obvious her mind was just playing with her.

*I'm safe.*

Her only regret now was that her intimate chat with Derek earlier probably hadn't been real either.

# CHAPTER NINE

"A word, please?" Derek said to Aidan, all the while eyeing Clarice, who continued to be stunned into silence.

Aidan nodded, and both the bears exited the bedroom, leaving Clarice behind.

Aidan's timing couldn't have been worse, Derek thought. Throughout his conversation with Clarice, he could tell that she did feel strongly for him. He could sense her mood: a mixture of yearning and affection. Her hormone levels suggested a physical reaction to his presence. He could smell the pheromones in the air. As she looked at him, her pupils dilated, her cheeks turned flush, and her entire body seemed to invite him in.

Although there was nothing practical about it all, he knew he wouldn't have been able to resist her much longer if Aidan hadn't turned up. Something told him that she wouldn't have either.

"She's human," Aidan remarked.

"Yeah, I know."

"She's seen us." Aidan paced around the hallway while transforming back into his human self.

Derek followed suit so that they were both back in their human form and naked. Aidan shook his head in disbelief, then walked off towards what used to be his old room towards the back of the farmhouse.

Aidan pulled some jeans and a hooded sweatshirt out of the wardrobe and put them on after drying himself off with a towel. The roads weren't clear enough for a vehicle, so the only way to get to the farm would have been just like how Derek did it hours before: in shifted form, straight through the woods, braving the elements. That explained why Aidan arrived rather damp and riled up.

He threw a similar outfit in Derek's direction, who also got dressed in a rush.

Despite living vastly different lives - Aidan spending all his time away from home and Derek doing a lot more physical labor on the farm, the two brothers looked very much alike. They were both extremely broad and muscular as you'd expect bears to be and had the same shade of shaggy brown hair. It was a blessing in cases like these when either one of them found themselves in need of covering up after an unplanned shift that they wore the same size clothes as well.

"Do I want to know why she was in your bed?" Aidan gave him a suspicious stare.

*Always the big brother,* Derek thought, *no matter how little he shows his face around here, or how old we get.*

"Get your mind out of the gutter. She's a guest. Her car crashed in the storm, knocked her out, and I brought her back here to keep an eye on her."

"A guest, eh? That's all?"

Derek shrugged, unwilling to go into the details of the matter right this moment. Actually, he wished to cut the entire conversation short so that he could go back into the bedroom to see how Clarice was holding up after the shocking display the two brothers had just given her.

"Well, perhaps if we play dumb we can convince her she was just seeing things. That would be for the best," Aidan speculated.

Derek slowly shook his head, not really in response to his brother, but more to himself. Knowing what he knew now, that Clarice did indeed have some kind of connection with him, he couldn't see how secrecy was an option anymore.

"Anyway, why don't you tell me why you're here?" Derek asked instead.

"Can't I just visit my little brother anymore?" Aidan responded gruffly.

"The way you came bursting in unannounced suggests something else is going on," Derek said while scrutinizing his brother's face. There was something there, a hint of a frown he tried hard to disguise, but Derek could still see it. Whatever he'd been up to in the nine months since Aidan's last visit, it had taken a toll on him.

"Alright then," Aidan began. "If I'm going to tell you everything, I have one condition. Don't think for a moment I'm buying the 'she's just a guest' crap, okay? I'm not stupid. You'll let me know what's going on with the human, and I'll tell you what's going on with me."

"Fine." Derek sighed. Despite Aidan's abrasive and often bossy nature, it might be useful to get another perspective on Derek's predicament anyway.

"It's a long story," Aidan said.

They walked back down the hall, past the master bedroom where he could still sense Clarice's presence. Her heartbeat had calmed down significantly. Her breathing had slowed. Even without opening the door, Derek knew that she had fallen asleep again, which was just as well.

"What do you say we discuss it over some mulled wine?" Derek didn't wait for Aidan's agreement, but just headed further down the hall anyway until they made it into the dark lounge, and from there into the kitchen, which was invitingly lit up by an oil lamp. He opened a cupboard and pulled out a bottle of mulled wine mixture he had made earlier, pouring it into a pot to warm it up. Outside, the storm had barely had a chance to calm. The wind was still whistling through the trees and around the farmhouse, and it was still raining as well.

All the while, Aidan paced up and down the room. Whatever was going on with him, it wasn't good. Derek could tell that much.

He picked up two glasses and poured the deep red, fragrant liquid into them, handing one to Aidan. They sat down around the large round wooden table and sipped their wine in silence. Derek waited until Aidan looked a bit more revitalized. If there's one thing that made bears even less chatty than normal, it was cold weather.

"She's my mate, Aidan," Derek broke the silence at last.

His brother looked up from the half empty glass, one eyebrow raised.

"I know it's not ideal, being that she's human, but I know it in my gut, and I can't fight it." Derek averted his gaze downward while continuing to warm his fingers on the mulled wine in his hands.

"I see." Aidan cleared his throat. "What does she know?"

Derek shrugged. "Nothing. I'd been avoiding the issue completely and avoiding her. But when she crashed her car earlier today, I realized I couldn't stand it anymore. I can't let her go, Aidan."

Aidan ran his hands through his still damp hair and let out a chuckle. "Believe it or not, I know how you feel."

Derek looked up. It was his turn to stare at Aidan in surprise. "How so?"

"I've also met someone. *The one.*"

"Is that why you're here?" Derek asked.

"No. Yes. It's complicated."

"Don't tell me she's human as well?"

Aidan took one last gulp before putting the empty glass down on the table and crossing his arms. "No, it's nothing like that. Anyway, your situation requires sorting out first. She doesn't know anything you say, and yet she's just seen the two of us. That's bad. Very bad." Aidan's face took on a thoughtful, more serious expression.

"I suppose, but maybe she'll be okay with it. What do you think?" Derek hoped out loud.

"It's not about whether *she* will be fine with it. What about the Code? This goes beyond just you and your *girlfriend*. The survival of our species relies on complete secrecy, as you well know!"

Of course, Aidan was right, but the tone in which he said it grated at Derek. The last thing he needed right now was a lecture from his big brother.

"Not even you can turn back time on what's already happened." Derek's face darkened as he spoke. Clarice couldn't just un-see them in their bear form, neither could he ignore the immense pull she had on him. It seemed irrational and crazy, but he knew that if he couldn't have her, he wouldn't survive his loss.

His entire situation was so unprecedented that the only comparison he could draw was with bear couples where one partner passes. The other half of the couple often died of a broken heart shortly after. Mated bears literally grew old together, or they didn't grow old at all.

"Pour us another glass. I have something to say," Aidan started.

Derek paused for a moment, tempted to argue, but finally decided to just do as he was told. Moments later, fresh refill in hand, he sat down opposite Aidan again and waited.

"I've never told you what it is I do." Aidan leaned forward and ran his fingertip across the rim of the glass, wiping a droplet of mulled wine off it.

"You've never been home long enough to discuss it. Not that I mind, you know I'm not the social type," Derek remarked.

"Obviously I've been traveling, but I never mentioned my reasons. When Mum and Dad had their accident, I couldn't shake the feeling that something else was going on..."

Derek raised his eyebrow. "You think it wasn't an accident?"

Aidan forced a smile. "You've always been sharp. Yes, that's exactly what I suspected. Of course, I had no proof."

"And you do now?" Derek asked.

"Not yet. That's why I'm here, to look through their things and the old newspaper clippings I'd kept from way back when. But what I'm getting at is, some people approached me a while ago. That's how I met Heidi recently as well."

The way Aidan said her name, Derek knew that Heidi was the woman he'd hinted at before. Aidan's mate. "Right. What people?"

"Have you ever heard of the Sons of Domnall?" Aidan asked.

"Yeah, from the old stories," Derek said.

"It would seem that they don't just exist in stories."

Derek stopped mid-sip and put his glass back down, his gaze now completely fixed on his brother.

"They're a real threat. A group of humans who know our secret and are intent on rooting us out. We're trying to form a counterpart to that. I'm now working with like-minded shifters to protect our secret and keep our own safe against the Sons of Domnall. Our group is called the Alliance."

"And how do Mum and Dad fit into all that? You think their deaths are related to what you've discovered?" Derek ran his hand through his hair, trying to make sense of it all.

"It would explain a lot, wouldn't it? The problem with us bears is, we don't organize ourselves. We tend to keep to ourselves, and when something happens, there's nobody to help out or put two-and-two together. Those who lives in packs, wolves, for example, are miles ahead of us. There have been disappearances across the shifter world. And the evidence links it all back to human interference."

Derek was stunned. Living alone in this remote part of the world, it had become very easy to assume life was quaint everywhere else. The possibility that their parents' death hadn't been an accident like he'd believed all his life was a lot to take in. And to think that their way of life was in danger because of a secret society of human assassins... That was all crazy talk, wasn't it?

"Their activities have escalated over the past few years - or perhaps it's only after the recent truce with the wolves that we've started to share the necessary information across species to find out the full extent of what's been happening. That's why secrecy is so important, now more than ever before. That's why your human poses a huge problem." Aidan pinched the bridge of his nose while looking away at nothing in particular.

"Before you burst in, and I was talking to her, I felt it. Our connection is mutual. I assumed it wouldn't be, because she's human, but..."

"We've got to know for sure. A bear would rather die than to put his mate in harm's way, but who knows how it works for humans? I'm not sure we can trust her."

"I'm sure." Derek looked up from his glass, staring his brother right in the eye. He was sure, because hidden in the dark of the doorway another pair of eyes was staring at Aidan. Clarice had woken up.

# CHAPTER TEN

———— ◆ ————

When Clarice finally awoke, she was surprised to still find herself in that same bed, in that same room, with the same wooden furniture from her crazy dream earlier. The only difference was the dark corner where Derek had sat was empty now, and the candle on the dresser had burnt up even further.

The welt on her forehead hurt equally, her limbs were stiff as before, and the only thing she could hear was a low howl outside the window. The storm was still going on though its intensity had reduced quite a bit.

Enough was enough. If she stayed in bed, who knows what other crazy hallucinations her mind would come up with. Clarice fought against the residual lethargy in her muscles and rolled over onto her side, ready to get out from underneath the warm covers. Her legs seemed to work just fine, even if the rough wooden floor underneath her feet felt funny, tingly, as if her feet had fallen asleep along with the rest of her.

She got up carefully, swaying slightly as she tried to maintain her balance. Then, putting one foot ahead of the other, she slowly walked around the bed and straight towards the door. *Where was the bathroom?*

Clarice turned the handle, then stopped to listen for any sign of another presence inside the house, before heading across the hall to the first other door she could find. She heard nothing but the wind. The house itself was completely quiet.

As luck would have it, the first door Clarice tried was indeed the bathroom. The mirror allowed her a first look at the damage done to her head. It looked pretty bad. Shades of blue and purple colored her skin with a bright red cut in the center. She would have expected more blood, meaning that someone - Derek probably - had cleaned her wound after carrying her here.

*That was what had happened, right?* Or had that also been a dream?

Clarice washed her hands, shivering as the icy cold water prickled against her skin. She hoped that the cold water would wake her up, to help her filter through her memories to determine what was real and what had just been fantasy.

"I'm losing it," she said to her reflection, then shook her head and dried her hands on the fluffy towel hanging beside the sink.

Still confused, she left the bathroom again and was greeted by muffled voices coming from the far end of the corridor. Now that she felt a bit more limber, she tiptoed her way down the hall. She'd had no idea where in the house she was before, but as she neared the room at the end, she could see shadowy outlines of two armchairs and a sofa. Further ahead was a doorway with light filtering out of it. The kitchen.

Two broad-shouldered figures sat across the heavy wooden table she'd observed through the window during her evening walks around the garden outside. One was Derek, the other one she didn't know, but the similar build and hair color, as well as the familiar tone in which they spoke to each other suggested they were related. His brother perhaps?

She overheard them talk of secrets and of humans finding out. It was surreal, but it dawned on Clarice that just maybe, her memories from the bedroom earlier weren't just part of a crazy dream after all. She couldn't quite explain how she picked up on it, but a certain sadness hung around Derek, who sat with his back towards her. The other guy, Aidan, mentioned their parents' death, and it all started to make sense.

Although it was wrong to eavesdrop, she couldn't tear herself away from the conversation. As the two men spoke, she didn't just listen with her ears, but with her heart as well if that made sense. That added dimension was so different from anything she'd ever felt before; it made the act of spying irresistible. She stepped ahead and felt her perceptions of Derek's state of mind intensify.

"... A bear would rather die than to put his mate in harm's way, but who knows how it works for humans? I'm not sure we can trust her," Aidan said.

"I'm sure." Derek radiated confidence as he spoke. Their minds were somehow connected at that very moment. He knew she stood behind him, and she knew that he knew.

Although she initially hadn't been sure whether she wanted her presence to be discovered, now her concerns were wiped away. Derek turned and smiled at her. Her heart warmed at the realization that she at least had a little bit of insight into his feelings now, even if she couldn't explain why.

"You're awake."

"Yes." Clarice stepped ahead into the light radiating from the oil lamp in the center of the table.

Across the room, Aidan looked up at her, and she finally could have a proper look at him. A strong jawline, like Derek, messy brown hair and eyes that betrayed the capacity for great cunning as well as kindness. He was handsome in his own right but had nothing on Derek of course. He looked skeptical but didn't say a word.

"I couldn't help but overhear some of that," Clarice

started.

Aidan raised an eyebrow and folded his arms.

"I don't know what happened between us, or how any of this works exactly," she addressed Derek now. "But I do know it's not just a phase, or something that'll easily pass. I feel you inside me, trying to connect with me. I can't ignore it."

Clarice glanced back up at Aidan again. "Your secret is safe. I couldn't tell anyone if I wanted to. Plus, do you think anyone would believe me?"

Although Aidan's expression suggested that he wasn't yet convinced, that didn't matter to Clarice at all. It was Derek she was concerned with, and the look he gave her now was halfway between pride and primal lust. When their eyes locked, she could clearly feel his intentions. *You're mine*, she thought. Or was that his thought rather than hers? Either way, she didn't know how she was going to deal with all this stuff coming from him, without acting on her most basic instincts.

He stared at her, as she stared at him. So much to see, so many hidden depths in those brown eyes that had sought to avoid her earlier.

Aidan cleared his throat as he got up from his chair. "I think I'm going to give you two some space."

Neither Derek nor Clarice so much as answered him. In their newfound connection to one-another, any third parties, family or otherwise, clearly held very little importance anymore.

"You can sense me," Derek said.

Clarice didn't need to nod her answer, but she did anyway out of habit.

"I've been able to feel you for days," he added.

This revelation put a smile on her face. A smile, which as it turned out, Derek could scarcely resist.

# SCOTTISH WEREBEAR: AN UNEXPECTED AFFAIR

He got up, the heavy chair falling backward onto the stone floor with a loud crash. Neither of them flinched or looked back as he charged ahead, cupping her face with his large, surprisingly gentle hands and leaning down for their first kiss.

From the first touch of their lips, Clarice felt unlike anything she'd ever known. Fireworks, butterflies, electric jolts, all those terms could not begin to describe the sensations coursing through her veins. It was as if Derek's being infiltrated hers, irreversibly leaving his mark on her.

They couldn't hold back any longer, hungry kisses led to a feverish exploration of skin. His hard, muscular torso enveloped her in an embrace that made her feel tiny for the first time in her life. Tiny, yet safe, and dangerously out of control.

He ran his hands over her curves, taking his time, while his tongue teased hers, pushing her anticipation of what was yet to come higher and higher. He tasted sweet, with a hint of spice, and completely irresistible. The slight tickle on her face from his beard didn't distract. Instead, it heightened her pleasure.

As they continued to explore each other's bodies, slowly peeling layer after layer of clothes off and admiring their discoveries, Clarice knew that there would be no going back after this. She wouldn't be able to turn her back on how he made her feel.

The little glimpses into his life and past she'd gotten from the overheard conversation gave her some sense of the man. The rational part of her brain knew that there was so much more yet to find out. Would she like what she found? Her heart screamed yes while her mind was aware of the risks, but it seemed not to matter. Whether she liked it or not, fate had already set her on this path with no choice in the matter.

Having already removed his hooded sweatshirt and finding that he wasn't wearing anything underneath, she couldn't believe her luck. All the fantasies that had crept up on her during those dark hours just before it was time to get up in the morning were coming true. His body was a work of art. Hard, chiseled lines and fluid curves of muscle that could put a Greek god to shame.

Derek McMillan was the kind of man who could have easily been cast as a Gladiator in Spartacus, a show Clarice had watched less for its artistic merit and more for the eye candy. The only difference was that he wasn't as smooth and artificially well-oiled as the actors in the show, which Clarice thought was a good thing.

Here in front of her stood not a photoshopped fantasy of a man, but a real one. Hers.

As he started to remove one of the last barriers between them, Clarice's t-shirt and jeans, it occurred to her that this was usually the point in new relationships that she'd dread the most. Although she didn't like to dwell on her insecurities, she couldn't always suppress the worry that a new partner might not like her as much naked as they seemed to with her clothes on. She always feared to see a little flinch or frown, or worse, complete indifference as Alan had shown towards the end.

Derek was unlike any other partner Clarice had been with, though. He didn't just continue on the path they'd set for themselves, kissing, tasting, and worshiping every inch of her exposed skin. He did so with an enthusiasm she couldn't even have foreseen in her wildest dreams.

When she looked at his expression, as he circled her nipple with his tongue, she couldn't see a hint of hesitation or disappointment in him. Everything was right between the two of them, just as it should be. They were both equally in awe of the perfection they'd found in each other.

# SCOTTISH WEREBEAR: AN UNEXPECTED AFFAIR

He stopped what he was doing when he noticed her staring at him, then cupped her face again for further kisses. The urgency with which he pressed his lips against hers made her heart ache for him. Never before had she felt so wanted, so needed, so...

"I've never felt this way before," she whispered.

He didn't answer, not using words anyway. Instead he scooped her up into his arms, sweeping her off her feet figuratively as well as literally. Only two words entered her mind, their connection growing even clearer than before. *Me neither.*

She felt weightless and unusually small again as he carried her through the dark lounge and down the hall, back into the bedroom she'd woken up in just minutes earlier. He laid her down on the soft covers, crawling on top of her on all fours. She was ready, as was he, to consummate their union in every possible way.

# CHAPTER ELEVEN

———◆———

Derek gazed down at Clarice's face. She looked beautiful, almost angelic if he ignored the bruise on her forehead. Her hair was fanned out over the pillow, and her eyes glistened in the soft candle light. The rest of her was equally perfect.

He'd never thought much about it before, what his dream woman would look like, but he knew already that Clarice was all he'd ever want. Her endless curves invited exploration of a more tactile kind, whether using fingertips or even his lips, and he could no longer resist her. Both bear and man wanted just one thing, to claim her and make her his.

It was impossible not to think of her in terms of his mate, the one fate had picked out for him, but even otherwise she was an attractive woman. The fact that she didn't act like she knew made her even more irresistible. Derek appreciated beauty like the next guy - bear or human- but had never had much patience for vanity.

The sweet scent of her arousal, the one he'd got but a hint of earlier, filled the room completely now. She was ready, aching for him as much as he ached for her. He noted how much her pupils had dilated, and how her cheeks had flushed to a deeper shade of pink.

She parted her legs, not brazenly, but almost involuntarily as if she was acting on instinct alone. It was a sight to behold. Her entire body seemed to invite him in while her eyes begged for further affections. Meanwhile, she was on her own journey of discovery, tracing her fingers across his biceps, and his firm, muscular chest, exploring the inked patterns on his shoulder.

He ran his hand over the ivory skin of her cleavage, taking care to be gentle with her. She wasn't the first female he'd been intimate with - even if it had been a while - but she was his first human and seemed all the more fragile for it.

As much as he tried, one part of his anatomy refused to entertain the notion of a gentle coupling. His cock had swelled to a size that was impressive for a bear, never mind a human. He hoped beyond hope that he wouldn't hurt her when the time came.

They'd reached that moment, which hung right in between endless possibility and painful anticipation. His hand traveled downward, circling her belly button, then moving on further until it reached the soft, inviting curls of her mound. So silky. Like a cub's fur. He slipped his finger in between her folds, thrilled to find that she was already wet for him.

"Stop teasing me," she pleaded, as she struggled to keep her urgent breaths under control.

Her fingers twitched, fingernails scraping skin for just a moment, before she ran her palm across and down his chest, over the ridges of his washboard abs. It was then that she finally touched his cock for the first time.

He was rock solid, had been for a while already, but the tension in his manhood was threatening to grow out of control now. As her fingers closed around his thick shaft, his mind was wiped clean of any remaining thoughts and speculations. Nothing mattered anymore except her pleasure.

Derek closed his eyes and took a deep breath in an attempt to swallow the desire to break free from her touch and plunge into her already. No, there could only be one first time, and he was going to do things properly.

He pulled away from her and crawled downward on all fours. Although her lips continued to tempt him, he wanted to taste a different part of her now. He kissed, nibbled and licked his way down, edging ever closer to those curls he had touched earlier. Every touch of his lips was met with a moan of hers.

She was vocal, yet another thing about her that he was pleased to discover.

He gently parted her legs wide enough to allow him to position himself between her thighs. Then he dove in for his first taste. Her sex was slick with sweet nectar, which he lapped up hungrily. She writhed against the sheets as he licked her outer lips first, then circled inward further and further until he finally slipped his tongue inside of her.

She tasted of honey, made of the sweetest summer flowers. The perfume of her arousal surrounded him and seduced him in a way that nothing - and no one - had ever done before. He didn't pleasure her orally as a favor to her, but because his deepest, most powerful desires demanded that he do so.

Clarice grabbed hold of the sheets, tugging at them violently as he continued his exploration of her most intimate depths. A fever-like feeling descended over Derek, clouding his mind with a red haze that made it impossible for him to think clearly. His inner bear was in charge, and somehow he knew exactly how to push Clarice's buttons.

As he alternated between licking her deeper and teasing her clit with the tip of his tongue, she reacted more and more intensely until finally she had reached the edge of her control. With her back arched, and hips raised up against his face, her moans had turned to cries, and her ragged breaths paused just for a moment.

"Oh my God!" she cried out while reaching for his hair,

tugging at it just hard enough to be pleasurable in a primal, almost painful manner.

He pulled away to get a better look at her expression but knew better than to stop his affections completely. With two fingers inside of her, and his thumb resting against the base of her clit, he drove her all the way over the cliff and into sweet relief.

With that, they'd unwittingly completed half of the journey all fated mates must undergo to finalize their bond: a selfless gift, the pleasuring of one partner by the other without expecting the same in return.

But as soon as she'd caught her breath, Clarice no longer seemed satisfied lying on her back. Derek observed her as she leaned up on her elbows and let her eyes focus on him again. She licked her lips - a gesture that he knew would keep driving him crazy as long as he was alive - and beckoned him to crawl up on top of her again.

"That was amazing," she breathed against his lips, before leaning further up for another taste of him. "Let's see what else is in store for us tonight."

Derek shuddered as her hand closed around his cock again and directed it straight at her slick entrance, his head coating itself in her sweet nectar. She bucked her hips, causing his thick cock to press against her harder though he couldn't quite enter her yet. He worried about hurting her, but the look in her eyes told him he had no choice but to proceed. She would accept no less than all he had to give.

He lowered himself, waiting as her body adjusted to him. The sensation as he finally entered her hot pussy was indescribable. It was as if he hadn't just entered her body, but invaded her mind as well. Her pleasure became his pleasure. They fed off one another, snowballing until it combined into one, and neither could tell anymore where one individual ended, and the other began.

Much to Derek's surprise, as well as Clarice's, judging from the expression on her face, her body accommodated his entire length and girth with ease. *As though we're made for one another*, Derek thought. *We are*, Clarice responded.

He started to move, each thrust of his met by a twitch of her hips. Even with her legs spread wide, he felt the stranglehold her pussy had on him as if trying to keep him inside of her as long as possible.

Derek loved how she felt against him; she provided the softness that his hard muscle lacked. Yin and yang, feminine and masculine, so different and yet so perfect together. With every move of his, he couldn't keep his eyes off the effect it had on her curves. He loved how her full breasts quivered when he pushed into her, as though they were teasing him, begging for attention.

He dove down and took her nipple into his mouth, eliciting a more primal groan from her lips. She was helpless again, pinned to the bed by his large physique, her thighs spread as wide as they would go, feet attempting to lock around his waist but having difficulty hanging on.

She reached out for his shoulders, running her fingernails over his tattoo. Her touch gave him shivers. Every move, every affection was as if it had been carefully choreographed. One paused, and the other took over, their bodies laboring away towards that common goal: complete surrender.

It started deep inside him; a twitch, which grew into a whirlwind of intense sensation that soon filled his whole body, before spilling over into hers. Sticky like honey, their pleasure clung to everything as it progressed, filling their veins, until their entire beings had been set alight.

A deep, primal groan left his lips, met by a cry from hers. Their movements sped up for a couple of strokes until Clarice's nails dug deeply into Derek's back. He shuddered into her, his cock twitching as he buried his seed into her depths.

When they opened their eyes again, they found themselves sitting upright: Clarice was held up firmly in Derek's strong arms. Their connection was complete. Selfless pleasure followed by the exchange of fluids and synchronized release.

They were spent, yet he refused to let her go, continuing to cradle her in his embrace until at last, their bodies relaxed, and they decided to lie down. Derek on his back, Clarice pressed up against him with her arm across his chest.

Clarice rested her head on Derek's shoulder and sighed deeply. Derek could hear her heartbeat slow down until it almost reached its normal rhythm.

"You must have a ton of questions," Derek remarked, as even Clarice's breaths had calmed back down.

"I imagine perhaps so do you."

"You write?" he asked.

Clarice smiled and nodded. "And you bake cakes."

"Who doesn't like cake?" Derek retorted with a grin.

"Nobody, I imagine." Clarice frowned as she collected her thoughts, and then raised her head to look up at him. "How come you're in my head? Is it always like this?"

"As far as I've heard, yes. I had no idea it would work with humans as well..."

"Mhmm... It's weird. Nice, but still a bit weird." Clarice chuckled.

"You must know, I never planned for this. I never expected to find someone I'd want to settle down with." Although Derek knew she felt the same, it was still awkward saying that kind of thing out loud.

Clarice let out a short laugh. "To think I came here to

get away from people..."

"What's waiting for you back home?" Derek asked.

Clarice paused for a moment, her thoughts racing, though Derek couldn't pick up on any particular one of them. "Actually... Nothing much. My work is flexible, and I'd been planning to look for a different flat upon my return. The one where I'm living now already didn't feel quite right anymore."

Derek wanted to ask about the phone call that first evening, his worry that there was someone else in her life but bit his tongue. There was no need to pry further. She was here with him, and that was all that mattered. In time, they'd learn everything there was to know about each other.

He wrapped his arm around her tighter, enjoying the feeling of her soft, almost silky skin pressing against his side. She was his mate now, and nobody could get between them, especially once they'd make things official.

"I have to ask..." he started.

She raised her head slightly, looking him in the eye. "It's funny, knowing what you're going to say most of the time. Yes, I'd love to stay."

As he kept gazing into her amber eyes, Derek thought he could see a change in her. There was a new brilliance in her gaze, a sparkle. It wasn't subtle like you hear about but obvious to him like it would be to any other bear. No longer did she look completely human, but her eyes seemed to glow in the dark. Like the embers of a fire that had stopped burning brightly, but refused to extinguish itself completely.

"How does it work?" she asked. "You can change at will?"

"It takes a bit of practice to control the bear side of things, but yes."

# SCOTTISH WEREBEAR: AN UNEXPECTED AFFAIR

"There are so many stories about werewolves, but I'd never heard of a werebear before," she remarked.

"We like to keep to ourselves away from people. Wolves are much more common."

"So there are actual werewolves too?" Clarice sighed and rubbed her eyes with the back of her hand. Obviously she was still feeling the effects of her earlier ordeal, as well as the sweet exertion he'd just put her through.

"Yes, though I doubt you'll ever meet one. We don't exactly get along, bears and wolves."

Before she had a chance to ask another question, she was interrupted by a low rumble originating in her stomach. "I'm so sorry," she mumbled, an embarrassed smile forming on her lips.

"I'm the one who should be sorry. I hope you like stew?" Although Derek didn't want to let her go, he jumped into action anyway and got up from the bed. How could he be so selfish, forgetting about her basic needs in his eagerness to get her into bed?

She sat up as well, observing him as he hurriedly put on the bare minimum of clothes.

"Stew sounds great."

Derek waited as she put on her panties, as well as a t-shirt of his that was so big it came down almost to her knees. Then they both headed for the kitchen, hand in hand, certain that no matter how many questions still needed to be answered, everything would work itself out.

# EPILOGUE

Although Clarice had had the chance to get used to the idea of werebears for a few days now, the prospect of meeting Derek's only relatives, other than Aidan, was still weird and unnerving. They were bears as well, of course, and what little interaction she'd had with Aidan before he left suggested that not all bears would be too pleased that one of their own was pairing up with a human.

They had good reason to be suspicious if you took into account the stories they'd grown up on and the fact that they had few unique rules or laws of their own except the code of secrecy. At the same time, Clarice couldn't see how the powerful bond she shared with Derek could ever be considered bad.

Derek had quickly become her entire world.

Of course, she still had her writing; after a couple of days of rest following the accident she had been able to finish her novel and get it to her editor on time to meet the deadline.

She also still had Lily, her best friend, who found the idea of Clarice's whirlwind holiday romance quite bizarre. Clarice felt some regret that she couldn't confide in Lily, but she'd sworn to keep Derek's true nature a secret and so she wouldn't be able to break that trust no matter what.

Still, Clarice also felt bad that Lily couldn't be there on the day that her connection with Derek would be made official.

Bears didn't care much for tradition, and as such there were very few rituals and ceremonies they performed regularly. One of them, the most important, was the

80

mating ritual.

Derek had explained it to her as basically a wedding for bears and their mates. Because they lived in such isolated places and didn't interact with many fellow bears, mating rituals were small affairs, often only involving the couple themselves and perhaps the occasional relative.

Today would be no different. Derek and Clarice would perform the ritual, under the watchful eye of Derek's elder cousin, Elise and her mate, Jack. Aidan - although invited - couldn't make it, which was just as well because Clarice was nervous enough already.

She looked in the mirror one last time, scrutinizing the long chiffon dress she'd purchased for the occasion. Her brown wavy hair she'd kept down, adorned only by a few flowers Derek had picked for her earlier. He really was quite the romantic when he wanted to be. Her make-up was also kept to a minimum, just how Derek liked it, but Clarice had insisted on disguising the remnants of the bruise on her forehead with some foundation anyway.

*You're beautiful just as you are,* he'd said when she'd fretted over what to wear for today. Although it sounded like a cliché, he managed to say it in such a way that had completely convinced her.

Despite everything, it was still a bit surreal knowing that a man as gorgeous and built as Derek would admire her so completely. If she didn't feel it in her bones every time he was near, she would have had a hard time believing it. Things like this didn't happen to women like her, normally. Then again, normally, you'd never believe that shapeshifters existed either.

*It's time,* Derek's voice entered her thoughts. He was waiting for her in the hall. She could sense him clearly, even if she couldn't see him yet.

Elise and Jack would be waiting outside in the garden.

Derek had told her earlier that this was where the ritual was going to take place. The two of them would walk out together when the time came.

She smoothed down her dress, took a deep breath and opened the door. There he was.

Derek's eyes locked onto hers, and she felt herself fill with confidence. It was weird, different, how Derek could still her worries and insecurities just with his presence. She'd never felt that with any of her boyfriends from before, especially not with Alan. The more she thought about her past, the more convinced she became that everything up to this point had never felt quite real enough as if it had all just been pretend and make-believe.

*I love you,* she thought. He responded with a smile and offered her his arm.

Together they walked along the broad hallway, through the lobby and out the main entrance of the farm, where an impressively tall middle-aged couple waited for them, just as Derek had foretold.

The woman turned, revealing features very similar to Derek and Aidan - the eyes, the shape of her nose, all were familiar. It was obvious that they were related.

She smiled and nodded at Clarice. The man, Jack presumably, just waited in place without looking back at the two of them. A stone giant, Clarice noted with a smile.

Clarice and Derek walked across the tree-lined lawn together, taking their position across from the couple and turned to face each other. It was chilly outside, as one would expect the weather to be in early October in the Scottish Highlands, but the excitement of their upcoming union had caused Clarice's skin to burn up so much that the cold failed to affect her.

Elise stepped ahead and handed each of them a pouch. Derek had explained what to do with the contents already, so Clarice knew to open hers, taking out the first of the two items inside.

"Derek," Clarice whispered, her voice shaking with residual nerves. "Please accept this, a red rose, as token of my love, and along with it my promise to walk beside you as your mate and mother to your cubs, as long as we both shall live."

Derek's eyes remained fixed on hers, the intensity in his gaze filling her stomach with butterflies.

"I do," Derek answered, his voice slightly hoarse with emotion. "Clarice, please accept this token-" Derek pulled out a short, very aged looking dagger from his pouch and presented it to Clarice with both hands. "This blade, to keep with you for protection at all time, as a symbol that I'll always look after you as your mate and father to our family, as long as we both shall live."

As often as Derek had gone through the exact words with Clarice, their meaning had not lost gravity. If anything, she felt his intentions more deeply now than before.

"I do," Clarice responded. She wedged the dagger carefully in between her belt and the soft fabric of her dress, just as Derek had taught her to do earlier. Once back inside she would keep the weapon safe somewhere, available to her whenever she would need it - which hopefully would be never.

Now, it was time for the second item, something that was a lot more familiar to most humans, including Clarice. The rings. Clarice pulled the bigger one out of her pouch, weighing it in her hand. It was made of white gold and was very heavy; the peculiar spiral design ensured it would expand and become big enough to fit Derek's finger even after shifting.

Derek followed suit, holding up the much more

delicate counterpart meant for Clarice's finger. Hers was a simpler, non-expanding design, adorned by a cut ruby set on top.

"With this ring, I become yours, and you become mine." Derek slipped the precious ring around Clarice's finger, the sight of it sparkling against her pale skin almost taking her breath away. Although the design didn't look all that unusual to Clarice's eyes, Derek had explained that any bear would recognize it as a mate's ring, a clear sign that she belonged, even if not everyone would approve.

"With this ring, I become yours, and you become mine," Clarice repeated, putting the bigger, more masculine and complicated ring onto Derek's finger, while trying but failing to conceal the tremble in her hands.

Next to them, Elise's emotions took over, and a sob escaped her lips. "Remember when we did this, Jack?" she whispered. From the corner of her eye, Clarice could see Jack taking her hand into both of his. The stone giant evidently had a soft spot after all.

A few years down the line, who knew, perhaps Clarice and Derek would be the more experienced couple, remembering their own special day while observing another bear perform the ritual with his mate, Aidan perhaps?

Clarice looked up at Derek, whose face failed to hide the pride and admiration he felt for her. They were one now, officially. A lone tear collected in the corner of her eye as she realized the importance of what had just happened.

Human marriages ended in divorce more often than not, despite most people going into them with the best of intentions. With Derek, there was no doubt in her mind that they were truly destined to be together. Their connection would never fade because something held them together that ran deeper than the shallow infatuations people tend to mistake for love. Fate. Or biology, whatever you choose to believe in.

They would be mates forever, and nobody would ever come in between them. She tiptoed, and they shared a kiss, not because it was tradition, but because they couldn't help it.

Then, Elise came up to the two of them and congratulated them, hugging Clarice tightly and welcoming her to the family. Jack shook her hand, as well as Derek's but remained mostly quiet, nodding his congratulations at the two of them. *That went well,* Clarice thought, relieved not to have to deal with any disapproval from Derek's relatives.

As all four of them made their way back inside the house, the phone rang. *That'll be Aidan.* He'd declined their invitation, stating he had urgent business to attend to but said he'd give his best wishes on the day. She kept her senses locked on Derek as he walked into the kitchen and answered the phone, focusing as best she could to try and figure out if her assumption was correct.

"Hello?" Derek said.

*Yes, that's Aidan all right,* Clarice sensed, as she entered the room behind Derek.

Almost instantly, Derek's mood, which had been triumphant and celebratory until now, turned darker. She couldn't tell what was going on, but his emotions tugged and pulled at her, telling her that something had gone horribly wrong.

"I understand. I'll be there." Derek hung up and looked over at her.

*Problems?* Clarice thought. Derek crossed the distance between them, resting his hands on her shoulders upon reaching her.

"Aidan needs my help. His mate is in trouble. I'll ask Elise and Jack to stick around while I'm gone. I'm so sorry about this."

She nodded, sad to see him leave without the chance to celebrate their new status, but there was no room for jealousy or speculation in her mind. She could feel that the situation was serious, and the thought to question Derek's actions didn't even occur to her. There was no room for secrets between them, so in time, she'd hear all about today's troubles as well.

"Go. I'll be fine. Just..." She tiptoed to reach him again, wrapping her arms around his shoulders tightly. "Be careful," she whispered.

Derek returned her embrace, kissing her forehead a couple of times before releasing her again. "Of course. Everything will be fine." He forced a smile, but Clarice didn't feel it. There was a change about Derek, he was tenser than she'd ever seen him before, almost hostile, though of course not towards her.

He was readying for a fight, and there was nothing she could do to help.

*I love you, please come back to me,* Clarice thought.

*Always,* Derek responded.

With that, he made his way to the lounge to talk to Elise, leaving Clarice in the kitchen.

*Everything was going to be fine. It had to be, right?*

# - THE END -

# Scottish Werebear

## A DANGEROUS BUSINESS

# CHAPTER ONE

———◆———

All was not well in Rannoch, Scotland. Heidi Blackwood felt her heartbeat speed up, and the urge to protest grew ever stronger in her chest. *How the hell had this happened?*

"You may not like the idea of leaving, but we need one of our own inside the Alliance. You said so yourself," Eric Blackwood said while giving his daughter a strict look.

"Yeah, but..." *I never thought it would be me*, Heidi thought. Her father's news came as a bit of a shock. Whenever the topic of the Alliance had come up, Heidi had always expected one of the young males of the pack to be chosen as their representative to the Alliance. Never once did she think it could be her.

"I've made the necessary arrangements. You are to travel to Edinburgh and join them. I've spoken to their local leader, Jamie Abbott, already." Her dad sounded firm. He wouldn't be receptive to any arguments she would think of, and she didn't have anything sensible to add, either. She just needed a moment to let the information sink in.

Of course, he was right. They needed someone they could rely on to join the Alliance. Who could be more reliable than Heidi herself? She'd learned at an early age that if you wanted something done right, you had to do it yourself. It was time to put her money where her mouth was.

She took a deep breath and tried to focus.

"I'll pack my things." Heidi turned on her heel and headed out of the living room of the cozy log hut where she lived with her parents, and up the stairs to her bedroom.

It may have been years since she had been of age technically, but the Wolves of Rannoch didn't follow the same rules that human society did. She would be considered her father's daughter first of all and her own woman second, no matter how old she was. Only her marriage to an eligible wolf would change that, but Heidi had no intention of throwing herself into yet another situation where she'd be forced to dance to someone else's tune.

In a way this assignment was a blessing in disguise, Heidi thought. She wondered if her father had picked her because he'd sensed that she would soon outgrow Rannoch and its strict rules. Or perhaps it was simply because he trusted her more than the others. She wanted to think it was maybe a bit of both.

As she started throwing clothes and a few weapons into an overnight bag, she wondered what the other members of the Alliance would be like. Jamie Abbott was a bear, she already knew that.

The rivalry between bears and wolves was one of the main reasons her father had pushed for one of their own to join the Alliance in the first place, even though they'd had a truce between their species for the past few years. She'd heard whispers over campfires about other, more unusual species of shifters inside the Alliance, but couldn't be sure if those were just rumors. Bears and wolves, that was the most likely scenario.

She also wondered what it would be like to stay in Edinburgh. She'd visited the city a few times, but had never actually lived away from home. It could be exciting, an adventure, something a little different. But if Heidi was completely honest with herself, it was also a little scary.

# SCOTTISH WEREBEAR: A DANGEROUS BUSINESS

Twenty-two years she'd spent in this room, in this house, safe in the knowledge that there was an entire pack surrounding her who would do anything to protect the alpha's daughter. Not that she'd needed protection – she was strong, taller than most of the other females her age, and broader as well. She was no pushover and had gotten into plenty of scraps growing up. She was used to winning, even when fighting some of the boys in her pack.

But the outside world was largely a mystery to Heidi. Bears, especially. She'd never even met one, though of course that would change shortly.

It didn't take her long to pack a few changes of clothes and a good selection of knives and other weaponry she thought might come in handy, but she spent much too long poring over all that *other stuff*. A photo album, her favorite books. She even found herself holding her old diary, which she hadn't written in for years but which now felt like too precious a thing to leave behind.

No, she was going to make a fresh start in Edinburgh. Plus, what would the other members of the Alliance say if they found all these girly mementos in her things? They wouldn't take her seriously, and she couldn't have that.

She hurriedly put all her old stuff into the top drawer of her dresser and zipped up the bag. She was ready.

A deep breath later, she picked up the bag and closed the door of her bedroom for what would be the last time in a good while. She had no idea when she would return, and did her best not to think of that too much.

Duty called. It was an honor that her father had picked her to represent them in the Alliance, and she would do her best to live up to his expectations.

Downstairs, beside her dad, Heidi's mom was waiting with her arms crossed. Clearly she was unhappy that Heidi was to leave, but she'd had no choice in the matter. An alpha's decision-making powers were absolute, even within the home.

"You just be careful, all right, darling?" Heidi's mom, Rebecca Blackwood, gave her a warm hug. Her voice betrayed the emotions welling up in her chest.

"I'll be fine, really," Heidi responded, trying to convince herself as well as her mom.

It was difficult not to be emotional, and all of a sudden, during this very rare embrace, it struck Heidi how much shorter and smaller her mom actually was. She felt fragile, sniffling slightly as she tried to keep the beginnings of tears in check.

"Call when you get there, promise me."

"Of course," Heidi forced a smile as she extricated herself from the continuing hug. Things were getting awkward now and if she didn't leave soon, she'd be crying puddles herself. It was important to Heidi to leave Rannoch with her head held high. No longer the little girl, but a she-wolf with an important job to do. An opportunity like this didn't come along every day.

Her dad cleared his throat and gave her a much more stoic, pat-on-the-back style hug when she approached him.

"Good girl. Do your job, follow orders, and do us proud. But always remember why you're there: in the end it's always us against them." He nodded at Heidi, and she thought she could see a little glimmer of something in his eyes as well. Pride? Worry? She wasn't quite sure what it was, but she knew she'd never seen it before.

"Yes, Dad." Although she couldn't guess what exactly was going on in her father's head, she understood his words perfectly. She was to make sure that the Alliance served the wolves as much as it did the bears and other species.

As long as it was humans against shifters, it would be

easy to pick sides, but if she found out that the Alliance was in any way favoring one of the other species over wolves, she had to make sure her father was notified. She had to be his eyes and ears inside the Alliance.

"Now be on your way, before you miss the train." Eric Blackwood nodded at Heidi one last time, signaling it really was time for her to leave.

So Heidi picked up her stuff, along with the few provisions her mom had packed, and headed straight out the door without looking back even once.

With her head held high, she marched towards the edge of the settlement, where one of the pack's jeeps was waiting. The drive was short and quiet – she didn't exchange a single word with the young wolf who was driving. Honestly, she was so lost in thought for most of it that she didn't even remember who it was.

The whole journey, including getting off at the station and waiting for her train to Edinburgh, passed in a blur. She had no idea what would be waiting for her, so her mind couldn't stop speculating about it.

Once in the train, she barely took note of the cloudy, rain-lashed countryside as it passed by at high speed outside the windows. Her attention was focused solely on the mobile phone in her hand, and the address and directions programmed into it. From the station, she'd take a bus, and a short walk later she'd arrive at the Alliance office.

What would it look like? A shiny modern affair, bustling with activity, dotted with fancy computer screens and complicated maps and things, like you see on detective shows? Or perhaps it was more of a secret lair type of place, hidden away in an old warehouse, complete with training facilities and a stockpile of weapons.

Heidi closed her eyes and tried to relax, forcing herself

to breathe more slowly. It would take a few more hours to get there, and somehow she was certain that she'd need all her energy then.

———◆———

When Heidi awoke, she had no idea how long she'd been asleep. The train was still mostly empty, only a few seats were taken in her carriage, and luckily nobody had sat anywhere near her. She didn't feel all that sociable.

At least her nap had helped her get her thoughts in order. She was on her own now, and she would manage. Somehow.

Not long after waking up did the scenery outside change as well. The lush green landscapes had made way for more built-up areas. They were getting close to the city. Village after village zipped past outside, and Heidi started recognizing some of the station names from her last trip to Edinburgh. Within twenty minutes, they pulled into their final destination and it was time to collect her stuff and disembark.

The bus ride also went seamlessly, even though she had been a bit worried about missing her stop. With the help of the phone, making her way to the Alliance address was equally easy.

After checking and double-checking that the house number matched what was in her phone, she finally knocked against the weather-beaten wood. A few flakes of faded blue paint chipped off and fell to the ground as she did so.

Despite her expectations being vague, the outside of the office didn't match up. It looked neither modern nor particularly mysterious. The building was old, in a downtrodden part of town, and plain ugly.

# SCOTTISH WEREBEAR: A DANGEROUS BUSINESS

Would the inside be any better?

Finally, a short wait later, someone opened the door. Her disappointments about where she'd found herself vanished instantly and were replaced by utter shock and disbelief, along with something else. Something more intimate.

His scent hit her first. A mixture of clean laundry and unmistakably male hormones made its way into her nostrils, setting her insides alight with a need she'd never felt before. His fragrance was different, unlike any other wolf she'd ever met.

The confused sensations she felt reminded her of the stories she'd heard, about when a wolf finds his one true mate. And yet, she wasn't elated like most of her peers would have been, she was royally pissed off. She's been sent on this important mission, and the first thing that happens is she wants to mate with a coworker? *Unacceptable.*

Heidi couldn't quite make out what the man who had opened the door looked like, only that he was tall, so tall he blocked out most of the light from inside the room. Two amber eyes burned into her with such intensity that she wanted - but couldn't bring herself - to look away from them.

*Damn. This was definitely the most inconvenient thing to happen to anyone, ever.*

"Jamie gave me this address," Heidi heard herself say. "I'm Heidi."

# CHAPTER TWO

———◆———

Aidan McMillan shook his head, before focusing on Jamie Abbott's face again. "Just now, when we're starting to make progress, you want me to partner up with a rookie? You know I work better on my own."

"If the Alliance is to be successful in its campaign against the Sons of Domnall, we've got to keep growing. And it's not like you're in the middle of anything in particular right now," Jamie remarked.

Aidan glared at him, still incredulous over what he felt was a rash decision he should have been consulted about. But Jamie was the team leader, a role he took much too seriously indeed. *Team leader, but not a team player,* Aidan thought.

"You'll meet Heidi soon enough, don't worry. I'm sure you'll find her to be a valuable addition to the team. In the meantime, how are you getting on with that human you've been questioning?" Jamie crossed his arms and stared Aidan down until the latter finally backed down with a dejected sigh.

Involving a newbie was the wrong call. Aidan was certain of it but if he gave Jamie too much shit, he might stop being the laid-back leader and exact his revenge by turning into a micro-managing prick. That was something Aidan was keen to avoid, given how much of his day was spent on his private investigation, instead of the official one.

"The human, Alison, yes. She's given me a couple of websites to check out which at first glance appear to be just the usual racist, skinhead crap, but some of the wording used indicates they're speaking in code. They keep referring to themselves as 'the Sons', so that's promising. She's hiding something, I'm sure of it, but I think her information is sound."

"Good job, stay on that," Jamie said.

Aidan nodded. He'd already created a log-in on one of the sites, a discussion forum, and posted a fake introduction of himself. Although he wasn't sure how this group worked, he hoped that if he made all the right noises, perhaps someone would be in touch to find out if he'd want to be involved beyond just spewing hateful nonsense on the Internet.

"Right, well, I had better make a move." Jamie checked his watch, probably just to make a point, and put on his coat.

Edinburgh could get quite chilly this time of year and bears weren't so resistant to the cold while in human form. Shifting, of course, was completely out of the question in Scotland's second busiest city.

"Later," Aidan mumbled, as he watched Jamie leave the dingy office space they'd recently moved into. Then he folded himself into his much too small office chair and opened a browser window on the outdated desktop computer on his desk.

In addition to reading as many existing posts as he could on that skinhead website, he'd also been going through old articles about a certain event that had happened almost seventeen years ago to the day: the death of Aidan's parents. That's what he returned to.

He knew the words of most of them by heart already. Suspected car accidents on the far away Isle of Skye didn't get a lot of news coverage, so he'd been going through the same handful of articles again and again. Aidan felt like he was close to discovering something new in all that old information, but he wasn't quite sure if that was just because his frazzled brain was playing tricks on him.

*Heidi, the rookie,* Aidan scoffed to himself. Sure, he'd meet her, he'd force himself to be civil enough in person too, but no matter what Jamie and the Alliance wanted, his thoughts were still his own. A very dainty name for a girl joining a covert task force out to hunt shifter killers. Aidan could just imagine her: a fragile little thing who'd worry more about the state of her hair and nails than the mortal danger in which they may find themselves.

After reading the end of the Google search results about the accident, he logged onto the skinhead website again. To his pleasure, one of the most prolific members had already commented on his introductory post. The greeting was full of national-socialist symbolism, with a few marked differences.

Along with calling themselves "the Sons," the fact that they didn't refer to foreigners as much as "animals" or "monsters" signaled to Aidan that they weren't just ordinary skinheads. If only he could gain their trust somehow.

He browsed through the older discussions, adding to his existing notes about terminology to compile something of a glossary alongside other random observations he'd made. Every day he ended his shift with a quick read-through of all the new material, in an attempt to assimilate and learn about their "culture" to the point of it becoming second nature to him. There was no way of knowing if he'd need to apply it all someday soon, if he indeed managed to meet any of these people in person.

A knock on the door interrupted him. *Damn, was that her already?*

Aidan got up, his chair creaking loudly as though relieved to be rid of the burden. He quickly crossed the half dozen steps towards the door, and turned the heavy lock until it released with a loud click. He tried his best to force himself into a more neutral facial expression, but he'd always had a hard time keeping his emotional state under wraps.

As he pulled the door open, revealing a wind-blown female figure outside, he had even more trouble keeping himself in check.

The statuesque silhouette standing in front of the doorway was less dainty and a lot more Amazonian than his expectations had allowed for. Long strawberry blond hair blew in the wind and two eyes cut through the darkness, staring right at him. But none of that explained how he felt – not even her irresistibly sweet perfume could explain it. He was frozen in place, helpless and enchanted, his massive frame blocking the entire entrance.

"Mr. Abbott sent me here," she said, while shaking the odd fallen leaf off her coat. "I'm Heidi."

"Right," Aidan responded, barely.

"So..." She placed her hands on her hips and cocked her head to one side.

The pause that followed wasn't just awkward, it was painful.

"Are you going to introduce yourself, or...?"

Aidan had trouble focusing on her words, such was the immense pull her presence had on his inner bear. The beast was going crazy, fighting against his human side, desperate to break free and pounce on her.

"Oh, sorry. Aidan. Please come in." Though his feet felt like they were made of lead, Aidan stepped aside at last, allowing her into the office.

She eyed him suspiciously as she stepped inside and quickly pulled the door shut behind her.

They say there's nothing less flattering than fluorescent

light, but Aidan couldn't recall ever seeing a more radiant sight than the woman who stood in front of him now. Her strong build suggested she came from a healthy lineage. She was a fighter. Intelligent yet slightly hostile green eyes stared at him; clearly, she did not suffer fools kindly and was used to being in charge wherever she went.

"So you're the rookie," Aidan remarked, more to himself than to her.

She frowned and pressed her lips together to form a tight line. Yep, a dominant personality, this one – as beautiful as she was strong-willed. Although she looked younger than him in years, she was no girl, but all woman.

It didn't seem like it at the time, but Aidan was usually good with the opposite sex. He was a reasonably witty conversationalist, and could usually get a laugh or two out of even the most difficult audience. It certainly helped that his large, muscular frame meant that most women found him attractive as well.

All that was wiped away now. In front of Heidi, Aidan felt helplessly stupid, like anything that would come out of his mouth would be all wrong.

*Work*. He should play it cool and talk about work.

"Welcome. You can take that desk." Aidan pointed at the unused table set against the far wall of the office.

Their eyes met again. Hers looked strangely fiery, even if they were a cool shade of green, and distrustful.

"Thanks," she said, her intonation making it sound like a question rather than a statement. He observed her as she walked to the dust covered desk and placed her overnight bag down onto the ground beside it.

Her gait suggested she was strong, flexible, but even that coat couldn't disguise that she had curves in all the right places, especially around the hips. She certainly didn't seem fragile, which pleased Aidan's inner bear to no end.

# SCOTTISH WEREBEAR: A DANGEROUS BUSINESS

"Do you have anywhere to stay?" Aidan asked finally, after watching her inspect her new workplace for a few painful seconds. He had no idea what expectations she might have had of the place, but was pretty sure the reality would have been a disappointment either way.

She turned and shook her head. Her expression didn't give him much to go on, except she didn't look all that pleased to be here.

"No problem. There are rooms upstairs. The stairs are through there." He gestured at the door near what was now her desk.

As usual, Jamie had been economical with the details about Aidan's new partner. Would it have killed him to mention that she was going to live here as well? He might have made sure the place looked a bit more presentable. No, actually that was a lie. Aidan would have done nothing of the sort, he would have left things as messy and dirty as they were now, because up until the point of actually meeting Heidi, he would have loved nothing more than to see her run right back out of the office, never to return.

"Thanks," Heidi repeated herself.

"Say, I was just going to head out for the night, how about we grab a bite to eat? I know this great pub nearby. Best fish and chips in town. My treat," Aidan suggested.

It immediately occurred to him that his offer might seem way too eager, but it was too late to worry about that now, since he'd already blurted it out.

"Through here?" Heidi asked, while turning the knob on the door leading to the stairs, as though she never even heard his invitation. She didn't wait for an answer either, and reached over to pick up her bag again before marching off into the dimly lit stairwell.

"Yeah, just take any room, they're all empty," Aidan called after her, just before the door shut behind her.

*Very smooth, you idiot,* he thought to himself while shaking his head. He could already tell that an uphill battle lay ahead if he was going to get along well enough with Heidi. She might be his mate, but she certainly wasn't all that friendly about it.

# CHAPTER THREE

———— ◆ ————

Heidi didn't know what to do. Should she take up Aidan on his offer of dinner? It would be the civil thing to do, and yet she really wasn't sure she was up to spending her evening socializing. All she really wanted was to crawl into the steel framed bed in the sparsely furnished room she found herself in, and hide under the covers.

So this was where she was going to stay and work...

It wasn't anything like what she thought a home ought to look like. Clearly this place could benefit from a feminine touch.

And Aidan? He seemed unusual, very unlike the boys she grew up with in Rannoch. Oddly enticing, like he was carrying a deep, dark secret that was just begging to be uncovered.

*No way, that's just the hormones talking.*

Heidi still couldn't believe that the first guy she ran into on her first stint in the outside world was going to be her mate. Fate was clearly playing a very cruel joke on her. She wanted to punch something - someone - and yet... She had to admit that he was rather handsome.

After lifting her bag onto the bed, she started unpacking the few belongings she had chosen to carry. All of it fit easily into the very impersonal steel filing cabinet in the corner - the only thing that could even be interpreted as storage in this room.

She hid her assortment of weapons underneath her clothes, and slammed the drawer shut with a loud crash that echoed off the bare walls.

There wasn't a sign of anything remotely nice in sight.

The bed was made of tubular steel with the occasional patch of rust breaking through the lacquer. The filing cabinet would have been primer gray at one point, except the paint had started to flake off, revealing the bare metal underneath. The room had no carpeting, dirty walls that probably hadn't seen a fresh coat of paint in years, and a bare bulb where a lampshade should have been.

The flooring provided the only source of color: a sea-green type of slippery vinyl that reminded her of the old school in Rannoch.

*What a dump.*

And the downstairs wasn't any better either. Worn desks with computers that looked at least ten years old, and all of it dusty. Didn't anyone ever clean this place? And was it just Aidan and Jamie working for the Alliance in Edinburgh, anyway? Quite a depressing presence for such an important city.

Heidi rubbed her eyes, which had gotten a bit sore after the long trip, and tried to focus on her last exchange with her dad before leaving.

*Do your job, follow orders, do us proud,* that's what he had said. *In the end, it's always us against them.*

It made perfect sense when she was still home, and she had been reasonably confident she would do a decent job. Now, she wasn't so certain anymore. How was she going to focus on her job, when a coworker provided such a big distraction?

Heidi took the mobile phone out of her pocket and stared at it for a while, before finally dialing home.

"Hello?" Heidi's mom answered almost immediately. She must have been sitting by the phone, waiting for this call.

"Hi, Mom," Heidi responded.

"You made it? Did everything go okay? How was the

trip?" So many questions, and Heidi didn't feel like answering them in much detail at all.

"Fine. I'm fine. I just wanted to let you know I'm here, before going out to dinner with the Alliance people."

"Oh, sure, darling. Well, take care of yourself, you're in the big city now."

After the emotional goodbye earlier today, this long distance exchange with her mother was difficult for Heidi. She struggled to keep it together, to answer concisely without letting the concern in her mom's voice tug at her emotions.

Between her confusing feelings for Aidan downstairs, the depressing room, and the uncertainty of whatever lay ahead, Heidi felt completely alone. This wasn't the beginning of an adventure as much as it felt like a banishment away from everything she knew.

"I will, Mom. I'll be fine," Heidi said, hanging up before one solitary tear escaped from the corner of her eye and rolled down her cheek.

This was hopeless. The longer she sat here on her own, the sorrier she would feel for herself and she did feel quite hungry... She dusted herself off, wiped her face with the back of her hand, and headed back downstairs. She could only hope Aidan hadn't left yet.

———— ◆ ————

"So, this is the place," Aidan said triumphantly, pointing at the gilded sign outside the historic looking building. Its name, The Coach and Horses, was written across an old fashioned illustration of the same.

*Supposedly* the best fish and chips in the city, though perhaps Aidan had just said that in an attempt to impress her, Heidi thought.

"Great," she responded, but her tone didn't quite match his excitement. She wasn't comfortable with the idea of sitting through dinner with the man, not because she didn't trust him, but because she couldn't trust herself.

"So where is - what do I call him? Mr. Abbott?" she asked, as they stepped through the wooden paneled door and into the cozy interior of the pub. It wasn't very busy inside, but Aidan opted to lead the way towards the back of the pub where there were even fewer people.

"Jamie. He... well, he keeps his own schedule. I should probably let him know you've arrived, though," Aidan said, while pulling out a chair for her at the nearest unoccupied table that caught his fancy.

"Sure." Heidi observed Aidan as he took out his phone and tapped out a quick message.

His movements, even while they were just walking the short distance between the office and the pub, seemed deliberate. Like he never did anything without a purpose. He gave the impression of a born predator with an iron focus. That's probably what struck Heidi the most about him, when she allowed herself to really watch the man. The wolves she grew up with, even those a generation before Heidi, were a lot more playful than Aidan seemed.

But his body language changed significantly when he was talking to her, like he wasn't being himself. They hadn't spoken about it yet, but she assumed that the strange pull she felt towards him was throwing him off balance as much as it did her. He was just a lot better at concealing that fact.

"Hi."

Heidi looked up to find a cheerful looking girl in a too tight white t-shirt and black apron featuring the pub's logo smiling down at her. "Ready to order?"

"Oh. Hi, Aidan, I didn't see you there," the girl added.

She blushed and looked away at her notepad, while scratching the side of her face with the back of her pen.

"I'll have the usual, please," Aidan said, while putting his phone away again. His eyes glanced up at the waitress, but then almost instantly settled on Heidi.

"You said the fish and chips were good here, right? So I guess that's what I'll have. And a Coke, please," Heidi said. Coke was the first thing that popped into her head. A big change from the largely homemade offerings of Rannoch, plus Heidi didn't drink, never had.

"Two fish platters, a Guinness and a Coke, coming right up." As soon as she finished repeating the order, the girl made a quick escape, and they were on their own again.

All the tables around them were empty, and despite the ambient noise of conversations, and cheers for some football game on the TV nearer the entrance, they might as well have been completely alone.

"What brings you here, anyway?" Aidan made a first attempt at small talk.

"What is a girl like me doing in a place like this, you mean?" Heidi teased, and immediately regretted it. This wasn't how you handled a professional dinner with a new coworker, not at all. *Stupid.*

"Something like that."

"I guess I want to make a difference," she said.

"Me too."

They stared at each other for just a moment too long, until Heidi caught herself and looked away. This really wasn't how she had imagined her first night in Edinburgh would go. She felt an urgent need to express how weird everything felt. So far away from everything she had known all her life.

She wondered if Aidan felt a similar conflict of

emotions towards her.

Did he even feel their connection like she did? All the stories she'd heard growing up told of these bonds being mutual. Always.

On the other hand, the way the waitress had acted around them just now suggested that perhaps he was just a little bit of a player. Perhaps he couldn't feel it. She'd be damned if she was going to be the first to say something if that were the case.

"Fancy finding you here," a male voice interrupted her thoughts.

Heidi looked up to find another huge man towering over their table. He was almost as broad and equally athletic as Aidan. The two were roughly the same height.

"Jamie." Aidan's voice sounded cheerful enough, but Heidi could detect a hint of displeasure in him anyway. "Meet Heidi. Heidi, this is Jamie Abbott."

"Oh, right," Heidi mumbled, while getting up and offering her hand to her new boss. Their boss.

She felt her cheeks burn up a bit, as though she had been caught. In this light, neither of them would be able to see that, right?

Jamie took her hand, shaking it firmly. "Welcome to the team, Heidi. Sorry I couldn't be there earlier when you arrived. I had some things to attend to."

"No problem. Nice to meet you."

Jamie pulled up a chair and joined them. "Organizing a welcome dinner without inviting me, huh? I'm surprised, Aidan."

"I couldn't let her go to bed hungry on her first day, could I? Just trying to be civil," Aidan protested.

Their banter would have seemed light-hearted to the casual observer, but Heidi found herself having a little extra insight, at least into Aidan's feelings about the matter.

# SCOTTISH WEREBEAR: A DANGEROUS BUSINESS

He wasn't pleased at all that Jamie had turned up.

On the one hand, neither was Heidi, but on the other, she did feel a bit relieved. With him around, at least she'd be forced not to do anything stupid on her first night away from home.

Jamie ordered his dinner as well, along with a beer of some description, the name of which Heidi didn't recognize. The three of them chatted until the food arrived.

Apparently it wasn't just the two - now three - of them that were stationed in Edinburgh on Alliance business. There was another guy, their computer expert, Kyle, who was away visiting family. Heidi was the first female on the team. Quite the responsibility, she thought.

Throughout dinner, Heidi felt occasional glances and intermittent stares originating from Aidan's direction. Whenever Jamie asked her something, and Aidan was just observing, he kept observing her. It was unnerving, especially since she felt her body react involuntarily.

A persistent heat collected inside her lower abdomen, making her skittish and uneasy. She already knew Aidan could tell - that explained the dark stares - but could Jamie as well? Surely he'd be able to smell the change in her, if he paid just a little attention?

It was embarrassing to say the least but she couldn't control it. By the time dinner was done, and it was time for her to retreat to her room, she was relieved to get away from Aidan at least for the night.

How long until she could no longer control her urges? How long before *he* decided it was time to take action, even if she didn't?

# CHAPTER FOUR

---·◆·---

After Aidan and Jamie had walked Heidi back to the office, leaving her there by herself with much difficulty, Aidan was much too restless to head home and go to bed himself. He said his goodbyes to Jamie, and instead he opted for a walk towards the center of town. The Alliance premises, which occupied one of the many downtrodden buildings near the harbor, was only a fifteen minute walk away from the city center.

The Alliance was on a budget, but that was only part of the reason why their office was in one of the less scenic areas of what was otherwise a very attractive city. Edinburgh attracted many tourists every year, and the Alliance was hell-bent on keeping a low profile. Luckily, these same tourists rarely ventured beyond the Castle, the Royal Mile and select other sightseeing hot spots in the area.

The diverse crowd made Edinburgh a nice place to stay for people - or bears - who enjoyed the company of others, but didn't like them to stick around long enough to ask awkward questions.

Aidan wandered the familiar streets heading towards the Old Town, passing by busy pubs and restaurants, many of which he'd visited previously. But he wasn't looking to join the bustling nightlife. He was after solitude - a chance to clear his head and think about all that had happened today. And of course, about Heidi.

Rather than turn onto the Royal Mile that led to Edinburgh Castle, he crossed the street and continued straight on towards Holyrood Park, a huge green patch right in the middle of the city that also contained Arthur's Seat, the distinctively shaped hill that could be seen from pretty much anywhere in Edinburgh.

Although it was a popular destination for tourists as well as anyone else looking for a bit of privacy like he was, it did get very quiet at night. It was the one place where Aidan occasionally allowed himself to shift, but only on dark, starless nights.

Tonight was one of those nights. He could hardly control the urge to let his bear out, and as luck would have it, the moon as well as stars were hidden behind a thick cloud cover typical for this time of year. Scotland was pretty well known for its wet and unpredictable weather, especially when the last of the late summer warmth had left the land.

By now, early October, there was very little chance of the weather clearing up, so Aidan felt safe to be himself, if only for a little while. The Code of Secrecy all shifters adhered to was important to Aidan, that's why he only did this very rarely. Too much had happened in recent years to be lax about shifting in full view. Even just a single human witnessing a transformation was one human too many.

When he reached the edge of the park, his brisk walk turned into an impatient jog. After ensuring he was completely alone, he hid behind some shrubs and got undressed, concealing his clothes in the fallen leaves. Then he closed his eyes and breathed a sigh of relief as his instincts took over.

Fur sprouted where there previously had been none. As did claws and teeth, strong and sharp enough to tear flesh and crunch bone. His body grew to almost twice its original size and when he opened his eyes again, the world around him seemed to have changed along with him.

Things made more sense now.

Aidan had never expected that he'd come face-to-face with fate today. If he was completely honest, he had never really believed that there was one true mate for every bear out there. It was a strange and wondrous thing, the feeling of knowing beyond a shadow of a doubt that someone was meant to be yours.

Heidi.

She'd tried her best to hide it, to pretend like everything was all right and she didn't feel the way he did, but she couldn't hide her physical reactions to his presence. She couldn't control her hormones, the slight blush of embarrassment when they were interrupted at the pub, the flutter in her heartbeat when she'd caught him staring at her from across the table.

If only Jamie hadn't shown up when he did, perhaps Aidan wouldn't have been alone tonight. After wandering much of Scotland, and parts of Europe on his own as though he didn't need anyone else in his life, he felt a strange urge to share this place with her.

She wasn't ready for it though, he knew that. He would give her some space to come to him. Fate had decided that they be together, but that didn't mean they had no choice in the matter at all. She had to come to the conclusion herself that this was what she wanted.

He deeply breathed in the fresh air in an attempt to calm himself. The scents of grass and heather, along with a bit of salt from the sea hung in the air. He enjoyed the feel of the soft muddy ground under his paws, he even allowed himself to scratch at one of the bigger trees in the area - something he didn't do normally for fear of humans discovering the marks.

Throughout his little expedition back to nature, Aidan kept his ears open for any sign of human activity. He was good at hiding in the darkness, but he was never careless.

# SCOTTISH WEREBEAR: A DANGEROUS BUSINESS

Carelessness got you killed, he knew that.

Just as he was ready to leave again, his sensitive hearing picked up another presence further up the hill. Someone out for a late night walk up Arthur's Seat, perhaps? Two pairs of footsteps and muffled voices traveled down to his position. A couple, out for a quiet stroll?

Aidan stayed extremely still, and crouched down behind some of the shrubs set alongside one of the walking paths circling the hill. Sure enough, after a ten or fifteen minute wait, two men appeared in the distance. They were carrying flashlights to help them walk the difficult terrain, but Aidan would have seen them even without.

He ducked down behind the foliage, and just listened.

"Brother, I don't know if this is wise. It's been a while since we've had any action."

"That's exactly why it's time. Plus, those animals aren't going to wait for us to be ready. We should mobilize the old guard, as well as recruit a few new soldiers."

*What the-?* Aidan's heart started to beat faster. The way they spoke was eerily similar to some of the chatter on the message board he'd signed up on earlier. Could he accidentally have stumbled across a couple of members of the Sons of Domnall, just as they were planning to ramp up their activities?

"What about weapons?" asked one of the men.

"Leave those to me."

"All right. I'll start recruiting then."

"Good man. I'll be in touch when the leadership has formulated a plan."

Aidan took care not to disturb the shrubbery around him but couldn't resist a peek at the two figures ahead. Both of the men were white, one in his thirties, the other perhaps two decades older. They wore football shirts,

Aidan could just about make out the logo of one of the main clubs in the city.

They gave each other a quick hug and pat on the back, and the younger one walked on up the path. The older man turned to go back to from where they had just emerged, giving Aidan the chance to get a better look at his face just for a moment.

Something about him was familiar, but he didn't think he'd ever met the man. Aidan was good with faces, so to come across someone he thought he might have seen before, without being able to identify when or where, was unusual.

*Who was that? And why did he look so familiar?*

Aidan waited as both of the men vanished from view and even their footsteps faded away in the distance.

The conversation he'd overheard was vague and didn't even fully prove that they were who he suspected. Still, Aidan knew in his gut that this was the real deal. This was significant. He ought to report what he'd seen to Jamie.

After staying out of sight behind the bushes for another ten minutes, just in case, Aidan hurried back to where he'd left his clothes. He transformed back into his human form just as a slight drizzle started to fall.

It was during times like these he regretted having to act human for most of his life. As a bear, he wouldn't have cared at all about the rain, but there was hardly anything worse than trying to wear clothes on top of damp, shivering skin.

As soon as Aidan was dressed, he wrapped his coat around himself tighter to ward off the cold, and rushed back through the streets he'd walked earlier. Not home, but straight to the office.

# SCOTTISH WEREBEAR: A DANGEROUS BUSINESS

———◆———

A few strong cups of coffee later, Aidan had opened the familiar news articles concerning his parents' deaths again. His recognizing the older one of the two men in Holyrood Park had something to do with the accident, he could feel it, but he couldn't pinpoint just why that might be.

Despite going over everything again and again, hoping for some kind of connection to form in his mind, he'd made no progress. Aidan already knew these pages by heart, so looking at them any further seemed like an exercise in futility.

Instead, he sat quietly in his chair, his eyes closed, and tried to remember everything he knew about the case. There was something missing. Something that the computer couldn't tell him. And then he realized what it was: the local paper that used to be delivered to the house when he was growing up didn't show up on any of the websites he'd found! He didn't even know for sure if it still existed.

Just after the accident, Aidan had collected every mention of his parents in the Isle of Skye Gazette. Every article and their obituary. The short feature on McMillan Farm that had served as a sort of memorial for his parents who, although private, had been well liked by the local community. He had to obtain those clippings to see if they could shed light on the matter.

Aidan checked his watch; 4 AM. It would be hours before either of his two colleagues would turn up to start their day. As soon as it was a halfway decent time, he would phone Jamie to let him know he needed to take a few days off. That would be the only way to put his racing mind at rest.

He crossed his arms and leaned back in the rickety office chair, in an attempt to catch some shut-eye. He couldn't find any peace though. In between images of the two men he'd seen at the park, glimpses of when he first saw Heidi mere hours ago infiltrated his frazzled mind.

Aidan hadn't wanted a partner, and especially not one new to the business. But knowing that she was safe upstairs made him feel more at home in this dingy office than he did whenever he visited the farm where he grew up. That was the thing about losing one's parents before their time: it could sour the idea of family... of home.

If he could just figure out just how their deaths fit into the grand scheme of things, perhaps he could move on and have a family of his own again. Perhaps that's why fate had sent Heidi his way now. Perhaps it hadn't been a coincidence, but perfect timing instead.

# CHAPTER FIVE

It had been a long, largely sleepless night, followed by a painfully early morning. Heidi had stared aimlessly into the darkness of her room, until she must have dozed off for a while without realizing. The vivid images of Aidan, shirtless, hovering above her with a hungry look in his eyes had felt so real. When he leaned down to kiss her, it was as if she could taste his essence on her lips, feel the tickle of his breath against her skin.

Like he had actually been there with her all night.

Although even in the midst of these most intimate of dreams she was still painfully aware of how inappropriate their affair was, she hadn't been able to resist him. He had made her feel something she had never known: a sense of belonging and purpose that had nothing to do with her duty to her pack, but that answered a deeper need within herself. For just a little while, she had stopped feeling so alone in the world.

Morning came in the form of a panicked awakening sparked by… Well, Heidi wasn't sure by what, exactly. The building was quiet, it was still dark outside, and everything indicated that she was on her own.

All she knew for sure was that she had a throbbing headache, and felt uneasy about what the day had in store for her. But she couldn't bear lying in bed anymore either, so she got herself up, tried to stretch the lethargy out of her tired limbs and reluctantly climbed down the stairs.

*Coffee, that would solve everything!* Heidi could only hope that she would be able to find everything on her own, until one of the others came into the office.

"Oh!" Heidi exclaimed as soon as she stepped into the office, finding Aidan already sitting there poring over various printouts and websites on his computer screen.

He quickly closed whatever he had open on the PC, and rotated his chair to face her. "Morning."

He was wearing exactly the same clothes as yesterday. *Weird. Had he been here all night?*

"You're up early..." she remarked.

He just smiled, bleakly. Yeah, she was sure of it now, he had never left. If he hadn't looked so focused on his work just now, she might have wondered if coming back into the office was just an excuse to be in the same building with her. He seemed to have other things on his mind, though.

"Is something wrong?" she asked at last.

"Wrong? Not at all. Why don't you grab a seat and we can go over a few things." Aidan pointed at the wobbly looking chair sitting in front of what was going to be Heidi's desk and pulled out a few files and notes from the mess of paper in front of him. "Oh, if you want to grab a coffee, I've made some already."

Indeed the scent of freshly brewed coffee had already made it into Heidi's nose, so she quickly poured herself a cup and got her chair. As she sat down beside Aidan, something told her that this, the matter-of-fact workaholic investigator, wasn't a front, but really him. It was strange to admit it, but she liked it. Here was a guy who could take things seriously when required, unlike some of the boys she'd grown up around.

"Excuse me for jumping right into things, but we're in the middle of an investigation, as you will already know."

"The Sons of Domnall. Yes, I know," Heidi responded, trying her utmost not to get distracted by his presence so nearby. If she reached out just a little, she would accidentally brush against his arm... *Stop it!*

"Well, we've been trying to get close to them, at least on the Internet. We have an informant who has shared a couple of websites, and one of those hosts a message board that I have joined, pretending to be someone with - shall we say - similar interests and convictions." Aidan flipped open the first file, and showed her some print-outs from the websites in question.

"Okay." Heidi took the first sheet and studied the screenshots. The whole thing was quite vague, nowhere did it mention that these people knew about shifters, or were out to hunt them down. Of course they'd keep that kind of content locked away from the general public...

"They present themselves as ordinary right-wingers; racists and bigots," Aidan clarified, before she had the chance to voice her observations.

"I see."

He showed her another few sheets of paper which contained conversations - presumably printed from the message board, as well as a glossary containing phrases and words the members had used regularly.

"Has anyone made contact with you?" Heidi asked.

Aidan looked up, meeting her gaze with his. Their eye contact was almost painful, making her heart race and stomach flutter. Heidi quickly looked away again and reached over to pick up her coffee from the desk, knocking the cup over in the process and spilling the remainder of its contents across the floor.

"Oh, crap, I'm so sorry!" Heidi jumped up instantly, picked up the cup and set it aside, before looking around for a towel, or a cloth of any kind.

Aidan just observed her for a moment, before reaching into one of the drawers of his desk, taking out a large pack of paper napkins.

"Here you go," he said, his voice a lot gentler than it had just been when he was briefing her. How had he managed to switch from complete pro to warm and friendly in a split second?

His finger brushed past hers ever so gently when he handed her the napkins, sending shivers down her spine. She flinched and retreated instantly, but somehow something had changed in her. She felt like he was still touching her, even though they were at least three feet apart from one another.

*No way, that was stupid.* She was just tired, and the lack of sleep was starting to mess with her mind.

While she tried her best to contain the mess on the floor, he seemed to go right back into work-mode as if nothing had happened.

"One of the regular members of the message board has sent me a couple of messages, yes. Nothing beyond that, but I'm hopeful." Aidan took a deep breath, before continuing. "But that's not why I came in last night."

"No?" Heidi asked, while picking up the coffee-soaked napkins and putting them into the trash.

"I overheard a conversation, while I was out for a walk after dropping you here. The details are inconclusive, much like these websites are, but my instincts tell me there's something more to it. I may have accidentally stumbled across two of their members..."

Heidi stopped what she was doing and stared at him. *Wow, could it be?* Obviously this was what she was here for, to make a real difference, but she hadn't heard of the Alliance actually making much progress yet. To find that Aidan had come across some potential real life members of the Sons of Domnall on her first night in the city was incredible. She couldn't wait to tell her dad the good news.

"That's amazing! Does Jamie know? What are we going

to do, follow them?" Heidi asked.

Aidan shook his head throughout her questions and raised his hand, making a calming gesture. "There's no point in doing anything until my suspicions are confirmed. But there is something else..."

"What's that?" Heidi thought she could pick up on a vibe that told her he was about to share something significant.

"I think I may have recognized one of them," Aidan's voice was low, clearly this information was something he had intended to keep secret.

She didn't respond straightaway, and before she had the chance, the lock on the front door clicked, revealing a wind-blown Jamie Abbott.

"Morning, guys! You're up early!" Jamie greeted them with a wide grin, which to Heidi looked a bit off.

"That's what she said," Aidan remarked dryly while getting up from his chair.

Heidi nodded and smiled back at Jamie, while trying to figure out if she was just tired and hence seeing things that weren't actually there. He was nice enough, had been last night as well, but something made her feel like he was hiding something from the two of them. Perhaps she was just picking up on Aidan's emotions, who clearly preferred being alone with Heidi over having Jamie around.

*It's all in your head, woman!*

"I'd like a word, please," Aidan told Jamie, who nodded and followed Aidan into the stairwell, leaving Heidi on her own.

While the two were outside, Heidi wondered why she wasn't more curious about their exact conversation. Her instincts told her that Aidan had taken Jamie aside not to hide something from her, but to handle him. Why she would think that, she wasn't quite sure. It must have been a fated mate thing, some failsafe that ensured mates trusted each other implicitly.

Instead of pondering their strange relationship further, Heidi picked up some of the papers Aidan had showed her and started to read. She went through the glossary, the transcripts of various conversations between suspected Sons of Domnall members that had taken place on that message board, and finally, she studied the beginnings of a members list Aidan had put together.

They all used aliases, which didn't mean much to Heidi. Nobody had put up their own picture either, but Aidan had somehow managed to put together a few relevant details about each one of the people he'd followed online. Their profiles contained suspected locations, as well as age ranges for some of them based on turns of phrase or slang they used. Aidan had also added certain special skills to some of the profiles. If this information was true, it was impressive work. She did wonder if half of the details were just wild guesses, though.

By the time Aidan and Jamie appeared again, Heidi had already switched on her computer and started browsing the website and message boards herself.

"Heidi?" Jamie called out to her.

"Yes?" She got up and joined the two men in front of Aidan's desk.

"Aidan has just briefed me about an important development in our investigation. Unfortunately he has a family emergency to attend to, so he's going to be away for a few days. In the meantime you and I will work together."

Heidi looked up at Aidan, then back at Jamie. *A family emergency?* It didn't feel right, but from the look in Aidan's eyes she knew not to question Jamie's explanation. She would find out what was really going on when the time was right.

# SCOTTISH WEREBEAR: A DANGEROUS BUSINESS

Jamie led her back to her desk and took a seat beside her, while Aidan busied himself stuffing various items into a worn leather shoulder bag.

She turned around, observing him for a moment. *Be safe*, she thought. Aidan looked up and shot her a subtle smile just when their eyes met. As though he had heard her. That couldn't be, though... could it?

"Let's go through the rest of these files together," Jamie said.

She turned back again and responded with a quick nod. "Okay."

Jamie opened another folder and handed it to her. Inside were pictures and names of people - shifters - who had gone missing under mysterious circumstances. She didn't recognize any of them, but felt deeply sad seeing their faces anyway. The list read "Suspected Sons of Domnall Victims" across the top.

Behind the two of them, the door creaked open, and then fell shut with a click, and Heidi felt that Aidan had gone.

# CHAPTER SIX

———————◆———————

The drive from Edinburgh to Aidan's home on the Isle of Skye was a long one. Six hours in the best of conditions, without taking any breaks. But these weren't the best of conditions...

By the time Aidan made it to the island, a storm was lashing the rugged landscape, making conditions treacherous at best, lethal at worst. He knew his brother Derek would have taken precautions, so he wasn't worried about what he'd find there. Still, it didn't help that the thick clouds overhead had made dusk arrive much earlier than normal.

The stores were always fully stocked with food, as well as firewood and other supplies they would need to weather a storm. Especially at this time of year, shortly before winter would properly set in, the farm would have everything he'd need. Although he didn't visit home nearly often enough, he could always count on a warm enough welcome, including good food, courtesy of his brother.

The landscape on the island was starkly beautiful: barren hills, covered with a smattering of heather and tough grasses, broken up only by the occasional patch of woodland. The black cliffs that rose up from the center of the island stood proudly against the dark gray skies, like timeless giants, bearing silent witness to whatever went on around them.

He kept on driving, despite the winds trying to push his car off the narrow road and into the nearest ditch, until finally Aidan had to admit defeat. With the woods surrounding McMillan Farm already in view, he parked his car to make the rest of the journey on foot. The trees were old, weathered - a legacy from Aidan and Derek's ancestors who had planted the first of them two centuries ago when they first settled here, and downed branches would make driving conditions even more treacherous up ahead.

The storm had brought in cooler air from the north, and rain and sleet would seep into Aidan's clothes, chilling him to his core. He knew what he had to do: if he wanted to make it home safely, he had to shift.

Still in the car, safe from the elements, Aidan got undressed. A deep breath later, he stepped out into the icy cold, and let his instincts do the rest.

The entire process was over in less than a second; the cold was a brilliant motivator for quick shifts. He started to run in the direction of the farm, his paws carrying him over the mossy, wet ground much faster than human feet could have. Plus, he didn't have to worry about the cold creeping into his muscles, slowing him down.

Although the roads would be empty in these conditions, he kept off them anyway out of habit, which was just as well because his car wasn't the only one out this evening. A gray hatchback stood still in the middle of the road just inside the woods, its lights still on and filtering through the rain.

Aidan's heart started to race. He checked the car from afar first, then investigated it up close once he realized there was no sign of life anywhere around it. He could smell blood. Human. But whoever had been in the car at the time of the accident wasn't around anymore.

He decided to get back on course to his original destination, home. Aidan couldn't explain it, but he felt that something had gone very wrong.

————— ◆ —————

Still anxious, Aidan entered the farmhouse in a rush. Coming up the drive, he had seen that most of the house was dark, save for a dim light in the bedroom and the kitchen. The storm must have knocked out the power. When he found the kitchen empty, save for a pot bubbling away on the fire, he proceeded down the hall and burst into Derek's room. Nothing could have prepared Aidan for what awaited him.

In the bed sat a woman, her mouth wide open in shock. The bright red bruise on her forehead stood out against her pale skin. Aidan stared at her, equally surprised, then spied his brother's form lurking in the corner of the room, as if he'd been guarding the female.

"Aidan. Bad timing," Derek growled.

"Well... This is awkward," Aidan responded.

They weren't very close, Aidan and his brother, but Aidan just couldn't imagine Derek and this woman... Derek had never shown interest in the opposite sex. While Aidan had been the more curious one, Derek had been content tending the farm on his own. *So, what was different about her?*

"A word, please?" Derek said. Aidan agreed and they both exited.

"She's human," Aidan said as they made it into the hallway, shutting the bedroom door behind them, and immediately shifted into his human form again.

"I know."

"She's seen us." The more Aidan thought about it, the more he realized the disaster he had gotten himself into. It was obvious that the car wreck on the road had belonged to this woman; she had the cut on her head to prove it.

And yet he had marched into the house as a bear, expecting that Derek was on his own like he always was. *Stupid.*

They moved into Aidan's old room and got dressed. As Aidan continued to question his brother, and Derek kept insisting that she was a guest who had rented one of the cottages, he was certain that there was something else Derek wasn't telling him. So what if she was a tourist? So what if she crashed her car? None of that explained why she was in Derek's bed rather than her own.

It was then that Derek turned the tables on Aidan and started asking *him* questions. *Why are you here?* There was something in Derek's tone that made Aidan defensive. As if he had to have a reason to come home.

Still, being vague about everything wasn't going to help any. As Aidan and Derek finally headed into the cozy kitchen for some much needed warmth and nourishment, Aidan felt it was time to share at least some of his recent activities with his brother.

He was going to tell him about his job at the Alliance, but it was Derek who spoke first.

"She's my mate, Aidan." Derek's words explained everything.

He started to clarify how he felt, but Aidan didn't need further details to know exactly what was going on. The way Heidi had made Aidan feel from their very first meeting onward had driven him to act out of character too. Now that the woman, whose name turned out to be Clarice, had seen the two of them as bears, there was no turning back either. Derek wouldn't let her go, that much was obvious. He couldn't, just as Aidan couldn't ignore his feelings for Heidi.

When it was Aidan's turn to speak, he indeed opened up to his brother. About the Alliance, and their work with the Sons of Domnall. Aidan didn't believe in fear-mongering, but it was only sensible to inform people, and especially Derek, so that he could prepare himself.

But Aidan's concerns about exposing his real self to a human didn't fade. Derek would never be able to do anything to harm Clarice, the woman, because she was his mate. But would the same rules apply to her? He tried to tell Derek about the dangers that existed nowadays. How the Sons of Domnall had actually been hunting shifters, so the Code of Secrecy all shifters lived by had become doubly important. You never knew who was watching, or whom to trust. As far as Aidan was concerned, any human was a potential threat.

"I'm not sure we can trust her," Aidan insisted.

"I am," Derek responded.

Something in Derek's eyes had changed, a glow that hadn't been there before. Bears' eyes glowed when they were in danger, angry, or otherwise riled up. But Derek's body language wasn't threatening. When a female voice started to speak from behind Derek, all was explained.

Clarice, the human, had woken up and found her way into the kitchen. As she started to speak, Aidan could see that there was something more to them than what he'd witnessed of human relationships. They acted like mates, seemed to know the other's thoughts. She said their secret was safe with her, and sounded pretty damn convincing.

Aidan decided to give them the benefit of the doubt, for now. What was he to do, anyway? Tell the Alliance? Try to scare Clarice away in the hopes that she wouldn't return? In his work with the Alliance, Aidan had seen what happens to shifters who lose a mate. It wasn't pretty. There was no way he could do that to his own brother.

"I think I'm going to give you two some space," Aidan said, sensing that his presence was no longer wanted.

# SCOTTISH WEREBEAR: A DANGEROUS BUSINESS

Neither of them responded, in fact they acted like he had never even been there.

Aidan walked down the hall straight to his old bedroom. He'd come here for a reason, and the unfortunate incident earlier had thrown him off track long enough. He didn't think either Derek or Clarice would come looking for him tonight, but he felt compelled to lock his door anyway.

Once safe, he switched on an emergency lantern on the bedside table. It wasn't bright, but it was enough for Aidan to start emptying the large wardrobe that contained all his old things.

On the top shelf, behind stacks of old woolen sweaters and other winter clothes, sat an old cookie tin. This is where he'd kept all of the newspaper clippings just after the accident. He hadn't looked at it in years, and opening that box was never easy for him.

He carried it over to the leather arm chair in the corner and held his breath as he flipped the lid open. Inside, everything was as he remembered. Newspaper articles, sorted by date of publication, and bundled according to which paper they'd come from. And a sealed envelope.

He weighed the envelope in his hand. It was heavy, which was only natural considering its content, and inspected the seal. The red wax was still intact, and looked exactly the same as the day when their cousin, Elise, had handed it to him for safekeeping. He set it aside and continued to rifle through the contents of the box.

Underneath all the papers, he found the gold locket his mother had always worn. The policeman who had come to the farm to notify them of what had happened had given that to him. Although not strictly relevant to his mission, he opened the pendant anyway. Inside, exactly as he remembered, was a photograph of his dad on the left and one of Derek and himself, when they were only boys, on the right.

It hurt. Seeing these things always hurt.

He quickly shut the pendant again and placed it back into the bottom of the tin, and started going through the various clippings instead. It didn't take him long to find exactly what he was looking for: one of the first articles in the Isle of Skye Gazette, titled *Tragic Road Accident Claims Two Lives*.

The article was accompanied by a photograph of the wreckage, along with a man in a firefighter uniform. Bingo.

Aidan squinted at the picture, but it remained as grainy as ever. He was certain that this was the same man he'd seen in Edinburgh the other night. Neither the caption, nor the article mentioned him by name.

This could not be a coincidence. After all these years, following instinct alone, he finally had some proof: their parents' death had been no accident.

# CHAPTER SEVEN

———◆———

Heidi's second morning at the Alliance office wasn't perfect, but at least she'd slept well enough. Somehow, knowing that Aidan was going to be gone for a couple of days had helped her relax.

She was up by seven and headed straight down to find the office eerily quiet. After figuring out how to work the coffee machine, she settled down into her chair and looked through the files she'd started working on yesterday. The news that Aidan might have found actual Sons of Domnall members running around Edinburgh had been very exciting indeed.

The one thing she didn't understand was why Aidan had run off all of a sudden, giving Jamie some nonsense excuse about a family emergency. She couldn't explain how she knew, but there was no family emergency. It had something to do with the job, she was convinced of it.

It was too bad they hadn't had the chance to talk further until Jamie came in, or she might have known more about what exactly Aidan had seen, and what he thought it meant. Still, just because Aidan wasn't here, didn't mean Heidi had to sit around doing nothing. She knew about the websites, she had read the files Aidan and Jamie had given her, and she was plenty motivated to get started and make some real progress.

She had only taken a few sips of her hot coffee by the time she logged on to the main website. *A profile*. She needed to create a profile for herself, just like Aidan had done. Heidi made a few notes, picking phrases from Aidan's glossary that she felt would make her sound authentic.

Although the member profiles of the other people on the website were vague at best, Heidi opted to fill out the "gender" field anyway. Perhaps they'd be more inclined to talk to a new *female* member? That was how the world worked, wasn't it?

Once her profile was set up and her introduction typed out, she sat back, lukewarm cup in hand and admired her handiwork. Not a bad start.

Rather than wait around for responses - she couldn't imagine any of these people would log on so early in the morning anyway - Heidi started working on something else that had been bothering her ever since she'd arrived day before yesterday: the state of the office.

She began with her new desk, but as soon as she'd gotten into the swing of things; tidying up papers, throwing away random bits of rubbish, and wiping the top down with a moist cloth, she found it hard to stop just there. She moved on to the coffee maker and stationary cupboard, then finally sorted out the final empty desk in the corner of the room, until everything looked clean.

Everything except Aidan's and Jamie's desks. She didn't dare touch those.

Just as Heidi poured herself a second cup of coffee, Jamie arrived.

"Morning," he said, as he started removing his coat, hanging it up on the shabby rack near the door.

"Morning," Heidi responded, observing the man as he walked across the office, straight to the coffee maker, pouring himself a large one. She counted six heaped teaspoons of sugar, and although she really wanted to comment on it, she kept quiet. *He's the boss. None of my business.*

After the first sip, followed by a satisfied sigh, Jamie

turned in Heidi's direction and caught her still staring at him.

"What?"

Heidi glanced away, embarrassed he'd busted her. "Nothing."

"Oh, the coffee? Did you want a refill?" Jamie asked, in between further sips of what must have been the sickliest sweet hot beverage Heidi had ever seen anyone drink.

"No, it's nothing, really." Heidi felt her cheeks burn up. *Crap.* She might as well explain herself, before he drew even worse conclusions. "Just, I've never seen anyone add that much sugar..."

Jamie let out a laugh and wandered over to his desk, placing the cup down and taking a seat in the much too small looking office chair, which groaned under his weight.

"That's the thing about bears, we have a giant sweet tooth," he remarked, while picking up his cup again and holding it in both hands.

*Bears...* Heidi's heart started to beat faster. That was right, Jamie was a bear; the first one she'd ever met. In all the confusion over the past few days, she never stopped to wonder about working in such close proximity with a bear, when for the most part, their species didn't get along very well. Perhaps that's why Aidan didn't trust Jamie fully either...

"No need to look so uncomfortable. We don't bite." Jamie winked at her, and leaned forward to switch on his computer. "In fact, Aidan and I fully stand behind the truce. We're better off working together, don't you think? As it is, the humans outnumber all of us."

The way he said it: *Aidan and him... As if... Holy Crap!*

If Heidi had managed to maintain at least some of her composure earlier, every last bit of it was gone now. She felt her chest tighten and her airways narrow. *That meant*

*Aidan was a bear, too!*

"Heidi? Are you all right?" Jamie asked.

Her vision blurred a bit, her head went fuzzy, and although she could hear his chair creak as he presumably got up, followed by footsteps in her direction, she couldn't bounce back and act normal.

"Fine. I'm fine!" she heard herself say, but it didn't sound convincing even to her own ears.

Of course Aidan was a bear. That's why he smelled different. That's why he was pretty much the same height and build as Jamie, taller as well as broader than most wolves. How the hell had she not noticed that before?

"Here, have some water." Jamie handed her a half-empty plastic bottle, which she accepted with trembling fingers.

"Thanks," Heidi mumbled.

*Deep breaths,* she told herself. *Deep breaths, calm down...* How could she calm down, though, when for some stupid reason she the man she was meant to mate with was a bloody bear?! Not just a colleague, but a bear on top of it! There had to be some way out of this mess. There was no way she would ever be able to show her face in Rannoch again if she paired up with a bear.

When the world came back into focus, she could see Jamie towering over her, with a concerned expression on his face.

"I'm okay, really," she said, while returning the water to him. "Low blood sugar. I haven't had breakfast."

"Ah, well that's understandable. How about we head out and rectify that, huh?" Jamie suggested.

Although it had been just an excuse, Heidi's stomach was indeed growling as well. She nodded, and got up to grab her things. She was still a little wobbly on her feet, but determined to follow along with her chosen cover story.

# SCOTTISH WEREBEAR: A DANGEROUS BUSINESS

What Jamie had said was proven true after reaching the nearby cafe: bears evidently did have a massive sweet tooth. While Heidi opted for a full breakfast with extra sausages and bacon, Jamie ordered a huge stack of pancakes just for himself.

*Bears...*

———◆———

Later that afternoon, Heidi was still upset about the bear thing, obviously. But at least Aidan wasn't around to send her instincts into a tailspin. She'd been resisting him so far, how hard could it be to continue? Perhaps if she just worked hard enough, she could keep herself focused on the job alone.

Growing up, she'd heard a lot of stories about bears. They're lazy, greedy, anti-social... But now that she was working more closely with one, she had to wonder how much of that stuff was true.

Jamie seemed to be quite a reasonable person, save for his strange appetite and occasional grouchiness. He was easy enough to work with, and patient as well. So was Aidan, though. Kind, caring, and just reserved enough to be mysterious... And so very sexy. *Stop it! Stop getting distracted! You're not mating with a bloody bear!*

Heidi took a deep breath and tried to focus on her screen again. Luckily, her earlier prediction about females getting more attention online had proved to be true. Just eight hours after first signing up she had already received a bunch of responses from other members on the suspected Sons of Domnall message board. It was way more than Aidan's introductory post had received in days.

A lot of it was small talk, racist-style, but some people seemed eager to chat with her in more detail. She kept reading up on them, looking through Aidan's notes as well as existing discussions on the website, hoping to absorb as much of it as possible, while occasionally typing out hopefully authentic-sounding responses to everyone who had gotten in touch.

Time seemed to pass quickly, until finally later that same evening, the unthinkable happened: a private message arrived from one of the senior members of the forum.

*A few of us are getting together tomorrow. Just drinks among friends, would you like to come along?*

A sense of achievement welled up in Heidi's chest, or maybe nerves. Perhaps a bit of both. This was huge, exactly what they'd been working towards. Never once did she expect to get results this quickly, though.

"Hey, Jamie," Heidi called out, while waving at him excitedly.

Jamie looked up from his phone - who knows what he had been doing on there for the best part of the last hour. "What have you got?"

"I've got a way in with these people. They've invited me for drinks," Heidi explained.

Jamie got up from his chair and walked up behind Heidi, looking over her shoulder at the screen. He took a moment to read through the message, then Heidi showed him the discussion she'd been having publicly on the forum.

"Wow, great work." He patted Heidi on the back and pulled up a chair next to her. "Just a couple of things..."

"Yes?" Heidi asked.

"These are potentially dangerous people, but I don't have to tell you that, do I?"

"Indeed." Heidi nodded.

"And they're expecting you to go in alone, presumably."

"Presumably."

"How are your fighting skills?" Jamie asked.

Heidi shrugged. She'd been training for years, with various weapons as well as hand-to-hand. Everyone in Rannoch knew how to fight. "I'm pretty decent. Easily the strongest in my class."

Jamie smiled. "Your father did tell me that, but I wanted to hear it from you. Very well, then. Keep it simple: in and out, say a few hellos, try to remember as many faces and names as you can, then report back to me. Do not under any circumstance engage them, understand?"

"I understand." Heidi forced a smile. She understood the potential danger she could get into. If they were Sons of Domnall members, and they suspected any foul play at all, things could go very badly for her. She only hoped she was a good enough actress to convincingly disguise her true intentions. "No problem, I'll handle it."

"Good girl." Jamie got up and gave her a final nod. "I suggest you take it a little easy tomorrow, so you're well rested for the meeting in the evening."

# CHAPTER EIGHT

———◆———

Although the storm had calmed down overnight, Aidan hadn't been able to catch much sleep. Yesterday's discovery had been simply too exciting, and his mind kept racing to come up with a plan to identify the man in the picture. So, Aidan was already up and enjoying a hearty breakfast in the farm kitchen by the time anyone else stirred.

"Morning," Aidan greeted his brother, who had wandered in topless and half asleep.

"Mhm," Derek responded, while pouring two cups of coffee.

Behind him, a slightly disheveled looking Clarice came into the kitchen and eyed Aidan suspiciously. "Morning."

She was wearing a t-shirt big enough that it could pass as a nightie. One of Derek's, no doubt. Aidan nodded at her and started clearing up his used dishes, keeping them in the dishwasher. *Awkward* seemed too weak a word to describe the current atmosphere.

"I'm sorry if I seemed hostile last night," Aidan attempted to break the ice. "I was just concerned. This is all new to me."

"I understand," Clarice responded.

"No reason to be concerned," Derek added, while putting his arm around Clarice's shoulders. They did look happy together, like there was nothing else in the world that they could ask for. This was the kind of happiness you only saw between true mates.

Aidan shot them a bittersweet smile. His own mate was hundreds of miles away. A day's drive, but even when they were in the same room together, the distance between them seemed insurmountable. She had to come to him willingly, he reminded himself. He couldn't - wouldn't - force her.

"So, did you find whatever it was you were looking for last night?" Derek asked. He had a way of getting right to the heart of things.

Aidan glanced at Clarice, then reminded himself that they wouldn't have any secrets between them anyway, so he might as well tell both of them together.

"Yes. Have a look." Aidan sat down again and leaned over to retrieve the clear plastic folder with the newspaper clipping he'd found out from his shoulder bag, which was hanging from the back of the chair. Placing it down on the table, he slid it forward as Derek and Clarice both pulled up some chairs and sat down as well.

"This man." Aidan tapped on the picture with his index finger. "I saw him in Edinburgh two days ago. Overheard him discussing an attack."

"Wow." Derek picked up the folder and squinted at the picture, then passed it to Clarice. "You're absolutely sure?"

"I never forget a face."

"What does it all mean?" Clarice asked.

"Where do I begin? What does she know?" Aidan asked Derek.

"I overheard quite a bit last night, sorry about that." Clarice averted her eyes.

Derek took her hand and squeezed it encouragingly. "There shouldn't be any secrets between us. It's fine."

"So, I suspect that this man, and the one he was with in Edinburgh are members of the Sons of Domnall."

"Those are the people who hunt shifters, right?" Clarice asked.

Aidan nodded. "Yes. If he was around when our

parents were killed, it wouldn't be such a big stretch to think he might have had something to do with it. Maybe he found out who they really were somehow."

"Right..." Derek scratched his chin, like he often did when lost in thought. "One thing doesn't make sense to me. If he figured out Mom and Dad were bears, why not kill us too? Why let us live?"

"That, I don't know... If I find him, I'll make sure to ask him that." Aidan shook his head. That was strange indeed. He hadn't even considered that point. Trust his brother to find holes in his seemingly air-tight theory...

"So now that you've found this, what's next?" Clarice asked.

Aidan looked up at her. "I find out who he is. Get a name."

"Of course." Clarice sat back and held her coffee in both hands, staring at nothing in particular in the distance.

"Well, if I'm going to be successful, I'd better be off. Who knows what the storm has done to the roads." Aidan took the folder, put it back in his bag and got up. "I'll let you know what happens."

Derek got up as well, and the two brothers hugged each other goodbye.

"Clarice." Aidan nodded at her.

"Bye, Aidan," she responded.

Aidan picked up his bag, slung it over his shoulder and made his exit.

———— • ————

The small town of Portree, about an hour's drive from the farm, might be the biggest settlement on the Isle of Skye, but it was still small by most people's standards. With a population of just under 2500 people, you could drive through the place in minutes.

Still, it was exactly here that Aidan expected to find his answers.

He drove up to the fire station, the only one on the entire island and hence the one that would have dealt with his parents' accident. If anyone knew who the man in the photograph was, it would be these people.

Everything looked quiet. There was no sign of any activity inside, and no cars parked in the marked bays next to the building. Aidan walked to the main entrance only to find it locked. Of course. Fire stations in small towns like this didn't have permanent staff, they just called people in whenever there was an emergency.

On the wall next to the bright red entrance door, there was a sign with a phone number to call if one needed assistance. Aidan took out his phone and dialed without hesitation.

"Hello?" a female voice answered after just a couple of rings.

"Hello there, I'm here at the fire station and I was wondering if I could talk to someone to help me identify one of your former firefighters?" Aidan responded.

There was a pause, and a low crackle in the line.

"To what end?" the woman asked.

To what end indeed. Aidan couldn't very well tell her the whole truth, so he opted for a partial version of it.

"Around fifteen years ago my parents were killed in a traffic accident on the island. I would like to speak to the man who was there. I have a photograph."

"I see..." she paused again. "Fine. I will be there in a little while."

The call was cut with a rustle and a click, and Aidan was left pacing the fire station parking lot back and forth on his own. He hoped she would be willing to help him out. And if she did, he hoped that the man in the photograph had actually been a real firefighter, not just someone dressed in a fake uniform.

But that wasn't his only concern: Derek was right. Why kill their parents and leave Derek and him alive? If the Sons of Domnall were trying to cleanse the world of all shifters, they should have come to the farm and finished the job just as soon as they found out that his parents had left two sons behind.

"Mister?" A voice called out to him from behind.

He turned to find a middle-aged woman standing a few feet away. She looked to be in her fifties, her long gray hair tied into a pony tail, and slightly dusty clothes that could only be described as 'sensible'.

"Forgive me, I was doing a bit of gardening when you phoned." She stretched out his hand towards him for a handshake.

"No problem. Aidan McMillan," he introduced himself.

"Helen Brown," she responded, while scrutinizing him over her small red-rimmed reading glasses. "Please tell me again what's the matter."

"You probably wouldn't remember, but fifteen years ago, my parents, Gillian and Matthew McMillan were killed in an accident on the A850..."

"I remember. Terrible business."

"It's been very difficult for my brother and me to come to terms with it, especially him since he was only a teenager when it happened. So, I was hoping to speak with the man who recovered the wreckage."

"I understand." She pushed her glasses further up the bridge of her nose and rummaged around in her handbag, retrieving a bunch of keys. "Why don't we discuss this inside?"

Aidan followed the woman as she unlocked the door,

and walked into the dark, empty fire station. Through the hallway, towards the left, she opened another door leading to an office, where she offered Aidan a seat.

"How about a cup of tea?" she gestured at the kettle in the corner.

Aidan nodded and sat down, while taking in his surroundings. There were photographs on the walls, group shots with little captions that were hard to read from where he was sitting.

"So who is this fellow you're trying to find then?" the woman asked, while dropping teabags into two empty mugs. "Sugar?"

"Yes please. Two. Well, as I said, I have this photograph. I apologize, it's not very clear..." Aidan took the folder with the newspaper cutting out of his bag and placed it on the desk ahead of him.

The woman leaned over to look at it, then turned back to face the kettle when it clicked to tell her the water had boiled. "I see. Don't think I know the man."

"If you could take a look again, I'd really appreciate it."

The woman turned around again, mugs in hand, and slid one of them towards Aidan. "You understand I can't just hand out contact information for former firefighters. It's against the rules."

Brilliant. The rules. "I just wanted to ask him a few questions. Thank him for his assistance in the matter. That's all."

She wrapped her fingers around her mug and cocked her head to the side. Then she looked up across the room, seemingly aimlessly as she spoke. "I want to help you, I really do, but I can't jeopardize my job here. It's a nice bit of extra change, you understand. Especially since my husband has had to stop working, it's been a great help to us."

"I understand. I don't want to cause any trouble for you." Aidan sighed.

"I think I need more milk in my tea, but I'm all out. Be a dear and wait here while I get some more..." The woman placed her mug down on the desk, while still staring across the room, then walked out, leaving Aidan on his own.

What had she been looking at so intently? Aidan scanned the wall behind him, then got up for a better look. There it was, another one of those group photos, this one labeled "Portree Fire Station, 1998". Among the dozen or so men portrayed, in the back row, third position from the left, there was a familiar face. Much clearer than the newspaper photograph, and unmistakably the same man that he'd seen in Edinburgh, only a bit younger of course.

The caption underneath gave Aidan everything he'd come here for. He counted the names written underneath. Back row, third from the left: Lee Campbell. He repeated it a few times in his head. *Lee Campbell, member of the Sons of Domnall, shifter killer.*

Aidan never forgot a face, and rarely forgot a name, especially one so important, but he felt the need to record this new find anyway. While listening out for footsteps signaling the woman's return, he quickly whipped his phone out of his pocket and took a picture of the entire group photograph, and another one of just the caption containing the names.

Who knows, perhaps this Lee Campbell person hadn't worked alone. Perhaps someone else in this picture had something to do with the accident?

Aidan quickly emptied his cup of tea, retrieved the folder with the newspaper clipping from the desk and stuffed it into his bag. He left without even catching a last glimpse of the woman who had helped him.

If he hurried, he could still make it to the town hall,

and hopefully get some more information about this Lee Campbell character, before starting his journey back to Edinburgh. If all went well, he would even be able to catch a good shut-eye before going back to work in the morning.

# CHAPTER NINE

———◆———

Everything had seemed okay, at least at first. Heidi kept going over it in her head but still couldn't understand exactly where things had gone as horribly wrong as they had. One moment, she was being introduced to people over drinks and small talk, the next, they were dragging her into a dark alley with a bag over her head and stuffing her into a van.

And now, who knows how many hours or days later - it was hard to keep track of time when locked up in a windowless room - Heidi still had no idea what these people wanted from her. Nobody had come in to talk to her, nobody had even given her anything to eat or drink. She was parched, starving, and close to giving up.

Despite how things turned out, she still was pretty sure she hadn't slipped up. Throughout the brief meeting at the pub, she'd stayed in character perfectly. So how did they know to suspect anything? Were they perhaps just being cautious?

The worst part was, the longer she was stuck here, the more her inner wolf fought to come out. If her captors only had a vague suspicion so far, a transformation would definitely push them into action. They would kill her, Heidi was certain of it. These were not people you messed with, especially if you were a shifter.

A loud click and creak interrupted her panicked thoughts, and the heavily reinforced door swung open. *Finally.*

"So, young lady, are you ready to tell us who you are yet?" The older guy she'd met at the pub walked in, flanked by two of the younger ones who had also been there earlier.

Heidi tried to focus her frazzled mind, so that she might remember every detail about these people. Although it was dark, her vision was much better than that of the humans, so she barely stirred, just observed from the bed she'd been shackled to.

Shaved heads, all of them, making it hard to figure out what their original hair color would have been. The younger guys had lots of tattoos, the sleeve type that covered their entire arms - at least as far as Heidi could see. The older one - she estimated him to be about fifty - also had a tattoo on his arm, but one of those old school, simpler ones. A couple of swallows holding a banner with the initials A. C.

"Not talking yet, I see. We have ways of making people change their minds," the older guy, presumably their leader, hissed.

"I don't know what you're talking about. I'm just concerned about where this country is headed, like you are. We can't stand by while we're overrun by those animals-" Heidi rambled.

"Quiet! There's something not right about you... You're not a copper, are ya?"

Heidi blinked a few times. They think she's police?

"Look, you invited me. If you thought I was up to no good, why do that?" Heidi pleaded.

"How did you find out about the message board?"

That was a good question indeed, one that she hadn't rehearsed an answer for... "A friend... a like-minded friend tipped me off to it. He said he'd come across it while browsing. He's a lot better with computers than I am, I don't know..." Her stomach growled, painfully. *Focus. Don't shift.*

"What friend?"

Heidi pressed her lips together tightly. She had nothing. If she mentioned any of the handles of other members of the message board, she had no way of knowing if this guy knew those people personally and would be able to verify that she was lying. There was only one name, one username that she knew for sure didn't belong to any of these people's associates... Aidan's.

"He goes by 'Fight4Independence', that's all I know," Heidi whispered. She felt bad that she had to ruin his cover too, but she had to give these people something, anything to go on that would sound plausible. This way, perhaps she'd get out of this yet, or at least buy some time to think up an escape plan.

The man didn't respond, just turned on his heel and left her cell again, followed by his two silent henchmen. A loud creak and click from the lock later, and Heidi was alone again.

Heidi breathed a sigh of relief. At least they had just questioned her and not done anything to hurt her. Perhaps they'd believe her story, and let her go. *That was still possible, right?* Or maybe they were planning to just let her rot here until she starved to death...

She flopped back onto the hard mattress and covered her eyes with the back of her hand to soothe the dull ache that had started to develop in her temples.

Ironically, the decor of her cell wasn't so different from her accommodation at the Alliance, with one exception: the mattress was even worse. She curled up on her side and tried to ignore the poking from the springs trying to break free from their flimsy covering.

If she could stick to her story, perhaps there was still hope, but with every passing moment, it became more and more difficult to stay positive. Unless she could get out of here soon, there was only one possible outcome. Sooner or later the wolf would win. And the man with the swallow tattoo would come in and put her down like a rabid dog.

Heidi thought back to what had led her here. Leaving Rannoch for the first time, saying goodbye to her family for who knows how long - potentially forever, considering her current situation. The Alliance office, and… Aidan.

Aidan, who had received her on that first night in Edinburgh, and made sure she got a good meal in her at a time when she felt more alone than she'd ever felt. She could almost taste that first meal all over again.

Aidan, who by all accounts seemed to be a complete professional, and capable member of the Alliance, but who hid a passion she'd never known before - the brooding looks he'd given her over that first dinner were as clear a sign as she needed.

And yet, he hadn't acted. He'd kept his distance, and treated her with respect. Was it because he was a bear and she was a wolf and he knew nothing good could come from it? No, if that had been the case, he wouldn't have been so kind to her.

She knew that if they gave in to their instincts and paired up, it would go against everything she'd been taught. It would even go against the rules put in place by the truce between their species.

Just because they were working together as part of the Alliance, didn't mean their species had all of a sudden forgot centuries of rivalries. If she followed fate and paired up with Aidan, she could never go home. She would never see her family again.

But as things stood now, and she was faced with the very real possibility that she'd never see any of them again, what hurt more? Realistically, the moment she left Rannoch, she'd changed forever. She would never be her parents' little girl again. She already didn't conform to what was expected of a she-wolf in Rannoch. She didn't want to play second fiddle to a man who would decide everything for her and their future children.

She wanted Aidan.

More than anything, it dawned on her that perhaps that was why fate had chosen him for her. They were mates, which meant that everything she had felt, he had felt too. He would have wanted to claim her from the moment he saw her, but he didn't. He had waited.

Tears started to burn in the corner of her eyes as she let her imagination take over. If they got together, he'd continue to respect her like that, she just knew it. He would treat her as an equal, not as a submissive. Perhaps that was why wolves didn't like bears and vice versa, their ways of life clashed too much. But Heidi wasn't an ordinary wolf...

In a last ditch attempt to keep her emotions in check, she tried to quit crying, but it was pointless. Tears were flowing more heavily now, running down the side of her face and into the dirty mattress. Perhaps this was for the best. If she vented like this, perhaps she could stay in control of her animal side a little bit longer.

Heidi lay there, curled up and motionless except for the occasional sob, until her body and mind tired and pulled her into a confused dream-state. Visions of Aidan filled her thoughts.

*He opened the door to her cell, came inside and scooped her up in his strong arms. As he lifted her, the world spun out of focus and what had been just dirty bare concrete turned into a lush, green forest. Like the one in Rannoch. She looked up at his face, and saw that he was smiling down at her.*

*"I'm so glad I found you," he said.*

# SCOTTISH WEREBEAR: A DANGEROUS BUSINESS

*She smiled back at him, closed her eyes and wrapped her arms around his shoulders. Those strong, muscular shoulders she'd previously only stolen glimpses at, but never touched. She'd been missing out.*

*Her head rested against his chest, which might as well have been made of steel. Rock hard muscles, all over. What a specimen. Gorgeous. All hers.*

*"I'm getting you out of here, don't worry," Aidan whispered in her ear, before stealing a kiss on that most sensitive of spots just down the side of her neck.*

*It tickled, and she couldn't suppress a giggle. "I know. I'm waiting for you."*

*That heat she'd first felt when she sat across from Aidan on her first night in Edinburgh in that pub had made a return. An intense fire burned in her, lighting up her lower abdomen. There was just one way to soothe it. One man who could soothe it.*

*She opened her eyes again and found Aidan staring down at her. His normally brown eyes had turned a deep, dark black. Just looking into them gave Heidi shivers.*

*The air seemed to prickle with tension, like the kind you feel in the calm before the storm.*

*His scent overwhelmed her senses. Sweet with a bit of spice. A little woody, like a forest in the fall after shedding all its leaves.*

*She chuckled.*

*"What?" he asked.*

*"You bears, you even smell sweet." Heidi grinned up at him.*

*Aidan let go of her, but she didn't fall. Heidi felt like she was floating in the air in front of him. He cupped her face with both hands, closed his eyes as she did too. His breath tickled her lips, making the wait almost unbearable, but she didn't stir.*

"All right, missy," A voice shouted, dragging her painfully out of her fantasy just as it was about to hit its climax.

Heidi opened her eyes to find the same man with the

swallows standing in the doorway.

"I need you to tell me who this 'Fight4Independence' person really is."

One of his silent minions dragged a chair into the cell, the bare metal of its legs scraping against the concrete floor, making the hairs on the back of Heidi's neck stand up.

"Did you hear me? Who is 'Fight4Independence'?" The man repeated.

*Crap.* "I don't know the guy, okay? I just met him online," she tried to explain, but something told her, a vague answer like that wasn't going to satisfy this guy...

# CHAPTER TEN

———— ◆ ————

Aidan entered the office bright and early in the morning, only to find it empty. *Where was everyone?*

The clean coffee cup on Heidi's desk was dry, unused. Aidan wondered whether to go upstairs to see if she was still in bed... But that would have been too creepy, so he decided against it.

He made a quick call to Jamie instead, who picked up just when Aidan was about to give up.

"Hello?"

"Jamie. I'm back." Aidan sat down at his desk, and impatiently tapped his fingers against the already worn surface.

"Great timing, Heidi has made some progress while you were away." Jamie sounded uncharacteristically excited, especially considering the time.

"Has she? She's not here."

A crackle interrupted the awkward silence.

"She's not upstairs, either?" Jamie asked at last. His tone had changed, gone was his excitement, instead it had been replaced by... concern?

Aidan's chest tightened, and a feeling of dread came over him. He rushed to the door, up the stairs and into the room where Heidi's scent lingered the strongest. Her bed looked unused, the pillow was still fluffed up and her duvet was neatly folded and placed at the foot-end of the mattress.

"Goddammit, Jamie!" Aidan shouted into the phone. "She hasn't been here all night!"

"I… Shit. I'm coming in." Jamie hung up and Aidan

stood helplessly in the center of her room, phone still in hand. His bear wanted to come out, roar in anger and tear up the place. Where was she? Why hadn't she come home?

She had looked strong enough, Aidan had no doubt she would have been a good fighter, but the city could be a dangerous place for a lone shifter. They had files filled with names downstairs of shifters at least as capable, if not more so, who had disappeared without a trace. The last thing Aidan wanted was to have to add her name to one of the files. He wouldn't be able to stand it.

Aidan paced around the room, trying his best to control his breathing and suppress the urge to shift. After regaining a little bit of focus, he rushed back downstairs and powered up Heidi's computer in an attempt to find out what she had been working on.

Before Jamie even turned up, Aidan had read through various messages between what he assumed was Heidi's ID on the message board, and some of the regular members. They had been very chatty, much more so than they had been with him when he first joined.

"What the fuck where you thinking?" Aidan shouted, as soon as Jamie finally came through the door. "She hasn't been here a week and you let her meet with these people? She wasn't ready!"

"Watch your tone!" Jamie responded. "She seemed capable enough, and the job was simple: go meet a couple of people for drinks in a public place. Nothing more than that. Perhaps she's just hungover and..."

"I'll use whatever tone I see fit!" Aidan slammed his fist down on the desk, making it shake dangerously in the process. "She hasn't even slept in her bed! Whatever happened last night, she never made it out of there."

"Don't talk to me like it wasn't my call to make. In case you forgot, I'm the team leader. And you weren't even around!" Jamie responded.

Aidan took a couple of deep breaths and tried to control the rage that had bubbled up into his chest. He balled his fists and released them a few times, but he couldn't calm down. Jamie was right, though. Aidan had gone off on his own before even training Heidi properly. He'd had good reason to, of course, but still... How could he not feel responsible for what had happened?

"Okay, let's think about this. The last thing the Alliance needs right now is to make enemies of the Wolves of Rannoch." Jamie slowly wandered over to his desk and sat down and rested his head on his hands.

"What?" Aidan looked up again in confusion.

"Rannoch. That's where she's from."

"What the- You're telling me she's wolf?" Aidan couldn't believe his ears. This was a disaster. The woman fate had selected for him was gone. In his haste to run after ghosts from his past, he hadn't even realized the most basic details about her. He hadn't noticed she was a completely different species, and from Rannoch, no less!

He'd heard about that place, a secretive community of wolves living deep in the woods, far removed from human society. She wouldn't know the first thing about how the world worked, and probably jumped head-first into a dangerous situation with the bloody Sons of Domnall! He should have known. This was all his fault.

"Jesus Christ, Jamie. Would it have hurt you to let me know?" Aidan asked at last.

"You already weren't thrilled about her coming here, it seemed unnecessary to complicate matters further. Plus I figured you'd have noticed from her scent."

"Her scent..." Aidan shook his head. "How the fuck do I know what a wolf smells like? Fuck."

"Anyway, enough of this. Rather than continue to

blame each other, let's figure out how to fix this," Jamie suggested. He looked terrified, as though there was something else he wasn't sharing, but Aidan decided to let it go for now.

Perhaps there was still time to sort this out. The one thing he did know was that he couldn't trust Jamie with this, not fully, anyway. And if by chance Lee Campbell was involved in Heidi's disappearance as well, Aidan really needed help he could rely on to ensure he'd get the chance to capture the man himself. There was only one other person he would entrust Heidi's life with: Derek.

———◆———

By the time evening came around, Jamie had pulled fellow Alliance team member Kyle back from his vacation, and Aidan had managed to get in touch with Derek, who was on his way as well.

The office was buzzing with activity, and eerily quiet at the same time. All three of them - Aidan, Jamie, and Kyle, were each completely absorbed in their work, so they barely spoke to one another.

"I've got it!" Kyle finally broke the silence.

Aidan looked up, his eyes burning from staring at his screen for so long.

"What is it?" Jamie asked, who had gotten up to take a look at what Kyle had found.

"I've managed to hack into the phone company's server." Kyle pointed at his screen. "There. That's the cell tower Heidi was connected to when her phone went dead."

"All right..." Aidan rolled his chair up to Kyle's desk and took a look. It was just a number, a code, it might as well have been Greek to him.

# SCOTTISH WEREBEAR: A DANGEROUS BUSINESS

"So cross-referencing the tower ID, with the grid, here," Kyle opened another screen, and showed his two colleagues a map of Edinburgh, which was divided into zones with equally confusing looking numbers in them. "It seems Heidi was roughly in this area." Kyle circled one of the zones with his index finger.

"Okay, well… that's something." Aidan scratched his head. "Jamie, you said she was going to meet people for drinks. A public place, a pub?"

"Yeah, a pub."

"How many pubs are in that area, there?" Aidan braced himself for the answer. This city - as well as most of the country - actually, was famous for its numerous drinking establishments.

"Let's see…" Kyle clicked a few buttons, and super-imposed another map over the grid he'd looked at earlier. "About… thirty?"

"Thirty." Jamie let out a dejected sigh. "We don't have enough people to canvas thirty pubs in time to figure out where she went. Not without drawing attention to ourselves anyway."

"Perhaps we don't have to… What else do we know about these people? If they've taken Heidi at the meeting, they would have done it somewhere where they felt comfortable. Somewhere, where nobody would have called the police on them… They're nationalists, right? Separatists. How many of these pubs are independent, not owned by large breweries - especially not English breweries?"

"About half are free houses, not tied to any brewery."

"How else can we narrow this down? How about location? It's unlikely Heidi would have been taken from a pub that is in full view of a main road…"

"That leaves us with five. Five unaffiliated pubs that are set back from main roads." Kyle sat back, crossing his arms. "That's not half bad. Good thinking there, Aidan!"

The printer in the corner purred into action, and soon spat out a list with all the addresses. Jamie got up to retrieve it, read through it, and handed it to Aidan.

"Let's go, then. No time to waste."

———————◆———————

The first two pubs on the list didn't feel right to Aidan. He couldn't catch a whiff of Heidi's scent there either, so they quickly moved on to number three.

After picking up his brother, Derek, on the way, they parked up a few buildings down and walked up to the third pub. There was a Scotland flag in the window, and the place had a particular vibe to it that made Aidan suspicious.

"This could be the one," he remarked.

Jamie, next to him, nodded. "Very private, service alley leading to the back. I agree."

They decided to split up, with Jamie heading inside to look for clues there, and Aidan exploring said alley, while Derek went back to the car to keep an eye on the surrounding area. Aidan had barely made it to the back of the building, before he found what he'd been looking for.

Right next to a stack of piled up garbage bags, was unmistakable proof that they had come to the right place. A discarded hair band, a couple of strawberry blond hairs still attached to it. He picked it up and immediately caught Heidi's scent. She'd been here.

He made a quick call to Derek, telling him this was the place and to stay put. Then he decided to head inside to join Jamie, who had taken a seat at the bar.

Inside the dimly lit establishment, Aidan immediately saw that the crowd looked right too. The clientele was overwhelmingly male, working class, a lot of tightly cropped or shaved heads around the place. They fit the profile down to the combat boots and occasional nationalist tattoos. And they were all were staring at him.

Actually, both Aidan and Jamie stood out like sore thumbs. Considering how built they were, of course, it would take a lot more than wearing your hair the wrong way for any of these people to confront the two bears. After a quick greeting, they ordered whatever was on tap and immediately started commenting on the football playing on the flat screen overhead like they came here all the time.

All the heads they'd turned initially looked away again. A decent knowledge of the local sports scene was apparently enough to appease the crowd.

Although Aidan knew that time was of the essence if they wanted to get Heidi back in one piece, he also knew that patience and stealth were called for here. By the third round, they'd gotten a few of the regulars involved in an in-depth discussion about coaching decisions and seemingly blended in.

It was then that a familiar face walked in the front door and ordered a scotch. It was the younger guy from the park.

Aidan subtly signaled to Jamie that he was their man, then sent a quick text message to Derek in the car as well:

*Found our guy. We'll follow him when he leaves, and once we get there, keep Jamie out of my way.*

The two bears watched him from the corners of their eyes. As soon as he left, they'd be on his tail, and hopefully he'd lead them right to where Heidi was being held.

# CHAPTER ELEVEN

—————◆—————

"Answer me! How do you know 'Fight4Independence'?" The man shouted again, while his two younger partners stood silently behind him, their arms folded.

Heidi flinched with every outburst of his. Not because she was scared of him, per se. She was more terrified that if he did anything more than just raise his voice at her, she couldn't fight the urge to shift anymore. In her current state, hungry and mentally as well as physically exhausted, she'd be able to take on one, maybe two of her captors, but only if they weren't armed. If any of them had guns, she'd be down in no time.

"I told you, I don't know him in person, we met on the Internet," Heidi repeated herself for the umpteenth time.

"Why did you try to join us? Who do you work for?"

"Nobody! I just agree with your philosophy and wanted in on the action!" Heidi covered her face with her hands and tried to focus on deep, even breaths. Hyperventilating wasn't going to do anyone any good.

She had no idea how long she'd been locked up, and the hunger pangs that had been coming and going for what felt like hours were making a painful return. How much more of this would she be able to take? Like most animals, her wolf side couldn't stand being trapped.

"If you won't talk willingly, I'm going to have to find a way to make you..."

Heidi looked up to find the two silent henchmen taking a few steps in her direction. This was bad. She could feel a familiar itch develop in the pit of her stomach. Once they were on her, she wouldn't be able to control her body's urge to protect itself.

She closed her eyes again. *Come on, Aidan, if you're looking for me at all, now would be the time to find this place...* Just as she'd completed her thought her sensitive hearing picked up a disturbance elsewhere in the building. It was too faint to make out what it really was, but it sounded out of the ordinary.

Was she starting to lose her mind? Was her imagination playing tricks on her?

The noises - footsteps, the occasional thump and scream - came closer and closer, until she could pick up on actual words.

"Where is she?" someone who sounded suspiciously like Aidan demanded.

"Who?" Another voice retorted.

"Stop messing me about, where's the girl?"

Heidi swallowed her concerns, as well as her fatigue. When she opened her eyes and stared right at her main captor, she was back in control and revitalized.

"You might want to call back your goons," she warned, keeping her voice steady and low.

"Oh yeah? Why is that, lassie?" he taunted.

"They lay a finger on me, and..."

"And?"

Heidi felt her eyes burn up as she looked around the room. Even the most casual observer would clearly be able to see them glow in the dark. One of the younger men flinched back, but the other one, and the guy in charge didn't react at all. This wasn't the first time they'd seen a shifter readying for a fight.

"I knew it," he said, a subtle smile playing on his lips. "There was something not right about you. We're done here. Take care of her."

His two underlings exchanged a quick glance, and then

approached her again. They weren't going to deal with her using just their bare hands, though. This time, one reached around, retrieving something from his belt. A hunting knife.

Heidi held her breath and waited for them to come closer. If all they had were knives, she'd be fine. This is what she had trained for. Guns, however...

The footsteps reached outside the door, followed by a loud crash of metal against metal. The wooden frame splintered, and the reinforced door flew open, revealing a slightly red-faced Aidan, holding a hand-held steel battering ram.

*Are you okay?* His eyes seemed to ask as they exchanged a quick look. Heidi responded with only a smile. Her heart fluttered at the sight of him. He had come to free her. *Her hero.*

Her three captors turned to face this new threat, giving Heidi the perfect opportunity to get involved in the fun. Within a split second, she'd allowed her animal side to take over. The shackles that had kept her tied to the bed fell off her much sleeker paws, as did the clothes she'd been wearing. She pounced on the first person that came her way.

There was no room in her mind for moderation, for keeping things clean. Her sharp teeth tore through flesh and crunched bone, until her prey was left in a puddle on the floor, whimpering in pain.

The other two looked back at her in horror, but didn't have time to dwell on what had just happened, because Aidan was coming at them with the steel ram he'd just used on the door. The young one flew back against the wall at the far end of the cell, leaving only the senior one still in one piece.

That's when things calmed down very suddenly.

# SCOTTISH WEREBEAR: A DANGEROUS BUSINESS

"Lee Campbell, I presume… We have some unfinished business," Aidan said in a low voice.

"I'd been wondering when you'd turn up."

Despite adrenaline still coursing through her veins, Heidi decided to sit down right in between the two incapacitated men to just observe. *How did these two know each other?* This must have been one of the men Aidan had seen at the park, the one he said he'd recognized.

"Then you know what this is about?" Aidan asked.

"I got a call from a friend in Portree the other day…"

Aidan nodded, as if that explained everything.

The other henchman, whom Aidan had thrown all the way across the room, groaned as he tried to reach for the hunting knife that was lying on the floor mere feet away from him. Heidi quickly intervened, and with a growl kicked the knife out of his reach. *Watch yourself or you'll get mauled like your friend,* she thought.

"Back in 1999, Skye. Your parents," the man Aidan had identified as Lee Campbell said.

"That's right." Aidan placed his hand on Lee's shoulder and shoved him backwards across the room, until he reached the bed. As Lee sat, Aidan grabbed the steel chair and positioned himself across from him. "Why?"

"Why…" Lee let out a chuckle. "Why do bad things happen to good people? Why is life so unfair?"

"If your organization killed them simply for what they were, then why let me and my brother live?"

Heidi held her breath. This man had killed Aidan's parents? That was it, Aidan's deep, dark secret. That was why he was so focused on his work with the Alliance.

She thought of her own parents, and felt her earlier rage flare up again on Aidan's behalf. Hidden underneath the controlled exterior, Heidi saw signs that Aidan was struggling with his emotions as well. The animal inside him wanted revenge, while his human side needed answers. Every muscle in Aidan's body had tensed up. His heartbeat was racing, she could hear it clearly from across the room.

"For who they were? No, son, they didn't die for who they were, but for *where* they were and *when.*"

Aidan frowned. "What are you saying?"

"Wrong place, wrong time. Just bad luck. A coincidence," Lee clarified, and shrugged. "They saw something they shouldn't have. Believe me, had I known there was more to them than that, you wouldn't be here right now."

Heidi couldn't believe her ears. As slick and organized as all of her people thought the Sons of Domnall were, they seemed to be a rather confused bunch. Killing shifters without knowing they were shifters, just because they couldn't keep their shenanigans secret without being overseen by random bystanders. Wow.

Aidan gave her a knowing look, like he could read her mind.

*Kill him, he deserves to die,* Heidi thought. Aidan subtly shook his head. *Not yet.*

"I've thought about this moment for years. Fifteen years, to be exact. What I'd do to you once I found you." Aidan folded his arms and stared at Lee, who looked unusually content for someone who had just been captured by the enemy.

"Do what you must, sonny."

"I could kill you right now, but what good would that do anyone? No. I think you'll be of more use alive..."

Aidan got up and retrieved a pair of handcuffs from his pocket. Lee didn't struggle, he barely even reacted when Aidan cuffed him with his hands behind his back. The entire scene was surreal, and for a moment, Heidi wondered if she had perhaps passed out due to hunger and was just imagining everything.

"Is this the guy?" another man said as he burst into the room. The similarities between Aidan and him were uncanny, even if he did look like a wilder, more feral version of him. Scruffy beard and longer hair, but their body structure and even their walks were alike. They had to be related, brothers perhaps.

"Derek. Stand down," Aidan warned him, placing his hand against his chest.

Behind Derek, Jamie came into view, wiping his brow with the back of his hand. "What's the status here?"

"Heidi is secure. One guy in critical condition," Aidan glanced at the bleeding man Heidi had sharpened her teeth on earlier. "Another with a few bruises and this one here, Lee Campbell, senior Sons of Domnall member. Captured."

"All right. We've had a few runners, half a dozen or so, two casualties, three prisoners who are somewhat unharmed," Jamie responded.

*Holy crap, casualties?!* Heidi had been aware of the risks of this work, but it was still surreal hearing her boss report actual deaths in such a matter-of-fact tone. The Alliance was a relatively small set-up, especially in Edinburgh, but they clearly knew how to get their hands dirty.

"You," Jamie addressed Heidi directly now. "You can't go out like this."

Heidi instinctively flinched at his strict tone, and hated herself for it immediately. Jamie was her boss, but he wasn't her alpha.

"Relax, she's not going to," Aidan butted in.

"Fine. Let's get out of here before anyone else sees us. Kyle has already brought the van around." Jamie grabbed Lee Campbell by the arm and dragged him out of the room. Behind him, Derek paused for a moment, but then made his exit as well, stopping only to drag out both the incapacitated henchmen out by their arms. Finally, Aidan and Heidi were on their own.

"You, umm... I should give you some privacy," Aidan mumbled, while watching Heidi pick up her clothes between her teeth. He turned around and headed for the door as well. Heidi channeled all her energy into one final instant shift and followed Aidan to the door, placing her hand on his shoulder.

"Wait."

He paused, allowing Heidi to catch up properly and face him. She didn't care that she was butt naked. She didn't care that they were surrounded by filth. All she cared about was that she was finally reunited with the man she knew she was going to spend the rest of her life with.

She wrapped her arms around his neck, and pressed her lips against his.

If he was surprised at her sudden change of heart, he didn't show it. Instead, he held her tightly in his arms, and responded to her kisses with an urgency that matched her own. His touch was electric, and his kisses...

Tears started to stream down her face.

"I thought I'd die in here. That I'd never see you again," Heidi whispered.

"Impossible. I wouldn't have let that happen," Aidan responded.

He cupped her face, just like he had done before in her dreams, and gazed into her eyes.

She could see hidden depths in his brown eyes that hadn't been there before. Or perhaps she never actually had allowed herself to look.

In the short time she'd known him, he'd seemed totally independent. She had never been really sure he felt their connection as intensely has she had, but there in his eyes, she found a different Aidan. The teenager who had lost both his parents to a stupid coincidence, who all of a sudden was forced to grow up. She saw Aidan, the man, who felt that he could never truly rely on anyone but himself. That's why he hadn't told Jamie the truth about why he had to take off for a couple of days. Who could be charming if he wanted to be, but had never let anyone come too close.

Until now.

"You have very green eyes, has anyone ever told you that?" Aidan remarked.

Heidi laughed, then tiptoed and kissed him again. "What happens now?" she asked.

Aidan stole a glance down at her naked chest and gave her another one of those sexy, brooding looks he'd given her at the pub on her first night. "How about you cover up and we get out of here?"

"What about the prisoners? And Jamie and all?" Heidi asked.

"They're not going anywhere. You've been locked in here for over a day, if that's not deserving of a little time off, I don't know what is."

Heidi smiled. "Fair enough. Before anything else, I could murder another one of those fish platters from that pub."

"What, raw man flesh didn't sate your appetite?" Aidan teased.

"Nah, I prefer my meat cooked." Heidi released Aidan's neck, and walked back across the cell to get her clothes, all the while feeling his intense stare on her naked body. Oh, she could definitely use some time off, but had a feeling it wouldn't involve much relaxation.

# CHAPTER TWELVE

Aidan hadn't been able to keep his eyes off Heidi while she got dressed inside her cell. He hadn't been willing to let go of her hand as they walked out of the dark, damp warehouse where she'd been locked up. He had had a taste of her lips, and both man and bear needed more of the same.

When he'd seen her shift and attack one of her captors, he had to admit to himself he'd been impressed. She had held up remarkably well in captivity. When faced with four blank walls and no way out, it was easy to lose hope and lash out. She had kept her cool though, and waited for the right moment to attack. When she did, it had been a glorious display of the force of nature. Cruel, efficient, beautiful.

As much as he hated him for it, Jamie had been right. Heidi was capable. A great addition to the team and the Alliance overall. If only he didn't feel so goddamn protective of her.

The connection between the two of them hadn't been as clear as he'd heard about in other fated couples, but every time they were in the same room together, their bond seemed to grow stronger. When he'd just reached the hideout, he could feel her presence. He knew she was alive, and scared.

When he'd found her, he could even hear glimpses of her thoughts. He was used to keeping secrets, mostly from Jamie, but even from Derek. Still, it seemed nice to have someone in his life who would always know what he was thinking. Someone who would understand him no matter what.

Although she'd said she wanted to return to the same place where they'd eaten on her first night in town, they didn't quite make it there. The first kebab shop on the way proved too tempting. Grilled meat could do that to a person, especially one who was also a wolf.

Aidan watched her eat, no, inhale the food. The color returned to her cheeks, making her look all the more tempting.

"What?" Heidi looked up from the now empty wrapper that had only moments earlier contained a lamb wrap.

"Nothing." Aidan grinned and made no attempt to look away.

"No, seriously. What are you staring at?"

"I love watching you eat. Wait, that sounds creepy, doesn't it?"

"You ought to work on your lines, sweetheart. *Creepy* is an understatement." Heidi grinned back at him.

"Still hungry?" Aidan teased.

"You're impossible. And no, I think I'm done," Heidi responded.

Aidan got up to pay for the food, when his phone buzzed. Jamie. He'd seen Aidan's message stating that he was taking Heidi home for some much needed rest and agreed. They wouldn't be expected back at the office until the next morning.

"Who was that?" Heidi asked when Aidan shoved his phone back into his pocket.

"The boss. Time off approved."

"Gee, I wonder how we will pass the time?" Heidi blinked at Aidan quasi-innocently.

"I have a few ideas." Aidan offered her his hand and off they went, straight to his place.

—————◆—————

"Wow, this is nice!" Heidi remarked, after Aidan had unlocked the front door and stepped aside to let her enter first.

"Welcome to my humble abode." Aidan gestured around the cozy living room. "Make yourself at home."

"Oh, I intend to. I've had enough of cold, musty cells for a while. And that includes the bloody Alliance building with what you people so generously refer to as "rooms" upstairs."

Aidan let out a laugh. "Oh, that. Yeah... I lasted one night when I first arrived. Went house hunting the very next day."

Heidi took off her coat and placed it over the backrest of the sofa. Then she turned to face Aidan again.

"So, where were we earlier?" she asked in a low, seductive voice.

Her question unleashed a whole load of explicit thoughts in his mind. She was here with him, and willing. Why wait? Why hold back any longer?

Rather than voice his desires, he picked her up in one swift move and carried her through the living room, down the hall and into his bedroom. She giggled the entire way, and once on her back in his bed, looked up at him with those big, bright green eyes of hers until he could resist no more.

He got up onto the bed on all fours and kissed her again. And again, until both their lips got sore.

As her hands roamed over his back, setting him alight from within, he raised himself up again and moved down lower, grabbing the collar of her t-shirt between his teeth. He pulled, hard, until the fabric gave way with a loud tear.

# SCOTTISH WEREBEAR: A DANGEROUS BUSINESS

The glimpse he'd gotten earlier after she'd shifted back was still burning in his mind, and he couldn't wait to get her back to her natural state. After ridding her of her top entirely, as well as her bra, he tore her jeans off her using just his hands.

Heidi was also getting into the swing of things and started clawing at his clothes. Within moments, they were both naked.

She really was a beautiful woman. Tall, with long, shapely legs, and endless curves in all the right places. Some men liked their women petite and slim, but Aidan was not one of them; he liked to play rough, and that was only possible with someone who could match his passion.

In Heidi, he'd found everything he could ever hope for. As he started to explore her soft, silky skin with his fingertips and lips - occasionally his teeth - the looks she gave him betrayed that gentle love-making was the last thing on her mind either.

Their union would be spectacular, that much was certain.

But first, he needed to taste her. The scent of her arousal hung heavy in the air, intoxicating him completely. His bear roared with excitement, and tried to push him to hurry up with the foreplay, and get on to the main course already, but he chose to resist just a little bit longer.

Heidi had other ideas though, and wrapped her fingers tightly around his thick shaft. "I need you. Oh God, I need you so badly," she breathed.

As she started to pump him, slowly at first, she never once broke eye contact.

Aidan closed his eyes, and tried to fight the building tension within him. He wouldn't cum. Not yet. Oh, hell!

He opened his eyes again and grabbed her wrists tightly, forcing her arms up above her head. No more touching. If she wanted him, she could have him. Right now, and when they were done, they would go again, and again, until she'd be too tired to give him that look. The one she was giving him right now.

This stare, it wasn't a request, it was a command. She demanded that he take her.

He couldn't hold off any longer and positioned himself between her thighs, pressing the head of his cock against her tight entrance. She was slick for him. Ready. But nice girls from Rannoch didn't go around fucking boys in their spare time. He didn't need to ask to know that he was her first. It was painfully obvious.

Heidi shut her eyes when he lowered himself on top of her, and her body finally made way for him.

She cried out, but when she looked at him again he could see that it wasn't a cry of pain.

He started off slow, rocking his hips into her, until he felt her relax. This was new for her, and he felt grateful - no, he felt proud to be her first. They would remember this moment forever.

As he settled into a more comfortable rhythm, her body started to react. Each thrust of his she met, her moans getting louder and louder. He loosened his grip on her wrists and her arms wrapped around his neck, clutching him tighter against her naked chest.

Their excitement turned more and more feverish. He focused on the rhythm, the in and out. Her body twitching and bucking upward in waves.

He felt her heat grow, her reactions turn more skittish and involuntary. She was heading up the cliff, and he was going to push her over the summit.

Heidi's hands twitched, fingernails dug hard into Aidan's back. It didn't bother him – if anything, it got him more excited. She turned rigid and groaned loudly, while dragging her hand down across his shoulder blade. The metallic scent of blood hung in the air, but rather than slow, Aidan sped up.

The sting on his back made his arousal grow. He plunged into her faster and faster, as she helplessly lay on her back panting through the remainder of her orgasm.

He finally reached the limits of his own control and jumped off that cliff after her, filling her with his hot seed, while sweet pleasure washed over him, paralyzing every one of his muscles. The room had suddenly turned so very quiet, while they both tried to catch their breath.

Neither of them stirred until Heidi started to nibble on the side of his neck.

"That was amazing. I never expected it to be *that* amazing."

Aidan smiled as he lifted himself off her. Without saying a word, he gathered her up in his arms and carried her into the spacious bathroom for round two. They could both use a hot shower after all they'd been through today, and he'd make sure to clean her out properly with his tongue... Virgin no more, he was intent on showing Heidi just how much more amazing stuff they could do to one another. After all, she was his now, and he was hers.

———◆———

Aidan stole a glance at the sleeping beauty beside him. Yes, she was a wolf, and he was a bear, and that complicated matters significantly. They would have an uphill battle ahead. But looking at her now, blissfully asleep on his pillow, he felt like none of that mattered.

The Alliance didn't approve of inter-species relationships. No doubt Heidi's parents would have a fit if they found out. But was it any of their business, really? She had come to him, she had accepted him. Once they made it official, what could anyone do about it?

Bears didn't have a lot of laws and traditions, but one that was carved in stone was that you didn't mess with a bear's mate. Wolf society was much more regimented and bound by a whole barrage of rules, but in this respect their cultures intersected: the bond between mates was considered sacred.

Plus, if it was good enough for Derek and Clarice, whose bond had been finalized only moments before he had called Derek away, it would be good enough for Heidi and him.

Aidan carefully lifted Heidi's arm off his chest and got up. There, inside the top drawer of the bedside table next to him, he already had everything they would need... Aidan retrieved the sealed envelope he had carried home from McMillan Farm. Its contents clanged together. The jingling sound was muffled by the thick parchment surrounding it, but he could still hear it.

"What are you doing?" Heidi said behind him, and rested her hand on his bare back.

Aidan turned around, envelope still in hand. "Here," he said. "Open it." Although he knew this was the right way of handling things, he was still anxious about how she would react. Was it too soon?

Heidi rubbed her eyes and sat up straight in the bed. Then she took the envelope from him and slipped her finger underneath the lip, levering the red wax seal off the paper underneath. She held her breath and looked inside.

"Oh! Are these what I think they are?" she whispered.

"These belonged to my parents," Aidan said. "Since they were designed for bears, yours may not fit quite right, but I'm sure we'll work something out."

Heidi took out the smaller of the two rings, and held it

up to get a better look at it. "It's gorgeous."

"As are you." Aidan took a deep breath. "So, what do you say? Will you be mine forever, as I'll be yours?"

She blinked a few times, yet failed to hide the tears collecting in the corner of her eyes. "Of course. I love you."

"I love you, too."

# EPILOGUE

———◆———

"Morning," Jamie said as he walked into the office, shaking off his umbrella and leaving it in a bucket in the corner.

Aidan and Heidi exchanged a quick look before responding. *He wouldn't be able to tell what's going on, would he?* Heidi wondered, while instinctively reaching for the ring hanging from a chain around her neck. His mother's ring. They'd showered before coming in, but still she felt like the whole world would be able to smell the sex on them. And she'd heard it said that something happened to couples after they were fully mated. That other people would be able to tell.

*No way,* Aidan responded. *We've been careful.* His hand was resting on his pocket where she knew he'd kept his ring. Maybe one day they'd feel safe enough to wear them openly, but not yet.

Heidi suppressed a smile. It was nice, having Aidan in her head. Where earlier she'd been able to catch only glimpses of his mood, it was reassuring being able to communicate with him, without even saying a word out loud.

"So where are we with the prisoners?" Jamie asked.

"They're secure in the basement. We've been questioning them one by one and so far none of them are in a mood to talk," Aidan said.

"How about you, well rested?" Jamie asked Heidi.

"Yeah. Fine. Ready to get back to work." Heidi smiled at him, let go of her chain, then looked back down at her computer screen.

"Good. Carry on." Jamie sighed and started on his

176

usual morning routine, walking over to the coffee maker, and shoveling spoonful after spoonful of sugar into his cup, before pouring the black liquid over it.

"Aidan, I want you to bring in your informant, what was her name? Alison." Jamie stirred his coffee and turned around while taking the first, careful sip.

"Do you think that's wise? Shouldn't I meet her out in public, as usual?" Aidan asked.

Heidi pretended not to listen, but stole a glance in Aidan's direction anyway. *Who was this Alison person?*

*Our informant. Human,* Aidan responded.

"She's been instrumental in identifying the websites. Don't you trust her?" Jamie asked.

"I suppose…"

"Well then perhaps it's time to question her properly, both of us, capture it on video." Jamie took another loud sip, then walked over to his desk and sat down with a loud creak.

"It's your call."

"Bring her in."

Aidan leaned forward, grabbing his phone off his desk and scrolling through his address book.

"Oh, where's your brother… Derek, was it?" Jamie asked. "I didn't have the chance to thank him for his help yesterday."

"Derek left bright and early."

*Of course he did,* Heidi thought. *Aidan had basically called the poor guy away from his honeymoon to help out with her rescue.*

"That's a shame. Nice guy. We could've used him on the team..."

"Uhuh," Aidan responded, while playing with his phone again.

Jamie sat back and looked around the office, pausing on both of their faces for a bit too long. The extra attention made Heidi nervous, but she resisted the urge to fidget with her chain again.

"Guys. It's okay, you know..." Jamie started, "It may be controversial in some circles, but you have nothing to worry about here."

Heidi tried to swallow her worries, and looked up at him as coolly as she could manage. "Worry about what?"

"Right." Jamie grinned and diverted his attention to his computer, which had just switched on. "Worry about what, indeed... Excuse me for a moment, I am going to pay a little visit to our guests downstairs."

While Jamie gathered up some notes and a pen, along with his half-empty cup of coffee, Heidi tried her best to remain calm.

As soon as he was out the door, she pulled her chair across the office, right next to Aidan's.

"He knows! Despite being careful, he still knows!" She couldn't believe it. Aidan was right, they *had* been careful. So how did he figure it out?

"I'm not surprised. He's been doing this kind of work for a long time. Good instincts," Aidan responded.

"Now what?"

"Nothing. We can't very well undo what has happened. Neither can we force him to forget."

"But the way you act around the guy, like you don't trust him. Are you sure he won't rat us out?" Heidi asked.

"I don't think he would."

"So why didn't you tell him why you were really driving up to Skye?" Heidi insisted. "Why keep secrets?"

"Because it was none of his business. And because Jamie Abbott isn't his real name. I've only been able to uncover records for *one* Jamie Abbott living in Scotland, and he's been dead ten years."

Heidi was speechless. Jamie wasn't who he said he was?

That was huge, and strangely, Aidan seemed quite calm about the entire affair.

"I don't understand. Either we're all on the same side, or we're not."

"I've found nothing to suggest he's disloyal to the cause, all I know is that for some reason or other he's chosen to live under an alias. Trust me. Things will be fine. He won't tell a soul." Aidan placed his hand on Heidi's shoulder and gave it a gentle squeeze.

"Fine. I trust you." Heidi closed her eyes and rested her head against Aidan's hand. Amazing, how such a simple gesture could put her mind at ease. She *did* trust him, and her own instincts were usually right about people too. During their time working together, she'd never felt unsafe around Jamie. He had his secrets, but then that might well be a bear thing, because Aidan had his too. Maybe one day, with Aidan's help, she'd understand why bears were so secretive...

"What do you say, we head downstairs to observe Jamie as he has a go questioning the prisoners? We might learn something." Aidan got up and offered her his hand.

"Sure." Heidi accepted his gesture, and together they left the office, ready to embark on whatever new adventures might lie ahead.

# -THE END-

# Scottish Werebear

## A FORBIDDEN LOVE

# PROLOGUE

———◆———

It had started like any other day. The boy couldn't wait to get out of the house and head to the beach at Applecross Bay. It was his favorite place in the world and nothing or no one could keep him away.

"Don't go in the water, all right? You'll catch a cold. And keep an eye on your brother." The boy's mother called after him from the veranda but he barely reacted, just kept his eyes fixed on the horizon. "Did you hear me?"

"Yes, mom." He took his little brother by the hand and dragged him along the narrow pathway through the dunes, around the s-bend uphill until their mother was out of view and they reached the crest of the hillock that stood between them and the windswept beach. He was twelve years old, old enough to know not to go into the icy waters. Old enough to take his brother to the beach. Not that his mother had realized that fact – she still acted like he was a baby.

It was chilly and cloudy, a typical Scottish summer's day, but the boys were used to it. Applecross Bay was where they were born, where they belonged.

"Shall we finish that sand castle?" asked the smaller of the two, who couldn't have been older than seven or eight years old, looking up at his older brother with big blue eyes.

"Don't be stupid, the tide will have washed everything away overnight," the older boy responded.

"So we start again. Make a better one?"

The older boy shrugged. "You do it."

"Okay, I will."

They walked on further, downhill and finally across the damp sand until they almost reached the water. The beach was vast and pretty much empty, like most of the surrounding countryside. Some might say this place was desolate or lonely, but to anyone who knew better it was magical and full of endless possibilities.

The older boy let go of his kid brother's hand and watched as he ran the rest of the way, plastic bucket and spade in hand, ready to leave his mark on the landscape. Let him build another stupid sand castle. Let it get destroyed again when the high tide rolls in.

He had other ideas, as he tightened his grip around the net in his hand. He was going to climb the cliffs that marked the edge of the beach and catch some dinner. Sandcastles were for kids, but gathering food, that was a much more respectable and grown-up activity.

A quick look back at where his brother had started digging in the sand revealed that all was still as it should be. The beach was empty as always. Why was his mother so paranoid about them coming out here? It made no sense. Nothing ever happened here, and his little brother knew better than to get into the treacherous waters.

So he pushed onward against the strong winds coming in from the sea, straight towards the shiny black cliffs where he knew a lot of crabs and other wildlife liked to hide. He had seen a lobster there previously, and today was the day he would catch it. He was determined.

Anyone could pick up crabs from the beach; that required no skill. But lobsters were a lot more skittish and cunning.

The boy's determination grew as he clambered up the slippery rocks heading for the crevice where he'd seen his prey before. If only he could shift already, it would make things like climbing up rocks a lot easier. But he wasn't ready yet.

It was around the thirteenth year that the bear side would become strong enough to assert itself. How he wished he could just skip this last year and become fully bear already. But time neither waited nor sped up for anyone, unfortunately.

From the corner of his eye, the boy saw a movement. An animal? Perhaps a bird, trying to hunt for the same thing as him?

Looking back down at the beach, he saw his little brother was completely oblivious to anything around him. He just kept filling his little bucket and turning it over to make turret shaped piles of sand, haphazardly positioned next to each other. It was childish. Amateurish.

So the older boy once again focused on the task at hand. He wasn't about to give up that lobster to a seagull or something. No. That would be unacceptable.

But when he looked around again he saw that the earlier movement hadn't been a seagull or other animal. Further up the cliff, gazing down at him, sat a girl. Red hair blowing in the wind, framing a freckly face featuring two piercing green eyes. She was pretty, for a girl, and about his age.

"Hi," the redhead said.

The boy paused for a moment. Was he imagining this? Nobody ever came here, except a few of the locals. And he'd never seen her before. "Hi."

"Nice place. You live here?" she asked, while wrapping her arms around herself as though she was trying to keep warm.

"Uh-huh. Where are you from?"

"Edinburgh. We're only here on vacation."

"Aha. Edinburgh," the boy repeated after her, hoping it

made him sound knowledgeable. The truth was he'd never been to Edinburgh, or even spent much time away from his home just across the dunes at all.

"What's your name?" she asked.

"Jamie. Yours?" he responded.

But she didn't answer. Instead she got up on top of the cliff and looked back at something - he wasn't sure at what, because he was too far down to be able to catch her line of sight.

"Hey, I need to go. My dad gets real upset when he doesn't know where I am. See you around, maybe."

Before he had the chance to think of anything else to say, she had climbed over the other side of the cliffs, and ran off into the grass-covered dunes leading away from the beach. Perhaps he should follow her, try to get to know her. But he couldn't bring himself to move, so he just stood there watching as she got smaller and smaller and finally vanished over the top of the hill.

It was the strangest thing. When she was gone and out of sight, he wasn't even sure anymore if she'd actually been here or if he'd just imagined her. Nah, that was dumb. If he was going to imagine someone, he'd imagine someone totally different, not a *girl*. He didn't like girls much, thought they were mostly daft and spent way too much time fussing about stupid things like ponies and whatnot. No, he definitely wouldn't dream up a girl if it was up to him.

The entire incident had distracted him sufficiently that he didn't feel up to the task of hunting his arch nemesis, the lobster, anymore. So he climbed down the cliff from the end where he had just come from and walked across the beach towards the beginnings of his brother's sand castle.

The beach was empty again. Totally empty, like it

usually was. The bright red plastic bucket and spade were lying in the center of the oddly shaped circle of sand turrets. There was no sign of his brother.

*Weird, had he gone back?*

The boy traced their steps back to the path they had taken across the dunes. *He must have just gone home, right?* As he got further and further away from the water, his heart beat faster and a sense of panic built in his chest. Why would he just leave? He wouldn't. They'd only just gotten here and his castle was far from finished. There's no way his little brother would have left his bucket behind either.

He was completely out of breath by the time he made it home. His mom was sitting on the porch, reading her morning paper. As soon as she noticed him, she looked up and smiled.

"Hey, Jamie. That was quick. Where's Matty?" she asked.

He didn't know what to say to her exactly, how to explain it. At this moment Jamie realized two things: his brother was gone, and he'd never spend time down at the beach again.

# CHAPTER ONE

———————◆———————

It was late and most of Edinburgh's popular pubs were starting to close. Jamie Abbott didn't feel like heading home yet, but figured he might as well try to rest before another undoubtedly long day at the office.

A confusing maelstrom of thoughts plagued him. He had worked for the Alliance for years, laboring away day after day without much to show for it. Until now. Now they'd captured some actual members of the illustrious secret organization of humans who were trying to eliminate shifters the world over: the Sons of Domnall.

Three of them in total were being held in the basement underneath the Alliance office, while the rest had gotten away. Jamie thought about their unwillingness to talk. They may have made progress identifying and attacking what could very well be the base of the Sons of Domnall in Edinburgh, but what if they wouldn't learn much as a result? The only one who had said anything to him during questioning was the man in charge, who Jamie's colleague Aidan had identified as Lee Campbell.

Jamie knew better than to ask Aidan how he had uncovered the man's identity or what history they shared. If Jamie started digging into Aidan's private affairs, he could be certain to receive the same treatment in return. That was something Jamie was keen to avoid. Although Jamie was the senior Alliance member at the office, technically, when push came to shove that wouldn't mean very much to Aidan. Bears weren't good at dealing with authority figures like wolves were. They valued their autonomy too much, so team work didn't come naturally to them.

As Jamie had tried to gain further insights into the Sons and their activities in the city through intense interrogations, Campbell had been a constant source of frustration. He liked to speak in riddles. Jamie wasn't sure anything the man had told him was true. His gut told him that the one thing Campbell had definitely not lied about was that the Sons would plan a counterattack. They didn't take kindly to people, shifters in particular, interfering with their affairs and taking their members - brothers, as they called them - prisoner.

But Jamie and his people had always been careful. The building they occupied was owned by another, much more senior Alliance member, who had registered it in the name of a shell company. As far as the outside world was concerned, it was an administrative office for a shipping company.

After wandering the largely empty streets for about fifteen minutes, Jamie made it home. An impressive wooden door led to the ground floor of a Victorian house that had been converted into flats.

Jamie had been occupying this space for the better part of three years now. Despite splurging on the finest furniture to make it as comfortable as possible, he barely spent time here. Somehow, no matter what he did, he found it impossible to feel at home anywhere.

Jamie lived for his work, just like everyone else at the Alliance seemed to do. After hours, Jamie felt like he was waiting. For something, or someone. *The girl? How ridiculous.*

He took off his leather jacket and hung it neatly on one of the elegant dining chairs he never used. Then he checked his mail, even though he already knew that all he had waiting for him were bills.

It was four in the morning, according to the wall clock at the other end of the combined living and dining space. Jamie settled down in the armchair facing the TV that hung above the defunct period fireplace, but didn't switch it on.

How could he convince those people to talk? They were fanatics who truly believed in their cause and that made them dangerous.

*Hell, we truly believe in ours too, don't we?* Jamie sighed deeply and rubbed his temples in an attempt to soothe the dull ache that usually started to build up in there around this time. He knew he was exhausted, but he also knew sleep wouldn't find him just yet.

He closed his eyes and went through a few breathing exercises he'd found online. With his eyes still shut, he breathed in sharply, then exhaled in a slow, controlled manner for as long as he could stretch it. Rinse and repeat.

It wouldn't work, he already knew that, but he was nothing if not persistent in everything he did.

After a few breaths like that, he opened his eyes again and started to look at the switched off TV. Jamie felt his body relax, the tension he'd been carrying around in his limbs slowly dissipating until his body was ready for sleep. The previously clear shape of the television blurred in front of him as he continued to stare at it.

His mind refused to cooperate with his body's demand for rest, though.

He needed to get those men to talk.

Perhaps they knew something that would help him.

Jamie's eyelids grew heavy until he gave in and let them fall shut again. He was surrounded by darkness, but only for a moment, before the blackest of black made way for the gray late summer's day that always came to him at this time of night. That day at the beach, back when he was only twelve years old. The day his brother had gone missing.

The pain of the loss stabbed him right through the heart, as it had done back then, when he first realized what had happened. But that wasn't the worst of it. The worst thing was that his baby brother was only a small part of what plagued his mind.

*The girl.*

He couldn't get the girl out of his head.

It made no sense at all. Why was he so fixated on her? He didn't remember when exactly the memories had started to change, because it had been so gradual at first. As the years had passed, so had his recollection of that day. Every night when these glimpses of so long ago infiltrated his mind against his will, the girl had aged right along with Jamie.

They'd been probably the same age back then. Tonight what Jamie saw wasn't an awkward twelve year old, but a full-figured redhead in her thirties, like him. And so lifelike, too. Her green eyes sparkled in what little light could escape the hazy clouds overhead. Her smile could stop traffic, it was so radiant. Her ample curves invited further scrutiny, but Jamie resisted the temptation, as usual.

Sometimes he did allow himself to focus on her beauty, just for a bit. But the guilt always got him in the end. It wasn't worth it. How could he fantasize about some girl he might have very well just imagined there on the beach, when his actual, real little brother had vanished without a trace?

How could a creature so beautiful have existed in the exact same moment as a loss so terrible?

His inner bear kept insisting that if only he found her,

everything would become whole again. Secretly that was why he'd joined the Alliance in Edinburgh rather than anywhere else, because that's where she'd said she lived. If he found her, perhaps he'd find *him* too. But if he found *her,* did it matter?

Jamie frowned, furious at himself for even questioning the importance of figuring out what had happened to his brother. Angry for all the pain the disappearance had caused to his parents, who had never been the same since. Guilty over his own selfishness and carelessness. It had all been his fault, after all.

Breathe in deeply, hold, slowly release. *Who was she, though?*

Breathe in, and release. *Why was she so important?*

Breathe and release.

———◆———

When Jamie awoke, he had no idea just when he'd fallen asleep, or for how long. He wasn't rested, but it was enough. He got up and stretched himself. Sleeping in a chair wasn't ideal, but it was better than not sleeping at all. A big mug of sweet instant coffee later, he felt ready for the day that lay ahead.

He would question the prisoners some more today. And today was the day Aidan would bring in their human informant, Alison, for more thorough questioning as well. Perhaps she knew more than she'd initially shared. Jamie was also curious about how she knew about the websites in the first place. She'd been too vague about that in the past. Either way, it was time for Jamie to step in and take control of the situation before the Sons got the chance to plan anything.

The first order of business would be to set up an

appropriate area for them to question Alison. There was no way he would let her into the main office, and he certainly couldn't use the basement where the prisoners were kept. Perhaps one of the rooms upstairs...

Jamie could be the most single-minded and focused person in the morning, but come nightfall, his thoughts went everywhere at once. Somehow it was easier to keep the bear part of him under control when the sun was out. It was his bear who was suffering more than his human side.

Now that it was morning, the world made sense again. Jamie grabbed his things and made the trip to the office on foot like he often did when the weather allowed it. A bit of drizzle like today wasn't enough of a deterrent.

"Morning." Jamie greeted the rest of the team as he swung the door open. Aidan and Heidi were already sitting at their work stations, while their resident computer genius, Kyle, was pouring himself a cup of coffee in the corner.

"Anything I need to know before getting things ready for Alison later?" Jamie asked.

Aidan looked up from his desk, as did Heidi. In the couple of days since her rescue, both of their behavior had changed drastically. They'd been distant toward each other earlier, especially Heidi, but now they seemed to have connected in a way one doesn't often see. Like they understood what the other was thinking without voicing it.

Jamie knew what it meant - they were mates, despite belonging to different species - and he'd tried to talk to them about it, but they were intent on keeping a low profile. Jamie couldn't blame them. Wolves and bears didn't ordinarily get along and there would be many who would oppose the idea of interspecies mating.

He suppressed a smile as he watched them exchange a

subtle glance. They were talking to each other, communicating with their thoughts alone. Rather than worry about their connection distracting from their work here, Jamie was certain it made them more valuable to their cause. He would never have to second guess their loyalties, as long as they were on the team together.

"No progress on the prisoners. We've been keeping the lights on in their cells to confuse their sense of time in the hopes that it would help us break them," Aidan said.

"I see. Perhaps the girl can give us something that'll help."

Aidan shrugged. Jamie could tell from his demeanor that he didn't think bringing the informant in would make any difference. But it was Jamie's responsibility as team leader to steer this investigation forward. If he was called in by the Alliance Council, he wanted to be able to say that he hadn't left any stone unturned. They'd given him this chance to make a difference at a time when he was completely lost. He owed it to them, as well as himself to do the best job he could.

"Very well, I'll get things ready for the interrogation," Jamie said. "Kyle, walk with me?"

Jamie pushed the door leading to the staircase open and waited while Kyle caught up, steaming cup of coffee in hand. "I'm thinking of converting one of the upstairs rooms so we can use it for interrogations. The one closest to the back entrance. I want you to think about recording solutions."

Kyle followed him up the stairs as the door slowly shut behind them with an ominous creak.

"Right. I'm assuming you don't want to make things too obvious?" Kyle asked.

"Hidden cameras. Multiple angles."

"Sure thing. I have some equipment lying around that

would be perfect. It'll take me a couple of hours maximum to set everything up." Kyle said.

"Wonderful. Let me know if you need any help." Jamie smiled. They'd all struggled to get along initially, but the team was finally pulling together as one. If they wanted to be successful in their fight against the Sons of Domnall, they needed to keep this up.

# CHAPTER TWO

———◆———

"This is a bloody disaster," Alison Campbell whispered, while sinking back into the sofa and shaking her head.

"Yep," her brother Gareth, who was sitting opposite her, confirmed.

"How did the Alliance find them, you think?" Alison asked.

"No idea, perhaps someone talked. Or perhaps they managed to sniff us out somehow. Who knows what these animals are capable of?" Gareth shrugged.

"Are you sure they're just holding dad and the others prisoner and they haven't actually killed them?" Alison had been talking to someone from the Alliance in an attempt to create her cover, but her contact was so distant, so cold, that she couldn't get a read on him. She was told that their entire race was made up of dangerous killers, but she hadn't been able to gather any real evidence of just how ruthless they could be.

"We don't know anything for sure. But it would make sense for them to try and squeeze him for information first. That gives us a little time before they realize he won't talk." Gareth ran his hand over his tightly cropped hair. He looked a lot like their dad when he did this.

"Shit. Well, how the hell will we find out where they're keeping him?" Alison wondered aloud.

"That's up to you, isn't it? You've got to find out where their base is."

Alison rested her face in her hands. *Damn.* "Did you guys *have* to capture one of theirs? This would have never happened if you hadn't taken the girl," Alison argued, tears welling up in her eyes.

"In case you forgot, they got awfully close to us thanks to the information *you* gave them!" Gareth retorted and crossed his arms. Alison hated it when he did that; when he gave her that cocky look like he knew everything.

"I had to give them something, otherwise how would I earn their trust?" Alison asked.

"Did you have to give them the message board, though? A lot of the guys feel that that cut awfully close to home."

"I can't be posing as an informant, if I don't *inform*, can I? And it was you who made the first move to meet with her. You could have just kept her at arm's length and they would have given up sooner or later." Alison felt the anger take over.

Her brother had never taken her particularly seriously. In fact, he probably hated that their dad had chosen her to get close to the Alliance by posing as an informant in the first place. Well, too bad for him. Dad had trusted her to get the job done, not him.

"Still, you're playing a dangerous game with these people, and now we're facing the consequences."

"I've done whatever was asked of me. You can take your hindsight and stick it somewhere."

Alison and Gareth stared at one another, neither in the mood to back down.

"If you've done such a great job at earning their trust, how come you've only ever met one of them? How come you don't know where their base is or even what their full names are?"

"This stuff takes time. Patience. Not that you would ever get that through your thick skull. And plus, our guys were no match for them at the warehouse. Don't you think we ought to arm ourselves a bit better before we can even think of acting?"

"Well you better hope it doesn't take too long, or we'll never get Dad and the others back. As for weapons, they're on the way. Don't you worry about that."

Alison gave him a dirty look and picked up her bag. If she had to stay here with Gareth one more minute, she'd be tempted to clobber him over the head with something. Such was her relationship with her brother – he really knew how to push her buttons.

Wallet, phone, all was in place, so she zipped up the top and threw the strap over her shoulder, ready to make a quick escape when her phone rang, stopping her in her tracks while she checked who it was.

*Aidan.*

"Keep quiet, it's them," Alison warned her brother, who still had a disapproving scowl on his face.

"Hello?" Alison answered the call.

"Alison. It's Aidan."

"Hello, Aidan. What's going on?" Alison asked, while keeping her eyes glued on Gareth.

"We've made some progress in our investigation and I've been asked to bring you in to see if you can shed some light on a few things..."

"Bring me in?" Alison repeated.

"Yeah. I'll text you the directions. It's time we had a more formal chat, what do you say?"

"Sure. Fine. I'll be there." Alison hung up and stared at her phone for a moment while she collected her thoughts. "They're bringing me in," she said triumphantly when she looked up at her brother again.

"So?" Gareth asked.

"So it seems they *do* trust me sufficiently now. Fingers crossed this goes well and we can get Dad back soon." Alison grinned and looked down at the flickering screen.

# SCOTTISH WEREBEAR: A FORBIDDEN LOVE

One new message. She was to meet Aidan in half an hour, at a park only a couple of blocks from the cafe where they'd met last time. He would take her the rest of the way.

Gareth didn't comment, and Alison didn't wait for him to. She had already been ready to leave before the call, and now she definitely didn't feel like sticking around. She'd grab a bite to eat, then head to the meeting point as instructed by Aidan.

Perhaps she still had a chance to fix things.

———— ◆ ————

Alison reached the meeting point ten minutes early and spent the time sitting on a park bench, watching the world go by. It was cold, but she was well prepared and didn't mind the fresh air. Today was a rather ordinary late October day, and Edinburgh's inhabitants as a whole didn't seem to care about the chilly weather either.

Mothers pushed buggies with small children. A group of construction workers passed by her bench on their way further into the park to eat their packed lunches. Of course they couldn't hold back the obligatory inappropriate remarks once they noticed her.

All of these people acted like everything was fine. It wasn't their fault, obviously, nobody had told them about the threats that lurked in the city - and everywhere else in the world for that matter. They had no idea about werewolves, and other dangerous creatures that could attack at any moment. They had no reason to fear the dark.

Alison knew better though, thanks to her dad and his work with the Sons. All their lives, she and Gareth had been taught about the various monsters that threatened humanity. Wolves, bears, lions. These were the three types they knew about, but it wasn't too farfetched to consider that perhaps there were other kinds of hybrids too.

The one thing Alison was certain about was that they were all predators and that human society was no place for them to reside.

She felt herself grow a little jittery, like she normally did shortly before her meetings with Aidan. She wasn't sure which of the three shifter species he belonged to, though she suspected he was a bear due to his impressive height and build. Either way, she wasn't fooled by his calm and controlled exterior.

Most were-creatures were savage animals unable to control the urge to kill. That's what her dad had told her. And that made Aidan a dangerous exception.

"Alison." Aidan's familiar voice interrupted her dark thoughts and made her flinch slightly.

"Hey." She jumped up, not to greet him per se, but more because seeing him tower over her bench put her in too much of a disadvantage if anything were to go wrong.

"Ready?" he asked. "Please give me your phone." Aidan held out his hand.

Alison nodded, and did as asked. He switched the mobile off, opened the back cover and removed the battery just like he'd done before earlier meetings. After he put all of the separate components into his pocket, he gestured at her to follow him out of the park.

They barely spoke while they walked, but Alison couldn't resist the urge to pry.

"So you said you've made some progress?" she asked, while trying to keep up with Aidan's long strides.

"That's right." He looked down at her, probably considering exactly how much information to share with her. "One of our own was taken, but we got her back. With interest."

Alison nodded and kept quiet. Aidan wanted to be vague, and that was fine. Today he was going to bring her into the Alliance hideout, and that was already a massive step in the right direction. Alison didn't want to push her luck.

"How about this weather, eh?" Alison attempted a bit of small talk.

"Mhm." Aidan looked left and right, then scanned the area behind them. "You weren't followed, were you?" he asked finally.

"No. Who would follow me?" Alison asked. God, she hoped Gareth hadn't actually followed her. That was exactly the sort of thing that could ruin her cover.

"All right." Aidan started to walk again and Alison followed, through the narrow alleyways in the old town. Left, right, zig-zagging around the historic buildings, until finally they made it to the other end of the city where the buildings started to look more modern.

Perhaps he had been trying to confuse her, so that she wouldn't remember the route they'd taken. That wasn't going to work, though, Alison thought. She'd lived in Edinburgh for most of her life, ever since her family had moved here when she was just seven years old. She knew this part of town like the back of her hand and no matter how much they walked in circles, she would know exactly how to get to where they were going.

Plus, unless he blindfolded her, she would be able to read the street signs and remember the landmarks.

After walking around seemingly aimlessly for about fifteen minutes, he led her further away from the center of town and towards the harbor. The streets no longer featured pretty old buildings, but bland warehouses and offices, most of which had been constructed in the sixties and seventies. A lot of this area was empty, abandoned. It was the ideal location for a hideout.

Finally, they reached their destination. An old warehouse that didn't stand out in the least. It was as rundown and dilapidated as all the others in the area. The paint was flaking off the woodwork, and weeds made their home in the cracked concrete of the facade. Bingo.

Aidan knocked and waited, though not very long, until the door was unlocked from the inside and swung open.

It was dark inside, and it took Alison a moment before her eyes adjusted to the low lighting. Inside stood a man, at least as tall as Aidan, if not slightly taller. The sight of him took Alison's breath away. He was gorgeous, and also a little familiar...

It was the eyes that got to Alison the most. A pair of almost sparkly blue eyes that pierced the darkness. She couldn't shake the sense of déjà vu. Where had she seen those same eyes before?

The man opposite her was frozen in place as they stared at one another, until what felt like minutes later Aidan cleared his throat, breaking the silence and dragging both of them back into reality.

"Err, I'm Jamie Abbott. You must be Alison Carter."

Alison reluctantly accepted Jamie's outstretched hand. As soon as their fingers touched, a jolt of something - excitement perhaps, or nerves - hit her right in the chest. She didn't know why, but was certain Jamie had felt it too. It was difficult not to say something about how strange she felt.

A subtle smile played on Jamie's lips as she let go after their handshake. As if he understood...

# CHAPTER THREE

———◆———

Meeting the human, Alison, for the first time was a huge shock for Jamie. For a moment he wasn't certain if he was actually awake or had somehow found himself in a vivid dream, like the ones that plagued him every night.

That face. Those green eyes and soft feminine curves. Alison was literally the girl of his dreams. As stupid and cliché as that sounded, it was true. She was the girl from the beach, he was certain of it. There was no way that this was a mistake. He'd seen her face every single night for as long as he could remember.

He'd wanted to ask her if she knew him too, but with Aidan around that seemed too weird a question, so he'd just shaken her hand and introduced himself instead. The look on her face had told him that their meeting was significant for her too. Or had he imagined that?

Shortly after he'd regained his composure somewhat, he'd stepped aside and let Aidan and Alison pass him and head upstairs. Luckily Aidan had understood that Jamie wanted him to take lead on this after all. Jamie found himself sitting opposite the radiant redhead in their newly set up interrogation room. The harshness of the fluorescent light overhead made her hair light up like it was on fire. He was glad that he didn't have the best view of her feminine curves while she sat there, half-obscured by the table, or he'd have even more trouble concentrating.

Aidan asked the questions Jamie had come up with earlier, and Jamie observed. He caught himself staring at her so intently that his eyes burned from forgetting to blink.

He looked down at his right hand which rested in his lap. It was warm where her fingers had touched his. Like they were still touching.

What did it mean? Had he lost his mind?

"Could you tell us again how you found out about those websites you mentioned to me before?" Aidan asked. His tone indicated that he wasn't expecting much of an answer, but Jamie didn't care.

He wasn't sure he wanted to know how she knew either. He just wanted to hear her voice as she answered.

"I worked part time for a hosting company a while back. Tech support. They had some issues with their software which I sorted out. That's how I found out," Alison responded.

Her voice sounded clear yet melodious, like she was singing her answers, not speaking them. He'd definitely lost his mind. Perhaps the years he'd been suffering from insomnia were finally catching up with Jamie.

"Those websites are quite vague to the untrained eye. How did you know that you'd found something worth sharing?" Aidan looked up from the list of questions, scrutinizing Alison.

Jamie tried to read her body language, but he kept getting stuck on tiny, irrelevant details. The dimples in her cheeks. The freckle on the tip of her nose. Her curvaceous lips which begged to be kissed...

"While sorting out their issues, I gained access to the private messaging system," Alison said. She glanced over in Jamie's direction.

Yes, she felt it too. Jamie could tell.

He knew for sure that she was the girl he'd dreamed about as recently as perhaps twelve hours ago. But did that automatically mean that she was also the same girl he'd actually talked to on that beach so many years back? How could he be certain? He had to ask her, but not with Kyle's comprehensive video surveillance system running in the background.

"What did you learn exactly?" Aidan asked.

"That they're dangerous. They want to hurt people."

"What people?" Aidan pushed.

"I'm not sure. The words they used are confusing. Animals. Monsters. I figured they're a bunch of crazy fanatics." Alison blinked a few times, then focused her green eyes on Jamie again.

He couldn't look away. He could barely breathe.

"How about we take a break, huh?" Aidan suggested, while picking up and straightening out the papers with his questions and notes.

Jamie nodded without even looking in his direction, and Alison leaned back in her chair, relaxing visibly as she folded her arms across her chest. With Aidan leaving the room, this was Jamie's chance to talk to Alison. Unfortunately he still had to deal with the cameras Kyle had installed everywhere somehow...

"Can I get you a coffee?" Jamie asked.

Alison looked up at him but didn't reply. Her eyes locked onto his and he was lost. They would have sat there opposite each other, just staring at one another indefinitely if Jamie's phone hadn't broken the spell.

He stole a glance at the screen. Damn. "I'm sorry, I need to take this. I'll be right back," Jamie mumbled, while getting up and rushing out the door, leaving Alison behind. Of all the times for his superiors at the Alliance to phone up, they had to pick this exact moment. Typical.

"Hello?" he answered.

"Abbott. Any progress?" the strict voice on the other end demanded. Alliance council member Adrian Blacke had never been one for small talk.

"The prisoners have kept their mouths shut. We're questioning another lead right now, the human who gave us the websites." Jamie felt his heart rate go up as he thought about Alison. It was his duty to report on what they were up to, but if it were up to him, he'd rather keep Alison's presence a secret. Thanks to his own demand to have video in place in the new interrogation room, he didn't have that option anymore. Blacke would see the footage sooner or later.

"I see. We will send in someone to take those prisoners off your hands within the next 48 hours. You're not equipped to keep them there, and if they're not talking to you anyway, perhaps we'll have more luck."

"But... we're not done questioning them yet," Jamie interjected.

"You have two days. That's all," Blacke said. With that, the conversation was over. The decision to transfer the prisoners had already been made and there was nothing Jamie could do or say to change that.

At least they didn't want to take over Alison's interrogation as well. Yet.

Jamie was still agitated when he slipped the phone back into his jeans. Coffee, that's what he needed.

He headed down the hall and through the door at the end, locking it behind himself, then rushed down the stairs leading down to the office. Aidan was already there and nursing a cup of the steamy hot liquid while going over some of the video footage with Kyle.

"How about the other angle, show me the other angle," Aidan remarked, leaning in closer as Kyle complied with his request. This could take a while. Good.

Jamie stuffed a couple of packets of sugar and creamer into his pocket and emptied the remaining coffee waiting in the coffee maker into two mugs. Then he headed back up the same way he came without disturbing any of the others. He had to get back to Alison, and learn whatever he could before Aidan cut his break short.

Back upstairs, he opened the door to the interrogation room and was relieved to find Alison exactly where he'd left her. Not that she would have had anywhere else to go.

"I wasn't sure how you take it, so here you go," Jamie said, placing the mug as well as the packets he'd brought in front of her on the table.

"Thanks," Alison whispered.

That voice... It made the hairs on Jamie's arms stand up straight, but in a good way.

He watched as Alison fixed her coffee. She had the most elegant fingers, like a concert pianist. He couldn't stop staring at her, she was mesmerizing to watch.

Alison took a first, tentative sip and closed her eyes.

What could Jamie say to her? How could he get her out of this room without raising any suspicion? And if he did, how could he resist the urge to let his inner bear claim her right then and there?

Jamie cleared his throat and Alison looked up from her mug. "This is a bit awkward, so I'm just going to come right out with it," he mumbled.

Alison blinked, waiting for Jamie to continue. He had to force himself to look away or he was convinced his words would come out jumbled up in the wrong order. *Focus, or she'll say no.* He had to make sure his question would at least make some sense.

"I was wondering if you'd like to have dinner sometime." Jamie held his breath while she seemed to mull things over. It was as though time had stood still and the ability to breathe had left him.

She bit her lower lip for a painful few seconds. "Sure," Alison said at last, to Jamie's relief. "I'd like that." She shot him a quick smile that seemed to make everything better.

"Brilliant. Here, take my number. Aidan has yours, I gather?" Jamie said, while sliding one of his business cards over to her. That was the first hurdle done with.

"Yeah, he does." She'd barely finished answering him, when Aidan opened the door, ready to continue.

Jamie sat back, calmer now, knowing that after today's questioning, he'd have the chance to see Alison again in a much more intimate setting. Perhaps then he'd be able to find the answers to all the questions that had plagued him since her appearance on his doorstep earlier.

Aidan shuffled his notes, looking at which question he'd left the conversation at earlier, and proceeded to ask Alison whatever else was on his sheet. A lot of the questions were rephrased repeats of the ones asked earlier, designed to catch her out if she wasn't being truthful. Tedious, but necessary.

Throughout the rest of the afternoon, Jamie continued to sit quietly at the table, watching her answer everything as best she could. She was so patient, so helpful, it was almost surprising. A lot of people might have gotten frustrated at the amount of detail Aidan asked for over and over, but not her.

She was perfect.

When the last question had been asked, Aidan shot him a quick glance and raised his eyebrows to check if he had anything to add. Jamie just shook his head. They were done for now.

Whatever else he needed to get from Alison, he'd get on his own time, without the additional set of eyes and hidden lenses pointed at the two of them.

# CHAPTER FOUR

The interrogation had been intense for Alison, and yet... The answers had rolled off her tongue easily and she thought she'd appeared confident and honest and above all, genuine. The thing was, she'd also shared a lot more than she initially planned to.

Such was the effect Aidan's boss, Jamie, had had on her.

Where did she recognize him from? While walking back with Aidan, who again took a convoluted route leading away from the office, probably in an attempt to confuse her, she couldn't get Jamie out of her head.

It had all seemed so simple before: she was going in to give them some vague answers, while memorizing as much as she could about the office and the people within. Despite Aidan's best efforts, she knew exactly where the Alliance building was located and would be able to find it again in a heartbeat.

The next step was to take all that information and hand it over to her brother so that he could mount a rescue for their dad and the other two guys.

The last thing she'd expected was to get a dinner invitation from the Alliance leader. And why the hell had she accepted? Things were simple no longer.

He seemed to be taken with her, so much so that he didn't interfere or interrupt her even once when she was answering Aidan's questions. He only listened, observed. It was as though he felt bad, putting her in an awkward position like that. There was something more to Jamie Abbott, and Alison needed to find out what.

Perhaps it was lucky then that she'd see him again. Her fingers closed around the business card he'd given her. She fished it out of her pocket and held it up to her nose. It smelled of him, strange as it seemed. Like an expensive cologne, but one she'd never had the pleasure of coming across before. Sweet, heady, sexy.

If Aidan was a bear, then Jamie must be one too. They looked similar enough.

Was she really going to go on a dinner date with a werebear? How utterly ridiculous. That was a risk Alison normally would never take, and yet she couldn't have refused. What if he only wanted to lure her out on her own to capture her too? No, if they'd wanted to confine – or worse, kill - her they could have just gotten it over with right there in that creepy little room where they'd questioned her.

Instead they'd let her go on her merry way afterward.

Now that she was alone again, back in the park where Aidan had picked her up a good four hours earlier, she didn't know anymore what she was going to do. Her brother needed two things to rescue their dad: weapons, which would arrive soon enough, and Alison's help in locating the prisoners.

Gareth was out for blood. He wouldn't ask questions, just shoot on sight if anyone opposed him.

There would be casualties, a lot of them. The Sons would strike hard, and aim to reduce the Alliance numbers by any means necessary. Both Aidan and Jamie would be in real danger. The more she thought about it, the more uneasy she grew over the prospect of another confrontation.

Earlier she might have worried about the two men in her life and whether they'd survive the fight. But now, another concern played on her mind more: Jamie's safety.

# SCOTTISH WEREBEAR: A FORBIDDEN LOVE

She couldn't give Gareth the location, at least not yet.

Alison wasn't sure how long she'd sat there thinking things through, but she was no closer to clarity. It had gotten dark in the meanwhile; time to head back home. She reluctantly got up from the park bench and started walking on autopilot.

Soon after, she reached her flat and came face-to-face with a furious Gareth as soon as she'd unlocked the door.

"Where the fuck have you been?" he demanded.

"You know where." Alison dumped her things on the sofa, but as she was heading towards the bathroom, Gareth held her back by her arm.

"You've been gone for hours. No updates, your phone is dead, what the hell am I supposed to think?"

"They made me switch it off," Alison explained, realizing that possibly she should have remembered to switch it back on after they'd let her go, but Gareth didn't need to know about the time she'd spent reflecting on things at the park.

"Well? Where is their base?" Gareth asked.

Alison straightened her shoulders, hoping a more confident posture would make her seem more believable.

"They shifted the meeting elsewhere at the last minute, so I don't know yet. But I do have some good news." Alison wasn't sure whether to be all that candid with her brother, who no doubt would get even more agitated at what she was about to say, but it was all she had to share. "I met the guy in charge, and he seems to have taken a liking to me and asked me out..."

Gareth was speechless, but only for a moment. "You're joking. Don't tell me you've agreed?"

"Put aside your ego for a moment and think about it — we need more information in order to rescue Dad. I've found a chance to get closer to at least one of the animals who are holding him, and you want me *not* to act on it? Have you lost your mind?" The angrier Gareth made Alison, the easier it was for her to sound convincing and distract from the fact that she was hiding information from him.

She stared him down with her hands on her hips, as he glared back at her with fire in his eyes.

"You're going to get into trouble, you know that? This isn't a fucking game." Gareth shook his head and ran his hand over his cropped hair.

"I will be absolutely fine, if you don't drive me nuts first!" Alison insisted.

"Then at the very least I should be there. Follow you. When is this ridiculous date going to happen?"

"Hell no! I can't be expected to maintain cover with this guy if I have to worry about you and your temper lurking in the shadows behind me. And I don't know yet. He's going to call me."

"Whatever. You're going to get yourself killed or worse at this rate."

Alison wanted to argue more, but bit her tongue. At least Gareth had backed off somewhat from the idea of spying on her date, and if she fought on, she might say something she'd regret later. If Gareth got wind that she was keeping stuff from him, she would be in a world of trouble.

"Clearly you're going to do whatever you want to, but keep your goddamn phone on when you meet this guy, all right?" Gareth grumbled.

Alison nodded, and watched as he picked up his leather jacket and headed for the door. *Good riddance.* She needed time alone to think about how she was going to fix things.

# SCOTTISH WEREBEAR: A FORBIDDEN LOVE

———— ◆ ————

As it turned out, Alison didn't get much of a chance to mull her situation over after all. Shortly after Gareth left, she received a phone call from Jamie who suggested drinks and dinner. The man sure was eager, but Alison knew better than to complain.

Sure, he was supposedly the enemy, but Alison was a woman first and Sons member second. It was hard not to feel flattered to have a guy like Jamie fawn over her and call her just hours after meeting for the first time. She accepted his invitation and immediately started sifting through the contents of her wardrobe to find the perfect outfit to wear.

She wanted to impress him, and she didn't know for sure why. Alison had tried her best to justify her impulses by convincing herself that a successful date would give her a better chance to earn his trust. But she did sort of like him, and she certainly was attracted to Jamie. Perhaps the danger he represented had made him more enticing somehow.

Or perhaps she *had* lost her mind, as Gareth had accused her of earlier.

None of that changed the fact that she hadn't been out on a date in a while, and really could use the boost to her self-esteem. Jamie had been quiet earlier in the afternoon, almost a bit shy and awkward, which seemed unusual for a guy as hot as him. Hopefully that had been the case because Aidan had been there too, and when it was just the two of them, he'd loosen up a bit.

Alison had trouble reconciling her conflicting emotions as she got dressed and made up for her date. She wanted things to go well, because it would help her mission, but she couldn't ignore her ulterior motives.

In the past whenever she'd seen a scenario like this portrayed in movies and TV shows, Alison had not been able to imagine ever being in a situation like that, playing a femme fatale who seduces an enemy, just because it was her job.

She wasn't that type of girl, or so she'd thought. Never mind the fact that she wasn't slim or beautiful enough to play the role, she didn't think she was a good enough actress either. Her aversion to her mark would be written all over her face if she ever found herself in a similar situation. She never once had imagined the possibility of losing herself in the fantasy she was only meant to act out.

Eight o'clock came around and Alison was as ready as she would ever be. She'd chosen a flattering A-line skirt and heels, and a pretty blouse that she felt accentuated her best feature, her cleavage.

Alison's hair had always had a mind of its own so she'd given up on trying to tame it years ago. Tonight also, she had just brushed her curls lightly, and kept them untied. A final check in the mirror, and she was out the door.

She didn't think it wise to give Jamie her home address, so they'd agreed to meet at a pub of his choice. Like most things in the center of town, it was only a short walk away from where Alison lived, so she found herself wandering again the same streets that she'd just traveled earlier.

After what had been a cloudy, rather gloomy day, Alison was surprised to find the skies clear overhead. A sign?

The full moon lit up the streets, giving everything from the damp pavement to the historic buildings a mysterious, magical feel.

Tonight wasn't an ordinary date; it was more meaningful than that.

# SCOTTISH WEREBEAR: A FORBIDDEN LOVE

There was a chill in the air that filtered through Alison's long woolen coat and stung against her legs. The streets looked surprisingly empty for this time of night. Normally you'd find couples walking arm-in-arm, tourists rushing back to their hotels after finishing their sightseeing for the day. Tonight it seemed to be just her and the moon and stars up above.

Alison breathed a sigh of relief when she saw the lit up sign of her destination in the distance and sped up for the final stretch. Her heels clicked loudly against the cobbled pavement with every rushed step. She pushed against the door and felt the warmth of the pub interior try to escape around her as she stepped inside.

There he was. Alison's heart skipped a few beats when she spotted Jamie sitting by himself in one of the booths lining the wall. He gave her a quick wave and she forced a smile. Here goes nothing.

"Hi," she said, offering him her hand while bracing herself for the inevitable jolt that would pass through her as soon as they touched...

# CHAPTER FIVE

———— •  ————

"Hope you found it okay?" Jamie asked while Alison opened her coat, revealing the outfit she'd chosen for the occasion. She looked breathtaking and smelled even better. Should he say so? Would that be too much of a cliché?

"I'm a local, remember?" Alison remarked with a smile that brightened up the entire room.

He'd felt uneasy about the date before she'd arrived, but all his concerns had melted away once in her presence.

"Of course, yes," Jamie mumbled. "Can I order you anything while you get comfortable?"

"Whatever you're having looks good to me," Alison nodded at the half full pint of draught beer in front of him. He'd arrived early of course, having been way too restless to stick around either the office or his home. His habit of finding comfort among crowds of strangers was a hard one to kick.

"Sure."

Jamie waved at one of the bar staff, who came over immediately to take his order.

"So I didn't expect you to call me so quickly," Alison teased. The way she looked at him when she'd said it didn't suggest she minded. If anything, she looked rather pleased to be here. Through the varied scents hanging around the place, Jamie couldn't ignore hers. Irresistibly sweet and intoxicating.

"Well... Life's too short to put a good thing off, don't you think?"

The incredibly efficient twenty-or-so guy who had taken his order appeared again with Alison's drink, placing it on the table in front of her. "Can I get ya anything else?" he asked.

Jamie shook his head. "Thanks."

"You're right. Life *is* too short," Alison repeated.

The scent of her arousal was more pronounced the longer she sat in front of him. If Jamie didn't bring up their history now, he'd never manage the presence of mind to do so later.

"I do have to admit, though, that I'm afraid I had a hidden agenda asking you to meet me here..." Jamie said.

Alison cocked her head to the side and folded her hands on the table. Those green eyes staring at him almost made Jamie lose himself again. A deep breath helped him regain focus.

"Applecross Bay, 1995." Jamie paused and observed Alison's reaction.

She pressed her lips together and all the color seemed to drain out of her face. Her eyes darted back and forth between Jamie's and random spots around the room. She reminded him of cornered prey, and although it was in his instinct to always maintain an advantage in any confrontation, he felt uneasy about putting her in this position.

"That's it. That's why you looked familiar," she whispered.

Alison loosened her hands and rested her face in them for a moment, before looking up at Jamie again through the gaps between her fingers.

"I guess that's it then," she said, under her breath.

"What?" Jamie asked. His mind was racing. Although he was certain that he'd been dreaming of her every night since, it was still a shock to hear her admit that she'd been there. He hadn't lost his mind after all.

"The game's up, eh?" She blinked a few times and

Jamie could see that her eyes had glazed over slightly.

She was visibly upset, and although he should be furious that this woman had had anything to do with what had without a doubt been the very worst day of his life, he couldn't muster anything other than sympathy. She'd been only a child back then, like him.

Jamie reached across the table, resting his hand on top of her arm. To ignore the intense attraction he had for her, especially while touching her was a tall order, but he managed to suppress it somehow. "Alison."

She sniffled and reached into her handbag, retrieving a pack of tissues with her free hand. After struggling to get one out of the wrapper, she dabbed the corners of her eyes with it.

"I can't explain it, I should be angry. I should demand answers. I should... I don't know. Really, I just want to know what happened," Jamie whispered.

"And I should be scared right now," Alison responded, a thoughtful, though still teary-eyed expression on her face. "But..."

"So let's talk. Figure it out." Jamie gently squeezed her arm, enjoying the warmth as it filtered out of her skin and into his fingertips. It was too easy to touch her, so tempting to do so much more...

"He's safe, you know. Your little brother. I don't know where he is now, but he's safe," Alison whispered.

"Matthew. That was his name. We used to call him Matty." Jamie took Alison's hand, threading his fingers through hers. He hadn't said his brother's name out loud in years, it had hurt too much. For some inexplicable reason it felt good to open up to *her* of all people.

"I know. Matthew." A lone tear ran down her cheek as she looked up from their entwined hands resting on the rugged wood of the table. "It was Dad's idea. I had no choice but to go along."

"I know. It's okay," Jamie tried to comfort her. His own pain paled in comparison to the regret and guilt emanating from her. It was heart wrenching, to sense her emotions so keenly.

"It was all part of an experiment. You see, Dad was convinced that every child is born innocent, and if introduced to the right sort of surroundings at an early age, they'd grow up exactly the same as any of us. Matthew was one of the first," Alison explained. "And my name isn't really Carter, it's Campbell."

Alison tried to pull her hand back, but Jamie couldn't bear to let go. "But then your name isn't really Abbott either, is it?" Alison asked.

"No. It's not. I didn't want anyone to look up my history when I joined the Alliance. Whatever happened in the past, it's none of their business." Jamie looked away and pinched the bridge of his nose to ward off another one of his persistent headaches. "Campbell... Any relation to-"

"Lee Campbell. He's my dad," Alison interrupted.

As huge as that revelation was, it didn't surprise him. They looked at each other in silence for a few seconds.

"When I get back to the office in the morning, am I going to find him where I left him?" Jamie asked.

Alison bit her lip, hard. "I haven't told anyone. I was supposed to, but I just couldn't. It doesn't make any sense."

In a way, it made a lot of sense to Jamie. She hadn't been able to do her job and reveal the location of the Alliance building, just like Jamie knew he wouldn't be able to reveal Alison's real identity to anyone within the Alliance. He'd rather take a knife and slit his own throat than to betray her. That could only mean one thing...

The more he thought about it, the more things fell into place, and it also explained why he hadn't been able to get her out of his head ever since that first meeting twenty years ago. They were fated. Back then he hadn't been able to shift yet, so he couldn't sense the connection as strongly as he did now, but his inner bear had seen her once and the memory had never left him alone. They were meant to be.

"What do you know about us?" Jamie whispered and leaned across the table. It was difficult being so close to her, surrounded by her scent, without taking things further, but he didn't want his eagerness to startle her.

"Only what I've been told. That you're half man, half animal. That human morality doesn't apply to you, only animal instinct."

Jamie let out a chuckle. "That latter part isn't quite true, but all right."

"Sometimes you turn into... a bear?" Alison asked, her eyes wide with either curiosity or apprehension. Perhaps a bit of both.

"Yeah. A bear. Let me guess, you people watch Wolf as a documentary?" Jamie joked. "True, we feel certain instincts a lot more keenly than ordinary humans do, but we're not immoral or out of control. Well perhaps in *some* scenarios we like to let go a bit... If you get my drift. But we don't go around killing people indiscriminately."

"It's hard to know what to believe. Most people don't even know you exist. I can't go to the library and do research, except in the horror section."

"Fair point. But then that's because when people do find out about us they tend to pick up their torches and pitchforks..." Jamie grinned.

Alison pulled away and folded her arms, scowling at him.

Jamie regretted teasing her so much, but he couldn't help it. It had been the only thing he could think of to try to cheer her up. At least she'd stopped crying.

"I'm sorry. It's just hard to know truth from fiction," Alison remarked.

"I'm sorry too. I'm not being fair to you. You're taking all this very well, I must say." Jamie smiled at her, and felt his excitement surge to new levels when she reluctantly smiled back.

"All this stuff you feel right now, there's a reason for it..." Jamie started. "I feel it too."

"Oh?"

"It's one of the main differences between us and humans, save for the turning into an animal bit. Our relationships work a bit differently than yours. When a bear finds his mate, they connect on a deep, almost subconscious level."

"Is that what this is? Does it ever fade?" Alison's eyes widened and Jamie was once again shocked at how green they were.

"Bears mate for life," Jamie replied.

"This is insane. I feel like I could wake up any moment now and find that all of it has just been a crazy dream." She picked up her glass and took a big sip.

"I know. We should hate each other, instead we're sitting here, having a pleasant chat over a couple of beers..." Jamie smiled at her, hoping she'd reciprocate. He ached to see her smile again.

"I feel like I want to do more than chat," Alison whispered, then covered her mouth as though she was surprised she'd actually said that.

Jamie let out a laugh loud enough that some of the people seated nearby turned to see what was going on. Her body's visceral reaction to his presence had been obvious to him from the start, but she had no way of knowing that of course.

"Oh believe me, I know what you mean." Every fiber in his body yearned to get close to her. To feel her skin against his...

He could barely take it anymore. Something had to be done or his heart would explode out of his chest.

Alison kept her eyes fixed on Jamie as he got up from his seat and joined her on her side of the table. She didn't protest as he slid his hand around the back of her neck and leaned in, drinking in her scent before allowing his lips to touch hers.

"Wow," Alison breathed, then wrapped her arms around his shoulders and returned his kiss with a deeper, even more passionate one.

It was as though all the fuses in Jamie's mind blew all at once. If they hadn't been out in public, he would have ensured that their clothes would come off that very moment, in shreds most likely. A warm feeling overwhelmed him that was so unusual, alien, that he couldn't identify it at first. Then he realized its meaning: after twenty years of yearning after the same woman during every one of his sleepless nights, he'd found his home.

Jamie pulled back, and gazed into those familiar green eyes once more.

"Now what do we do? About the others, I mean," Alison asked.

"Honestly? I'll be damned if I know." What could they do? To say that both sides would be unhappy about their pairing was putting it lightly. At the same time he knew that this was just the start for them. There was no way he'd let her go after waiting all this time. "I guess we'll have to be careful. How good are you at keeping secrets?"

Alison pressed her lips together, all the while maintaining eye contact. It was as though with that first kiss, the remaining distance between them had been bridged, permanently. She wanted him as he wanted her, he could see it in her eyes. The time for talk had passed.

*Let's go then*, Jamie thought.

Alison couldn't hide her surprise at hearing him in her head, but quickly recovered and nodded. She was ready.

# CHAPTER SIX

This was not how Alison imagined her evening would go. Not at all.

She glanced up at Jamie, who'd rested his arm around her shoulder as they walked, protecting her from the winds that had grown even colder during the short time they'd spent at the pub together. None of it made any sense. He was meant to be the enemy. She was supposed to fight the shifters, not go home with one of them.

And yet, she couldn't help herself. Her hormones, or whatever it was that made her feel this way about Jamie had overridden her capability for rational thought.

He'd tried to explain it to her, the connection bears form with their mates, but she still didn't quite understand how it worked. If it was a bear thing, why did she feel it too? She should turn around and run, to leave him behind and never look back, but she couldn't. It was as though she no longer had a choice in the matter. Her decision making privileges were revoked indefinitely.

Her brother would be furious. She couldn't imagine what her dad would say.

In fact, she should be upset as well. After all, it was her life that was being affected the most. But as she walked through the dark, empty streets alongside the powerful half-man, half-bear that was Jamie, she was actually happy. She felt the glances of the occasional passerby, intimidated by Jamie's presence and it filled her with pride to be his. For him to be hers.

Sure, they'd only just kissed, but it hadn't been like any other first kiss she'd shared with a new lover. She had never felt this way. She had never had this sense of belonging, this feeling of complete and utter safety, like the man she was with would walk through hell and back to protect her.

Jamie would.

She shivered against the cold and his arm drew her against him tighter. Alison closed her eyes and drank in his scent. The same perfume that had clung to the card he'd given her earlier that day, only stronger and more overwhelming.

They were getting close to their destination, she could tell by the way his steps sped up. He was eager to get her home. In the crudest of terms she knew he was eager to get in her pants, and she didn't mind at all. She was equally keen to get in his.

It didn't make any sense. But it felt right.

Her heart jumped when Jamie paused in front of one of the terraced Victorian houses that lined the street. He retrieved a bunch of keys and guided her up the front steps. It was nicer than the little new-build flat where she lived. A lot nicer. So much for all the talk she'd grown up with about how shapeshifters lived like animals.

During their short conversation at the pub it had become clear that a lot of what she'd grown up with had just been plain wrong. Just like Aidan hadn't acted like a senseless monster around her during all the times he'd questioned her, neither had Jamie. He seemed to be just a guy. Sure, he'd be a lot stronger than a normal man, but there was nothing too strange about him so far.

Jamie unlocked the wooden front door and switched on the light inside the hall.

"Welcome to my humble abode," he said.

Funny guy. There was nothing humble about the stylish furnishings that greeted her.

As she turned to face him, his hands were already on her. She wanted to close her eyes, but she didn't want to miss out on the view either. His blue eyes seemed to pierce her soul as he looked at her. Nobody had ever looked at her like this. Not Clive, to whom she'd given her virginity behind the bike shed when she was still in school, or her most recent lover Ian, a Sons member like her dad and Gareth. Nobody.

She shut the door behind them and let out a surprised shriek when Jamie gathered her up in his arms and carried her down the hall. He knew exactly where he was going of course, it was his house, and she could very well guess.

The bedroom was as nice as the rest of the house, a large wooden bed standing proudly in the center of the room. The sheets, curtains, everything matched as though it had been chosen by a professional decorator. But he didn't care about keeping things tidy, just deposited her in the middle of the bed and climbed on top, kicking his shoes off as an afterthought.

She understood now, this is was but a taste of what lay ahead. The one scenario in which bears apparently like to *let go*.

"What's funny?" he asked, leaning down to nibble on her lip.

Alison grinned against his lips. "I'm beginning to see how having a strong animal instinct can come in handy."

"Just you wait, I'll show you animal instinct."

She could do little more than giggle as he got to work on her clothes, unzipping her skirt and tugging it off her in one swift motion. He did the same with her blouse, flipped her over to rid her of her bra and panties and finally unzipped himself.

"Wait a minute, you're not thinking of keeping all *your* clothes on, are you?" Alison demanded.

He paused for a moment and looked down at himself, then at her naked form in front of him on the bed. "All right, all right."

She turned onto her back again and observed as he undressed. Everything about him was perfection, from the sculpted abs to the well-pronounced pecs. If it wasn't for the lustful way he looked at her, he was beautiful enough to give any girl an inferiority complex.

Aidan and Jamie had been the only shifters she'd met so far, so Alison had to wonder if they were all this fit.

"To think you were going to hold out on me..." Alison teased and ran her hand over his firm chest.

"In a rush to see and do it all, are we?" Jamie grinned at her, then hooked his arm through the crook of her knee and flipped her over again.

Jamie got on top of her. The heat of his body against her bare back and buttocks made her shiver. He gently pushed her unruly locks out of the way and started kissing and sucking on her neck.

Alison moaned into the pillow. God, he knew exactly what to do to drive her crazy. The stubble on his chin prickled against her skin, giving her goosebumps.

He was right though, she was in a rush. Clearly, so was he. Throughout the short time they'd spent at the pub together, she'd felt her senses heighten to his presence. She'd been attracted to him from the moment she first laid eyes on the man, but what she'd felt while they were talking earlier was way more intense than any attraction she'd ever known.

By the time he'd all but ripped her panties off, she was beyond ready.

He leaned onto one side and ran his other hand all over the soft curves of her body. His erect cock pressed eagerly against her ass cheek while he explored the curvature of her hips, then reached around her side and gently tweaked her nipple between his fingers.

Every touch of his set her alight.

She leaned up onto both elbows, allowing him free reign over her cleavage and breasts. All the while, he continued to lavish every inch of her shoulders with kisses and nibbles.

Then, unwilling to delay the inevitable any longer, he adjusted himself between her legs, spreading her wide and guided his thick cock towards her slick entrance.

"Oh!" Alison exclaimed, as he pushed against her, forcing her open.

He was big. Bigger than she'd ever had. It burned, but pleasantly so when he entered her.

Jamie filled her so entirely, she found herself lost in a haze of pleasure. He wrapped one arm around her waist and lifted her off the bed.

She was utterly helpless in his arms when he started to thrust into her, slowly at first, then faster and faster. His finger found its way around her hips and into her folds from the front. It didn't take him long to locate her clit.

Alison closed her eyes and just hung on. She could hardly move in his iron grip, neither did she need to because he was already doing everything right.

Jamie sped up further, thrusting into her more intensely than before. Her body took everything he had to give without protest. The burn from his initial penetration faded and was replaced by a growing pressure on her G-spot.

She cried out with every one of his strokes as her pleasure rose to new heights.

"You're the most beautiful woman I've ever seen," Jamie whispered against the back of her neck, sending shivers down her spine all over again.

"You too. Most beautiful man, I mean. Oh God!" Alison responded, his intense thrusts forcing her to pause after every couple of words.

She couldn't focus anymore, couldn't think. It was as though her mind was wiped clean of anything other than their union. He was completely in control of what was happening to her and she was just along for the ride.

He kept fucking her with deliberate movements, all the while manipulating her clit.

She was there, so close, and he seemed to know it somehow. He could tell.

Jamie pushed her down onto the bed for the finale, grinding into her from behind and getting rid of the last shred of self-control she had left. The pillow muffled her final cry as the sweet relief of orgasm washed over her. Rather than pausing or hesitating, he continued on, releasing his hot seed into her shortly after.

They stayed like that, with him on top of her cradling her in his arms again. Sweaty and sated, hoping to drag out their moment of mutual bliss. Neither of them spoke a word for what felt like an eternity, it would have ruined the moment.

Finally, he slipped off to one side, giving her limbs some rest, though he never let her go.

"You're amazing," Alison mumbled, once she found the energy to talk.

"You are," Jamie responded.

He held her tighter, his breaths slowing further and further until she could tell he'd drifted off to sleep. In another situation she might have minded, she might have felt alone to have a new partner fall asleep so soon after making love for the first time. But somehow, everything was different with Jamie.

She carefully lifted his arm off her and sat up in the bed

to watch him.

Something about him had changed. He didn't look as serious as he did when awake. He looked completely calm and at rest, even the otherwise permanent crease between his eyebrows had smoothed out. Alison wasn't sure how she knew, but this moment was significant. A sign of complete trust.

She could watch him for hours like this, no matter how creepy that sounded. Unfortunately, she didn't get the chance to just yet.

"What's funny?" Jamie said when he opened his eyes only moments later.

"You look so sweet when you're sleeping." Alison grinned down at him.

"I didn't sleep!" Jamie protested, and sat up himself.

"Yeah. Sure."

"Really!" Jamie insisted. "Anyway, this is unacceptable. I asked you out for dinner, didn't I? I'd better keep my promise."

Alison watched as he got up from the bed and found some takeaway menus in the bedside table.

"Pizza?" Jamie asked, with an apologetic frown on his face. Perhaps he'd wanted to take her somewhere nice, but they'd been so preoccupied with one another, they hadn't noticed the time. It was too late to go out now and besides, Alison didn't want to leave.

"Perfect," Alison said.

Jamie took the menu and left the room to place the order, leaving Alison alone with her thoughts for a moment.

What a night.

In the span of just a few hours, she'd gone from confused about the idea of dating the enemy, to understanding they were soul mates, now and forever. She ought to feel guilty about betraying her family, but somehow, she didn't.

Instead, Alison still felt terrible finding out she'd been instrumental in the abduction of Jamie's brother, Matthew. His capacity for forgiveness in the matter had amazed her. Matthew's disappearance had left a gaping hole in his being. That much was obvious from the way he'd talked about that day. No matter what he said, it was at least in part her fault. She'd do anything to help make things better.

"Done. It'll be here in half an hour," Jamie said, as he came back into the bedroom, phone in hand.

"Really. I wonder how we will pass the time," Alison teased, while obviously checking out his naked body from head to toe.

That was all the encouragement Jamie needed to get back into bed.

# CHAPTER SEVEN

It was just another late morning at the Alliance office. Two days had passed since Jamie's first date with Alison, and although he'd made no real progress questioning the prisoners no matter how hard he tried, Jamie felt invincible.

He and Alison hadn't been able to stay away from each other and had spent every spare hour together. Gone were the days when Jamie didn't know what to do with himself once his working day was over.

Gone also were the sleepless nights, the endless restlessness and unnerving dreams that threatened to spill over into reality. He was a changed man, who no longer lived to work, but worked to live.

"What time is the pick-up?" Jamie asked Kyle, who had been coordinating with their contact at the Alliance Council.

"Depending on traffic on the M1, probably early afternoon," Kyle said, without looking up once from his computer screen.

Kyle was the odd one out at the office. Not only was he a black bear unlike Jamie and Aidan who transformed into brown bears, he was a bit of a nerd and awkward around people, especially women. His pale complexion stood out against the darker hair, a testament that he was less outdoorsy than the others on the team.

Though Kyle could fight if he needed to, his main weapon was his brain and Jamie was thrilled to have him on his side. In fact, perhaps Jamie could utilize Kyle's particular skill set for something of a more delicate nature...

Jamie looked over at Heidi, who was reviewing the tape from Alison's interrogation on her own. Aidan was out running a few errands, which made this one of the rare times Heidi and Aidan weren't joined at the hip. She was distracted, so Jamie decided to pull Kyle aside for a private chat.

"Kyle, a moment?" Jamie waved at him, then opened the bottom drawer of his desk and picked up the brown cardboard dossier he always kept in there.

"Sure. What's up?" Kyle approached Jamie's desk.

Jamie handed him the file. "This one's off the books, but I would appreciate if you could look into this case for me when you get the chance."

Kyle opened it and studied the photographs and reports inside. They exchanged a silent look. He understood. "Sure thing, boss."

Jamie breathed a sigh of relief. Just as he'd hoped, Kyle hadn't demanded an explanation or made things more awkward than they needed to be. Jamie watched him walk back to his computer as if nothing of note had happened.

It was only a matter of hours before they'd lose the prisoners. The Alliance leadership had some bigger plans for them that Jamie wasn't privy to, and it was a professional loss for their office. Perhaps he'd take another crack at Lee Campbell in particular. If only the man knew what Jamie had been up to with his daughter for the past two nights, it might wipe that smug grin off his face.

But Jamie didn't get the chance to head downstairs. A loud bang on the door disrupted the calm atmosphere of the office. Was that the transport already? Kyle couldn't have gotten their arrival time that wrong, could he?

"Open up!" An unfamiliar voice filtered through the heavy, reinforced front door.

Jamie jumped up to face the threat, as did Heidi. They exchanged a look, while Kyle furiously typed something into a message window on his computer.

"It's not our people. They're still about an hour away," Kyle whispered, looking up at Jamie with an alarmed frown on his face.

Jamie nodded, then signaled at Heidi to head to the basement. She didn't hesitate for even a second. For all their differences, Jamie had to respect the wolves' ability to follow orders, especially in a crisis. She was out of the room before the second, much louder bang on the door. Jamie waved at Kyle to position himself behind him, who did so after triggering the silent alarm they'd installed as a precaution months earlier.

Seconds later, the door started to creak and splinter under the repetitive impacts typical of the same type of manual battering ram Jamie and Aidan had used during their attack on the Sons' base. Whoever it was, they were determined to get inside and had brought the necessary equipment with them.

"The data!" Kyle shouted, as he sprinted back to his workstation and pulled the hard drive out of his computer. He hid it underneath the false bottom in one of his desk drawers, created just for this purpose.

"Get back, Kyle!" Jamie ordered.

The door swung open, revealing about a dozen determined-looking skinheads in full combat gear. *Crap.* Lee Campbell had been right. It was a counterattack.

"On the ground, filth!" The man in front bellowed, while pointing the muzzle of his weapon in Jamie's direction. If looks could kill... Green eyes, exactly the same shade as the pair Jamie had been gazing into for hours these past few days, shot daggers at him. This must be Alison's brother. *Shit.*

Jamie weighed his options. Should he comply or attempt to fight? They were outnumbered and outgunned. Shifters didn't use firearms, they rarely had the need to because of their greater physical strength compared to regular humans. Then again, large scale confrontations between the two were rare because both sides kept such a low profile.

There was no point to endanger Kyle and himself unnecessarily. Jamie grudgingly got down onto the ground and placed his hands behind his head. Kyle followed his example next to him.

"Good. Cuff 'em," the man ordered and one of his companions stepped ahead and reluctantly placed steel handcuffs around Jamie's wrists. From the solid clicking noise they made as they were tightened, Jamie could tell they weren't toys and would be impossible to break free from without help.

"Up on your feet," Alison's brother barked. "Tell us where you're holding our brothers, animal!"

Jamie got up and stared down at the man in silence. If they hadn't brought guns, this much shorter human would have been no match in hand-to-hand combat, even for Kyle.

"Don't worry, we have ways of making you scum talk." The man gave him a hateful look, then focused his sights on Kyle. "You. You tell me where they are!"

Kyle also didn't say a word.

Jamie knew how this would play out. Their silence would buy a little time, but these people would soon find their prisoners down in the basement on their own. Guarded only by Heidi, who also didn't carry a gun, they'd have no trouble freeing them.

After that, there was no way of knowing what these guys would do. The Alliance attack had resulted in two deaths, mainly because the humans hadn't known when to surrender. This strike was probably as much about revenge as rescuing their men, so once they'd found the cells, they might just kill Heidi, Kyle and Jamie for sport.

"They're alive," Jamie said at last.

Alison's brother shot him another hateful look. "Where? Or do I need to beat it out of you?"

Jamie felt his entire body tense up as instinct tried to take over. *Beat it out of him? Let this clown try.* He tried his best to remain calm, because if he shifted right here in front of a bunch of trigger-happy fanatics, he was certain he wouldn't survive it.

"Fine, have it your way," the man hissed, and stepped up ahead, until he stood right in front of Kyle. He held his weapon to Kyle's temple and turned to make eye contact with Jamie again.

"You tell me what I want to know, or your friend here gets it."

There was no doubt in Jamie's mind that the threat was real. These were the people who had been responsible for disappearances of shifters everywhere, and they'd think nothing of eliminating another one of their enemy.

If Kyle was afraid for his life, he didn't show it. Jamie knew it was over. If he gave up the prisoners, at least hopefully he could ensure Heidi didn't do anything to get herself hurt either.

"Downstairs." Jamie nodded in the direction of the door leading to the staircase.

"Both of you lead the way. Go on." Alison's brother prodded the muzzle of his weapon into Jamie's shoulder blade, forcing him ahead.

One of the armed intruders stepped ahead of them to open the door for Kyle and Jamie, while the rest waited for the two bears to step into the staircase.

"Don't do anything stupid, you hear?" The man warned, prodding his gun into Jamie's back again.

Jamie wasn't planning to. He'd go along with whatever these people wanted, just as long as it would keep his team safe. They went down the stairs into the dark hallway leading to the basement rooms they'd repurposed as holding cells. Heidi was waiting by the first door, tense, ready for confrontation.

"Oh, hell," Heidi said under her breath.

"Stand down," Jamie said, making a calming motion with his hand.

She didn't seem convinced, especially now that the men behind Jamie and Kyle came into view, but didn't argue.

One of the armed men stepped around the two bears, holding another set of handcuffs.

"It's okay, Heidi. Just give them what they want." Jamie watched while Heidi was being restrained.

Some of the other intruders started to fan out ahead, inspecting the doors leading off from the corridor. These rooms originally didn't have windows, so Jamie had ordered Kyle to install spyholes in the doors before securing each prisoner inside. The Sons members now benefited from the same, looking inside first and breaking down only those doors that contained one of their own.

"They're here," one reported, after peeking into the first cell.

Most of his associates scattered around to explore the rest of the rooms, leaving only two guys to guard the three shifters. This was as close to a chance to escape as they'd ever get, but still it seemed too risky to do anything rash.

"How the hell did they find our location?" Heidi whispered. She kept her volume so low, it would have been nearly impossible for human ears to pick up her words, but obviously Jamie and Kyle didn't have that problem.

"No idea," Jamie responded.

"Alison," Kyle mumbled.

Jamie tensed at his suggestion. "No way."

"He has a point. Our position has never been compromised before. Now these people turn up mere days after calling her in? It can't be a coincidence," Heidi remarked.

Jamie felt a red haze descend over his senses. It was an impossibility for Alison to betray him, put him in danger. But he couldn't very well tell these two that, could he? He couldn't reveal how he knew Alison was innocent. It was one thing for two shifters of opposing species to pair up, but a bear and a human? That was almost unheard of.

"I'm not convinced she's given us her real identity. Looking into it, there are precious few records mentioning an Alison Carter that fit her profile." Kyle gave Jamie a thoughtful look.

Jamie balled his fists and took a deep breath to regain his composure. He focused on Kyle again.

"We'll figure it out. But a good investigator rules out other options before being absolutely certain of a suspect's guilt. Remember that," Jamie said.

"Sure thing, Boss." Heidi nodded.

Kyle didn't look convinced, but didn't argue further.

This was a bloody nightmare. With the Alliance pick-up barely an hour out, he'd lost the prisoners. If they couldn't somehow recover the situation, the three of them could be killed. And who knew what the Sons would do with the intel they'd recover from the office eliminating them? This one incident could tilt the fight entirely in their favor.

Once the dust settled on today's events, the Alliance council would no doubt come to the same conclusion as Kyle and Heidi. It wouldn't be so difficult to figure out

Alison's real identity, and that would be the end of it. They'd come after her next.

Something had to be done.

# CHAPTER EIGHT

———— ◆ ————

Alison couldn't explain exactly what happened to her at around eleven that morning, but it wasn't good. Her stomach was in knots and even though it was an unseasonably nice, bright day, she felt trapped and skittish under the blue skies. Something was very, very wrong.

Was she coming down with something? Caught a cold, perhaps?

That couldn't explain her paranoia. No, it must be something else.

After pacing around her little flat for a good fifteen minutes, unable to find rest or figure out what she should do with herself, she finally knew she needed a change of scenery. Alison put on her coat and rushed out the door.

While wondering if a walk in the park would do her some good, her feet carried her forward almost involuntarily. She walked on and on until she realized she was getting close to the edge of town, heading toward the neighborhood where the Alliance building was located.

*Jamie.*

She had to see Jamie. He would know what to do.

Alison's throat felt tight, like an invisible hand had grabbed hold of her and squeezed her tight.

The closer she got, the faster she walked, until she was ready to break into a jog. It was crazy, like one of those dreams in which someone's chasing you. Of course that was silly. No matter how often she looked back, there was nobody in sight.

She was out of breath by the time she reached the door where she'd seen Jamie for the first time. It was shut and there was no sign of activity anywhere in the building. If she didn't know any better, the state the dilapidated warehouse was in would have suggested it was abandoned.

With her heart still pounding in her chest, she took a step back to look up. The windows were boarded up, so she couldn't see inside. *Damn.*

The entrance was offset from the main road in a narrow service alley. Perhaps she'd have better luck on the other side of the building?

Although she wasn't sure what was happening, Alison knew Jamie was in there somewhere. She could sense his presence nearby.

She hurried around the side of the building, turned the corner, and finally found a breach: the front door had been smashed in, the frame left in splinters.

This was Gareth's work. There was no other possible explanation. Somehow, despite Alison's best efforts to blow him off, he'd discovered the Alliance's location on his own.

Alison didn't know what she would find inside. She was unarmed and terrified. If Gareth didn't already know she'd been bullshitting him, he certainly would if she came face-to-face with him after wandering into the Alliance office, proving the fact she had known its location all along. But at least Jamie was still alive. She would have felt it if he wasn't.

Now what? Call the police?

"Hey, what are you doing here?" a familiar voice made Alison jump.

She turned around and found an equally frazzled looking Aidan looking right at her. "Long story. They've been attacked!"

Alison pointed at the broken door and waited while Aidan inspected the damage and peeked inside for a moment. He seemed different, much less stoic and controlled than usual.

"I know. The silent alarm was triggered a short while ago, when I was already on the way back. That doesn't explain why you're here though." Aidan gave her a suspicious look, then glanced back up at the building.

Aidan had never particularly warmed towards her and always seemed a bit suspicious. Turning up at the scene of an attack wasn't helping. She had to find a sensible explanation... Screw it, she had nothing. Jamie had made it clear that the truth wouldn't be particularly popular with anyone, including his own people, but it was the only chance she had of earning Aidan's trust.

"This is going to sound really crazy, but Jamie and I are mates. I felt he was in danger." Alison's bottom lip was trembling while she spoke. She still felt the risk, and if they didn't hurry up, things could get a whole lot worse.

"Okay." Aidan looked away from her again, fished his phone out of his pocket and read something on its screen.

"Really. I know it's not acceptable, considering I'm not one of you, but-"

"Calm down. I believe you."

*Wow, that was easy.*

"My mate is inside too," Aidan added, looking up from his phone to make eye contact with her.

Finally his demeanor started to make sense. They were in the same boat together. He'd been brought here not by some silent alarm, but the same feeling of uneasiness that had spurred Alison into action. The alarm had just served to confirm the danger he'd already sensed himself.

"So what do we do now?" Alison wondered aloud.

"We're going in, of course! Backup is arriving shortly." Aidan put the phone away, straightened his back and started marching towards the door.

*Shit.* This was it: the moment of truth. She knew she couldn't do anything to betray Jamie, but Gareth was in there. Despite everything, he was still her brother. Her dad was in there too, more than likely.

She had to pick a side and it would no longer be possible to keep her relationship with Jamie a secret from the rest of them either.

"Wait! What do you mean, *shortly*?" Alison rushed into the building behind Aidan. She wasn't going to be much use in a fight, but considering everything was already unraveling around her, perhaps she could use her position to her advantage.

"Ten minutes, tops." Aidan scanned the empty office space. Wherever Gareth and the guys were, it wasn't in here.

Alison felt Jamie more keenly, and her feet wanted to carry her ahead to his position, making it nearly impossible to focus. Every second they wasted discussing what to do increased the risk of escalation inside. She had to be proactive, and get Aidan on her side.

"I haven't been entirely truthful with you." Alison turned to face Aidan, who paused. "I don't have time to get into it now, but they know me in there. I'm going to stall them, try to get them away from your people if possible. You stay out of sight until the backup gets here and then surprise them."

Aidan's jaw tightened. He wasn't happy to find out she'd played him, but seemed to accept this wasn't the time to argue about it. "Fine. Don't make me regret this. I don't have to tell you what will happen if anything happens to Hei- them."

Aidan's threat didn't faze Alison. If something happened to Jamie, she wouldn't be able to live with herself anyway. "Okay then." *Here goes nothing.*

Alison looked back at Aidan one last time before heading for the door leading out of the cluttered office space. It creaked heavily as she pushed it open, making her flinch. Hopefully nobody had heard her.

She listened for any movement up or down the stairs. She knew that she'd been kept upstairs during her interrogation. That must mean that the prisoners had been locked up downstairs...

Alison tiptoed down the steps until she heard muffled voices, though she couldn't make out what they were saying exactly. There was another door at the bottom of the staircase, which led into a dimly lit corridor.

Alison pushed the door open. Its shrill squeak sent shivers down her spine. There they were. Heads turned in her direction and she recognized the faces of the two armed guards waiting in front of one of the doors leading off the hallway.

"Lads," Alison mumbled.

The two skinheads exchanged a look and then shrugged and nodded at her. So far so good.

"Gareth called me in, where is he?" Alison asked, hoping they wouldn't detect the slight tremble in her voice.

"In there." One of the men gestured at a door further down the hall.

Alison kept her shoulders straight as she marched onward past the pair of them. She managed to steal a glimpse out the corner of her eye at the door they were guarding, but there was no window to see inside. That's where Jamie was, she could feel him. Hopefully he could feel her, too and then he'd know that she was here to help.

Her feet felt like they were made of lead as she forced herself to move ahead, when all she wanted to do was rush inside that first room to make sure Jamie was okay. Assuming there was nobody else inside the room where the Alliance people were held, the current scenario was ideal for a rescue. As long as she could keep most of the Sons out of the way.

Could she risk a quick message to Aidan to let him know? No way, the two geniuses by the door were probably still gawking at her.

She pushed against the door the guards had pointed out to her and was greeted by a half-dozen surprised faces clad in combat gear, along with three in civilian clothing. The room looked depressing, barren except for a bed and mattress. Paint peeled off the ceiling and walls, revealing damp patches in the concrete. This must have been one of the cells where the Alliance had held their prisoners.

"Alison," Lee Campbell said. "What are you doing here?"

She cocked her head to the side, then jumped ahead to give him a hug. "Dad! I'm so glad you're okay."

Tears burned in her eyes. This was an impossible position to be in. Of course she was glad he was unharmed. He was her father. But since the first night with Jamie, he wasn't really her family anymore.

She let out a sob as his arms tightened around her. "It's okay, darling. It takes a whole lot more than a few days of confinement to bring me down!"

"Sis..." Gareth's voice spoke behind her. "What *are* you doing here? How did you know where to find us?"

She didn't move, just sniffled into her dad's shoulder for a moment while considering her answer.

Of all the familiar faces she'd seen coming into the room, one had been missing: her ex, Ian. Perhaps...

"Ian called me, thought you could use some help handling the prisoners. After all, I'd spoken to some of them before," Alison said, while turning around and smiling at Gareth. "Good to see you've got the situation under control."

"Right." Gareth stared at her in silence for what felt like forever, but then turned to face one of the other former prisoners, inspecting the bandage on his leg. "I think we should get Bob, here, to a doctor as soon as possible."

"Can I have a look?" Alison asked. She'd had some first aid training, so it was only natural to ask.

Gareth stepped aside and waved her over. "What do you think?"

Alison's mind was still racing. If she could stall everyone in here until Aidan's backup arrived, perhaps she'd have a fighting chance of defusing the situation without endangering Jamie and the others.

"This might hurt," Alison whispered, as she carefully pulled away the cotton gauze covering some of the man's wounds. His leg was in a bad state, though there was no sign of infection so far and it was starting to heal a little.

"I don't think he should walk," Alison concluded, while making more of a show of inspecting his leg than strictly necessary. He probably could walk without any issue, but it was all she could think of to buy some time.

"Do you think you can use some of those blankets to make a stretcher of some sort?" Alison asked Gareth, who looked at their father for confirmation.

"Really? Can't we just prop him up and let him limp out of here?" Gareth argued.

"He's not bleeding right now, but if it starts we'll have no way of stopping it and he could be in real danger," Alison lied.

"She's right, better safe than sorry," their dad chimed in.

It hurt. He was supporting her in front of Gareth, yet here she was fighting for the other team. Then again, they wouldn't hesitate to kill Jamie if they knew about their affair. And for what? For being a different species?

Alison had to wonder if other than for reasons of vengeance, shifters had ever actually attacked and harmed humans. More often than not it had been the Sons who struck first.

She bitterly remembered the origin story of the Sons that her dad had told her when she was little, about a bear who abducted a human woman to be his bride many centuries ago. The story of Eileen and Bhaltair. The rescue team sent in by the woman's father, Lord Domnall, were the first of what was to become a long line of shifter hunters. But that was just myth, surely?

Since then, had shifters actually done anything wrong? Most of them seemed to live their lives in secret, separate from human society to prevent anyone from knowing the truth about them... Torches and pitchforks were never too far away when shifters revealed themselves as *different*, as Jamie had rightly remarked.

Alison was certain she was now on the right side of this fight, but she didn't want these Sons dead either. She'd grown up with some of them. She observed Gareth and his men fold and arrange the blanket, tearing strips to secure to bits of wood scavenged from what had been a bed frame only moments before. It took them a while, but in the end, they had a makeshift stretcher.

*Now what?* Alison had started to panic over finding another reason to keep everyone in here when the door finally flung open with a loud crash. The figures that entered didn't belong to the other guards outside. They weren't even human. Aidan's backup had arrived!

# CHAPTER NINE

———◆———

The change in the air had been gradual.

Jamie sat with Heidi and Kyle in a row on the bed, staring at the locked door. If they shifted, it would be no match for the three of them. They could easily break through, but they'd still have to take care of the dozen armed fanatics on the other side. It would be a suicide mission.

While he sat and tried to come up with some sort of a plan to keep his team – and mostly Alison – from any fallout from today's cluster-fuck, what had seemed like a hopeless situation started to change. He felt the change, a presence. It was faint at first but then the sensation grew until he could identify it: Alison.

She was here.

He felt her near the cell, exchanging words with someone outside. If he could feel her through the door, he was certain she could feel him, too. She had come here for him.

His optimism was short-lived as she passed by his cell. She was moving ahead, probably to confront the rest of the Sons who were further down the corridor tending to the prisoners. How would she be able to explain her presence? If they found out why she was really here... He dreaded to think of what would happen.

Jamie tried to listen to the conversation that took place in the other cell after Alison opened the door, but the walls were too thick even for his keen sense of hearing. All he heard were indistinct mumbles.

He couldn't stay still any longer and got up, pacing the

room restlessly.

"You okay, Boss?" Heidi asked, her eyes wide with concern.

She was a sweet girl, loyal to a fault.

"Fine." Jamie paused, listening for any sign of trouble next door, but there was none.

Still, Alison was upset — he could feel it. So he started pacing again.

"Aidan," Heidi whispered behind Jamie.

Had Alison brought him here? Or had he come in after her on his own accord?

"Heidi, I respect your wish for privacy, but if there's anything you can feel that'll help us, please share," Jamie said.

"What?" Kyle wondered aloud.

Jamie shot him a strict look in an attempt to keep him quiet. There was no time to explain.

"He's here," Heidi said, looking up at Jamie. "We'll be okay."

"Is he alone?" Jamie wondered. He knew he was able to communicate with Alison telepathically, but only when they were in the same room together. Perhaps Heidi and Aidan's bond was stronger because they'd been an item for longer.

Heidi closed her eyes and seemed to concentrate, hard. "No. I think the Alliance pick-up has arrived early."

"Shit, really? That's awesome," Kyle exclaimed.

"Get ready," Heidi said.

Jamie cleared his mind, as much as possible with Alison's fear leaching through the wall separating them, and prepared himself. Beside him, Kyle quickly took off his T-shirt.

"What? I don't want to ruin it. They don't sell these anymore," he justified when Jamie gave him a questioning look.

"Five... Four... Three..." Heidi gestured the rest of the countdown.

For the first time since Heidi's rescue, Jamie let the beast out. Ordinarily, he dreaded it. His bear form had always felt painfully incomplete, so he avoided shifting unless a situation absolutely demanded it. Now things were different.

The tickle that traveled the length of his body as brown fur started to break through his skin actually felt pleasant. A burn in his muscles signaled growth. Within a split second, he'd torn through his clothes.

Beside him, Kyle had transformed into his slightly smaller black bear form and Heidi stood on all fours, her razor sharp teeth exposed as she growled at the door. On her signal, they charged ahead, breaking through the door.

*Alison. I'm coming.*

Jamie lashed out at one of the two armed guards in the hallway, as Heidi and Kyle took on the other. At almost the same moment, a group of bears in varying shades of brown led by Aidan's huge bear form charged through the door coming from the stairwell.

Jamie didn't recognize anyone else, but gladly handed over his slightly bruised prisoner to one of the strangers who had arrived as part of the Alliance Council transport.

"The rest are in there," Jamie said, while leading the way. He had to get to Alison before any of the others did.

"The girl is one of ours," Aidan remarked behind him, giving Jamie pause.

Aidan knew?

Jamie cleared his mind and charged ahead, breaking into a run before crashing through the door.

"What the-" a Sons member on the other side of the door exclaimed.

# SCOTTISH WEREBEAR: A FORBIDDEN LOVE

Two of them carried the wounded guy they'd held prisoner on an improvised stretcher, so they couldn't react without dropping their comrade. The others were scrambling for their weapons.

Jamie went straight for Alison's brother, pinning him to the ground under the immense weight of his paws. Behind him, Aidan, Kyle and Heidi also charged in and neutralized some more of the intruders, growling, biting, and slapping weapons out of their hands, but making sure not to harm them too badly. The Alliance backup did the same until, after just minutes, they had disarmed and surrounded all of the Sons members in the room.

Most of them hadn't even fought back. The element of surprise was a powerful thing indeed.

In the center stood an unarmed man who hadn't been engaged so far: Lee Campbell.

"You didn't think it was going to be that easy, did you?" Aidan snapped at him.

He didn't reply, but he suddenly looked utterly defeated. Gone was the smug prisoner who had taunted Jamie and the others during every interrogation. He'd lost. It seemed as though the man had aged ten years in a span of seconds.

Next to Campbell stood Alison, shivering visibly. Jamie let go of Gareth and stepped up to her. She wobbled slightly, and seemed dangerously close to losing her balance as she looked down at him.

*Are you okay?* Jamie stretched his paw out in her direction, just in case she needed to steady herself.

*I don't know*, she responded, pressing her lips together tightly. This was a lot to take in. As much as Jamie and she had shared over the past couple of days, he hadn't transformed in front of her before.

She looked over at Gareth and her dad and tears

started to stream down her face.

"I fucking knew it!" Gareth hissed at Alison, attempting to get up. Heidi pushed him back down with her front paws. "You filthy whore!"

"Watch it," Campbell interjected.

"No, Dad! Enough! While you've been rotting away in this building, your favorite over there has been screwing the enemy!" Gareth groaned as Heidi shifted more of her weight onto his upper torso.

"That can't be. Alison, tell him he's wrong. Whatever you did, you were just doing your job, right?"

Jamie glanced around the room at everyone. Despite being in animal form, their expressions were clear as day. Surprise. Shock. Anger. This was bad.

"That's enough. Let's get them out of here." Jamie attempted to regain control of the situation.

"The girl has been informing for us. She brought me in to coordinate the rescue," Aidan explained.

A few bears Jamie had never seen before exchanged looks, as though they weren't quite convinced by Aidan's words, but nobody argued back.

Heidi jumped into action first, nudging Gareth up and snapping at him when he tried to turn around.

"You're going to pay for this," Gareth growled, while he was forced out of the door.

Reluctantly, Kyle followed suit and got his prisoner up as well, herding him out the room behind Heidi.

One after the other, the guys from the Alliance Council secured the Sons members, using heavy cable-ties as stand-in handcuffs and placing cloth bags over their heads. Jamie stayed behind with Alison and watched them as they led prisoner after prisoner from the room.

When the room was largely empty, a familiar human face entered. Adrian Blacke, wearing one of his trademark black three-piece suits. No doubt he thought his outfits made him look more authoritative.

"I don't have to tell you that we expect a detailed report of what went wrong here," he said to Jamie.

Blacke turned and scrutinized Alison from head to toe. "I suppose thanks are in order for your role in the rescue."

She nodded, but didn't say a word.

"I probably don't need to tell you that what you've seen here today is strictly confidential. Your loyalty will be rewarded. Similarly, if we find that you've breached that confidentiality, there will be consequences."

Jamie glared at Blacke, but quickly reined in his distaste for the man when he turned to face Jamie. "You'll monitor the situation, Abbott. And that report. Monday at the latest, understand?"

Jamie nodded. "Yes, sir."

Blacke stared at him a bit too long for comfort. Aidan and Heidi knowing about Alison were fine, but enough. Even if they disapproved, they wouldn't say a word. Kyle would probably remain loyal as well, but Blacke was dangerous. Jamie had to make sure he never found out the truth about him and Alison.

*Who the hell was that?* Alison wondered.

*Alliance council member,* Jamie responded. *Uptight bastard.*

They watched as Adrian Blacke left the room again, leaving the two of them alone. His footsteps faded as he walked down the hall, and back up the stairs where he had originally come from.

*I'm sorry it turned out like this,* Jamie thought.

*No. I'm sorry. I have to conclude that Gareth followed me and I led him right to you.* Alison turned to face Jamie again. Her eyes were still moist from crying earlier, causing her lashes to stick together.

He wanted to hold her, tell her it was all going to be

okay. But it wasn't. She'd lost her family today.

Jamie listened for any sounds, but the basement was completely quiet. They were on their own for now.

*I'm equally responsible. He could have found this place by following me as well,* Jamie thought.

*Are they going to hurt them?* Alison wondered.

Jamie had no answer. He and his team had never tortured the prisoners, just used basic interrogation techniques to encourage them to talk. Unfortunately Jamie had no way of knowing the lengths Blacke would go to if he thought it could help him extract information.

*I'm sorry.* Jamie closed his eyes and transformed back into his human self. He wrapped his arms around Alison, who melted into his embrace.

What had started off as an impossible situation for his team had been turned around into a victory. But Alison's loss made it feel hollow.

"I'm so glad you're okay. All morning I've felt like I had this black cloud following me around. Like something terrible was going to happen to you," Alison whispered.

"Really sorry about your dad and brother," Jamie responded, caressing her hair.

She didn't respond straightaway.

"I guess now we're even, huh? A brother for a brother."

Alison's inner turmoil tugged at Jamie's heart. He'd never wanted to get even. All he'd wished for, even after finding out her identity, was to make her happy. Right now that was clearly an impossibility, but maybe one day he'd get another chance.

"Let's go," she mumbled. "You ought to wear something, or people will talk."

Jamie forced a smile. "Don't worry. Nudity isn't as much of a taboo among shifters as it is among humans."

# SCOTTISH WEREBEAR: A FORBIDDEN LOVE

"Uh-huh." Alison wrapped her arms around herself and followed Jamie out of the room.

With a bit of luck, Blacke and his people would have already left, leaving Jamie free to deal only with his own team.

# CHAPTER TEN

---·◆·---

Alison caught up with Jamie as they reached the bottom of the stairs. Nudity might not be a big deal for him and his people, but if she kept watching his naked behind for much longer, her physical reaction to him would definitely make things awkward in front of the others.

"Aidan knows," Jamie remarked, as he glanced over at her.

"Yeah, I'm sorry. I had to tell him, or he would have never trusted me," Alison explained.

Jamie rested his hand on her shoulder. His hand felt so warm, almost feverish as it burned into her through her clothes. "That's fine. Don't worry about it."

Alison closed her eyes for a moment. She'd felt so torn between the two aspects of herself when everything went down that it had brought tears to her eyes. Deep down she knew she'd done the right thing, but it didn't make things much easier. She took another few steps with Jamie following closely behind.

"Did you know he's with the girl, what's her name? The one Gareth abducted," Alison remarked.

"Heidi? Yeah, I had guessed as much, though neither of them were willing to openly talk about it."

"Why's that?" Alison paused at the top of the stairs, nervous about facing everyone again, so their ongoing conversation was a convenient excuse to delay the inevitable.

"He's a bear, she's a wolf. It's complicated."

"Funny. I would have never thought you guys had issues like that within your ranks."

Jamie smiled at her. "We're a complicated bunch. Anyway – let's go in."

Alison took a deep breath. *Here goes nothing.*

Jamie pushed the door open and Alison flinched at the horrible noise it made.

"There you are," a shorter, dark haired man who sat at one of the desks said. "They just left with the prisoners." He nodded in the direction of the broken door.

"Good riddance," Jamie remarked.

Alison watched as Jamie walked right across the office, stepping over papers and other things that littered the floor. Nobody batted an eye. Aidan and that Heidi woman were sitting together at one of the other desks sorting through piles of loose paperwork, and the man who Jamie had just spoken to was already focused on his computer screen again.

"Kyle, what's the damage?" Jamie asked the man, while opening the bottom drawer of his desk and pulling out some sweat pants and a T-shirt, putting the former on first.

"Managed to retrieve the hard drive. Data's fine. Your monitor is cracked, but we've got a spare. Whatever papers they had planned to take, the Alliance guys handed 'em over to us before they took them all away."

Jamie nodded, then pulled the T-shirt over his head and returned to Alison who still stood awkwardly by the door.

"Guys, listen up," Jamie raised his voice slightly.

Aidan and Heidi looked up in his direction, as did the other guy he'd just identified as Kyle.

"What happened today was extremely unfortunate. I know you all have your own theories about how our location was compromised, but I just want to say that I take full responsibility. It was my job to keep this place safe, and I've failed you. The Alliance council will investigate, and Adrian Blacke will probably want to question every one of you individually. I can't tell you what to say, but-"

"Now hang on." Aidan got up. "They knew our faces from Heidi's rescue. They could have followed any one of us here."

"They could have, but they didn't." Jamie looked serious.

Alison's heart was hammering in her chest. Was he going to tell them everything? Could they trust these people to keep their secret? It was bad enough that Alison had lost everyone from her past, would the same happen to Jamie if his people disapproved of their relationship?

"Boss," Heidi said.

Jamie nodded at her. "Yeah?"

"I know what we said earlier, but it's obvious that Alison's help was instrumental in keeping us all safe. Aidan said as much already."

"Thanks," Alison mumbled.

"I agree. And that's what we'll tell Mr. Blacke if he asks. Unless the prisoners talk, we'll never find out how exactly they managed to track us down," the other man, Kyle, said.

"Glad to hear it. Thanks, Kyle. Heidi." Jamie nodded at all three of them, and they settled back into whatever it was they'd been doing before Jamie had interrupted them.

*What the hell had just happened? That was it? That was the entire briefing?* Alison couldn't believe her ears.

*Not wordy enough for you?* Jamie smiled at her. *They're good people. It'll be fine.*

"Okay then. Carry on while I make sure Alison gets home safely, all right? It's the least I can do after all she's done for us."

"No problem, Boss," Heidi responded. "We've got

this."

The other two men remained silent. All the while when Jamie was talking, so much was left unsaid their chat had been downright vague and confusing. Alison wished she could listen in on everyone else's heads too. Perhaps it was for the best that she couldn't, though, because finding out everyone's true feelings might just make things even weirder.

Still, Alison was kind of glad that the talk hadn't dragged out further. She needed to leave this place urgently and figure out what was next for her. For them.

*Let's get the hell out of here*, Alison thought.

Jamie grabbed his coat and marched straight to the door, Alison followed. She still couldn't believe that everyone had just accepted Jamie's non-explanation, after everything that had happened during the fight. Gareth had spelled out exactly what was going on between her and Jamie, and yet it hadn't made any difference?

These people were weird. Either very trusting, or very indifferent.

Outside, the weather was as nice as it had been all morning. As if nothing had happened. Clear blue skies, bright sunshine that even managed to warm Alison's back as they walked. Jamie seemed in a rush to get away from the Alliance building, as was Alison.

They walked at a brisk pace, turned a few corners away from the quiet streets of the warehouse district until finally risking a bit more affection.

"How do you know they're okay with us being together?" Alison asked. "The way you'd talked about it earlier, it seemed like we were breaking all your rules?"

"Heidi and Aidan have enough problems of their own to bother with ours. Aidan shared their secret with you during the rescue, so it's understood that I'd come to know. Kyle... I don't think he really cares, to be honest."

"What about that other guy, Blacke?" Alison asked.

"He's a problem, both for us as well as for Aidan and Heidi if he ever finds out about them. We'll cross that bridge when we get to it."

"And now?" Alison thought aloud.

"Now..." Jamie turned to her and cupped her face in his hands. "Now I take you home and we forget about all that's happened today."

"Okay," Alison whispered. "Not my place, though, I don't think I can stand going back there now, after everything..." The mere thought of it hurt and she again felt the prickle of tears in her eyes.

Her little flat was full of reminders of Gareth and her dad. Exactly the kind of things she needed some time and space from. It would take a while for her to get used to her new situation, no matter how much she believed that she'd done the right thing.

Jamie rested his arm on her shoulder and Alison felt at least some of her pain melt away under his touch.

"No problem. Stay with me." He leaned down and kissed her cheek, then the side of her neck.

His affections as well as his offer made Alison smile despite herself.

"I'd like that."

With Jamie's hand traveling up and around her neck, guiding their lips together, things didn't seem so bad anymore. For all that she'd lost, she'd gained something too. A future, with the boy she'd first met so many years ago and whom she'd never managed to completely forget.

He'd explained bears believe that fate brings couples together. It was tempting to think that everything that had happened, including his brother's abduction and her own crazy upbringing, had somehow served a greater purpose.

She would have never met him if it hadn't been for her dad and his radical affiliations.

He kissed her intensely, his hunger for her fanning her own.

*Not here*, she thought, and grabbed his other hand, running her fingers across his. His hand was so much bigger, stronger, and yet so very gentle and comforting as well. He managed to make her feel small, protected and safe at last.

Jamie's eyes darkened as he stared at her. His mind grew clouded with the possibilities that lay ahead once they reached his place. Glimpses of the imagery in his mind spilled over into hers: their naked bodies entwined, doing what they did best.

He didn't need further encouragement. Resolutely they started to walk again, keen to reach their destination only a few blocks away.

It didn't take them long, and they already had their hands all over each other by the time they reached the front door of his apartment. The first items of clothing ended up in the hallway, the rest were discarded by the time they'd reached the bedroom.

Jamie knelt down on the ground and forced her down onto her knees on top of the edge of the bed just in front of him. He dove into her without warning, tasting her sweet essence, covering her already wet lips with his mouth.

Alison grabbed handfuls of the pillow, moaning loudly as he explored her depths with his tongue. "Oh god, Jamie!"

He didn't pause or hesitate, instead licked her even more deeply.

Alison's legs threatened to buckle with the intensity of his affections. Out of breath and control, her mind went blank and she closed her eyes to focus on the pleasure he was intent on giving her.

*I'm sorry everything happened the way it did, but I love you,* she heard Jamie's voice in her mind.

She wanted to respond, to say that things would work out somehow and she loved him too, but she couldn't muster the energy. Every fiber in her body was primed, so ready to let go.

When he reached around and started to manipulate her clit, with his tongue still inside of her, it was all she could take. His hands were electric, his mouth was magical. He knew how to please her instinctively, effortlessly. She'd never had a lover like him before.

Her release sneaked up on her, making her knees shake until she sunk down into the soft mattress, shivering and moaning in between labored breaths.

*I love you too,* she finally responded, when she found her wits again.

He turned her over so they were facing each other and climbed on top of the bed as well. His hands cupped her face as he gazed into her eyes. His eyes were so blue, full of love and hope. In some ways he was still that wide-eyed boy from twenty years ago.

"Crazy to think we've only been together for a few days," he whispered. "I can't imagine a life without you anymore."

All the hairs on her arms stood up as he spoke.

"I know. Tell me this won't change. Tell me our feelings will never fade..." Alison demanded.

She knew what he was going to say, and that her question was unnecessary, but she couldn't get enough of his voice.

"Never. Our bond will grow every day, the longer we are together. Every day we spend together will be better than the last."

Alison closed her eyes and smiled, when his lips found hers once more.

They spent the rest of the night making love, until inevitably, the two of them fell asleep in each other's arms.

# CHAPTER ELEVEN

———◆———

"Morning, sleepyhead." Alison greeted Jamie with a smile on her face and steamy mug of coffee in hand.

Jamie smiled, and stretched out the lethargy from his limbs. What a night.

"You're up early," he remarked, stifling a yawn.

"Not quite. But I couldn't bear to wake you earlier, you really are too cute when you're asleep."

Jamie propped himself up on his elbows and gave her a sideways look. "If you say so. What's the time?" He leaned over and checked the alarm clock on the bedside table.

"Whoa, eight already?" Within a split second, he was up and halfway across the room, heading straight for the en-suite.

"At least have your coffee," Alison called after him.

"Okay."

He didn't have much time. Normally he'd have turned up at work by now. The others would be wondering where he was and what he was up to. It was one thing for him to be involved with a human, another to rub it in people's faces.

Jamie rushed through his morning routine and was ready in record time, though he did stop to take a big gulp from the mug Alison had poured for him. Extra sugar, just how he liked it. It was still hot, but just the right fuel to keep up his momentum.

He gave her a quick peck on the cheek, grabbed his coat and was halfway out the door when he noticed someone waiting by the front steps.

"Kyle! I was just heading out," Jamie said.

Kyle brushed away his explanation with a casual hand gesture. "We need to talk."

Shit, he wasn't about to get a lecture from a most unlikely source, was he? Jamie took a deep breath and straightened himself, well aware that with his shoulders pushed back, he towered over the man by at least a foot.

"You know that thing you asked me to look into?" Kyle asked, retrieving the brown paper dossier from his shoulder bag. The same one Jamie had given him just days ago.

"Yeah."

"I've made some progress."

Jamie allowed himself to relax a bit, though he couldn't quite read Kyle enough to figure out whether whatever he'd found out was good or bad news.

"Not here. Please come in," Jamie said.

Kyle nodded and followed him inside, waiting until the door had safely shut behind the two of them before continuing. "I've updated the file as you can see. Found a location."

He handed it to Jamie right there in the hallway.

"That's brilliant, great job!" Jamie eagerly took the file and started leafing through the new pages.

There was a map of a residential area in Glasgow with a red circle in the center, presumably the exact address, as well as pictures of the same area downloaded from Google street view.

There was also a photograph. It looked very recent. A pair of brilliant blue eyes that rivaled his own, the same shade of brown hair as Jamie remembered. It was unmistakably him.

"That's him. He goes by the name Matthew Argyle now," Kyle spoke deliberately, maintaining eye contact with Jamie throughout, which was unusual for him. "It took me a little while, putting two-and-two together. But here ya go."

Jamie looked down at the photo again. Despite the passing years there was no doubt in his mind that this was his little brother. He flipped the page over to find a print-out of an old newspaper article detailing the disappearance. The highlighted portions attracted his eye immediately.

'... Matthew (Matty) Brown, vanished from Applecross...'

'... his brother, Jamie Brown, and his parents...'

Kyle was still staring at Jamie's face when he looked up from the article.

"He's confused, as far as I can tell from his online activities. Doesn't quite understand where he belongs. It's time to bring him home," Kyle said, his tone uncharacteristically confident and sure of himself.

It was as though, just for a brief moment, Kyle was the one in charge. Jamie nodded.

"Well then, see you at the office." Kyle smiled at him briefly and opened the front door, leaving Jamie behind clutching the file.

He couldn't help himself and opened it to the photograph again. There he was. Matty. He'd been so young when he'd gone missing that one of the only things Jamie remembered about him was his obsession for sand castles. What was he like now? Would he even remember the family he'd been taken from so many years ago?

"Jamie." Alison appeared behind him, resting her hand on his back. "You've found him! Congratulations!"

Jamie turned to face her, his heart warming to the radiant smile on her face. "Don't congratulate me yet. What if he doesn't know who I am? I'd just be some stranger trying to take him from everything he knows all over again."

# SCOTTISH WEREBEAR: A FORBIDDEN LOVE

Alison wrapped her arms around Jamie's neck. "That's not going to happen. He'll be pleased to see you again, I can guarantee it."

Jamie felt that she really believed every word of what she was saying, but that didn't change the concerns that still weighed on him. *What if Alison's dad was right and Matty had grown up all human?*

"I'd better go now," he said, then kissed her goodbye again.

So much to do, so little time. If Jamie was going to go see Matty in Glasgow, he had to ensure everything at the office would be fine during his absence.

"He was wrong, you know," Alison called after Jamie. "My dad. I didn't think about it before, but... They took a few children like your brother, then all of a sudden they stopped. If his assumptions were correct, and they'd been able to reeducate those kids, why not keep going?"

Jamie turned back for a moment. She made an excellent point.

"Why indeed. I wish I could have asked him that."

"Yeah." Alison looked down at the floor, pressing her lips together. "Me too."

Jamie smiled at her, and caressed her cheek with the back of his index finger. "Will you be all right here while I'm at work?"

"Yeah. I'll be fine. I was thinking perhaps I'll move some of my things in if you don't mind."

"I don't mind at all. All this stuff-" Jamie gestured in the direction of the living room. "I don't care for it. None of it means anything. Would be nice to have something a bit more personal in here."

"Great." Alison smiled at him. "See you in the evening then."

"I can't wait." With that, Jamie turned the handle and

stepped out, ready to tackle whatever would land on his plate today. Although a part of him didn't want to leave her alone, he knew that the time spent apart would make their reunion at night all the sweeter.

Funny, how just a week ago he would have been in a rush to leave in the morning, and would aim to delay his homecoming as much as he possibly could at night. He'd been drifting, waiting endlessly for something to change.

He'd been alone, suffering the loss of his brother as well as the girl who had turned his world upside down so long ago. Now his wounds were well on their way to being mended.

His subconscious had been right: *find the girl, and he'd be whole again.* He'd found the girl, and before long he'd be reunited with Matty, too.

# - THE END -

# Scottish Werebear

## A NEW BEGINNING

# PROLOGUE

———◆———

As they exited the dunes and reached the beach at Applecross Bay, Matty had to smile.

His big brother, Jamie, had been right. Overnight, the sea had washed away their last attempt at building the most awesome sand castle anyone had ever seen. They'd have to start all over again.

Rather than feel discouraged, he was excited. Some of the turrets hadn't turned out quite right yesterday. Today, he would build an even better castle. And Jamie had told him to do it all by himself, so he would try extra hard.

He was only seven, but he didn't need anyone's help to build the best sand castle of the season.

Without paying too much attention to where Jamie was going, Matty got to work. Filling buckets of damp sand, and turning them over into perfectly formed shapes.

It was cloudy, a bit windy but not too cold. It was a perfect summer day.

"That's a nice castle," a voice interrupted him.

Matty looked up to find a tall man standing beside him, his hands on his hips and head cocked to the side as if he was inspecting Matty's work in great detail. Next to the man stood a woman with pale gray eyes and equally gray hair.

"Thanks. I'm not supposed to talk to strangers, though."

The man smiled at him and nodded. "That's a good rule to have."

Matty focused once more on his work, shoveling more

sand into his bucket, excavating what was going to be the moat of the castle.

"Listen, Matthew," the woman spoke softly.

"You know my name?" Matty looked up again, focusing on her face this time.

"I'm Molly. You've never met me before, but I know your parents very well. They've asked me to take care of you should anything happen to them."

Matty frowned scratching his face, leaving streaks of damp sand behind on his cheek.

"Where are my parents?" he asked.

"I'm very sorry to be the one to tell you this, but..." the woman hesitated, glancing anxiously over at her male companion.

"Your parents have met with an accident. They didn't make it," the man said in a matter-of-fact tone.

Matty turned his head and looked across the empty beach, his heart racing. There was no sign of Jamie; no brotherly advice within reach.

"But I just saw mom. She was just there, at our house!" Matty protested.

"I know, darling. These things don't ever make sense," the woman said.

They really didn't. How long had he been building this castle for? It felt like he'd only just arrived at the beach.

"I don't believe you." Matty threw down his trowel and bucket and jumped up, ready to run home.

The man had other ideas and stepped up to him, grabbing him by both his arms and keeping him firmly in place. "No you don't."

"I want to go home! Let go of me!" Matty fought hard against the tears prickling in his eyes - big boys didn't cry after all, but the man's fingers tightened painfully around his arms.

"We're sorry to tell you like this. But there's nothing there for you anymore."

"Where's Jamie? Jamie!" Matty cried out.

"Jamie has gone back to the house to take care of things now that your parents are no more. But he's only a boy himself; he can't take care of you as well," the woman explained.

The man meanwhile loosened his grip on Matty's arms. "Be a good boy and don't make this any harder than it has to be. Wouldn't you want your parents to be proud of you?"

Matty nodded, biting his bottom lip. He would be a good boy. For his mom and dad.

With his head hanging low, he walked in between the two grown-ups across the beach, not up the path Jamie and he had taken earlier which led to their home, but another one that led to Applecross village.

"Wait, my bucket!" Matty suddenly remembered.

The man grabbed his arm again and shook his head. "You won't be needing that where we're going."

Matty turned one last time, seeing his red bucket and spade abandoned in the pale sand, surrounded by turrets and walls that were going to make up the best sand castle of this season, if not ever. He didn't even get to finish it.

Life *was* unfair.

The rest of the walk was silent. Matty wondered if the two adults were communicating in their thoughts like his mom and dad were able to do. Every so often, when they did say something, they seemed to disagree a lot. Probably they couldn't hear each other unless they spoke.

After the long walk through the dunes, the woman directed him into the back of a big silver car waiting in the village parking lot, while the man took a seat behind the wheel.

From the back seat, Matty looked around the village; the shops were still closed, and there was no sign of anyone around. The roads were empty as well as they drove off. There was no one to wave goodbye to. No one to notice he was leaving.

Matty didn't know where they were taking him, but he'd adjust somehow, for his parents and Jamie.

He had to be a big boy now.

# CHAPTER ONE

———◆———

It was an ordinary November morning in Gartcosh, a sleepy village near Glasgow. At least, Matt Argyle assumed it was, because, from the safety of his home, all mornings seemed quite similar. He had a deadline and was expecting some groceries to be delivered, but other than that, today was going to be no different than yesterday or the day before.

Matt lived alone, ever since Molly, the woman who had raised him through most of his childhood, had left this house to him. He was glad to have it, because he couldn't imagine living anywhere else. The tall fences offered some measure of privacy, but, just in case, he never stepped out of the house until after nightfall.

He hadn't left his property in years.

Just as he turned on his laptop, Matt was interrupted by an unusual sound. A mechanical hum that seemed to creep ever closer. It wasn't any of the cars his neighbors drove. No, he'd recognize those. This was something bigger.

Matt got up and peeked out the curtain. A large moving truck pulled into the road and stopped in front of the empty house next door. His heart started to beat a little faster when two men got out of the cabin and started to pile up boxes of stuff on the pavement.

It had been nice, safe, knowing that the house adjoining his backyard was unoccupied. Now it looked like that was about to change.

His anxiety grew when he started to speculate about who might be moving in there. What if it was a family with children who would inevitably drop a ball or some other toy over the fence and expect to come in and fetch it? What if the parents expected to be all sociable and get to know him?

*No way, he couldn't have that.*

Along with the tension of what might be, Matt felt an old feeling creep over him. This is what always happened when he least wanted it to. His skin started to itch a bit, and the muscles in his shoulders, arms, and legs seemed to throb and pulsate.

*Shit, not now!*

He closed his eyes and tried to will the odd sensation away. It was all in his head; he knew that. The itching, the funny feeling as if his body tried to outgrow his own skin. If he didn't get himself under control, the transformation would be complete, and he'd find himself unrecognizable.

He'd turn into a bear.

Obviously, that was impossible, but somehow his mind refused to accept the truth and continued to feed him these outlandish delusions.

It always happened when he felt threatened or under pressure.

As he opened his eyes again, he saw a modest little car pull into the road beside the truck. He held his breath for the moment of truth: the opening of the driver side door. Two shapely legs clad in denim stepped out first, then the rest of his new neighbor came into view.

She was beautiful. Her shoulder length auburn hair framed a heart-shaped face with dark, mysterious eyes that Matt couldn't bear to look at for more than a second. She was curvaceous, feminine, mesmerizing.

He only managed to catch a short glimpse before she rushed off to the backside of the truck, gesturing wildly, probably at the two men unloading her things.

This changed things. He wasn't sure how exactly, but he could feel it in his bones.

*Wait a minute; he wasn't really considering meeting this woman, was he?* That was simply ridiculous. He hadn't talked to any of his other neighbors in ages, not even the ones he'd known all his life.

He didn't have time for this, not today. Matt shook his head, as if to rid himself of all these strange thoughts. He had a deadline to consider, a report to write.

And anyway, it would be best for everyone involved if he stuck to his routine. What difference did it make anyway who moved in where? His house was his own; nobody could change that.

Matt sighed and forced himself away from the window. With his laptop under his arm, he retreated to the farthest part of the house, the small room at the back where he'd spent most of his childhood. It didn't have any windows, and the loud hum from the truck up front only just managed to infiltrate it.

So what if she was pretty? He was hardly relationship material.

Matt plugged his headphones into the output of the laptop and cranked up the volume, drowning out the remainder of the noise coming from outside and got to work.

———◆———

As soon as he hit 'send' on the report, many hours later, he sat back and crossed his arms. He'd finished the job, somehow, but the image of the new woman next door had never quite left him. It was maddening. How was he meant to function like this?

Just with her presence, she'd upset the entire balance of

everything. He'd skipped lunch as well as dinner, something he'd never done before, simply because he didn't think he could regain focus if he accidentally spied her through the kitchen window.

He'd missed the delivery of groceries that he'd scheduled for the evening, because the music he'd been listening to had blocked out the doorbell.

Still, he couldn't stay in the back room forever. He needed to blow off steam somehow.

After preparing a quick bite, he noted with relief that there was no activity outside. Even the usual neighborhood kids playing ball in the street had gone home already, so he headed to the back of the house again and looked out at the unfinished project awaiting him.

For a few nights now, he'd been working on building a patio with a barbecue pit in the backyard. The print-out with instructions he'd found online had said it would be spacious, and the barbecue could cater to 6-8 people. Not that he was planning on using it for entertaining, but he was rather fond of grilled meat and had a very healthy appetite himself.

Of course, the new neighbor changed a few things. For one, he'd have to grow a hedge of some sort for extra privacy. Luckily, this was the right time of year to order the plants.

He didn't mind the extra work, after all, he enjoyed having things to do at night when sleep was hard to come by. Gardening had proved a welcome outlet for his energy as well as creativity. But it would cut into his area a bit, leaving less space for the seasonal vegetables he wanted to plant in spring.

But there was no point debating it. Matt picked up the instructions again and started collecting his materials. Everything he needed for the patio had already been delivered. The ground had been cleared and mostly leveled, so all he had to do was lay the stones tonight, and he'd still be right on schedule.

So he got to work. He managed to carry a dozen stones across the yard and had just begun to lay them down when something roused his suspicion. It wasn't a sound as such, more of a vibe. A presence.

He was being watched.

Just as he was trying to convince himself he was being paranoid, he turned towards his new neighbor's house and was immediately greeted by a rustle and muffled curse. She was there.

*Shit, now what?*

It was too dark to see properly, but that didn't deter his brain from showing him fuzzy images of her stumbling backward behind the wooden fence. Like infra-red imagery captured by a hunting scope, except he wasn't seeing them with his eyes. Of course, that wasn't possible. His brain was playing tricks on him.

Still, he couldn't take the risk, and he rushed inside. From the safety of his dark back room, he looked through the gap in the curtain while rubbing the cold out of his hands. In his eagerness to get the project done, he hadn't even realized how cold it was tonight.

Her side of the fence wasn't lit up, so there was no way of knowing for sure whether she was still there, not scientifically anyway. But now that his mind had captured her presence, he seemed to be able to track her a little.

*That's impossible.*

He kept scanning the fence for a few minutes until his instincts told him she'd gone.

This was too much to deal with. Even his safe haven, his personal backyard wasn't secure anymore. Something had to change.

Matt took to the one outlet still open to him. The world-wide-web. The answer ought to be out there, hopefully.

With a swiftness his fingers hadn't shown all day during his work, he typed out his experience - anonymously - aiming to publish it for the world to see on a discussion forum he often lurked in. For someone with delusions such as his, what else could he do? Where else could he go for help?

He finished his piece with questions: Was there hope? Should he try harder to ignore her? Or was this a sign that the status quo simply wasn't sustainable anymore? Perhaps he should go with it, and give in to the irrational desire to watch her, admire her, perhaps try to reach out to her even?

He didn't know right from wrong anymore. Either way, he definitely was in trouble.

And for a change, others shared in it.

In the past, he'd mostly held back, reading other people's posts instead of writing his own. He'd come to recognize some of the names of regulars who liked to comment. There was the cheerleader who supported everything and everyone, no matter how ridiculous. Next came the troll and the pessimist, each leaving their standard comments. *Go for it. Ignore her; there's no hope. Etcetera.*

The more helpful members were less prolific in their responses, but he waited for them anyway.

After an hour of waiting a few comments had come in that didn't offer much other than sympathy. Oh well, maybe later...

# CHAPTER TWO

———◆———

"Be careful with that, please!" Leah blurted out as she noticed the two movers unloading the truck containing her belongings a bit more enthusiastically as she would have liked.

They barely took notice and continued their work at the same pace, one all but flinging each box out of the back of the vehicle, for the other to catch and set down on the pavement.

*What's the point of labeling things as fragile if they're intent on throwing them around?*

Leah took a deep breath and headed for the door, clutching the key to what was going to be her new home tightly in her fist. *If anything's broken, I swear to God I'll give them an ear full and demand damages.*

Money wasn't the issue as such; Leah was most concerned about the supplies she needed to make a living from now on. Homemade candles and bath products can't just be replaced instantly by throwing money at the issue. These things take time and effort to recreate.

Her heart still hammered away in her chest as she looked around the empty hall, living area and open plan kitchen. It was a nice little bungalow, in a nice little village. Picturesque was the word. A far cry from the flat she'd called home ever since moving out on her own after her dad's death.

As she came back out, the truck was mostly unloaded, with only the larger pieces of furniture remaining inside. She bit her tongue and let the two men do their job as they saw fit, noting that despite shifting everything inside of the house at record speed, they hadn't scuffed a single wall or door frame.

The curtain-less windows facing the modest front yard revealed that the sun was out. Odd not just for the time of year – mid-November - but also for the area. It wasn't for nothing that Scotland had the reputation of being cloudy and wet most of the year. Some stereotypes were true. But today was a perfectly bright, icy day.

Leah felt chills run down her spine and remembered that she should probably switch on the central heating. The house had sat empty for a while the rental agent had told her. Although everything looked in good condition, you could never be certain that everything would work as expected.

Luckily, everything seemed to switch on as it should, and soon she could hear the hot water stream into the large radiator below the living room window.

Leah halfheartedly told the movers where to put all her belongings, though they had pretty much done everything on auto pilot based solely on the meticulous labeling system Leah had stuck to while packing. Kitchen boxes in the kitchen and so on. *Obviously*.

Though she did do a few spot checks to make sure the contents were all intact, she couldn't find anything amiss. Soon after, the older one of the two movers presented her with a clipboard containing a form for her to sign. Then they were off, and she was left alone in her newly rented bungalow, surrounded by boxes and wrapped up furniture.

Unpacking would be a thankless task. One Leah didn't have the energy for just yet. Anyway, it wasn't like she had a job to go to come nightfall; she'd quit her night shift position at the call center a month ago.

And so the only two boxes she did open up properly were the ones containing the electric kettle and mugs, and of course, her bedding so that she could catch some rest later. Thanks to the groceries she'd picked up on her way, she soon had a steamy cup of tea in her hands as she sat down on her still wrapped up sofa.

*Made it.*

It was hard not to feel just a little bit nervous about the big step Leah had taken today. She'd been ready for a change. Ready to slow down and live life somewhere quieter, on her own terms. But was this the right decision? Or the right time?

Her homemade bath supply company was just starting to pick up steam, and the internet was a fickle place to do business. What if her orders dried up suddenly? What if her savings ran out before she was able to make things work?

She took a deep breath, and then a big sip of her hot drink and tried to suppress all those doubts and worries that were attempting to claw their way to the surface.

*Everything will be fine.*

She closed her eyes and forced her nerves to calm, when the doorbell rang and made her spring into action yet again.

"Yes?" Leah asked, while opening the light wood front door.

"Hi!" a woman sporting a wide smile and larger than life platinum blond curls greeted her on the other side. "I'm Caroline- but everyone calls me Carrie. I noticed you moving in and thought I'd say hello and welcome you to the neighborhood!"

Leah reluctantly met the woman's outstretched hand, who warmly shook it while continuing to flash her teeth at her.

"Thank you so much. I'm Leah."

"It's nice seeing this old house in use again. It's been

empty for so long..." Carrie's voice trailed off towards the end of the sentence, as if there was something she was thinking that she didn't want to share.

"It seems to be a nice area. I've been meaning to get out of the city for some time," Leah responded.

"Mhmm. It certainly is. Very good for families. Do you have children?"

Leah shook her head.

"Oh well. Maybe later, aye?"

"Right."

Carrie hadn't taken her eyes off Leah throughout the short exchange, except to inspect the as yet barren hallway behind her. She was clearly curious what this house looked like on the inside, but Leah was in no mood to invite her in. Nobody was going to come in until everything was set just how Leah wanted it.

"Anyway, I live just next door. If you ever need anything." Carrie pointed to the neatly kept house towards the right of Leah's bungalow. "I'm sure you'll meet the rest of the neighborhood shortly."

"I'm sure." Leah smiled. "So, who lives there?" Leah pointed at the other house next door to her towards the left. Its exterior was equally polished, but the windows were dark almost as if they were boarded up from the inside.

"Oh... I suppose *him* you probably won't meet. Matthew Argyle," Carrie's voice suddenly didn't seem so upbeat anymore. "He doesn't tend to mingle."

"Oh yeah? How come?" Leah tried not to sound too suspicious but was having a hard time to disguise the concern that she'd been tricked into putting down a rather sizable deposit on a house right next door to a difficult neighbor. Or worse, a pervert.

"It's not that he's not a nice guy; he's fine enough.

Grew up with him. He just doesn't really socialize. Not sure what happened to him, but ever since old Mrs. Argyle passed and left him the house, he's been really withdrawn. It's a shame."

"I suppose the death of a parent can do that to a person." Although Leah was still a little suspicious, she did feel bad to have judged her new neighbor so harshly before even finding out the first thing about him. She'd had a difficult time when she'd just lost her dad years ago, so she could sympathize.

Eight years in a bad part of the city had clearly taken their toll and hardened her up. That was part of why she'd moved here, to get out of the hustle and bustle and allow herself to smell the roses more. If there was one thing she didn't want - despite herself - it was to start off on the wrong foot with her new neighbors.

"Well, thanks anyway and lovely to meet you. I'm sure we'll see each other around," Leah said her goodbyes to Carrie, who shot her one last bright smile before turning on her heel and heading back home.

Leah glanced to the left once more at the dark windows of Matthew Argyle's house before wrapping herself up tighter in her sweater in an attempt to ward off the persistent chill in the air. Perhaps she ought to make the first move. It must be a lonely existence, living all on your own in your mother's house after she had passed away.

Yes, that was exactly what she should do: go over there and introduce herself. In time. Perhaps in the morning.

———◆———

The first night in her new home was oddly surreal.

After unpacking only the bare essentials, Leah had ordered a pizza and soon after crept into bed. She'd been tired, exhausted actually, but sleep still didn't find her.

Leah lay awake, staring at the ceiling for hours when a faraway noise had attracted her attention. Her flat in the city was right next to a railway line on one side and a busy road on the other, so silence was a luxury she had not been able to afford before.

This new place was exactly the opposite. The silence was deafening, making Leah take notice of every little creak and rustle that did manage to infiltrate her bedroom.

In the end, it was a click and squeak that roused her. The sound hadn't come from inside the house, but it was still too close to ignore. Leah grabbed a throw from the foot end of the bed and wrapped around herself and crept up to the window to see what was going on.

Next door, the light in the back yard was on, and she could make out a shadowy movement through the gaps in the wooden fence separating her garden from Matthew Argyle's. As night had set in, it had apparently brought a mild fog with it, giving the entire scene a mysterious glow.

Why the hell would anyone be out in their garden at crazy o'clock at night? And in the freezing cold too!

Leah held her breath as she opened the window as quietly as she possibly could. The previously muffled sounds became clearer, and she could hear not just his footsteps, but also the occasional thump of heavy objects being set down on the soil, as well as metallic scratches. *Is he digging a hole?*

She remembered her earlier suspicions about the man, and simply couldn't stand not knowing what he was up to, barely ten feet away from her on the other side of that fence.

*I can't sleep anyway; perhaps the fresh air will do me good...*

Leah slipped on a pair of sneakers and exited through the back door. She again tried her best to be stealthy, walking on the grass instead of the pathway to dampen her steps. Within moments, she reached the same bit of fence visible from her bedroom window.

The activity on the other side had moved further away, but she could still hear Matthew pacing about.

*Just a little peek...*

Leah stepped up to the fence, her shoes sinking into the soft soil of the flower bed and looked through one of the many gaps between the wooden slats.

Although he had his back towards her, Leah felt validated in her nosiness already. As soon as she'd found out about her reclusive neighbor, a mental image had started to form. Her assumptions couldn't have been more wrong.

His broad shoulders, as well as deliberate movements with which he lifted one of the heavy paving slabs and carried it across his lawn didn't fit her expectations at all. He was strong to the extent that he made the hard labor look effortless.

In the dim light, as well as disguised by fog, Leah couldn't properly judge his wardrobe, but at least she could tell he wasn't wearing rags. His hair was closely cropped and thus looked neat enough. So he wasn't the unkempt spend-the-day-in-a-bathrobe type recluse at least.

And then he turned around.

Leah forgot to breathe and stumbled backward onto the lawn.

His strong jaw matched the rest of his physique. *Handsome* didn't quite describe him. And those eyes... A warm almost fiery amber, kind and yet infinitely sad.

That was the reason she'd stumbled in the first place. He seemed to be able to peek right into her soul, even though there was no reasonable way for him to even see her behind the fence. *Was there?*

As soon as she'd regained her composure, a confusing few seconds later, she was back at the fence, but her new neighbor was nowhere to be seen anymore.

Shame... Leah would have loved to catch another glimpse of him before heading back inside.

Despite everything, especially the mystery of why Matthew Argyle thought it appropriate to do a bit of landscaping in the middle of the night, her decision was final now. She was definitely going to make the first move and introduce herself the first chance she got.

# CHAPTER THREE

———◆———

The next day, Matt's doorbell rang, but he ignored it, instead keeping his head down and eyes locked onto the laptop screen. He never bothered with callers, unless he was expecting a delivery, so this wasn't unusual.

What was unusual was that for a change he knew exactly who stood there at the other side of his front door. It was the woman. He could feel her presence, just like last night. And that simple fact still didn't make any sense to him.

But then again, a lot of things in Matt's world didn't make sense. Like why the majority of the people on the discussion forum he'd posted on at night thought he should just be honest with her. What did they know?

He rubbed his eyes, but the alphabets on his screen continued to dance around in front of him. There was no way he could concentrate.

"I'm sorry to disturb. I'm new in the neighborhood and just wanted to say hello," she said. He could just about hear her muffled voice even though he was as far back inside the house as he possibly could be.

That was nice of her, but he couldn't risk it. Just the sound of her was putting him on edge. The hairs on his arms and legs were already standing up straight, readying themselves to grow.

"Anyway, perhaps you're busy, so I'm just going to leave this here," she continued.

*Wait, leave what where?* He got up and walked out of his office heading towards the entrance hall, then stopped in his tracks. What was he doing? If he got any closer, she'd see him and know he was avoiding her!

He waited, holding his breath until finally he heard footsteps move away from the door and down the steps of his porch. Another five minutes later, he finally dared to open the curtain of the porch window just enough to see outside. There was a basket on his foot mat. Of course, he couldn't tell what was inside from here.

It was still light out, and he had no way of knowing whether he was being watched, so he closed the curtain again and turned around to get back to work. But knowing that there was something out there, something *she* was trying to give him... He had to know what it was.

Barely an hour later, he'd again tried and failed to finish the article he'd begun writing that morning. Instead, he'd been reading and re-reading the reactions to his post on the discussion forum.

'If she's worthy, she'll accept you.' *Rubbish.*

'Wouldn't it be worse to always wonder *what if?*' *Ugh!*

The worst part was they were probably right in their own way. And he couldn't ignore that basket any longer without losing his mind completely, so he gave in to temptation. He returned to the front door, making sure through the curtain that nobody was around, and retrieved it.

A sweet sort of scent hung about it, and it wasn't just from the food he knew to be inside. Inside, he found a piece of heavy paper the size of a business card, a bar of soap that smelled of Christmas and a stack of carefully wrapped butter shortbread with a red ribbon tied around it.

Hello.

Matt turned the card over in his hand, hoping for something more, but that's all it said. Weird.

*Seriously? You're the one who didn't even open the door for her, and you think* this *is weird?*

It was still nice of her, though. Matt untied the ribbon holding the shortbread together and took a bite. *Amazing.*

Only then did he take a closer look at the rustically shaped soap. It didn't seem shop bought and along with the cinnamon and hints of orange peel, there was a strong scent of something else in there as well. *Her. No, it can't be, can it?*

The material of the label was identical to the very concise card, which should have been the first thing for him to notice if he hadn't been so distracted.

On the sticker on the back, there was a website and a phone number.

When he pulled up the website on his laptop, he had to smile. This was actually quite clever. On the face of it, she'd just packed together a couple of things, little gifts. But between the lines, there was so much to learn. He couldn't help but assume that she'd done it this way deliberately.

As the site loaded, her picture greeted him from the right-hand column. She looked even more beautiful in it than he could have guessed from the short glimpse he'd caught of her yesterday. So she made soaps. That explained a lot.

He'd always had a keen sense of smell, as well as a whole other host of instincts that often overwhelmed. One of them was a tendency to see mysteries and secrets everywhere. Why had she even tried to make contact? Why give him anything in the first place?

Last night had been fairly easy to explain away: he was

out making noise in the middle of the night, and she came to the fence to investigate. Simple. But this was something entirely different. Perhaps his strange night time activities had made her curious to find out more. She must be wondering what sort of a person she's ended up living next to; that was only natural.

*Still...*

Matt's brain wouldn't stop speculating.

He pushed the basket and its contents to the side and focused on his laptop once more. What if these people were right? Maybe he should just get over himself already.

Her website was still open in the background. Her smile was radiant and inviting. He hovered over the speech bubble labeled 'get in touch' underneath her picture for a moment and found that he'd clicked it without consciously deciding so.

What to write? Seeing as she'd kept things very simple, he ought to do the same.

**Hello & Thanks.**

A rush of excitement passed through him as he hit 'send.' What if she doesn't realize who it was from? Again, a stupid thought... If it reached her, she would know.

That last thought was what allowed him to go back to his original plan for the day: the articles he was supposed to submit the next day. It was just as well that a reply wasn't forthcoming.

———◆———

Ever since Leah saw the short message in her inbox from a certain "M. A.", she couldn't help feeling some sense of accomplishment. She didn't know the man, obviously, but somehow she could tell that simply sending her a 'hello' back was a big step. She wasn't even sure why she cared, considering she had moved there in search for a simpler life, not a more complicated one.

Trying to strike up a conversation with a reclusive, yet rather attractive neighbor definitely counted as complicated.

Still, she couldn't help feeling pleased. He had responded, so the lines were now open, sort of. Unless he was just trying to be polite...

Despite thinking about what to do or say next for most of the day, there was plenty of work to be getting on with. An engineer turned up to connect her TV, phone and broadband which took up the better part of the morning.

She was glad to no longer to have to rely on the rather patchy mobile signal. There was no network in her bedroom, bathroom, or most of the lounge; she'd learned that pretty quickly. Only along the front windows and in her kitchen did her mobile work properly.

Once the telecoms guy had gone, she had to start working through a couple of orders, necessitating a trip to the nearby post office. And then there were the boxes... the never-ending boxes that needed to be unpacked.

Only by the evening did she have the time as well as peace of mind to reply.

### I'm Leah. Nice to "meet' you.

Send.

She was about to put her phone down on the coffee table and settle into the freshly fluffed up cushions on her couch to watch some TV when it dinged. That was fast! Almost as if he'd been waiting...

Matt, likewise. I saw you move in.

It wasn't much as a response, but it was something. Had he been watching her? Oh crap, what if he asked about her peeping through the fence at night? That would be so awkward! Perhaps it would be best to face that particular topic head-on...

Leah typed out her next response with trembling fingers. *Fingers crossed he won't take offense!*

> So I guess you like gardening? I'm more
> indoorsy, a city girl.

*Did that sound stupid? Too late now...* Leah sent the email and waited, holding her breath.

> You seemed pretty outdoorsy last night...

They say it's hard to catch the intent behind written words, but Leah was sure she could sense the dry humor in his observation. *Oh hell, if you want to play it like that!*

> It was short-lived. I changed my mind once my
> toes started to turn blue.

Although she thought herself quite witty upon sending the mail, she wasn't so sure when nothing happened for a few minutes. Why wasn't he responding? She placed the phone next to her on the sofa and switched the TV on. Perhaps she'd missed the point of his message completely and turned him off.

While flipping through the channels, her phone finally lit up again with a notification. She bit her lip as she opened it.

### Check the same spot.

What the hell? What was he talking about?

Leah crossed her lounge and headed straight to the bedroom window overlooking the place where she'd stumbled at night. Sure enough... the same basket she'd left on his doorstep was waiting there, a string attached to its handle.

She put on a coat - dusk was setting, and she'd only been half joking about the blue toes - and went out. Inside the basket was a stem of fragrant flowers; they looked somewhat like the orchids you can buy at the supermarket, but somehow more elegant. Underneath it awaited a bottle of red wine.

Leah stepped up closer to the boundary and looked through the gaps in the wood like she'd done the previous night, but there was no sign of movement on the other side. He must not be looking for an in-person chat.

*Okay then...* Clutching her prize in one hand, she also retreated and upon returning inside she picked up her phone again.

### Cheers :)

She was about to send just that, then changed her mind.

### ... Do you have Whatsapp? It seems odd chatting via email.

Now she sent it. Again it took a little while for a response to arrive, giving Leah the chance to open one of the boxes waiting in the kitchen and take out a wine glass. This time, she wasn't worried anymore. Her new neighbor had turned out a lot more agreeable than she'd expected.

Sure enough, the next message was a positive one:

Now I do :)

Leah wasn't sure whether it was the wine or just the thrill of having broken the ice, but from then on conversation flowed a lot more freely. She learned that Matt was a freelance writer, which enabled him to work exclusively from home. In turn, she shared some of her work history, how she'd slogged through years at a call center in the city while dreaming of becoming her own boss.

It was nice to talk to someone in a similar position; after all, freelancing wasn't all that different from selling stuff online, not if you looked at the basics. You might set your own hours, but you're still dependent on clients ordering stuff, no matter if it's an article or a scented candle. And in both lines of work, word of mouth was everything.

Time flew as they continued to talk. Before she knew it, the gifted bottle was mostly empty, and the clock showed 3 am. She hadn't even realized that the muted TV in front of her had been showing infomercials, probably for hours.

By the time they said good night, the former stranger next door had started to feel a lot like a friend.

# CHAPTER FOUR

When Matt awoke, a little later than normal, it was with a smile on his face. He'd taken a chance, responded to Leah's little gift package, and as a result, spent the better part of the night talking to a real actual human being. Sure, it had been via email and chat, but this wasn't some anonymous person on a forum, but someone who was right there across the fence in the house next door.

And yeah, if he was being totally honest with himself, he could have talked to real people otherwise also. There were the neighbors he'd grown up with, who probably would be happy to have a chat with him, but this was different. They knew the old him. They had expectations he wasn't able to live up to anymore.

Leah hadn't known him before. She only knew what he'd told her. And for some reason he couldn't quite fathom, she hadn't told him to go away and leave her alone. She'd interacted with him like normal people did with each other. Except in writing.

He'd never had any use for chat apps, but installed one on his phone at her request, and he was glad to have done so. It was a lot easier to carry a phone around the house than his laptop.

Looking at it now, lying on the table beside his bed, he was tempted to pick it up and wish her good morning. Did people do that? Would that be weird?

He resisted for now, getting up and making himself a cup of coffee instead.

Outside, life was going on as normal. Kids were leaving their homes and grouping together in the street with their bicycles, ready to head to school. The garbage truck was making its usual round through the neighborhood.

And next door, a familiar silhouette was walking to her car carrying half a dozen little parcels. Leah.

He leaned across the kitchen counter and lifted the curtain aside to get a better look. She must have gotten a few more orders overnight. Good. He hoped for her business to work out. She seemed like a smart, ambitious woman who deserved a break after years in a crappy job.

Funny. Only yesterday he dreaded seeing her around because it would just lead to him obsessing about her, but overnight she had become a welcome, even familiar sight. He couldn't look away if he wanted to.

The way the wind tussled her hair made him smile again. She tried her best to brush one particularly stubborn lock behind her ear using just her upper arm but was unsuccessful and dropped a couple of parcels in the process.

He should go out there and help her out.

Of course, he didn't, but he ought to. In his place, someone else came up to Leah and picked up the fallen packets. Permed blond hair and tightly fitted velvet tracksuit: Carrie, who had lived two doors down from Matt pretty much forever.

If only he could overhear the conversation taking place outside.

It wasn't that he disliked Carrie; it was just that the woman she had grown into was nothing like the little girl he'd played tag with in the past. She'd followed in her mother's footsteps and had become the main source of gossip in the neighborhood.

Matt didn't appreciate gossip, especially since he expected to be the topic of it more often than not. Nothing ever happened in Gartcosh that was worth talking about, so why not discuss the crazy guy who never left home?

The two women glanced over in Matt's direction, Leah with what looked like the subtlest of smiles on her face while Carrie's expression was hard with suspicion. Were they talking about him?

Leah finished loading her things into the backseat of her little car, while Carrie kept loitering around. Matt breathed a sigh of relief when Leah finally sat in the driver's seat and left.

He should remember to tell her to be cautious around Carrie. Whatever she told her would be shared with the whole village soon after. That woman had no sense of boundaries.

Carrie glanced over at him one last time then turned around to head back home. Matt also let go of the curtain and prepared himself for a productive day ahead. Hopefully, come nightfall, there'd be more conversation to look forward to. He'd be ready just in case.

———— ♦ ————

It had only been a couple of days since the move, but Leah was starting to feel at home already. The place was perfect, just big enough to be able to house all her supplies as well as stock, yet small enough to be cozy for just one person.

Leah turned the key with a smile on her face and admired her new living room. Everything was set up just how she wanted it. All the boxes were unpacked, all the paintings hung and framed pictures lined up on the mantle. If her dad could see the place right now, he'd be proud.

She glanced down at the phone in her hand. She'd been carrying the thing around all day obsessively, hoping for a message from Matt. A bit needy perhaps?

Still, she hadn't imagined the two nights in a row that they'd spent exchanging stories and random thoughts. It was nothing like her previous relationship, which had been with a man who had the emotional maturity of a clam. Matt was different.

Perhaps it was that they were communicating in writing, which made the two of them open up so much more than they might have in person. They'd shared stories of past loves and other things she'd never told anyone she'd only just met, especially not a guy. Perhaps they'd found it easy to connect because they'd both grown up in a single-parent household?

Body language was a wonderful, yet often distracting thing. It was interesting to do without it for a while. In the case of a guy like Matt, who was unnervingly handsome in person, it was probably a good thing she couldn't see him while "talking" to him.

Ever since Leah had started her online business, the ding of her phone would get her just a little bit excited. It could be a customer enquiry, or better yet, a new order. But none of that could compare to the thrill she felt when she saw a new message from Matt. He definitely had made an impact, though she couldn't be sure that feeling was mutual.

In fact, there came another message, the first one of the day: "Had a good day?"

Leah smiled as she typed out her response. "Yes indeed. Getting the hang of the local geography. Did you know there's a charming little antique shop right there by the village green? It's so cute I nearly died."

Leah carried her purchases, mostly groceries, into the kitchen and waited.

"No kidding? Isn't that where the post office used to be?" Matt replied.

She shook her head and let out a chuckle.

"You need to get out more. It's next door to the post office." As soon as she'd sent her response, Leah's heart sank. Did she honestly just write that to him? Oh, crap.

"You're funny. Maybe next time. ;-)" Thank God, he hadn't taken offense. Leah breathed a sigh of relief. Perhaps body language wasn't so overrated after all.

"It's a date," Leah replied, her heart fluttering just a little bit. She wasn't quite sure why, but for some reason, she had this irresistible urge to get flirty with him. This was the most overt attempt so far, though. How would he respond?

"In that case: flowers or chocolate?"

Leah bit her lip. He has taken the bait.

"Do I have to pick just one?" she asked in response.

"Right you are. You don't. A girl like you deserves both."

She was speechless for a moment. She'd started it, but now they'd both crossed that invisible line in the sand. They were no longer just neighbors being friendly. There was something else going on here, and it felt good.

"You know where I live :-)" Leah couldn't stop smiling. This new life of hers was shaping up to be quite exciting indeed.

"Flowers and chocolates for the lady. That can certainly be arranged."

"And don't think you can get away with just smooth talking me. I'll be heartbroken if you don't follow through. :-)"

"No worries. I'm a man of my word."

Leah felt like hugging her phone but resisted at the last moment. She wasn't a teenager anymore after all.

Was he as excited as she was right now? Maybe. Hopefully. Perhaps she should ask him. No, that would be a dumb attempt to look behind the curtain and ruin the magic.

Still, though, this thing with Matt made her feel good about herself. Ever since planning to set out on her own, she hadn't given herself permission to date. The baggage left over from the last man in her life had also played a part. Perhaps this thing, this weird long-distance type deal with the man next door was exactly what she needed.

It's easy to convince yourself you don't need anyone when everyone tells you you're crazy to leave your job. But Matt had been supportive, something Leah hadn't realized she'd wanted, and yet he wasn't about to take over her whole life to the extent that she would no longer be able to achieve her business goals. He might not be Mr. Perfect, but whatever was developing here sure seemed to fit perfectly into Leah's life.

She plopped down on the sofa and started typing again. Now that this initial hurdle had been crossed, there was a whole lot more for the both of them to talk about. The night was still young, and she didn't want to miss a moment of it.

# CHAPTER FIVE

————— ◆ —————

Leah had come home late. The custom order that had come in earlier in the day for two hundred spring themed wedding favor bags meant a trip into the city for supplies was in order.

She didn't mind the drive so much, nor the traffic, because she knew that at the end of the day she had a quiet home to retreat to. Hers wasn't a city life anymore.

So when she unlocked the door and stepped inside, she could breathe a sigh of relief. Here she was, away from the noise and confusion. Here she could relax.

Leah started to unpack her shopping. The much needed supplies were put away for later in favor of the groceries she needed right this moment. She popped a ready meal into the microwave and poured herself a glass of wine while waiting.

One of these days, she'd decide to learn how to cook from scratch as well, but not today. Leah had more pressing things to occupy herself with, such as messaging Matt, which had become a welcome ending to every day since they started talking shortly after she'd moved into the place.

"What a day," Leah started the conversation

"Oh yeah?" Matt responded instantly, as usual.

"I'd almost forgotten how busy the city can be."

"I wouldn't know. Cities aren't my thing."

"Anyway, glad to be back home. I'm enjoying a ready made lasagna."

"Say what? Sawdust with cheese on top?"

"We can't all be awesome cooks like you."

"Can't or won't?"

Typical. Won't leave the house but has opinions about everything. Leah let out a chuckle, then opened the camera app and took a close-up of her plate.

"If you serve it up nicely before eating, you can't tell the difference," she wrote as a caption to the picture.

"Wanna bet?" Matt wrote, along with a photograph of a very inviting looking steak covered in creamy peppercorn sauce. Damn. He was right, of course.

"Trying to make me jealous? Watch it, or I'm coming over there demanding a share," Leah responded, only half joking. Their daily exchanges had progressed from innocent small talk to merciless teasing and flirtations. What would happen if he allowed things to progress to the logical next step?

Would she be as comfortable with him in person? Perhaps... Or perhaps the chemistry they felt was limited only to characters on a screen.

"What makes you think there'd be any left?" Matt responded. Something told her that the day he let his guard down and allowed her in closer, there would be. But he wasn't ready yet, and she wasn't about to force things.

"Anyway, I stopped by this new micro-brewery on the way home. If you're nice, I might leave you a bottle," Leah wrote.

"I'm always nice."

Ha!

"Give me a moment while I sort out the kitchen. BRB." Leah put the phone down and got to work. The advantage of not actually cooking was that there wasn't much to tidy away afterward either. Soon she was done and keen to properly relax with a second glass of Merlot.

Leah retrieved the phone, switched off the living room lights and retreated to her bedroom. As comfortable as the living area was, her bedroom was her safe haven. It helped that it was also the part of the house closest to Matt.

"Okay, I'm back," Leah restarted the chat.

"You want to watch a movie together? Tune in to Channel 4."

Leah frowned; this was new, but why the hell not? She didn't have a TV in the bedroom, but then again she didn't need one. The Internet had everything, even live TV.

"Dracula?" Leah asked.

"What's wrong with Dracula? This version is a classic."

"All right then, just checking." Leah settled into her pillows and wrapped a throw around her shoulders. The air in the bedroom was chillier than the living room, but soon that wouldn't matter anymore.

In between sips of wine, and the odd comment or remark, Leah soon became immersed in the movie. It had been ages since she'd seen it last. The first time around, she'd dismissed it as silly and a bit camp. This time, though, something spoke to her; she could feel the attraction. How tempting it might be to give in to the darkness, to get close to a man (or vampire) so dangerous.

It was because he'd suggested it, and they were watching together, even though they were apart probably. That was what made her enjoy the film. Maybe one day they'd be in the same room, the same bed even? Leah could only hope so.

As the movie came to a climax, something sent a chill down Leah's spine. A noise. A clicking sound had disturbed her that hadn't come from the speakers on her tablet. She muted it and listened out for more.

"Hey, I just heard something," Leah typed.

"What?"

"A noise-" Leah barely managed to write that much when another, louder sound cut through the silence. Shit.

This was definitely close, maybe even inside the house.

She wrapped the throw tighter around herself and got up to investigate. Years living on her own in the city had made her cautious, but she wasn't a wimp. Like that one time someone burgled the flat next to hers while her neighbor was out. She'd heard the whole thing and called the police just in time.

*Damn. Footsteps*. She didn't even have anything to defend herself with! Hiding was the only remaining option.

Leah snatched the phone from the mattress and got underneath the bed. Zero bars, all she had was the Wifi. So much for that plan. She opened Whatsapp again.

"There's someone in the house," she messaged. "I don't have a network. Call for help." Her bedroom door creaked open just after she managed to send the final message. She tightly pressed the phone against her chest and held her breath. Her heart was beating so hard it was all she could hear.

Maybe they won't find her. Maybe...

She let out a short shriek when a hand closed around her ankle and pulled her backward.

---

Matt stared at his phone for a second. Call for help? Was this some kind of weird joke?

He didn't get much time to analyze the situation. A distant scream pierced through his entire being. It wasn't loud, and he doubted any other neighbor would have heard it. *Her voice. This was real. Shit.*

His body sprang into action before his mind did, and the transformation was over within a fraction of a second, leaving his clothes on the floor in tatters. It didn't matter what shape he was supposedly in; he knew he had to step up. There was no way he'd let her down.

Although he'd never been in any sort of scenario like this, instinct kicked in. If he charged in there without a strategy, this whole thing could end badly for the both of them. Instead, he opted for stealth.

He checked through the kitchen window, looking for any sign of activity. All seemed quiet now, except for a shadowy figure, loitering around Leah's front steps. There was no way he could get in without tipping this person off.

Matt headed for the backyard instead, opening his back door as quietly as he possibly could and listening for movement on the other side of the fence. Nothing. A quick check through the wooden slats suggested all was clear. This was to be his entry point.

With swift movements, he picked up his heavy wooden picnic table and placed it beside the boundary, before climbing on top and jumping over the top of the six-foot-tall fence, landing in the soft grass and crouching down immediately for cover.

There was no way anyone could have heard him unless they had the same super sensitive hearing he had. Looking down, the sight of massive furry paws where his hands should have been was distracting, but not enough to throw him off track. It's just a trick of the mind.

Some light filtered through the gap in the curtains, revealing two silhouettes standing across from one another. They seemed to be arguing, but he couldn't make out the words, so he crawled ahead and crouched underneath the window.

"She's just a human. We can't do this!" a younger sounding male voice whispered.

"She said this was the place. You've got to learn to follow orders, soldier!" this voice sounded older, more authoritative.

"But..."

"Decide quickly where your loyalties lie. With the Sons or the scum we're hunting. Because if you're not with me now, I'm going to take it very personally."

"Fine. Let's do this."

Shit, what exactly is it they're planning on doing with Leah? This didn't seem to be a regular break-in. For whatever reason, these people targeted Leah's house on purpose. But why?

"All right missy, you're coming with us," the younger guy barked.

Leah let out a muffled squeal.

"If you behave, we can take the gag off. Understand?"

She didn't react, or at least, she wasn't vocal about it. There was a pause.

"What do you want from me?" Leah whispered at last.

"Don't play dumb. You must have known this could happen - that we could turn up."

"I don't know what you're talking about!" Leah argued.

"Stop it, or I'll gag you again."

What the hell was all this about? Had Leah been hiding something? Perhaps there was a reason she'd abruptly moved out of the city and into this house. Not that it mattered, of course, Matt owed it to her, as well as himself to do something about this.

He got up just far enough to be able to see inside. Luckily, the darkness gave him a good amount of cover so the intruders inside wouldn't be able to spot him.

The two men stood off to one side, again discussing something or other, then the older one headed out the bedroom door, leaving behind his uncertain companion, and Leah, of course.

This was Matt's chance.

He got up and checked the window. He could just

about get one of his claws underneath the bottom edge. It would give; he was sure of it.

Given the element of surprise was on his side, he could make it. He had to make it.

Matt gave it his all, pulling at the window, which opened up even more easily than he'd foreseen and jumped into Leah's bedroom in one swift move. The man swung around; his face turning white as a sheet when he saw Matt.

"Fu-" he exclaimed, but Matt didn't give him the chance to finish, instead disabling him with a strong blow to the chest.

Then he turned to check on Leah, who looked equally shocked. She was even more beautiful close up than he had dared to imagine. If only the circumstances of their first proper meeting had been better.

"Please..." she whispered, her voice completely choked with fear. "Shit."

"Don't worry. I'll keep you safe," Matt said, but it was no use. He could tell from Leah's expression that his words weren't getting through to her at all. In fact, she'd started trembling all over. Seeing her this way cut right into his core.

He wanted to console her, to convince her that everything would be fine now. But there was no time to worry about that, because the door swung open, revealing the guy who'd seemed to be in charge of the strange operation.

"I knew it! This is the right house," he said only partly triumphantly, while holding up both his hands as if surrendering and backing out of the doorway into the hallway. His right hand twitched subtly before reaching for something. Matt didn't want to find out what, instead charging for the guy and pinning him down onto the ground.

The second kidnapper hit the floor so fast it knocked him out instantly.

Two down, one to go.

But Matt never got the chance to take care of the third guy. Instead, he was faced with the last thing he ever expected to see: Another great big brown bear, flanked by a smaller, blackish one. What the hell?

"Matthew Argyle, I presume?" the first bear seemed to say. How ludicrous. Bears can't talk. And how would he know his name anyway? This wasn't even Matt's house.

"Uhh..." That was all Matt could utter. What in the world was going on? Had he finally lost his mind completely?

"Looks like we got here just in time," the smaller one, a female, remarked. Her snippy tone rubbed Matt the wrong way, no matter how bizarre the situation was.

"I had it under control," Matt stammered.

"I can see that," the female responded.

"Please come with us," the bigger male said. He had an inherent authority hanging around him, but Matt wasn't so easily deterred.

"I've got to check on Leah," Matt explained as if that would make these two figments of his imagination vanish into thin air, allowing him to focus once more on the task at hand.

But they didn't vanish. Instead, they exchanged a look and almost instantly morphed into humans. Very naked humans.

The man snipped his fingers, and, from the other end of the hallway, someone flung a couple of bundles of clothes at them, which they swiftly put on.

*Jeez, how many of them were there?*

"You're just going to stay like this, are you?" the

woman, who looked a lot less distracting now that she was wearing a pair of cargo pants and a black pullover, asked.

"Who are you people exactly? And why are you here?" Matt responded, ignoring her odd question.

"I guess a thank you was too much to ask. Be glad we came when we did, or these clowns-" The woman nodded at the kidnapper who was still lying at Matt's paws. "Would have taken you and the human woman as soon as their backup arrived."

Backup? What the hell was she talking about?

"Oh, you didn't think it was just the two of them and another standing guard, did you?" she asked.

"That's enough. Matthew. You'll have questions. We'll answer them to the best of our knowledge, but only once we get back to base. Margaret here will ensure your lady friend is all taken care of. All right?" the man took over.

"Okay..." Matt frowned. Margaret, eh? That name really didn't suit her; it seemed too old fashioned.

"I'm Henry, by the way. Let's go then."

The black-haired woman, Margaret, resolutely marched off into Leah's bedroom, and soon the two of them could be heard talking. Perhaps these guys were real then, not imagined.

Matt finally gave in and allowed himself to be escorted through the hallway and lounge and out of the house, where a bunch of dejected looking skinheads stood around with their wrists tied together, surrounded by even more big men and a couple of women wearing black commando gear.

Every single head turned in Matt's direction when he stepped out into the street. It was nightmarish, and hair-no, fur-raising.

"That's really him, isn't it?" someone whispered behind Matt.

"Yeah. He's been missing for so long everyone thought he was dead."

Were they talking about him? How did these people even know anything about him? He needed to find out exactly the how and whys of today's events; that was the only reason he was going along with these people. And Leah... he couldn't wait to come back and talk to her. In person.

# CHAPTER SIX

———— ♦ ————

It had to have been a dream. A crazy, surreal, impossible dream.

Leah kept watching the woman- she'd introduced herself as Margaret - as she spoke, but her words weren't getting through to her at all.

One moment, Leah had been remotely watching a movie with Matt, the next all hell had broken loose. Who the hell were the two men who had come into her house and tried to take her? What possible reason could they have had? They seemed to know something she didn't.

And who were the people who intervened, including this Margaret woman who had stayed back to talk to her? She'd introduced herself as being from some kind of covert police task force, but Leah found that hard to believe.

"It's strange, how our mind tries to trick us, isn't it?" Margaret asked.

"What? Oh, yeah, very strange," Leah mumbled, averting her gaze from Margaret's prying eyes.

Margaret continued to speak, and Leah made sure to nod and voice her agreement in all the right places. She was being handled, just like her supervisor in her old job used to do when she wanted Leah to take on more work for the same pay. Much like her supervisor, Leah could tell Margaret wasn't used to having someone disagree with her either, so it would be easier - and quicker - to just agree to anything she said while letting her own thoughts run rampant inside her head.

If the entire home invasion part of tonight wasn't bad

enough, Leah couldn't get one particular image out of her head. The bear.

She'd been terrified when the bear came in - after all, who wouldn't be - but there was also something strangely familiar about it. She could swear there was something familiar in its eyes, something that had had a calming effect on her...But how could that be? She'd never seen a bear before, well, not outside of a zoo anyway, so how could she possibly have recognized it?

And then, if that wasn't weird enough, the bear hadn't attacked her. Instead, it had gone straight for the intruders in her house. As though it was trying to protect her. That wasn't possible either, though, was it?

After what felt like hours of nodding her head like a bobblehead to all sorts of explanations of stress induced hallucinations, Margaret finally left Leah to be alone with her thoughts.

Still shaky with the after-effects of her insane ordeal, Leah headed straight for the kitchen to make herself a cup of tea. No, better yet, something a bit stronger. The morning was early enough that it still counted as night, or at least, that's what she told herself. Propriety be damned; she needed a drink.

As she poured herself a stiff one - Scotch that had been in her possession for much too long, she realized there was something else she needed as much, if not more. Her phone.

Matt would have seen the commotion outside her home and be desperate for some kind of update. Leah knew she would be if she were in his place.

Drink in hand, Leah rushed back into her bedroom. Where was the damn thing? Under the bed! That's where she had it last. She got down on all fours and found it soon after. No unread messages. Nothing.

314

What the hell? The last thing she sent to him was a call for help. Wasn't he, at least, a little concerned?

Sure, their relationship - if you could call it that - wasn't exactly traditional, but she'd felt that he cared about her at least a little. Had she been kidding herself?

Had it all been in her head? The little flirtations, the bond she'd felt toward him?

Then again, he wasn't anything like her previous lovers. He wasn't really normal, strictly speaking. Could she expect him to react like a normal guy would to an extra-ordinary situation like this? Perhaps not.

Leah took a deep breath, and a generous sip of the burning amber liquid she'd absentmindedly poured into a mug rather than a glass and decided to be the bigger person. She'd send him a message then.

I guess you're wondering what went on here tonight, eh?

Send.

Leah stared down at her phone for much too long, but nothing happened. There was no response, no matter how long she tried to hypnotize it.

Goddamnit. She had moved to this place in search for a simpler life. Two weeks in, she'd been the victim of a home invasion, come face-to-face with a life-sized bear inside her own home, undergone a weird brain-washing exercise courtesy of Margaret, who mysteriously showed up just around the same time as the bear.

And, to top it off, she'd developed a one-sided crush on someone she can't have. She had completely misread that situation. Bloody brilliant.

She threw the phone down onto the sofa in disgust and headed back into the kitchen. Through the windows, she could see that even the last one of the blacked out vans that had not too long ago been parked up outside her house had left, presumably taking Margaret with it. Good riddance.

As Leah poured herself another double, she wasn't shaken anymore; she was furious.

---◆---

An insomniac at the best of times, Leah hadn't even tried to go to bed that night, so come 8 o'clock, she was still up. The buzz from the two shots of Scotch had worn off for the most part, and last night's events seemed very long ago.

She began doing the one thing that usually seemed to help when she had some issues to work through in her head: cook up a new batch of product. Funny, how she hadn't attempted to cook a meal for herself from scratch, but thought nothing of combining all these strange ingredients to produce soap.

She'd been telling herself for a while now that a new scent was required but just hadn't found the right combination of fragrances yet. Perhaps today was the day she'd figure it out.

Leah laid out all her essential oils, pairing them up in groupings she hadn't yet tried together, and put on a pair of gloves.

Although December had just begun, she didn't want to do anything Christmassy, so she quickly pushed aside the spicier scents.

Something fresh, new. That's what she was after. Like newly cut grass or the first flowers of spring. Daffodils? Why not...

She was just getting into the spirit of things when the doorbell rang and dragged her back into the real world. God. Hopefully, it wasn't that Margaret woman again.

Leah took a deep breath and rushed out to open the door only to find her other neighbor, Carrie, waiting outside. Just great. She'd probably seen the activity outside her door at night as well.

Matt had said she was a gossip - though, screw whatever Matt had told her.

"Hi!" Leah greeted Carrie with an attempt at a wide smile.

"Hey, Leah, how's it going?" Carrie couldn't quite disguise her curiosity. Her eyes clearly darted back and forth between Leah and the hallway behind her, as though she was looking for something or someone.

"Yeah, not too bad, considering. I suppose you must have seen a bit of what went on here at night?" Leah said, hoping to speed things up by steering the conversation in the direction she expected Carrie wanted to head in anyway.

"I did wake up to an awful ruckus outside. Cars pulling in, people running back and forth. I hope everything is okay?"

"Someone broke in; can you believe it?"

"No way! In this neighborhood?"

"That's what I thought. I still don't know what they were after. It was lucky the police showed up when they did, or I don't know what might have happened," Leah said.

Carrie's eyes widened at her mention of the police.

"So it was the police outside? I didn't hear sirens or anything."

"Standard procedure apparently, when the intruders are still in the house," Leah explained. "I was hiding under the bed when they came in." There was no way she was going to tell Carrie the truth, but she felt she had to give her something in order to get rid of her.

"Oh, my word! You must have been terrified!"

"Yeah, it was quite something. Say, you haven't had issues like this before, have you?"

"No, nothing like that. This has always been a very safe area," Carrie mumbled, obviously impressed by Leah's version of events. "Well, do let me know if you need anything. I'd better be off making sure the kids are dressed for school..."

Good. Leah smiled and nodded at Carrie as she said her goodbyes. Hopefully, that would be the first and last time she had to tell that particular story to anyone.

Leah wrapped her arms around herself against the chill still coming through her open front door. She'd changed things a bit, but her new version of events was so much more plausible than what had actually gone down, it actually felt a bit real.

She glanced over to the left, in the direction of Matt's place. Unbelievable that he still hasn't made contact. After everything that had happened.

Leah took a couple of steps outside and peeped across the low hedge separating their houses. His place looked dark - not that that was unusual - but just a bit darker than normal. As though he wasn't even home. But how could that be, when he himself had admitted to her that he never left his house?

Well anyway, if he wanted to hide himself away from her also, that was his problem, not hers. Leah took a deep breath, suppressing the sting in her chest that had first developed hours before when she'd messaged him and not had a response.

She shook her head and walked back inside, returning to the neatly lined up bottles of essential oils she'd left in her otherwise pristine kitchen. Sniffing the various combinations one by one, none of them seemed quite right.

No matter how hard she tried to concentrate, it was no use, though. Angry or hurt, she couldn't stop herself from feeling something. Something that affected her ability to work.

Alone. Yes, that was it. Out here in this new place that had turned out to be not as safe as she'd hoped; she suddenly felt very alone.

# CHAPTER SEVEN

———— ◆ ————

After a short drive in the back of a windowless van, Matt reached the supposed base; an old warehouse that looked somewhat like an impromptu command center from any generic espionage movie. Were these guys for real?

There was a lot of activity. Blindfolded and handcuffed men were being led through the warehouse and locked away somewhere in another part of the building. At the same time, the entire team of people involved in the action - they identified themselves as "the Alliance" - deposited weapons, communication equipment, and other items on their respective desks.

Matt took a seat at an unoccupied table and just observed. It was like a strange dream, like he had found himself in the middle of a Hollywood movie, and he was the only one aware that none of this was in any way normal.

As Matt looked around, his brain tried to make sense of it all. These people were like him. He'd seen it.

That meant that either all of them were as crazy as he was, or that his self-identified delusions were true. He'd convinced himself that the things he experienced were in his head for so long, it was near impossible to accept the opposite.

And what about Leah? She didn't know anything about this stuff, so she had to be even more confused than he was right now. To think he burst into her bedroom fully shifted... No wonder she'd been shocked. And he couldn't do a bloody thing about it!

"It's really you. I can't believe it," a voice spoke behind

him.

Matt jumped up from his chair and turned to find a man with a vaguely familiar face stand before him. He reminded him of a very distant past. Could it be? He wanted to say something but couldn't find the right words.

"Matty! Shit, do you even remember me?" The man smiled, but his eyes didn't look happy.

"Jamie?" Matt asked after a few long seconds.

Relief washed over Jamie's face. "You do recognize me. I was worried. It's been such a long time, since..."

"What the hell is going on here?" Matt asked, but Jamie didn't get the chance to answer.

"Mr. Brown, is it? How wonderful to make your acquaintance." A slightly sinister looking middle-aged man wearing a suit reminiscent of 1920s gangster movies offered his hand to Matt. Where the hell had he come from? ? And how did he know his former name, a name he'd pretty much forgotten about himself?

"Blacke. Adrian Blacke."

"Uhh, my name's Matt Argyle, actually," Matt mumbled while exchanging a puzzled look with Jamie, who didn't seem too happy to see the strange man.

"It's so good to see a lost one of ours returned to his own people, don't you think, Abbott-" Why was he referring to Jamie by a different name as well? "Despite the trials of your difficult childhood, I trust you'll feel at home in no time at all." The man, Blacke, flashed a row of white, be-it crooked teeth.

"My childhood was fine," Matt remarked - his troubles didn't start until around his seventeenth birthday - but Blacke wasn't listening. Instead, he waved at Jamie, taking him aside and leaving Matt standing on his own just out of earshot.

Matt observed the conversation while instinctively

reaching into his right pocket. Empty. Damn, he should ask Jamie about his phone.

As the chat in front of Matt went on, it became obvious that Jamie didn't like this Blacke character much at all, and Matt couldn't blame him. The man had a strange vibe around him which Matt didn't appreciate either.

It took a few more minutes for Jamie to return, sporting a tense expression on his face.

"Is everything okay?" Matt asked.

"Blacke wants you to stay here for a while until I can arrange something for you locally."

"Arrange what?"

"A place, whatever. I told him you could just come back to Edinburgh with me, but-"

"Why do I need a new place? And what were those skinheads trying to do exactly?"

Jamie scrutinized him for a moment. "You mean, you want to go back? To the house they held you prisoner in?"

"What are you talking about? I wasn't held prisoner anywhere!" Matt felt himself getting riled up, causing his skin to tingle again, ready for another transformation.

"But they took you, from the beach, when we were kids," Jamie argued.

"That may be so, but Molly raised me as her own. I was never locked up or anything." Deep breaths. Calm down. Don't tear this new change of clothes as well.

"Then why didn't you try to escape, to come back to us?" Jamie asked.

"Dude, I was eight. After Mom and Dad died-"

"What do you mean Mom and Dad died?! They're not dead!"

Matt was shocked into silence for a moment. "That was a lie... Of course. A lie to get me to go along with them willingly." He sighed, relieved to feel his muscles relax before the unthinkable would happen again. "Okay, I think we have a lot of catching up to do."

"Indeed," Jamie agreed.

They didn't get the chance for it just yet, because, at that moment, the large bear/human who had intervened at the house turned up. Henry.

"Matt." Henry offered his hand. "Good to see you in your usual form."

Matt accepted the man's handshake and nodded. It felt good to be back to his normal self as well.

"I see your family reunion is well underway. I must say, when Jamie came to me with the information that you'd been located, I wasn't sure what to expect, but I never expected to capture so many of our enemies as well."

Enemies? Oh, he must be talking about the guys who had come to take Leah.

"Yeah, I'm not quite sure what went on there. I was hoping you guys had some insights to share."

"Perhaps we'll know more after our interrogations." Henry shrugged off Matt's question. *Just great.*

But, of course, that wasn't the only thing Matt was keen to learn about. As soon as Henry walked off again, he took the time to question Jamie about anything and everything that popped into his head.

That was how he found out that he was indeed a bear. A werebear - as was almost everyone in the Alliance, except for the odd werewolf here and there who had joined the fight. He learned about who the Alliance really was, that Jamie was in charge of a group of them in Edinburgh, and about their shared enemy, the Sons of Domnall. Slowly but surely the new information allowed Matt to piece together what must have happened to him when he was just a kid.

The one thing he couldn't figure out was how Leah had

gotten involved in this mess. Nothing in her reaction to his shifted self suggested she knew anything about what was going on. Even the main intruder's reaction to seeing Matt's bear form suggested it was him they were after, not her, which made very little sense. If it was the Sons of Domnall who had arranged for Matt's abduction as a child, then why did they break into the wrong house?

"It goes without saying that it's best not to repeat any of this to anyone. I mean anyone human," Jamie said after answering Matt's last question.

"Why?"

"It's one of our most important rules. If the human world came to know about us, well... you can imagine what would happen. That's why we don't even tell our own children until they're old enough to understand."

Matt certainly could imagine people would be shocked; Leah certainly had been. Shit, surely he could be honest with *her*, couldn't he? Then again, if he had known about any of this, his adult life might have been very different. It was only because of all the secrecy surrounding their kind that he had assumed all of this was in his head and started to pull away from everyone around him.

Perhaps it would have been better to get everything out in the open. It might help someone in his position... Still, he wasn't sure he could trust Jamie with everything going on in his head. He was his brother, sure, but he didn't really know him anymore, did he?

"So what if one of us, a bear, for example, hypothetically, were to get involved with a regular human? Then what?"

Jamie gave him a suspicious look. "I see. The woman whose house you were in..."

"Theoretically," Matt emphasized.

"It wouldn't be wise for someone like us to get

involved with one of them. It would be reckless and stupid."

Matt heard Jamie's words, but his tone didn't sound convinced. There was something his brother wasn't telling him.

"The only way to be with a human is to live like a human. To deny the bear inside you. Of course, it tends to want to claw its way to the surface in a lot of us, so I'm not sure that would really work."

"Uhuh."

Jamie looked around the room, and then leaned in closer to Matt.

"How serious is it?"

"As I said, I was just giving an example."

"Bullshit, I can see it in your eyes. I know-" Jamie paused when one of the females on the team walked past. "I'm not supposed to tell you this, but to hell with it, you're my little brother, and nobody else can guide you right now... I get it. Really, I do."

Matt waited while Jamie took a deep breath and continued. "We're in the same boat, you and I. I too have developed feelings for a human woman. It happens. And it is unwise like I said. If Blacke found out..."

"Blacke, right." Matt scanned the room, looking for the man in the three-piece suit. "He wouldn't approve?"

"We'd be in a whole lot of trouble. The Alliance council is very strict when it comes to protecting our secrets and with it the safety of our people. They would stop at nothing..."

"Okay, so what do we do?"

"Nothing. Do what your gut tells you to do, but for fuck's sake, don't tell anyone anything about what you're up to. By now Margaret will have assessed the situation, and probably convinced your girlfriend that she's been seeing things, and none of it really happened. You'd better hope she agreed to that version of events."

Damn. Matt dreaded to think what would happen if she didn't.

"What did you do? You told your girl about who you really are?" Matt asked.

"It's a long story; she already knew. But Blacke must never find out."

"I understand." Clearly, there was a lot left to be said, but this wasn't the time or the place. First, Matt had to focus on getting out of here without setting off too many alarm bells. He had to get back to Leah at any cost.

Suddenly, in just one evening, his entire life had changed. He'd left his house for the first time in years, found out about his true nature, and come face-to-face with the woman he'd been obsessing about for weeks. Finally, there was a chance there, a hope. If only she could accept him.

"Matt. I know what you're thinking, but you're not ready," Jamie interrupted his thoughts.

"What?"

"You've first got to learn how to control this thing. They'll never let you out there if you randomly shift without intending to. It's too risky. You could expose all of us."

He didn't want to hear it, but Jamie was right. He had to sort himself out. He could only hope that by the end of it, Leah would still be there, waiting for him.

# CHAPTER EIGHT

———◆———

The room was cold, uninviting, which was exactly the point. Matt felt his skin tighten with every breath, and it was difficult, no, near impossible to stay in control.

But Jamie didn't let up. He kept goading him, kept attacking. It had started off as a simulated boxing match just like yesterday's training, but today Jamie had taken things just a little bit further.

"You've got to withstand the urge, little brother," he taunted him while stepping forward, trying to get a right hook in. He was wearing gloves, but Matt's instincts didn't know that.

Sure enough, as soon as the leather hit the side of his face, Matt's back started to sprout fur, and a growl escaped his lips.

"That's not holding back, in fact, that's pretty much the opposite," Jamie remarked.

Matt balled his fists, but the feeling didn't subside. How could anyone battle the red fog that tried its best to overwhelm him? It didn't make sense.

"Take a deep breath, focus on something that relaxes you," Jamie added.

Matt closed his eyes and inhaled sharply. The cold air stung against the inside of his nostrils, reminding him of just the place. Applecross Bay, where they used to come as kids. The air was fresh there too.

The sensation subsided, so he opened his eyes again, just in time to see Jamie's other gloved fist fly at his face. That did it. Matt's body twisted and morphed, and within a split second, he was no longer the half-naked man, shivering against the cold of his cell, but a magnificent beast, towering over Jamie's still human self.

"Enough!" Matt growled, his right paw raised in the air as though he was about to strike.

Jamie lifted his gloves up in defeat. "Fine. How about we take a break, huh?"

Almost instantly, Matt's limbs and torso contracted again, and the fur made way for smooth skin once more.

"I gotta tell you, if you keep going through clothes like that, we're going to run out," Jamie remarked, nodding down at the pile of torn fabric on the floor.

*Damn* . Matt averted his gaze. He just wasn't getting it. He knew it was just practice. He knew his brother posed no real threat, and yet his body refused to believe it.

"Tell me again how long it took you to get the hang of this?" Matt asked.

"Pfft... I don't know. It's been a while."

"Do you remember when it first happened? The change, I mean."

"I think I was about fifteen. Dad had just started training me a couple of months earlier. I couldn't wait to finally shift. It seemed like the most exciting thing in the world to me. To finally grow up," Jamie said, a wistful smile playing on his lips.

"Oh yeah? I can tell you it freaked me the hell out when it first happened to me."

"That's just because you didn't know."

"Yeah, and it hurt like hell too," Matt added.

"Well, that's there. Those early days were pretty painful."

Jamie handed him another pair of track pants, which Matt accepted with a nod. He put them on and sat down on the floor resting his head in his hands. It just wasn't right. He was in there, being held essentially against his will, and in trying to fight the exact thing he'd been suppressing for all of his adult life, he'd shifted more often in the past forty-eight hours than he had done in years.

And meanwhile, he couldn't get one specific image out of his head.

Leah's expression when she'd seen him in her bedroom. The sheer terror in her eyes. It hurt, knowing he'd added to her ordeal by bursting in there looking like a big furry monster. He had to fix it somehow. But how could he do that while he was stuck in here?

"Anyway, how long? How long do you think it'll be before I can go back home?" Matt asked.

Jamie frowned at him, his head cocked to one side just like he used to do when they were kids, and Matt said something stupid. Just that look made him want to transform all over again and roar.

"You're not ready."

"Fine, I'm not ready, but you gotta gimme something! I've got responsibilities, and I'm losing my mind here," Matt argued.

"Bullshit, you've got a human girlfriend who is under close watch by Margaret and the rest of the team ever since you recklessly exposed the existence of our entire race to her," Jamie retorted.

"How was I supposed to know what I could and couldn't expose when nobody bloody told me what I was, huh?"

They stared each other down, two grown men who were bickering pretty much like how they used to fifteen years ago. In the end, it was Jamie who backed down.

"Look, I can understand the situation you're in, but you've got to understand that these people-" Jamie gestured at the door of Matt's cell; the main Alliance workspace was just on the other side. "Are scrutinizing your and her every move. If you make contact, you'll both be in trouble. You don't want that, do you?"

Matt sighed. No, he didn't want that at all. But he had to make sure Leah was all right.

"How about you focus on your training," Jamie insisted. "And I'll check in on Margaret every so often to figure out what's happening with your human."

Matt nodded. Okay. That was a fair compromise, for now.

Although he'd been at the base and interacted a bit with members of his own species for days now, it was still weird to hear Jamie talk about humans like they were so different.

Matt, who had grown up around only humans, was, of course, painfully aware of how badly he'd fitted in with them, but he still couldn't consider them the *other*. To him, it was Henry, Margaret, the rest of the team - even Jamie - who still seemed alien.

"And how about this. I've finally received the green light from the Alliance Council to let Mom and Dad know you've been found. They're thrilled, obviously, and can't wait for us all to get together once Blacke signs off on it."

Matt felt his heartbeat speed up. The revelation that his, no, *their* parents were still alive after all these years had been a good one, obviously, but he couldn't shake the worry that meeting him would be more of a disappointment to them than a joyous reunion.

He hadn't exactly grown into the sort of person - bear - they would have wanted him to.

"What's up? you don't look too happy to hear that?" Jamie asked.

"Nah, I am," Matt said, but realized immediately he'd failed to hide the doubt in his tone. "I just don't think I'm all that, if you know what I mean."

"Shit, are you kidding me? You're alive, which is pretty much all they've wanted all these years. And finally, I can show face at home again as well."

Matt had to grin. "Yeah, after over a decade of being the son who lost their other son?"

"Something like that." Jamie shot him a wry smile.

It was a rare thing, to recognize weakness in Jamie. He put on a hard front, but this little glimpse made Matt wonder if perhaps he wasn't the only Brown boy who had grown up a little messed up.

"So. Ready to get back to your training? The sooner you get the hang of this, the sooner we can all get back to our normal lives," Jamie said.

"Sure, just one more thing. Is that why you go by Abbot?"

"I didn't want to have to go through the same story over and over again. In these circles, everyone has heard of the Brown abduction case..."

Matt remembered how weird it was to feel everyone's stares when he'd first been faced with the Alliance team. "Fair enough."

"You know what?" Jamie asked.

"What?"

"You and I just had an entire argument without you sprouting fur or claws. That's not bad at all." Jamie grinned at him, then, without prior warning charged at him, pushing Matt against the wall with a loud thud.

It hurt, and the concrete might as well be covered in ice, but instead of responding with aggression, Matt focused on another image. Another source of calm. The image of Leah balancing an impossible number of little parcels in her arms on the way to her car.

He had to get through this. And if Jamie indeed managed to keep an eye on what Margaret was up to, perhaps it wouldn't turn out so bad.

She was fine; she had to be. Leah was a strong woman, and once he got back home, he'd explain everything to her.

Matt saw the next blow coming from the corner of his eye and ducked out of the way, causing Jamie to hit his fist into the wall.

"Damn," Jamie growled, as he turned around.

A glimmer of something different appeared in his eyes. A fiery amber, which Matt had only seen a few times before: in his own eyes in the mirror, when he'd felt his sanity slipping away.

"Gotcha! How does it feel to be pissed off, bro? Looks like you're very close to losing control yourself now," Matt quipped.

Jamie frowned. "Very funny, just you wait 'til I get you again, little one."

Matt scoffed. Little one? Matt was at least as tall, if not taller than Jamie was. And they were both built, more so than regular humans.

He stood his ground for the next attack, both his feet planted firmly on the ground. This time, when Jamie hit him, he felt it rattle his bones despite the gloves. He wanted to turn; he wanted to retaliate so badly, but he didn't budge. Only the slightest flutter passed over his skin, its texture changing only for a moment, before morphing back into its usual, human appearance.

"Better. And again," Jamie ordered.

Matt took a deep breath, fighting with every fiber in his body against the survival instinct that had developed in their kind over thousands of years. It's common wisdom in the human world, not to suppress your emotions, and yet that's exactly what this training was about.

How stupid this whole secrecy thing was, anyway. Everyone was afraid of the unknown, so if the objective was not to create fear in humans, wouldn't it actually make sense to be transparent?

None of this would have ever happened if people had just been honest with Matt while growing up. And now he had to pay for it, in this cold, dark, horrible place, with his very own brother trying to rile him up.

Ridiculous.

Matt's jaw tightened as he withstood another one of Jamie's assaults.

"Good job. Keep this up, and we'll be able to progress to the next stage: outdoor training," Jamie remarked.

# CHAPTER NINE

———◆———

For days, Leah had been keeping too much of an eye on the house next door - Matt's house. And yet, she hadn't seen the slightest curtain twitch or sign of movement at all.

It was nerve wracking.

By Thursday, his weekly grocery delivery came and went, and his door didn't open for that either.

That was the last straw for Leah, who had started imagining all sorts of horror scenarios.

What if he hadn't been ignoring her, but something bad had happened to him? What if he was unwell or worse and unable to respond to her repeated messages - or the doorbell? What if more of the same people who had come into her house to take her, had also broken into his place and successfully abducted him before those weird black commando gear people had turned up? But to what end?

It just didn't make sense, and not knowing where Matt was or what he was up to was driving her crazy.

So finally, before the delivery van from the local supermarket had even pulled out of their road, she picked up the phone for one last message.

"If you don't respond, I'm reporting you missing with the police."

She bit her lips and waited, tears stinging in her eyes. How long she should wait for, she wasn't sure, but it was all she could think to do.

When the phone buzzed, about a minute later, she got so startled she almost dropped it to the floor.

"Don't do that. Everything will be explained in time."

From terrified, Leah reverted to being angry. So all this

time he had just simply chosen not to answer her! The nerve. And what a weird, impersonal reply as well!

Fine. In that case, she didn't need to concern herself with this bullshit anymore.

Leah threw the phone onto the counter and started work on the order she should have been focusing on instead of obsessing about Matt.

———◆———

Day after day went by, and Leah kept on feeling low. It was like all the joy had been sapped from her, like nothing could make her smile.

And all because of a guy she hadn't even properly met.

It wasn't that she didn't have work to do and just set idle all day. Not at all. She had plenty on her plate. It was just that after a whole day of keeping busy, she had nothing to look forward to anymore. That's what she told herself anyway.

She had never had a large friend circle, only keeping a select few people close. Over the years of working at the call center, with all those night shifts, those few friends had drifted apart as well, so she'd mainly interacted with her colleagues.

In this new place, she had nobody. She certainly wasn't about to count Carrie as a new friend, no matter how often she chose to drop by for a chat - something that had been happening every other day or so since Matt's disappearance.

Leah hadn't told Carrie much about her contact with Matt, only that she'd left him a note to say hello. But for some reason, Carrie must have been suspecting something. That was why she kept coming over, kept prying, however subtly for information about Matt.

It was weird.

Still, the days kept on passing drearily, and Leah started to get used to the emptiness left behind by the uninhabited house next door.

On the tenth night, another strange, windowless van pulled into the street. It was late, so the neighbors would probably be asleep, but not Leah. She was making herself a hot chocolate in the kitchen and happened to be looking out the window when it happened.

The people in black were back.

She took a sip and observed a strange man she'd never seen before get out of the driver's side door and walk to the other side, opening the passenger door for someone else.

Matt.

Leah held her breath.

He was back.

The other man patted Matt on the shoulder, and then they embraced for but a second. The whole scene was eerie.

They seemed so similar. Their hair, their frames, even the way they carried themselves, as though no burden was too heavy to carry, no obstacle too tall to cross.

Her heartbeat sped up against her will.

What did she care if he came back? Matt had been toying with her all along, and especially since that night these people had first shown up.

Leah swallowed the lump that had developed in her throat upon seeing him.

That was when he turned around, and she panicked. Her kitchen was lit up like a stage while the street was much darker. He'd be able to see her much clearer than she could see him.

*Shit, shit, shit!* She quickly jumped into action and left, pretending to herself that she'd never even noticed any movement outside the window.

He'd assume she hadn't seen him, right?

*Way to play it cool, you idiot,* Leah chided herself.

After leaving the kitchen, she took a round of her living room and hall, making sure the extra dead bolts she'd had installed were securely locked, and the new alarm system engaged, then hid herself away in her bedroom. Although she wouldn't be able to sleep just yet - especially not now that she knew Matt was back home - there was no need to draw unnecessary attention to herself either.

Leah got into bed and held on to her steaming hot mug with both hands, yet chills kept running down her spine. Why was she so nervous all of a sudden? He was just a guy. Just like all the other guys, who take what they want without for once considering how the other person felt.

Her phone sat beside her, lifeless on the wooden bedside table, practically taunting her. He wouldn't try to get in touch immediately, would he? *Rubbish!* And she wouldn't answer him if he did either.

She put the mug down and brusquely shoved the mobile underneath the pillow beside her.

There was no way, absolutely no way that she would keep on sitting here staring at it, waiting for the buzz of a message. Not now. Not after all that.

———◆———

Morning came, and Leah felt like she'd barely slept, just sort of drifted in and out of a dreamless half-consciousness that hadn't provided much rest.

Matt was still there, after his late night arrival. She didn't know how she knew, but she could feel his presence nearby.

Despite her struggle to get through the night, she did feel somewhat lighter today, after nearly two weeks of having a dark cloud hang over her.

She'd been wondering what if he came back? What if he wanted to get in touch? He hadn't even sent her a single message. Knowing that he wasn't interested, perhaps could give her some closure and enable her to move on. That had to be it. She was feeling a bit better because she could close off that chapter of her life, not at all because he was back home.

It was still quite early, but there wasn't much of a point staying in bed if she couldn't sleep anyway, so Leah got herself up and into the kitchen, ready to start her day. The forecast had foretold clear weather, and she was hoping to finish work early so that she could catch a few rays sitting on her living room sofa before dusk would inevitably set in at around four-thirty in the afternoon. This time of year, the days were depressingly short, so any sunlight was precious.

While waiting for the kettle to boil, a rustling noise came from the front door, like something being pushed through the letterbox. Six o'clock was way too early for the postman, wasn't it?

She wrapped herself up tighter in her oversized knitted cardigan and left the kitchen to investigate. Indeed there it was, a little parcel on her welcome mat.

Leah picked it up and immediately opened the front door to get a glimpse of whoever had delivered it, but the street just looked dark and empty. A gust of cold wind made its way into the house through the open doorway, so she shut it again almost as quickly.

She weighed the packet in her hand. It was small, about the size of two small juice cartons taped together, but much lighter than that.

# SCOTTISH WEREBEAR: A NEW BEGINNING

*Should she open it?*

Her heart beat a little faster while deciding on her next move. She didn't like the idea of having a random stranger deliver something through her letterbox. What if there was something dangerous inside? Then again, it hardly weighed much, how bad could it be?

She returned to the kitchen and poured herself a cup of tea first. Nothing good can come from a decision made before the first cup of tea, as her dad used to say.

Once ready, she carried both the parcel and the steamy beverage with her into the living room and put both down onto the coffee table.

As cautious as she wanted to be, there was no way curiosity wouldn't get the better of her eventually. She might as well open the thing right away, rather than torture herself any further.

She peeled away the first layer of brown tape with her fingernail, then quickly unraveled the rest. Underneath, a layer of bubble wrap, and then a sealed cardboard box. If the picture on the front was anything to go by, it was a basic mobile phone.

Why would someone send her a phone? And for free, no less.

As she opened the seal and lifted the lid off the small box, a piece of paper fell out the side with a short message scrawled on it.

"Your phone is being monitored. Use this one instead."

Oh damn. It was from Matt, wasn't it?

She wasn't sure what to think. Had he lost his mind completely? What made him think that he could just waltz back into her life after vanishing without explanation for nearly two weeks?

That was it. She was going to give him a piece of her mind, and she might as well use the new phone to do it.

She opened the box fully and switched the gadget on. It only took a minute or so. It didn't have very many apps, or perhaps even a Wifi connection. The phone book had only one number programmed into it, labeled Matt.

Should she call? No, that would be stupid. They'd messaged back and forth plenty, but never actually spoken. Hearing his voice might just make her forget what she wanted to say.

Her moment of indecisiveness didn't last long, because the choice had already been made for her. The phone rang.

Her throat went dry when she saw the caller ID. It was Matt.

# CHAPTER TEN

———◆———

Why wasn't she picking up? It was early, but he knew she was already awake.

Matt put the phone down and scratched his head. They'd had a connection, hadn't they? Before everything went to shit, and he was taken by the Alliance for his so-called training. They'd felt something together; he'd been sure of it at the time, but now doubts were starting to develop.

He'd been away for what, little over a week? Had she dismissed him so quickly?

It made sense, in a way. He wasn't exactly a prize; he knew that.

And to make things worse, at a time when she was already scared to death, he'd climbed into her house full-bear and terrified her even further. Follow that with the Alliance's attempts at managing the situation - and their secret - by convincing her she never actually saw what she thought she saw...

No wonder she'd shut down and wanted nothing to do with him.

Or perhaps she hadn't found the phone yet. That could be the case as well. He'd seen her light on when he dropped the little packet into her letterbox, but perhaps she just hadn't picked it up and opened it yet.

He'd give it a little longer, then try again. It wasn't within him to give up on the situation so quickly, not without ruling out all other possibilities.

Matt took a deep breath and picked up his laptop. So many emails from his clients, their tone ranging from concern to anger right down to dismissal. He ought to write back to them immediately, apologize for his absence, make up some health related reason why he couldn't notify them sooner. Anything would do to salvage his reputation and get his work life back under control.

There was just one problem: none of it seemed important anymore.

He was a bear. Within the blink of an eye, he could turn and rip an attacker to shreds if he wanted to. What the hell was he doing here, typing inane reports about foreign currency fluctuations or what the latest budget would mean to small businesses? None of that stuff mattered.

Leah. She mattered to him.

He had to get in touch with her, explain everything - preferably in a way that the Alliance didn't find out about it - and make things right. Over the course of little over a week, he'd gone from never leaving his house to being stuck at the Alliance base and even heading into a nearby forest to train with Jamie outdoors.

He'd felt the reluctant rays of mid-winter sun on his face. The icy winds cut through his flesh, right to his bones.

He'd emerged from a shell he'd confined himself in for so long; it was unthinkable to just go back to the way things were.

And she - the woman who had given him the benefit of the doubt initially - was right there next door, yet so far away.

He tried her new number again, holding his breath as the phone rang. *Please, pick up!*

Then, rather than the expected recording informing him that the caller cannot be reached, there was a click and a second of static, before he finally heard a voice.

"Hello?" a female spoke softly at the other end.

He wasn't sure what to say. It was like he'd somehow drifted out of reality, and he wasn't actually on the phone with her.

"Leah?" he finally asked.

"That's me."

*Oh God*. She sounded irritated. Or nervous. Or both. He wasn't sure, not without looking at her.

"I'm so sorry," he blurted out.

"You vanished. No response to any of my messages, except just once, which was just plain odd,"

"I know. And I can explain; not that I'm trying to make excuses for any of this, I'm not..." Matt rested his forehead in his palm. How was he going to make this right?

She didn't respond immediately, just sighed.

"What did you mean they're spying on me?"

"It's a long story. Probably best we don't do this now. Who knows if they're listening in somehow, despite the new phone."

"Okay..." She didn't sound convinced.

How strange. This was the first time they'd spoken on the phone. He couldn't shake the worry that he'd say something to fuck it all up, but still her voice seemed familiar to his ear. Like he knew her way better than was possible after merely talking via Whatsapp for a couple of weeks.

"I know it doesn't seem like it right now, but I really care about you. I just hope you'll give me the chance to make things right," he said.

She sighed again, and the thought that he'd hurt and disappointed her affected him deeply.

"I'm not someone you can toy with. Just know that."

Her words stung even more. Matt closed his eyes and tried to focus, but his emotions were all over the place. He

LORELEI MOONE

had to do something more than this. Something compelling, that would show her the real him.

"I wouldn't do that. Please believe me."

"If you say so."

While he was away, he'd thought he'd just come back and explain, but this was way harder than he could have imagined. Her resistance was making him realize how fragile relationships could be. How one misstep could unbalance everything and destroy what trust they'd built up between them.

Was there even any hope? He didn't know the first thing about love or women even. He'd been away from it all for too long to know the rules.

He needed to think, to devise a plan to make it up to her. This was too impersonal, too distant.

"May I come over?" he asked. The question surprised him as much as it might have done her.

She didn't answer straight away. Matt wondered what would be worse, if she rejected him, or if she said yes, and he had to follow through on his word.

"Let me be totally honest," she started. Her voice was still soft but also determined. "The reason I answered your call was mainly to tell you that you just can't do stuff like this. You can't just disappear and expect things to be the same when you return. Things are definitely not the same for me."

Matt wasn't sure how to respond. "Just let me explain." He pinched the bridge of his nose to ward off the growing tension in his chest.

He'd trained so hard to get back home, to get this crazy urge to shift under control. He'd been kept locked up in a cold cell, even beaten up by his own brother, but none of that came even close to the amount of stress he was under right now.

He'd enjoyed his conversations with Leah; they'd made him feel normal. Knowing that they'd talk every night had made him feel wanted. The idea of losing all that was too much to bear.

"It's not the same. I understand that," Matt had to force each word to come out calmly when all he wanted to do was scream. "Leah."

"Yes?"

He could hardly hear her response through the haze that overwhelmed his senses, the rush of blood that tried to deafen him. It took all his focus, all of his strength to keep himself from shifting.

"Words can't explain how important you are to me. Allow me to prove it."

The silence between them seemed to last forever.

"Fine. Come over," she said.

Matt breathed a sigh of relief. She was giving him a second chance, even if he realized the battle was far from won.

"Thank you. I don't want to use the front door, just in case someone's watching. Meet me out back?" he asked.

"Whatever you say." With those words, Leah hung up.

Matt stared at his phone, which had gone dark in his hand. This was it. The moment of truth. Had he learned anything from his time with Jamie? Would Leah accept his apology? Would she accept *him*?

It took a moment to force himself into action. How ridiculous. This past week, he'd learned that he could fight. That he was at least four times as strong as a normal human man, but the thought of facing this beautiful, fragile creature next door terrified him. Despite all his strength, she could defeat him with just a look, or a word even. For some reason, she had all the power and he had none.

Still, this was what it meant to be a man, probably. To be faced with something seemingly impossible, and then do it anyway.

It was now or never. If he didn't follow through on this chance to make things right with her, after having to beg for it, she'd never respect him.

He ran his hands through his hair, checking himself in the mirror once to make sure he at least looked somewhat presentable, even if he felt like a failure at the moment.

Matt brushed himself off, put the phone down on the first surface he passed by on the way to the back of the house, and unlocked the French door of the sun room.

In the still dark backyard, he could still see that everything was how he'd left it. The paving stones waiting to be laid for his new barbecue area, the soil needed to top up the flower beds. All these reminders of projects that suddenly didn't seem important anymore.

The heavy wooden table which he'd used that night to climb over the top unseen and unheard still stood next to the fence as well.

Next door, a creaking noise signaled her arrival.

He took a deep breath and jumped onto the table, then cleared the top of the fence in one swift motion, without looking across first. Seeing her beforehand would no doubt throw him off and ruin his entrance.

A split second later, he found himself on the moist lawn he'd landed on just over a week earlier. This time, the object of his affection wasn't inside under threat. Instead, she stood right there in front of him, her arms crossed and gaze averted.

Before he could even say anything to her, so many conflicting emotions filled him, he found it hard to find the right words. These weren't his feelings, not even close.

That's when she looked up at him and allowed their

eyes to meet. No, they weren't his feelings. They were hers.

He wasn't concerned anymore about losing her, or how scared he'd been about explaining things face-to-face. His fears were nothing compared to what she'd felt all the time he'd been gone.

The transformation was over before he had the chance to stop it.

# CHAPTER ELEVEN

———— ◆ ————

When Matt had just lept over the fence, Leah didn't really want to look him in the eye. It seemed to intimate and made her feel too vulnerable.

And then suddenly, she didn't have a choice anymore.

There he was: the impossible. No matter how hard her brain tried to tell her that what she'd seen wasn't real, there stood the bear from that night when everything had changed. Seeing the metamorphosis with her own two eyes answered a bunch of questions and inspired a whole host of new ones.

"What the...," Leah mumbled.

The animal which had formerly been Matt looked startled, then immediately changed back into his former self.

Leah wasn't sure whether to believe what she'd just witnessed or take the easy way out of believing everything Margaret had told her. Stress-induced hallucinations seemed like a more plausible explanation than accepting that a person had actually just managed to shift their entire body-structure around to grow into a huge bear, fur, claws and all, and then back again into a human being.

"Shit, I didn't mean for that to happen," Matt stammered, both hands up in the air as he backed away from Leah.

She wasn't sure how to respond. As shocked as she'd been seeing his other form, he was still bloody distracting standing in front of her butt-naked. It took him a moment to realize what had happened and to pick up some of the shredded clothes off the ground between them and hold them up in front of the most pertinent parts of his exposed physique.

"I knew it. I knew that what I'd seen was true. I just didn't know how to explain it," Leah whispered, her eyes now glued on his chiseled chest.

He was a beautiful man. She'd already realized that the first time she'd laid eyes on him through the fence dividing their properties. But there was something else she couldn't look away from. There were scars, bruises, and scratches, which had barely begun healing, all over his skin.

Matt turned away, which revealed that his back was covered in more of the same blemishes.

"What happened to you?" Leah asked, taking a step forward.

He looked in her direction again, and then glanced down at himself.

"Oh, this? It's nothing."

"It doesn't look like nothing." Leah reached out for him, but he retreated instantly, hitting his back against the fence.

"I'm sorry. I don't know what I was thinking, coming over here explaining everything to you. What a great job I'm doing so far," Matt mumbled.

He seemed torn. Like part of him wanted to jump over that fence and run, and yet his feet weren't cooperating.

"Well, you have my attention now," Leah remarked.

Matt looked up, and, for the first time, they both allowed themselves to truly see the other. Their eyes were glued together, with neither in a hurry to look away. It would have been easier to back down, to not let the other see the vulnerabilities written on their faces.

But there didn't seem any more need to pretend.

"I thought you just left," Leah whispered.

"I had no choice," Matt responded.

Leah couldn't be sure how she did, but she could sense that it was true. "I know that now."

"I thought I lost you," Matt seemed to say, but his lips weren't moving.

Still, it was his voice Leah heard in her head. Perhaps now she was finally losing it and hearing things that weren't there. It felt real, though, and she didn't have the energy to question it beyond that.

She'd never been the emotional type, but this past week had done its best to chip away at her defenses. And now, after everything seemed to want to work itself out, she couldn't hold back the tears anymore.

"How is this even possible?" Leah asked, though she wasn't really after an answer just yet.

*Don't cry,* Matt's eyes seemed to say.

How ridiculous, eyes can't speak. Then again, if some men can turn into bears, perhaps those same men *can* also speak with their eyes.

"I'm not crying," Leah protested, but sounded so miserable, it was actually kind of funny.

"How about we go inside?" Matt suggested, but then looked down at himself and paused. "Perhaps I should wear something first, though. This is far from appropriate."

That was enough to push Leah's buttons, and she started to giggle.

"Oh yeah, it's all fine flashing a girl in her backyard, but you best wear something to come in the house."

Matt glanced up at her again, and then a smile broke through his previously stony expression as well. "Point taken. But it'll only take a second."

With those words, Matt lept over the fence again, leaving Leah behind on her own.

She still couldn't quite believe what had happened. All

of it was so far removed from what any reasonable person would consider possible, that laughing seemed like the most sensible response. He'd seemed genuine when he apologized, when he explained that he had no choice. And as much as she might have tried to fight it, his presence had an inexplicable effect on her. Like they were somehow meant to find a way to work through their issues.

He would explain what had happened these past weeks, and she would listen. That's all. No big deal.

*And then...*

Leah blushed before she could finish the thought. By that time, Matt was back, fully clothed and much quicker than Leah had expected him to be.

"I'm almost disappointed you found something to wear," she teased.

"Oh it's like that, is it?" Matt grinned at her.

They just looked at each other for a moment. With each passing second, the butterflies in Leah's stomach seemed to multiply, until she could take it no longer.

"Come in. It's freezing out here." She waved him over.

As Matt approached her, she could no longer recall what exactly it was they were meant to do or talk about. All she could focus on was his face, with those brown eyes which seemed to see right into her. His lips, just full enough to soften his otherwise masculine and angular face.

Rather than step aside to let him enter, Leah stood glued in place. How empty she'd felt while he was gone. And although she hadn't even heard his full explanation yet, everything seemed right again.

He stood right in front of her now, with barely a foot between them. It was only now that she realized how much taller he was. He towered over her and made her feel small, which was unusual, but she loved it.

Leah closed her eyes and inhaled. Sweet, with a hint of

pine. Was that his aftershave?

Either way, his scent went straight to her head. She couldn't resist him. She didn't want to.

Leah tip-toed and wrapped her arms around Matt's neck, and although he flinched for a moment, he soon returned the embrace. It was as though she could feel his heartbeat speed up along with her own. And the tension she felt grow inside of her fed off of his excitement too.

*I want to kiss you,* Leah thought.

She didn't expect a response, but when she opened her eyes again, there he was, leaning down to get closer to her eye level. Their lips finally connected, after the shortest of hesitations which only served to heighten her anticipation.

And then, Leah could feel him. Not just his lips against hers, his breath tickling her face, or his arms cradling her, but feeling his emotions. It seemed as though from the moment they touched, they had started becoming one.

She could see glimpses of what felt like memories coming from him. How he'd watched her move in and how he'd yearned for her ever since. She also saw bits of their time apart, how he'd worked hard to understand his true nature and figure out how to control it. The images didn't come in any particular order, but more like pieces of a giant jigsaw puzzle, which Leah managed to connect somewhat in order to make sense of it all.

Matt pulled away and immediately the stream of information stopped.

"Did you feel that?" he asked.

"Yeah."

"I guess that's how Mom and Dad did it," he mumbled.

"What?"

"Oh. I guess it's another bear thing. I've never known anyone else who could do it. Communicate like that, without words."

# SCOTTISH WEREBEAR: A NEW BEGINNING

"Ah." Leah had so many questions but couldn't quite focus enough to voice any one of them. She just wanted the connection back. To feel Matt as part of her own being again.

Luckily, she didn't need to spell it out for him because he was after exactly the same thing.

"We should probably take this slow," Matt whispered between kisses.

He didn't mean it, though. His mind was filled with images a lot more explicit than mere kisses, which spurred her own imagination into action. Before she got the chance to reply, she found herself floating. Not in a figurative sense, but she was actually up in the air, cradled in Matt's muscular arms.

"Whoa, careful!"

"Don't worry. I'm not going to drop you." His voice was hoarse with desire, giving her oh so delicious goosebumps. And with those last words, he carried her over the threshold of her back door, right into the hall leading to the bedroom.

She didn't care that her bed wasn't made. Okay, she didn't care *much*. It didn't matter that there was a pile of laundry on a chair, making the room look messy.

He certainly didn't seem to notice it as he marched straight to the bed and laid her down gently onto her back.

All Matt had eyes for now was her. If she focused, she could see herself through his eyes.

It was a strange experience and a completely new view for her. Her features seemed softer, more feminine and sensual than when she looked at herself in the mirror. Though it was certainly different, it was unmistakably her.

Could he see what she saw also?

Those eyes, a deep, warm amber so inviting she could scarcely look away.

The only thing more inviting was the promise of tempting flesh now covered by the button-down shirt he had on. She already knew what hid beneath the soft cotton and couldn't wait to discover the same by touch.

"I hope it doesn't hurt?" Leah asked as the first of the bruises she'd spied earlier came into view while unbuttoning his shirt.

"Can't feel a thing," he whispered against her neck.

"You're gorgeous," Leah breathed once she had finished with all the buttons.

"Your turn," Matt spoke in a low growl that made the hairs on the back of her neck stand up. Oh God, how could she resist this man?

He kneeled between her legs, giving her space to raise herself slightly, then he tugged her top off, leaving her barely covered by the rather sensible bra she'd worn this morning. It didn't stay on for long, though, his impatient fingers made sure of that.

Again, her mind was filled with images of herself, filtered by his consciousness. She'd always been confident enough in herself, but never felt as sexy as right now. Neither had she known this lust, this passion growing inside of her that was just begging to be let loose.

*I don't want it slow,* she thought.

He stared at her, his eyes quite a bit darker than normal.

*Your wish is my command.*

Leah closed her eyes and lay back onto the bed again while Matt tore off first her jeans and then his own. She was ready. She was his.

# CHAPTER TWELVE

It had been a while since the last time Matt had been with a woman. Quite a while actually; the last time he had been no more than a nervous teenager, impatiently fumbling in the dark.

Right now couldn't have been more different.

Leah made everything different.

He'd already known that her presence had made it so much more difficult to control the beast that lurked within him. But he could have never guessed just how hard it was to pace himself now that things had become a lot more intimate between them.

His bear didn't as such want to come out anymore, but he did have very specific wants and desires.

He wanted to possess her completely. To spread her wide and take her. Right now. No compromises.

Matt took a deep breath as he admired Leah's naked flesh in front of him. Flawless skin. Generous curves in all the right places. He ached to touch her all over, but at the same time, it seemed almost criminal to rush things.

There could only be one first time.

One first time for his lips to connect with the soft pink of her nipples.

One first time for him to taste her sweet nectar.

One first time for his cock to enter her.

He wanted to do it all, slowly, so that he would remember it forever.

At the same time, he heard her voice in his mind, spurring him on to take her. How he wanted to give in to her demands, to please her.

He reached down between her legs and gently explored her folds. She was slick with her own juices already, had been for quite some time; he'd been able to pick up on the scent of her arousal from the moment they'd first kissed out in the garden.

She moaned and pressed her hips up, forcing his finger to touch her more deeply. Then, as their eyes locked, something in him snapped.

He could hold back no more.

And so he spread her thighs wide and pushed his swollen cock against her opening. She was tight; perhaps it had been a while for her too.

Either way, it didn't matter. It was clear that this, what they felt together, was beyond anything either of them had experienced with any other partner. No matter what had come before, this was a new beginning; a new life of sorts.

When he entered her, an even louder moan escaped her lips. He felt a red haze descend over him, putting him in a kind of trance. He could feel her pleasure inside of him. He could hear the blood rush through her veins, the feverish pace of her heartbeat.

As he sped up, he could sense exactly how she wanted it: the faster and harder he went, the more intense her reactions were.

How beautiful she looked, her lips slightly parted, eyes full of desire for him. He so needed to hear her scream. To see those beautiful lips opened wider and gasping for air.

So he made it happen. Harder. Deeper.

His cock started to tingle and pulsate. He was getting close himself, which in turn seemed to spur her on.

Their climax came so quickly it almost snuck up on him. Leah hit the point of no return first, twitching, quivering underneath him as she screamed out his name.

He wasn't sure what happened next, only that he found

himself drowning in waves of bliss as he filled her with his hot seed.

Although he'd always been fit, it took a while for him to catch his breath.

"That was..."

"Yeah," she gasped.

"I love you," he whispered.

She pressed her lips together and stared at him with those big, dark eyes of hers. *I love you too*, he could hear her say in his mind.

He wasn't sure how he knew, but he was certain that now they had truly become one. Their bond would not be broken, not by time, distance or interference by other people.

This was it. They were a couple.

---

Matt wasn't sure when exactly he'd fallen asleep. It was unusual for him to fall asleep so easily, more so because it was the middle of the day. He hadn't slept at daytime since his childhood.

He looked over at Leah, who still snoozed beside him. Her dark locks were spread out over the pillow, but he could still make out how tousled they'd become during their passionate romp earlier. Watching her made him smile.

Despite being in this bed for the very first time, he felt at home. And it was all because she was here.

It hadn't been easy, getting to this point together. A lot had tried to stand in their way.

Matt thought about what brought them here. The glances stolen at each other through windows or fences. The messages back and forth that had sparked an initial friendship, which inevitably wanted to develop into something more.

He remembered their conversations, including the very first time she'd overtly started to flirt with him. He'd been an idiot, holding back, trying to deny his feelings in the hopes that simply talking to her would be enough. Fate, as well as Leah, of course, had had other ideas.

Flowers *and* chocolates, she'd said she wanted. He hadn't given her either so far. That had to change.

Now that they were together, he would give her whatever she'd want. He'd give her the world if he could.

Finally, Leah stirred, opening her eyes and blinking a few times as they adjusted against the bright daylight in her bedroom. In their hunger for each other, they'd never even closed the curtains.

"I fell asleep," Leah remarked.

"Me too." Matt smiled at her.

"I feel so... lazy." Leah stretched her arms but made no attempt to get up.

Recalling his earlier thoughts, Matt realized that although he still didn't have either chocolates or flowers to give her, the very least he could do was provide some caffeine.

"How about I make us a cup of tea?" he suggested.

"That would be lovely."

Matt leaned over and kissed her lips. So sweet. In all the frenzy earlier, he hadn't even stopped to notice her fragrance. Like vanilla and spring blossoms.

Then he got up and made his way to the kitchen. Although he'd only been in her house briefly once before, he could find his way blindfolded if he had to. Their bungalows shared the same layout, the only difference being the sunroom he'd added to the back of his house years ago.

He put on the kettle and out of habit scanned the street outside. It was quiet, save for one black van parked right in front of the house.

*Shit.* Had the Alliance found out about them?

Matt turned the kettle off and rushed back through the lounge towards the hall, then stopped dead in his tracks when he saw a very familiar figure.

"Henry." Matt turned to face him and folded his arms. His body squarely blocked the hallway leading to the rest of the house and with it, Leah. No matter what, these people wouldn't take Leah. No way. He wouldn't let it happen.

"Matt. You know why they sent me here?" Henry asked in a low voice.

"I can guess, and before you say anything else, no, you can't take her."

Henry sighed. "There's been a lot of enemy activity in the city, and everyone is on high alert."

"I don't care. I'm not going to let you take her." Matt felt his muscles tighten, his skin crawl. He was ready to shift and charge if the situation demanded it.

"Relax, I'm not going to take her." Henry ran his hand through his hair and started pacing around the room. "The truth is, I'm not happy with the status-quo. What happened to you, here, it's not right. None of this is right."

"Okay... What are you trying to say, exactly?"

"I have a plan to make things right, but it's going to take some time to set up."

"Shoot."

"Firstly, this is for you." Henry retrieved something from his pocket and handed it to Matt. An SD card, like the ones you put into a digital camera.

"You might want to keep that safe. I caught her red-handed taking pictures, so she wouldn't have had time to make another copy."

Matt weighed the little card in his hand, then looked up again. "You caught who? Taking pictures of what exactly?"

Henry cocked his head to the side. "Your neighbor, Caroline. I'm sure you can guess what she was taking pictures of without me spelling it out."

Matt swallowed. Carrie? He'd known she was a gossip, but to actually spy on the two of them? He would have never expected her to go that far.

"You seem confused. See, we finally managed to crack one of the guys who was at this house that night. One of the Sons of Domnall."

"Right..."

"He mentioned a female collaborator who had tipped them off."

No way. Carrie had sent those people here to attack Leah? And for what, to try to draw *him* out?

"That doesn't make any sense. Carrie and I grew up together. If the people who took me knew what I was, and Carrie is involved with them too, why would she send those guys after me now?"

"Who knows what these people were thinking. If one faction even talks to the other. Before you burst into the house fully shifted, these people weren't even sure you were one of ours." Henry shrugged.

"Anyway, so what do you want in return for this?" Matt nodded down at the card in his hand.

"It's not like that. I don't want anything in return. I want you to consider my idea carefully, and if you agree, only then do I want your help when the time is right."

"Tell me."

"I-" Henry took a deep breath. "I want to go public."

Matt raised an eyebrow.

"Think about it. None of this would have ever

happened if people knew about our kind."

"What about the whole secrecy thing Jamie was telling me about?"

"Oh, the Alliance will fight us every step of the way. That's why we've got to be careful until all the pieces are in place."

Matt scratched his chin. Was it a trap? Was Henry just probing him to see where his loyalties lie? But that didn't seem like the guy; he'd always seemed quite straightforward. An honest man. Margaret, now *her* he could imagine to do something underhanded like this, but not Henry.

"What do you need?" Matt asked, finally.

"People. Good, loyal people who believe that openness is the way forward."

"I can't help you with that. I don't even know anyone."

"That's okay. I just want to know if I can call on you when the time comes." Henry looked Matt in the eye as he waited for an answer.

Matt considered the idea and considered the man standing before him. Ever since he found out about his true nature, he'd questioned the same things, wondered if things wouldn't have turned out better if he had known about his true nature sooner.

And Henry... the frustration he had shown earlier about what he had been sent in to do here seemed genuine. Matt took a deep breath and decided to take a chance.

"Okay. I'm in," Matt said.

Henry exhaled, as if he'd been holding his breath the whole time while waiting for Matt's response.

"Right, well, that's good news. Just so you know, you won't have to worry about your neighbor snooping around anymore. I've got her in the back of the van already."

"Great," Matt said, though he still couldn't quite believe

Carrie's involvement in all of this.

"I'm going to head back now and tell everyone I found no evidence of you and the human woman being involved with one-another. You take care now."

"Okay, thanks," Matt mumbled, and watched Henry turn around and march out of the lounge, through the adjoining entrance hall and out the front door.

What a bizarre conversation.

Outside, an engine purred to life, and a vehicle - the van, most likely - pulled away and drove off.

"Who were you talking to?" Leah asked, resting her hand on Matt's shoulder. He hadn't even heard her walk up behind him.

"That's a long, weird story." Matt turned, and put his arms around Leah's waist.

She smiled at him and tiptoed to give him a peck on the lips. With her around, it was easy to think that everything was just going to work itself out.

"I'm not going anywhere. Now how about we have that cup of tea, and you tell me everything," she suggested.

He smiled back at her. "All right."

She took his hand, and they walked back into the kitchen together. A quick glance out the window revealed that all was quiet. As if Henry had never even come by.

# EPILOGUE

———◆———

It had been a long five-hour drive to Applecross Bay, filled with awkward silences. Leah was glad that Jamie, Matt's eerily similar looking brother, was driving. Not only did it give her the chance to admire the pretty scenery on the way, she wasn't even sure her little car would have made it this far.

Matt, who sat in the front seat next to Jamie, wasn't quite as receptive to the views; he had other things on his mind. Leah had been able to sense his concerns, obviously.

At last, they pulled into a gravel driveway leading to a solitary house nestled among the sand dunes surrounding the coastline. So this was where the two brothers were born.

"You ready?" Jamie turned the key to switch off the ignition and then turned to face Matt.

Matt didn't answer straightaway.

Leah squeezed his shoulder. *It'll be fine. They're your parents. They'll be thrilled to have you back.*

*I know, but... Ah, screw it.*

"Sure. Let's go," Matt said.

One by one they undid their seat belts and got out of the car. Jamie led the way up the gravel path leading to the porch, and Matt followed reluctantly. It was strange how similar the two brothers looked, and yet how different their personalities were.

Jamie was so serious, almost cold in everything he did, while Matt was a lot more sensitive and warm. Perhaps it only felt that way because Leah didn't know Jamie all that well. Or more likely, because she could tell he thought it unwise for her to be here with Matt. She was an outsider, after all, no matter how hard Matt tried to convince her otherwise.

Either way, Jamie's disapproval hadn't dissuaded her. Matt had been worrying about this family reunion for a while now, and she was set on being here for emotional support if nothing else.

As they climbed the steps, the net curtain beside the front door moved, and almost immediately after, someone opened the door.

"I don't believe it! You're really here!" a female voice said.

The elderly woman who appeared in the doorway was obviously Matt and Jamie's mother. The similarities between the three of them were striking, but it was Matt who had taken after her the most.

"Your father is inside. He's not been keeping too well, I'm afraid," Matt's mother said. "I still can't... When we last saw you, you were so little. We thought you were gone forever." Her voice cracked with emotion.

Matt seemed lost for words, and even Jamie didn't have anything to add. Not that that mattered to their mom, who couldn't stop talking.

"Anyway, I've made your favorite. At least, it used to be your favorite when you were little. You do still like Apple Pie, don't you?" she asked.

Matt nodded. "Thanks, Mom."

"Oh, you sweet boy." She reached out and put her arms around Matt. "Why don't we go inside and say hello to your father. And who's this?"

Suddenly Leah found herself in the foreground. Matt's mother stepped up to her and smiled. "Forgive the boys their manners; they've forgotten to introduce you!"

# SCOTTISH WEREBEAR: A NEW BEGINNING

"Leah," Leah said while offering her hand. "Matt's..." she wasn't sure how to finish that statement. Girlfriend sounded awfully juvenile.

"My fiancée," Matt chimed in and put his arm around Leah's shoulder.

Although they'd been inseparable ever since his return from the Alliance, they hadn't formally discussed the future yet. Hearing him introduce her as his fiancée made Leah's heart skip a few beats.

"Oh! How lovely to meet you," Matt's mom said. "What wonderful news, congratulations, you two! We've not just got our youngest son back, but a daughter as well. Jamie, you should take a leaf out of your brother's book and settle down as well. You're not getting any younger."

Jamie sighed. "Yes, Mom."

Leah couldn't suppress a smile. For someone as stoic and in control as Jamie seemed, it was hilarious to see this family dynamic.

Now that the introductions were over, they all moved indoors, Matt and Jamie's mother leading the way. The interior of the house looked like a time capsule left over from the 1970s. A lot of earthy tones and old-fashioned floral drapes. They probably hadn't changed a thing in years.

Leah glanced over at Matt, who silently took it all in. He seemed to recognize bits of the house and watching him as he made his way through his childhood home made her a bit emotional as well.

"David, look who's here," Matt's mom said as they entered the lounge.

Matt's dad, who had been watching TV up to this point looked up and cracked a smile which seemed to wrinkle up his entire face.

"My boys. Together at last. Don't mind if I don't get

up. The old leg's been giving me a bit of trouble lately."

"Dad," Matt whispered and walked up to the armchair.

The old man reached out for him, and they embraced awkwardly.

"And look, Matt brought his fiancée, Leah, as well." Matt's mom beamed.

"Ah, I see." Matt's dad smiled at Leah. It was awkward suddenly being the center of attention. "Welcome to the family, lass."

Leah smiled and shook his hand. "Sit down, everyone," Matt's mom said "I hope you're a tea drinker, Leah? I haven't catered for coffee."

"Oh yes, tea would be lovely."

Matt and Leah sat down on the sofa, while Matt's mom left the room, only to reappear shortly after carrying a tray full of cups, saucers and a teapot. Jamie sat further away, pulling up a dining chair for himself.

It was only natural that Matt felt awkward in the company of his folks. After all, they'd been separated for so long. They all waited in silence while Matt's mom distributed the cups and poured the tea.

Once everyone had a cup in their hand, and conversation slowly did get underway, suddenly it was Jamie who looked most out of place.

"Pie?" Matt's mom offered, and Leah gladly accepted a plate.

"Do tell us what you've been up to all these years? How have things been for you?" she asked Matt.

He answered diplomatically, leaving out the difficulties he'd faced in his adult life and focused on his teen years instead.

"How about work, son? What do you do for work?" his dad asked.

"I write, mostly articles and reports about financial

matters."

"Oh, a writer! That's wonderful," his mom chimed in.

The more they talked, the more comfortable the atmosphere became.

"And what about you two, have you set a date yet?" his mom asked, her eyes wide with anticipation.

Leah glanced at Matt and found that he was already looking at her.

*Have we?* Leah thought.

*You tell me*, Matt replied.

*Tomorrow if you're ready*. Leah smiled as Matt took her hand.

"Not yet, perhaps we can come up with something together. It would be no good unless you're both there as well," Matt responded to his mom.

"But of course, we'll be there. Wouldn't miss it for the world," Matt's dad said.

"First, though, what are you all doing for Christmas? Wouldn't it be lovely to finally have a proper family Christmas again? Unless you're going to celebrate with your parents, Leah?" Matt's mother asked.

Leah shook her head. "No plans yet. My Dad passed eight years ago."

"Oh, I'm so sorry to hear that. What about your mother?"

Leah shrugged. "She died when I was very young. It had been just Dad and me for as long as I can remember."

Matt squeezed her hand gently. Even though it had been years since the loss of her dad, talking about it still hurt.

"Ah," his mom said. "Well, it's been decided then. You must come up for Christmas. What do you think, Jamie?"

Jamie, who had been sitting silently in the corner, cleared his throat. "Umm, actually I have to work over the holidays. Sorry about that."

Weird. The Alliance were a strange bunch from what Leah had heard, but to work over Christmas was still a bit extreme. Was it just an excuse on his part?

"Oh, that's too bad." His mom's voice was loaded with disappointment.

"We'll definitely be there, though," Matt said.

"All right then." She smiled. "I'll do a roast like we used to have when you were little."

After this little hiccup, the conversation picked up again, leaving the previous awkwardness behind. Clearly the return of their lost son wasn't enough to repair whatever damage had been done to this family, but it was a start. There obviously was still a lot of love in this house, mixed in with old pain and regret.

The visit lasted for the better part of the afternoon, with everyone - except maybe Jamie - wishing for it not to be cut short. But the Alliance never waited, and he had to be back in Edinburgh early the next day, so they had to make a move.

Their goodbye was bittersweet, with Matt's mom getting emotional again. But at least everyone knew they'd be reunited again soon, for Christmas.

# - THE END -

# Scottish Werebear

## A PAINFUL DILEMMA

# PROLOGUE

———◆———

Henry checked his watch and shook his head, even though there was nobody to see him do it. This was the last straw.

Here he was, on what looked to be a perfectly pleasant winter's day, spying on one of his own. And why? Because Adrian Blacke, self-appointed leader of the Alliance Council himself had ordered him to. *Just ensure our secrets are being kept,* Blacke had said. *He's never lived according to our customs, with our rules. There's no way of knowing if we can trust him.*

Nonsense.

Hadn't Matthew Argyle and the human woman, Leah Hudson, been through enough already?

After being abducted as a child and sent to live with strangers, finally, Matthew had found out the truth about himself. And clearly - if the activity going on inside was anything to go by - he'd found himself a mate as well. Good for him.

But if Blacke had his way, Henry would march in there and arrest both of them for violating the secrecy requirement all shifters are meant to live by. Fraternizing with humans was frowned upon in the best of circumstances, but recently Blacke had reached new heights of paranoia and decided to outlaw it completely.

What was the point of keeping their existence secret, if their main enemy, the Sons of Domnall knew all about them anyway? They were growing in numbers, organizing themselves, and turning more militant by the day. And by staying in the shadows, the shifters were playing right into their hands.

It was much easier to convince people to fear the unknown when nobody argued for the other side.

Henry had had these thoughts before, but the more he considered it, the more certain he'd become. Education was the way forward.

A far away rustle brought Henry back to reality. Was someone else watching?

He focused on pinpointing the noise, just across the other side of the backyard he'd been surveilling himself. This could not be a coincidence. Had Blacke sent out another Alliance agent?

Henry silently made his way around the boundary fence, while listening out for more sounds. No, the other spy was human. Bears would never be this obvious.

It didn't take him long to scale the fence, land on the other side and follow the retreating human female who had almost reached the back door of her house. Before she had the chance to see him, Henry grabbed the woman from behind and covered her mouth with his hand. She let out a muffled squeal and tried to struggle free, but it was no use.

"Make a move, and things will end badly for you," he whispered in her ear.

She soon stopped squirming.

"Okay, just don't hurt me," she said as Henry removed the hand from her mouth.

Henry kept her restrained with one arm, and with the other patted her down for weapons. She didn't carry any, but she did have a digital camera in her pocket, which Henry retrieved and switched on to inspect its contents.

So his instincts were right. He flipped through the pictures and found that they were shots of the exact scene he'd witnessed earlier, along with some very damning pictures of things that had happened before he'd even arrived at Leah Hudson's house.

This bumbling human, no doubt the collaborator one of the Sons of Domnall guys had referred to during his interrogation, had actually managed to get a picture of Matthew mid-shift. It was bad. If Blacke saw this, things would end badly for Matthew and his human mate.

Henry stuffed the camera into one of the pockets of his tactical vest and tied the woman's wrists up with one of the plastic restraints he always carried with him.

"Your mates ratted you out. You're coming with me now," Henry said.

The woman's eyes widened in shock, but she didn't say anything.

"What's your name?" he asked.

She remained silent.

"Very well, don't tell me."

Henry covered her mouth with a piece of duct tape and dragged her to the backdoor of the house she'd tried to enter earlier. He listened out for any activity but didn't hear any. The place was empty. On the way through the house, he picked up a few unopened envelopes from a sideboard. They were all addressed the same person: Caroline Pratt.

The few framed pictures on display showed the same woman, posing along with other people, some of which looked familiar to Henry. Sons of Domnall members already captured by the Alliance. That's all he needed to know.

Henry wasted no more time, just checked that the road was empty before getting her to the van and stuffing her in the back.

He might not have followed Blacke's orders exactly, but at least he had something to show for his little excursion to Gartcosh this afternoon. Just as well. He'd made up his mind earlier about what was the right way forward.

In time, if his plan worked out, perhaps this stupid war between the Sons and the shifters would pass, but for now, she was still the enemy. Henry wouldn't feel bad about locking her up at the base and later handing her over to Blacke and his men.

What he wouldn't do was hand over the pictures she'd taken earlier.

He was done spying on his own people, especially those who'd been through so much shit already, like Matthew Argyle. Henry had joined the Alliance because he wanted to make a difference; to make the world a safer place for shifters. Instead of simply following orders he didn't believe in anymore, he was going to start a movement of his own.

He locked the van and observed the outside of Leah Hudson's house for a moment. As much as he hated to interrupt the lovebirds, he couldn't leave without talking to at least Matthew first.

If Henry's new movement was to be a success, he needed to gather support. Who better to talk to than the man who inspired Henry's decision in the first place?

Henry picked the lock to the front door and waited inside the living room.

———◆———

It felt like hours before Henry noticed any sign of activity inside the human woman's house. He'd always been a patient man, so the wait didn't bother him as such. What bothered him was that he wasn't at all sure how to broach the subject he wanted to discuss.

And what if it wasn't Matthew Argyle who found him

waiting in here, but the woman? He didn't want to panic anyone or create a scene. He just wanted to... What exactly *did* he want?

Henry wasn't sure, and time had run out to think about it any further, because a figure appeared in the doorway.

"Henry." Matt folded his arms.

"Matt. You know why they sent me here?" Henry asked.

"I can guess. And before you say anything else, no, you can't take her." Matt straightened himself further. He was on full alert, ready to defend his mate to the death if necessary.

Of course, Henry didn't make a move. That was not why he had come here.

"There's been a lot of enemy activity in the city, and everyone is on high alert," Henry tried to explain, but it didn't help get his point across.

"I don't care. I'm not going to let you take her."

Henry shook his head. It was only natural that Matt would be suspicious of his presence here. Even if he was planning to do nothing of the sort.

"Relax. I'm not going to take her." *Even if Blacke would have liked nothing better.* "The truth is, I'm not happy with the status-quo. What happened to you, here, it's not right. None of this is right."

This was not at all easy. Henry was used to being in control of himself and of any situation he got himself in. Years of Alliance experience had taught him to always prepare for whatever came next; to never follow impulse alone. Today marked a significant departure from said training.

"Okay... What are you trying to say exactly?" Matt still sounded suspicious - naturally. His body language was clear; as far as he knew, the threat was still very much present.

"I have a plan to make things right, but it's going to take time to set up."

"Shoot," Matt said.

Henry remembered his prisoner, out in the van. Perhaps if he started by explaining what had gone down earlier, he could win Matt's trust.

"Firstly, this is for you." Henry handed over the SD card he had taken from Caroline Pratt earlier.

It took a little explaining to get Matt to understand what had happened and how he'd got the SD card. Matt was obviously taken aback when he realized what Matt's prisoner had captured on camera. Luckily, the culprit was already under arrest so she wouldn't bother the two of them any longer.

Then it was time for Henry to bring up the one subject he had come here to discuss. His plans.

"I want to go public." Henry tried to gauge Matt's reaction. He looked surprised more than anything else.

"Think about it. None of this would have happened if people knew about our kind," Henry added.

Matt had a few more questions, which Henry tried to answer to the best of his ability. Yes, it went against the secrecy rules bears and other shifters had been following for centuries. Yes, the Alliance would oppose. But in the end, Henry believed it would be worth it.

"Okay, I'm in," Matt said after Henry had finished.

Finally, Henry could breathe a sigh of relief. His idea had legs, at least on the face of it.

Although he'd assured Matt that he wouldn't need anything other than his help when the time was right, there was no way of knowing how any of this would play out. Still, Henry's new movement had gained its first supporter.

# CHAPTER ONE

———◆———

Henry hadn't wanted a fight, but things had a way of escalating between him and Maggie.

"Why don't you trust me anymore?" Maggie folded her arms.

"Come on; it's not like that!" Henry argued, taking a step forward to rest his hand on Maggie's arm.

She pulled away just in time and shook her head. "Well, there's no other explanation. First, you go on the surveillance mission on your own, then you don't even involve me in the interrogation of that prisoner you took. Tell me, what am I supposed to think?"

Henry sighed. In a way, she was right. He *hadn't* wanted her to come along to Gartcosh to surveil Matt's house the other day. It's not that he didn't trust her, or didn't think she'd do a good job. Actually, he expected she'd do *too good* a job. She would have followed Blacke's orders to the letter, so they would have ended up with three prisoners, not just one. Caroline Pratt was a given, she was a Son's collaborator after all, but Maggie would have also rounded up Matt and Leah.

He and Maggie had been an item for years; Henry knew how she functioned.

As for the interrogation, he just couldn't risk Caroline cracking and mentioning the pictures she'd taken. Luckily, so far she seemed to hold up quite well and not said a word.

"Blacke gave me the order; it's only natural that I execute it," Henry excused his decision.

He had to come clean to her about what had happened, but with Maggie in the mood she was in right now, it wasn't the right time. She'd always been hot-blooded, and not particularly easy to reason with when she was ticked off.

"Did Blacke tell you not to take your partner along on the job?" Maggie demanded.

Henry remained quiet. Of course, he hadn't.

"I didn't think so."

She was hurt, obviously. And Henry couldn't blame her. But if there was one thing he had to give her credit for, she did take her work very seriously.

"Look, I didn't mean to step on your toes, but I can't have you questioning my operational decisions like this. When we're on the job, I'm in charge. That's just the way things are."

"Fine!" Maggie pressed her lips together. There was nothing agreeable about her body language.

"Now, shall we have breakfast? Wouldn't want to be late for work."

Maggie shrugged and marched out of their bedroom. Although he'd pulled the seniority card on her, this argument was far from over.

Today was going to be a long day.

———◆———

For much of the day, Maggie made it a point to steer clear of Henry, which was just as well. They weren't hiding their relationship as such, but they made it a point to always stay professional at work.

Henry liked to think of himself as a fair and capable leader. His agents trusted him - most of the time, in the case of Maggie - and he ensured not to give preferential treatment to his mate. Plus, bears weren't the sharing sort. They didn't wear their hearts on their sleeve like wolves seemed to do. In his unit, one's private life was just that: private.

Before lunch, Henry interrogated his latest prisoner - Caroline Pratt - some more. Nothing came out of it, just as he had come to expect from most of the Sons of Domnall members. Especially those that seemed to be authority figures of some sort were especially tight-lipped. Caroline's demeanor, as well as her role in the attempted second kidnapping of Matthew Argyle, made Henry suspect she wasn't just an informant, but perhaps a faction leader.

Then again, she wasn't in the loop on a great many Sons activities at all, or she might have already known who or what Matt was.

Either way, it was time to close the file on her and send her and the other prisoners across to Stirling, where the Alliance Headquarters were located. Henry wrote up a sanitized version of the events leading up to Caroline's capture, whatever little details he gathered during the interrogation, and that was that. Case closed. He'd inform Blacke's people shortly.

Once that was done, he grabbed a fresh sheet of paper and started to brainstorm about something else entirely. He'd had an epiphany outside Matt's house that day, but he hadn't taken the time to really think about it in depth. If he was going to set up a movement to counter Blacke's Alliance, he couldn't just wing it.

Who would be onboard with his idea? Anyone who - like Matt - had paired up with another species, obviously.

How would he find these people and convince them, though? Considering how notoriously secretive bears were about their personal lives, identifying potential recruits would be very difficult indeed. Henry didn't even know enough about his own team's relationships to be able to make an educated guess about whom to approach with his idea.

There had to be two recruitment phases: a slow start, relying on word of mouth, followed by a public call for support once they were ready to reveal themselves. Once his new movement was ready to go public, they might just attract complete strangers who agreed with Henry's ideology.

Henry sat back and looked at the sheet in front of him. Other than Matt, he hadn't been able to add a single name to his list of potential supporters. He crushed the paper into a ball and threw it in the trash.

What he was planning was big, too big for one person to orchestrate. He didn't just need supporters; he needed a partner to help him organize everything.

Henry looked up and saw her walk in. Maggie. Was she still angry at him? If he brought it up, would she be his partner in this new venture as well? There was only one way to find out.

"You ready?" she asked.

Henry glanced at his watch; five-thirty.

"Yeah, why not." He pushed the Caroline Pratt's dossier aside and got up. "Hey, how about we go out tonight? Somewhere nice."

Maggie cocked her head to the side. She pursed her lips like she often did when she was mulling something over.

*Definitely still annoyed about this morning* Henry thought.

"We'll go anywhere you like," he added.

Maggie smiled, and Henry knew he'd won at least the first battle of the evening.

———◆———

# SCOTTISH WEREBEAR: A PAINFUL DILEMMA

Henry waited until the waiter left before broaching the subject that had been on his mind most of the day.

"The work we do..." he started, then looked up to find Maggie already staring at him intently. "Do you ever wonder if we're doing all we can?"

"We're making a difference, aren't we? Only a few years ago, we had no idea about the threat against us posed by the Sons of Domnall. Now we're hot on their trail and arresting new people all the time."

"True, we're making progress. I do wonder sometimes if we're doing the right thing."

Maggie's eyes narrowed. "What are you trying to say?"

"The other day, the surveillance order on Matt Argyle," Henry said, hoping against hope that she wouldn't see this as an invitation to start this morning's argument all over again.

She paused for a moment.

"What about it?"

"It just didn't feel right. He's one of us, not the enemy." Henry ran his hand through his hair.

"God, is that why you didn't want me to go? Because you weren't sure it was the right call?" Maggie sat back and observed him for a moment. "You got an order; you followed it. I honestly don't see the problem. And if he isn't following the rules, he might as well be the enemy."

"You really think that?" Henry asked. This conversation wasn't going as he had hoped.

"I can't believe you're even asking me this. We signed up for this thing for the same reason: to keep our people safe. Things are getting worse. Disappearances, even murders. As many Sons members as we've caught, we have no way of knowing how many more are out there."

"True."

"It's not rocket science. Keep our true nature a secret

from humanity. What's so hard in that?"

Henry sighed. Maggie was a strong woman. That was one of her qualities which he'd always admired. The downside was that she could be incredibly stubborn. There was no convincing her of something she didn't already believe in. There was little point in discussing this matter any further.

"You're right. It's quite simple," he said. "Oh, the food is here."

Henry smiled at the waiter as he brought out their plates. Steak, medium-rare. Just what he needed.

He glanced over at Maggie again, who looked equally pleased to see the food.

For the rest of the meal, Henry didn't bring up his doubts about Blacke's policies anymore. It seemed Maggie was equally content to leave the topic behind as Henry was. Perhaps it had been the wrong time to discuss it, but at the very least she wasn't angry anymore about being excluded from the surveillance job.

As pleasant as the meal had been, the evening left Henry with a bitter taste in his mouth. By the time they'd gone to bed, doubts had started to overwhelm him. He turned to look at Maggie beside him, her eyes closed and features completely relaxed. How different she looked when she was asleep.

She wasn't onboard with his idea. This was a major setback, and unlike how Henry had hoped for things to turn out. But it was normal for couples to disagree on things. They had to get past it.

Somehow, Henry had to figure out a way to start the new movement himself, without her help. Blacke needed to be stopped somehow before he went too far, no matter what Maggie believed. They were a team in the office, a team at home, most of the time. But this was something he had to do for his own satisfaction and beliefs.

He needed to come up with a solid plan and gather support beyond Matt all on his own. Hopefully, then Maggie would see that Henry was right and join him after all.

# CHAPTER TWO

———◆———

This was not what Gail imagined her new job would be like. Not at all.

She held on tighter to the pile of document folders as she tried to keep pace with her new boss, Adrian Blacke, on the way to the holding cells located in the basement of the Alliance headquarters in Stirling, Scotland.

It was like a typical scene from a coming of age chick flick, only she refused to play the part of the clumsy heroine who would drop all her papers as her boss lost patience with her. That's not who she wanted to be.

Who *did* she want to be? Gail wasn't sure.

She followed Blacke through the heavy, reinforced doors, through the long corridor, stealing glances through the narrow windows in the cell doors. Inside each of them sat someone who had been deemed a danger to the shifter world, whether through threatening or violent behavior or by simply breaking one or more Alliance rules. It seemed like the latter group made up most of the prisoners here.

Their footsteps echoed against the concrete of the hallway as they made their way further into the belly of what her colleagues referred to as 'the dungeon'; a fitting name indeed for a place as unpleasant as this.

"Let's see what old man Campbell has to say for himself today," Blacke muttered.

After just over a week on the job, Gail knew better than to respond. Blacke had a habit of talking to himself when it was just the two of them. As if she wasn't even present.

They approached the cell where Lee Campbell was

being kept - just across from his son Gareth who had been captured at the same time apparently. His cell was one of the few with a dedicated guard; he was one of the most valuable prisoners here.

Most of the Sons of Domnall members they had captured were just small-time soldiers, but Lee Campbell was something else entirely. He was a leader of some sort, though his exact rank wasn't yet known.

Blacke nodded at the guard, who unlocked the heavy door and stepped aside. Gail followed her boss inside the cell, though it made her skin crawl to be here. This, coming down here, was one of the more unpleasant parts of her job.

She couldn't be sure what Blacke was planning for today, but his personal interrogations of Campbell had turned nastier and nastier over time. The more Campbell kept quiet, the more determined Blacke had become to make him talk.

"Morning," Adrian Blacke said, his voice low and sinister.

Campbell, who was merely sitting on the basic cot in the corner of his otherwise sparse cell, looked up. His eyes were blank like he wasn't actually present. His face was an unhealthy shade of grey, and the bags under his eyes seemed to darken with every passing day.

His deterioration wasn't all that surprising, considering they had kept him locked up in this windowless basement for weeks now. In an attempt to break his resolve, Blacke had instructed the guards to wake Campbell every two hours throughout the night and put him on a severely restricted diet.

Gail shuddered at the sight of Blacke, who continued to glare at the miserable looking man. Some days, the prisoners seemed more approachable and sympathetic than her boss did.

Blacke snapped his fingers, jerking Gail into action.

"Yes, sir?" she asked.

"A chair. Get me a chair."

Gail turned on her heel, eager to get out of the dingy cell, but her relief was cut short by the guard outside who had already arranged for a chair. Damn.

She dragged it inside with one hand, the steel feet making an awful kind of noise scraping over the bare concrete of the floor.

Blacke sat down without acknowledging her.

"Let's try something new today, shall we?" Blacke said. "We'll step things up, as they say."

Gail's insides twisted painfully. She really wasn't keen to find out what Blacke had in mind.

"Get me Agent Dumbarton," Blacke spoke in a low growl.

Gail nodded and finally made her escape from the cell. This was bad, very bad. Dumbarton was mean. One of those guys who didn't think twice before getting physical. Calling him into an interrogation could only mean one thing: Blacke planned to make good on his threats; he was finally going to have the prisoner tortured.

With every passing step, back past all those cells, through the doors and up the stairs, Gail couldn't shake the feeling of dread that her realization had inspired. She didn't want to be here.

That man, Campbell no doubt was the enemy, as were the rest of the Sons of Domnall. He'd kill her and everyone in this building if he had the chance. But this went too far. If they did this, they'd sink to his level and justify his beliefs that shifters were dangerous and needed to be rooted out.

Her hands trembled as she opened the door leading to

the main floor where all the agents had their desks. It didn't take her long to spy Dumbarton in a crowd hanging around the coffeemaker. He was the loudest of the lot.

"Agent Dumbarton," Gail addressed him, attempting to sound a lot more confident than she felt. "Mr. Blacke needs you in the dungeon. Cell 27."

Dumbarton gave her one of those looks. The ones that make you feel dirty and violated. "Sure thing, darling. Anything for you."

Some of the other agents chuckled. Pigs, the lot of them.

She didn't want to wait for what else he would say, instead made a run for the exit. Whether Blacke wanted her back down there or not, she didn't care. She wasn't willing to watch what was going to happen next.

Outside, the grey skies perfectly matched her mood. The only noise around was the groundskeeper who operated a leaf blower to clear away the last fallen leaves of autumn.

The Alliance headquarters was situated in a strange looking mansion built in the 1920s by Blacke's grandfather. Ever since he'd taken over control of the Alliance Council, this place - which thanks to its concrete and steel exterior looked more like a bunker or a prison than a luxury country retreat - had been used to hold council meetings and store prisoners taken by the various Alliance branch offices.

It was ugly, as were most of the people inside.

Gail took a deep breath, but it didn't help calm her nerves. The hum of the leaf blower stopped, as Gerry, the caretaker retrieved a pack of cigarettes from his pocket and lit one. Perhaps that would help.

"Gerry, excuse me," Gail called out to him.

He looked up, as though surprised that anyone was

talking to him at all.

She approached him, her knees weak as she did so. "May I have one?"

"Sure." He retrieved the crumpled packet and held it up for her.

"Thank you," she said.

He offered her a light and continued his work straightaway. Like most bears, Gerry was a man of few words.

Gail walked back towards the building, hoping that standing closer to its walls would offer some shelter against the sharp wintery breeze. She inhaled deeply, waiting for the smoke to relax her. It did nothing of the sort.

All it did was made her cough and feel nauseous. What a ridiculous idea. Why would a cigarette help her when she didn't even smoke? She put it out against the bottom of her shoe and leaned back against the cold concrete with her head down and eyes shut.

Gail wasn't sure how long she remained like that for, only that the sound of an approaching vehicle made her look up again. Black, windowless, Ford Transit. All of the HQ agents were on site, so this could only mean one thing: a transport bringing with it more unfortunate souls to be forgotten in the dungeon.

She didn't want to see who was being held in the back. She didn't want to think about what would happen to them, but rather than run inside, something made her stick around and watch.

The driver's side door opened, and her heart all but stopped.

Gail had never seen the man before during her time here. His broad shoulders looked like they could carry the world on them. He was most definitely a brown bear, bigger and stronger than her own subspecies. Although she knew nothing about him, when he turned around she could see in his eyes that he was different from all the guys working inside. He was meant to be hers. She could feel it.

Gail tried to swallow the last remnants of that horrible cigarette and dusted herself off.

"Hey," she said, but it came out all hoarse at first. "Hey!"

The man, who had already walked around to the back of his van, looked up.

"Can I help you?" Gail asked.

"Prisoner transport." The man barely acknowledged her presence beyond that, instead unlocking the backdoor of his vehicle.

Gail nodded. She did vaguely remember Blacke discussing an upcoming transport with other people in the office. Still, it was infuriating that he wasn't paying any attention to her at all. He was her mate; she just *knew* it. However, he seemed to be completely oblivious.

"Name? I'm Gail McPherson, by the way. Mr. Blacke's assistant."

That last bit of information seemed to sink in, because the man stopped what he was doing again and turned to face her.

"Agent Weston. Your boss is expecting me."

"I see..." Gail frowned. Why couldn't things just be simple? Not only was she stuck doing a job that wasn't at all how she thought it was going to be, here was a guy who didn't behave in the least how he was meant to. She'd heard about the instant attraction bears experience when they are confronted with their true mate. It was always mutual. Why wasn't it mutual now?

"I will let him know you're here," Gail said.

She paused for another moment, only to find that so-called Agent Weston was intent on ignoring her presence. *Fine!* Off she went to notify her boss of the arrival of Weston and his transport.

Perhaps once he was done doing the job he had come here for he would be more open to converse with her.

# CHAPTER THREE

———◆———

Henry was still in shock when he led Caroline Pratt into the Alliance Headquarters. That woman, Gail McPherson, who had introduced herself as Adrian Blacke's assistant, had awoken things in him he hadn't felt before. A connection. A certainty that he was meant to be with her.

But that couldn't be. He had chosen Maggie as his mate already, someone he'd known and worked with for years.

*This is just a silly infatuation,* he told himself. *There's no way this is real.*

Perhaps it was due to the recent disagreements between Maggie and him, most notably their differing views on their work. That had to be it.

Every relationship took work and dedication. Everyone had doubts sometimes. He just had to make sure not to give in to them.

"Prisoner transfer from Glasgow," Henry told the man manning the front desk. "Mr. Blacke is expecting me."

"Hold on, let me check." The man picked up the phone on the table in front of him and dialed a few numbers. "All right, you can go straight down. Is it just the one prisoner?"

Henry shook his head. There were more in the van. "Two more."

"Very well. Bill, give us a hand here, will ya?" The agent called out to one of his colleagues who had just passed through the double doors at the other end of the entrance hall.

The other guy, Bill, nodded and approached Henry.

"This one and two more prisoners as requested by Mr.

Blacke," the man behind the desk clarified.

"Understood. Follow me."

Bill led Henry along with his prisoner to another, less impressive door in the corner. Behind it was the staircase leading into the basement. They walked in silence, almost all the way to the end of the long corridor, cells on either side. One of the doors opened, and that same woman from before, Gail, almost ran into Henry.

"Careful, there," he mumbled, as he reached out to steady her by her arm.

Their eyes met, and he felt it again. The pull, the strange attraction he'd never felt before. *You're mine.* He immediately pulled his hand back again. How awkward. Had she noticed him stare?

"Excuse me," she whispered. She shot a cold stare at Henry's companion and marched off back in the direction of the staircase. Like she couldn't wait to get out of here. Obviously, he'd made her uncomfortable with his weird behavior.

"Nice one, aye. I wouldn't mind bumping into that myself," Bill remarked and stopped for a moment, looking back at Gail as she walked away.

It was distasteful. Henry balled his fists and took a deep breath. There was no point getting into a confrontation with this guy. And over what? Some misplaced feeling of protectiveness towards a woman who wasn't even his to protect. What a mess.

"Let's do this," Henry grumbled under his breath while prodding Caroline in the back to make her walk faster.

"What?" Bill asked, then shrugged when Henry didn't reply. "Here we are. You can leave the prisoner in here. I'll open up a couple more cells for the others."

"Great. I'll be right back." Henry left Caroline behind and turned back immediately. His feet seemed to carry him in a hurry back to the door at the end of the hall, up the stairs, and through the entrance hall back outside. As though he was stuck in a trance.

The fresh air helped clear his head. He was just going to do what he had come here for and stop obsessing about that woman.

With everything that was already on his mind, this was the last thing he needed.

Luckily, it seemed she had read his mind, because he didn't run into her again.

Within little under an hour, he had delivered the remaining prisoners and handed over their paperwork as well. He'd also been taken in to see Mr. Blacke himself, who questioned him on his findings regarding Matt Argyle's conduct. All in order, Henry had said.

That's as much as he was willing to divulge, and luckily, Blacke hadn't pushed him further.

If only Blacke knew what Henry was planning... For now, though, Henry's senior position in the Glasgow office afforded him a certain amount of trust from the normally quite suspicious Alliance Council leader.

Henry made a quick exit as soon as everything was settled. No matter how hard he tried throughout the lonely drive back, he couldn't get Gail out of his mind. Raven black hair, dark brown, nearly black eyes, and flawless olive skin. She was something else. When he closed his eyes, it was as though he could catch her scent again.

How was he meant to resist such temptation? When every cell in his body seemed to ache for her. He wasn't a womanizer. He couldn't betray Maggie.

Finally, about halfway through the drive, he couldn't take it anymore. Rather than continue straight to Glasgow, he took the next exit and just kept on driving. Through fields and small towns and villages, until he found himself at the shores of a lake. That's where he pulled over and got out.

It was getting late, the sun was setting, and a frosty wind battered the landscape.

He closed his eyes and inhaled deeply. The cold air stung against his nostrils and helped him gain clarity. His bear wasn't happy, and there was only one way to appease him right now.

About three hundred feet from where he'd parked the car were some pine woods. They'd provide shelter for what he had to do next.

As soon as Henry reached the first trees, he started to unzip his jacket. The rest of his clothes followed soon after.

It was freezing, but if he was going to make it back home after this without exposing himself, getting undressed first was as necessary as it was uncomfortable. He folded everything into a neat little bundle and left it underneath some fallen needles and branches.

Then he let the animal side take over. As soon as his fur had grown, he felt better. Now he was protected against the elements and ready to wander through the pine forest. He had a lot to think about.

What was it about that woman that the thought of her wouldn't leave him alone?

And was there any hope for his plans to tell the world about shifters? If Blacke got wind of what he was up to, he'd have him locked away and the key thrown away.

How would he get the support he'd need to execute his plans?

Even in bear form, glimpses of Gail kept popping into his mind. Why? Why couldn't he focus properly?

He wasn't sure how long he'd been running for, but in the distance, a familiar sight showed up, barely visible through the fog that had set in.

The large sprawling farm he'd grown up on. Home.

Why had he come here? He wasn't sure. But now that he was here, he might as well pop in.

There was a familiar scent in the air; his mom's famous pot roast. Was she expecting someone? It seemed like an odd meal to cook just for oneself.

Ever since his dad's passing, she'd lived alone on this large property. Henry wasn't sure how she managed everything, but every offer he'd made for her to move in with him and Maggie had fallen on deaf ears.

"Son," it was unmistakably her, who called out to him from the front door. "I've been expecting you." She stepped ahead into the light flooding the porch. Every time he saw her, her hair seemed to grow more white, her skin more fragile.

Henry hesitated. How was that possible? He hadn't even known himself that he would end up here.

"Mom. Thanks, but I won't stay long. Maggie will be wondering where I am."

"You didn't bring her along?" His mom reached out for him, and he leaned down, allowing her to pat the thick fur on his back.

Henry shook his head. "Just me."

"Very well. Why don't you freshen up? Dinner's almost ready."

Henry nodded and walked in through the spacious entrance, up the broad stairs leading to his old bedroom. Inside, he found a pair of jeans and a chunky hand knitted pullover already laid out for him. With a sigh, he let go of his bear and morphed back into his human self.

A heavy feeling overwhelmed him immediately. What was it? Sadness? Guilt?

The wooden steps creaked underneath his bare feet as

he made his way down.

When he entered the kitchen, his mom was already waiting, roasting tray in hand.

"I hope you're hungry." She smiled at him. "Son. What's troubling you? You don't look yourself today."

"How did you know I was coming?" Henry wondered aloud.

"I had a feeling... ever since I woke up this morning to milk the cows. I suppose a mother just knows."

That didn't make much sense to Henry, but he didn't want to question it anymore.

He followed her into the dining room and sat down at the large rectangular table. This place had always seemed disproportionate, too spacious for a couple and their only son. Now it was even odder, with his dad gone.

She started carving the meat and served him first, then herself.

"Eat. You look like you need it."

Henry nodded. He must have run quite a distance to get here. He wasn't even sure where he'd parked the car exactly. He'd have to find his way back by scent.

His mom observed him as he ate, taking only a couple of bites of the food herself. After a while, he couldn't stand being watched so closely anymore and put his knife and fork down.

"Something's on your mind," she said before Henry had the chance to say something himself.

He sat back and sighed. A lot of things were on his mind; she was right about that.

"You know, the work I do..." he started.

His mom pushed her plate away and folded her hands, resting them on the rough wood.

"To help our kind. With the Alliance," she responded.

"Right. Well lately, I wonder if it's really helping."

"I see. Do you want to quit; is that it?"

Henry shook his head. "No, I just want to make a difference, like I had hoped to."

"And you think the Alliance isn't succeeding at that?"

"I wonder if they're going down a wrong path. Something that'll do us more harm than our enemies are already doing."

"How so?"

"Did you know we're arresting our own kind now?" Henry also pushed his plate away. Talking about all this had ruined his appetite.

"For what?"

"For what... For taking a mate of a different species, that's the latest one. Did you know they're proposing to implant all newborn cubs with trackers now also? We haven't received the orders yet, but they're coming. They say it's for our safety, in case one of them gets taken, but who is to say it's not to keep tabs on them as well?"

His mom frowned. "Things have really changed, haven't they?" She shook her head.

"They have," Henry agreed. "I'm not sure I want any more part of it."

"Son. Only you can decide what to do. You must follow your instincts."

"Lately, I've been wondering if perhaps a lot of our problems wouldn't be solved if we started living out in the open."

His mom was silent for a moment. "Humans are afraid of what they don't understand."

"Exactly. If we can make them understand, through education, and dialogue, they'd have nothing to be afraid of anymore."

She shook her head again. "I don't know."

"We're not living in the Middle Ages anymore. Human

society is more tolerant now than it has ever been."

"You know better. It's hard to know what things are like outside these walls."

"I just don't know where to begin yet to make this happen."

She looked up and smiled at him. "You'll think of something. You always do."

Henry smiled back at her. It was good, being able to talk openly of all he'd been thinking about. He had hoped to have this conversation with Maggie, but obviously, that wasn't an option just yet; not until he had a solid plan in place.

# CHAPTER FOUR

———◆———

Ever since Blacke had mentioned the upcoming surprise visit to the Glasgow Alliance office, Gail had been struggling to keep her excitement under control. That's where the guy, Agent Weston, was based. The prospect of seeing him again made her giddy like a schoolgirl.

And perhaps, this time, he'd be on the same page and feel their connection as well.

She tried her best to keep her expectations in check, but it was no use.

Throughout the drive, she found it increasingly difficult to concentrate on the actual task at hand; organizing the documentation Blacke wanted to distribute regarding his latest pet project; a nationwide tracking program for young shifters. Project Safeguard, as he called it.

She had personally sent out memos to all the Alliance branches in the country a week ago. But that wasn't enough for Black, who insisted they must visit at least the nearest Alliance offices in person to ensure everyone's full participation.

Gail hadn't been keen for this new program to be rolled out. As much as Blacke insisted that his intentions were to track youngsters only in case they were reported missing by their parents, Gail couldn't shake the feeling that Project Safeguard could easily be misused as well.

She simply didn't trust Blacke. Gail glanced over at him sitting in the backseat of the spacious sedan beside her. He was furiously scribbling down notes of some sort. Preparing a speech, probably.

No matter what she thought about the tracker project,

he was going ahead with it, and she had no say in the matter. At least, it meant she had an excuse to see that guy again.

It had only been a few days since they'd first run into each other at HQ, but she'd had a hard time thinking about anything else but that first meeting. Agent Weston had infiltrated her every waking moment and some non-waking ones as well.

By the time the car turned off the motorway and entered the city, her heart was racing so much, it made her feel light-headed. She looked out the window, but couldn't properly focus on the buildings and streets they passed by. It all merged into a blur.

Fifteen minutes later, they stopped in front of an empty-looking, dilapidated building. Once you'd seen one Alliance branch office, you'd seen them all; that's what the agents at HQ had said. It was located in an old warehouse in what looked to be an old industrial estate. It had been populated during a time when the Alliance favored discretion over anything else, and completely unlike the HQ which looked a lot more intimidating.

The driver opened the door for Blacke, leaving Gail to get out from her side on her own. She quickly gathered all the paperwork off the seat and rushed to get to the front door and pressed the buzzer.

"Identify yourself, and state your purpose," a crackly female voice answered.

"Mr. Blacke, official Council business," Gail responded.

The door opened with a loud click, and she entered to hold it open for her boss, who was right behind her by now.

In front of them, a woman in full combat gear appeared. "Welcome, Sir," she said. "Shall I assemble everyone inside?"

Blacke nodded, barely slowing down on his way inside. The woman vanished as quickly as she had appeared, meanwhile Gail just tried to keep up with her boss, who clearly knew exactly where he was headed even if she didn't.

They soon entered an office space that looked quite similar to the one at HQ, though obviously not as grand and well-equipped. Half a dozen men and two women gathered around Blacke and Gail in a semi-circle.

"Welcome, Mr. Blacke, Sir," a familiar voice spoke behind them.

Gail could hardly contain her excitement. Agent Weston.

He nodded at her boss but didn't acknowledge her at all. Damn. So she was still the only one who could feel the attraction.

"Weston. Good, you're here. I have important matters to discuss. The files," Blacke turned to Gail, both his eyebrows raised expectantly.

Shit, the papers she'd been organizing. Gail shuffled through the things she'd carried inside and located the neat packets she'd prepared in the car. She handed them out to everyone in the room, finishing with Agent Weston. He still barely looked at her.

*What the hell?*

As soon as everyone had the documentation for Project Safeguard in front of them, Blacke started talking. He started off with the threat the Sons posed, about disappearances, and all that stuff Gail had heard so many times before. She retreated to a quiet corner and ignored Blacke's speech.

To keep from obsessing about Agent Weston too much, she started to read the top sheet of the papers she was still carrying. It was the handwritten notes Blacke had made in the car.

> Phase 1: Project Safeguard encourages families to volunteer for trackers (Blood & DNA testing as part of qualification process).
>
> Phase 2: Document families in detail, sending in teams as necessary to investigate their background and family tree.
>
> Phase 3: Classify everyone according to new points system (still to be devised, but non-participation in Phase 1 should count as a red flag), grading the purity of their bloodline. Refer to DNA tests carried out in Phase 1.
>
> Phase 4: Searchable database.
>
> Phase 5: Compulsory trackers for high-risk families.
>
> Phase 6: Activate audio transmission.

Underneath it was an incomplete flowchart with notes scribbled in the side, presumably behaviors Blacke didn't approve of, which he intended to record as part of the grading system.

Gail couldn't believe what she was reading. What he was proposing today was just the start of a much bigger, much more nefarious operation. Blacke was planning to divide up the shifter population, singling out families whose lineage he considered impure. To what end?

Didn't their kind have enough to worry about already, considering they were being hunted to death by the Sons of Domnall?

It was then that a single word in Blacke's speech caught Gail's attention. *Purity.*

# SCOTTISH WEREBEAR: A PAINFUL DILEMMA

She listened up just in time to hear him instruct the agents to start rounding up mixed couples in their jurisdiction.

"We've let these high risk behaviors slide for too long. But the shifter world is in crisis, ladies and gentlemen! We cannot afford to be so lax anymore."

Gail observed the crowd. Some, like the woman who had received them earlier, were nodding in agreement, while some others just seemed to be less convinced.

*This isn't right. This just isn't right,* Gail thought.

She felt a stare bore into her from across the room. Agent Weston. This was the first time she'd made proper eye-contact with the man. He was infuriatingly, distractingly handsome. Despite her concerns about Blacke's plans, she couldn't help but feel just a little bit excited to finally have Weston's full attention.

*No, it's not right,* a voice seemed to say in her head.

*I can hear you,* Gail thought.

*Yes.*

*Someone has to do something about this. Stop him before he goes too far.* Gail formulated the thought before even considering if she could trust him. Of course, she could, he was her mate after all. The feeling had to be mutual too; that's why he was in her head.

Mated couples could hear each other's thoughts; that's what all the stories said. Such is the connection when you find the one fate has picked out for you. Not that Gail personally knew a couple who could communicate telepathically, but that didn't make the stories any less true.

*We have to do something.* Agent Weston turned around to face the female agent who had greeted them before.

Before Gail could communicate anything else, she felt that their connection was broken. An immense sense of loss overwhelmed her, like a part of herself had gone

403

missing. *What the hell had just happened?*

"Keep up the good work!" Blacke nodded at the crowd and turned around to join Gail.

"If we hurry, we can make it to Edinburgh and back before nightfall," Blacke muttered.

Shit, she couldn't leave just yet, could she? This thing with Agent Weston was still unresolved. How could she go without talking to him properly? When would she see him again?

Gail turned to find him looking at her again, and immediately she felt more reassured.

*Go. I'll be in touch.*

She nodded subtly, hopefully subtly enough that nobody else could see.

There was no choice but to do what she was told right now. She didn't want to attract her boss's suspicion.

Before she had the chance to say or do anything else, Blacke had ushered her out of the room, down the hall and out of the building.

"We'll need another five information packs for Edinburgh," he said while getting into the back seat of the waiting car.

"Yes, sir."

The driver got in as well, and they pulled away swiftly, back-tracking their way through the same streets as before until they reached the motorway.

---

It had been a long day. The visit to Edinburgh was short, and the reaction of the agents there largely the same as in Glasgow. Some seemed convinced, others, not so much. Yet nobody argued or protested.

While she tried to stay alert, to assess which of the

agents seemed to take issue with Blacke's proposals, but all the while her mind was a couple of hundred miles away. Weston. She didn't even know his first name yet, and at the same time, the connection they'd felt had been undeniable this time.

Once they got back to the Alliance Headquarters, it was pitch dark outside. Blacke was unstoppable, though. Now that he had taken the first step and announced his plans to the two nearest offices, he wasn't ready to slow down.

"We fly out to London in the morning; book us some tickets," he ordered.

Gail's heart sank. London? She couldn't leave now, not when Weston was about to make contact with her. She paused for a moment. There was no other choice; she couldn't go.

"Umm, Sir?"

"What is it?" He frowned impatiently. Blacke wasn't used to having someone question him.

"I was wondering if I might stay behind. My father hasn't been doing well, and I'd hate to have something happen to him while I'm away." Gail felt bad having to use her dad as an excuse to get out of a work trip, but it had been the only excuse she could think of.

Blacke sighed. "Family is important. Very well. I'll have Agent Finch accompany me to London." Despite the words of understanding, he sounded displeased. Had her reason for staying back been any less important, she might have backed down immediately.

Gail smiled. "Thank you, Sir. I'll book your tickets immediately."

"Just don't let this become too regular. I need someone I can depend on. Occasional travel is part of the job, understood?"

"Understood, sir."

Gail breathed a sigh of relief as she returned to her desk to make the necessary travel arrangements. She could only hope that while Blacke was away, Weston would make good on his promise to get in touch.

Whatever plans he had to *do something* about Blacke's new project were only part of the reason of course. Really, Gail was just desperate to see Agent Weston again. Perhaps if they found themselves alone...

# CHAPTER FIVE

———— ◆ ————

Henry couldn't believe what had happened.

Just like that, during Blacke's short announcement, everything had changed. The Alliance Council leader had lost his mind; that much was clear. But at the same time, his words had presented Henry with a huge opportunity.

The tracker project was on. Although Henry had no intention of actually implanting young shifters with GPS transmitters as instructed, he was going to make sure to publicize the project as much as possible. He would talk to every shifter family he could get in contact with, in the hopes that most of them would be as suspicious as he had been when he first heard about it.

At the same time, the second announcement that it was now open season on mixed couples had even more potential. It had been only a few days since he had realized mixed couples were the ones who had most to gain if he started a counter-movement to Blacke's Alliance. He just didn't know how to get in touch with them.

If the Alliance started investigating people's private lives to the extent that Blacke intended, he would come across plenty of potential recruits for his new movement.

This wasn't without risk, though. He would have to figure out a way that he could identify these potential targets, and then keep them safe without Blacke or anyone else finding out what he was up to.

And then there was the other thing. The voice in his head. The connection he'd made with Gail. Completely by chance, he'd potentially found the partner he'd yearned for.

Of course, he still had to talk to her about everything,

but he was certain she'd join him. He'd felt her disgust, her outrage, as if it were his own.

Their relationship would be completely professional, of course. He'd have to find a way to keep his straying mind under control around her. Perhaps that would get easier in time. But he did need the help, and who better to have on his side than an insider in Blacke's own office?

It was perfect.

For the rest of the day, Henry was in a better mood than he'd been for weeks. He whistled to himself while planning to promote Project Safeguard, even writing up a flyer he wanted to get printed and distributed among the local shifter population.

On the surface, Blacke would be pleased with his efforts. Henry intended to be his star agent going forward. A true believer in his crazy ideas. The Glasgow office would lead the way and become an example throughout the Alliance.

When the time would come to reveal his new movement, Henry's betrayal would sting even deeper. How he looked forward to that.

"You're awfully cheerful today," Maggie remarked.

How long had she been standing next to him?

Henry shrugged. "Just getting on with work. Hey, could you get someone to run over to the printers and get these leaflets made up?" He handed her the sample he'd printed out himself.

Maggie paused. "Okay..."

"Oh, and tomorrow I was thinking of taking some time out to visit the farm to check up on mom," Henry added.

"You think that's wise? With everything we've got going on?" Maggie questioned him.

His good mood soured almost immediately. Why did she have to do this?

"You don't have to come. I only have one mother, though, don't I?" It wasn't fair for him to be too annoyed since his visit to his mom was mostly a ruse, but what if it hadn't been? What if he'd planned to go there purely out of concern for her?

Henry took a deep breath and bit his tongue. This wasn't the time to argue.

"Fine." Maggie shrugged and held up the print-out Henry had just given her. "I'll get this done then."

Henry nodded and focused once more on the paperwork ahead of him, even if his mind was struggling to get back on task.

———◆———

The following morning, Henry didn't bother coming into the office. After saying his goodbyes to Maggie at home, he made the drive up north straight away, heading for Stirling. Throughout the night, he'd been mulling over various ideas for getting Gail out of the office without raising suspicion in her colleagues, especially Blacke.

In the end, he'd decided to try the least invasive option first. Considering she was Blacke's assistant, chances were she'd answer his phone calls for him. If Blacke actually did answer, he'd report on progress with Project Safeguard instead.

As soon as he had the front gate of the large compound the Alliance Headquarters were situated in within his sights, he pulled over onto the soft verge. Henry took out his phone and dialed the number.

"Hello?" A male voice answered. The guy who manned the front desk, probably.

"Agent Weston for Mr. Blacke."

Just like that, the man had put through Henry's call.

Once again, there were certain advantages to his position within the Alliance.

"Mr. Blacke's office," a female voice said after only two rings.

It was her. It had to be.

"Weston here."

"Oh!" Was that surprise in her voice? Shock? He *had* told her he'd be in touch.

"Can I speak freely?"

"Uh, okay..."

"Is there some way you can get out of the office to talk?" Henry asked.

"I..." Gail cleared her throat, then continued in a much firmer tone, as though someone had just walked in on her. "I'm afraid Mr. Blacke is not available this week. Perhaps there's something I can help you with in the meantime?"

"How about you take an early lunch? Go for a refreshing walk through the grounds. I'll find you."

"No problem. I'll wait for your call." With that, she hung up.

They were on.

Although the road Henry's car was parked on was quiet, almost abandoned, he couldn't risk leaving his car here. He drove a little further ahead and pulled into an unpaved track leading into the forest surrounding Blacke's compound.

From here, he quickly prepared himself, leaving his clothes in the trunk of his car. Going in full bear would allow him a certain amount of stealth he could not muster in his human form. Within seconds, he was ready to shift.

Henry trudged through the forest, heading straight for the boundary fence. He closed his eyes and focused. Although Gail must have been at least a few hundred yards away from him, he could catch her scent already.

# SCOTTISH WEREBEAR: A PAINFUL DILEMMA

A few large trees near the fence allowed him to cross easily. From there, it was just a matter of following his nose. It didn't take long for him to find her.

*You made it,* Henry thought.

She held up a Tupperware box. *Lunch break, remember? So. Let's talk.*

Henry nodded. *We're the same, you and I. These new initiatives Black wants to implement... He needs to be stopped.*

*Yes.* Gail wrapped her arms around herself.

*I feel like I can trust you.*

She raised her head and stared at him. It was unnerving, like she could see through all the bullshit, right to his core. *You* can *trust me.*

*I had this idea, to stand up to Blacke. A new movement of people like us. As many fellow Alliance members as we can recruit, and regular people.*

Gail cocked her head to the side. *To what end?*

*Once we gain sufficient momentum, we go public. We'll blow the lid off the whole secrecy bullshit. We educate the human population, so they know not to fear us. We'll only be free if we can live out in the open.*

*Are you sure that's wise?*

Henry heard Gail's question, but he was pretty certain she wouldn't need much convincing. He could feel her growing excitement spill over into himself. Not only could he hear her thoughts - how, he wasn't quite sure - he could sense her emotions as well now.

*Think about it. Right now our people have so much to fear. Not only are the Sons after our blood, it's our own people, our own Alliance people who are surveilling us, to make sure we don't do anything wrong.* Henry paused, waiting for Gail's input.

*You're right. It's unacceptable.*

Again, her words didn't quite match her vibe. It was distracting. As much as she disapproved of Blacke's radical

411

ideas, she seemed... happy? It didn't make a lot of sense.

*I can't do this alone, though. I need a partner,* Henry thought.

*I imagine you do,* Gail answered.

*Will you help me?*

The more he looked at her, the more distracted he could feel himself become. His bear didn't often speak up, but right now, fully shifted, he had no choice but to listen to his primal call. She was beautiful. He wanted her.

Gail smiled and nodded, and Henry had to stop himself from pouncing.

No way, Henry wasn't about to let himself go off track. He'd always tried to be a good person; honest, loyal. He wasn't about to throw all that away. Henry swallowed hard and forced himself to shut down any remaining yearnings for the temptation that stood before him. Maggie would be waiting for him at home. He wouldn't betray her, or his own ideals.

*That's all? You want my help?* Gail asked, her mood wavering suddenly.

What a strange question. Henry observed her for a moment. Her eyes still tried to bore a hole in him.

*It's not going to be easy, but it's the right way forward,* he thought.

She nodded, then looked away. A strange melancholy seemed to overwhelm Gail and him along with her. They'd agreed to work together; wasn't that a good thing? Then why did she exude all this sadness? And why did it tear at him so much? He had to fix it, but he didn't know how.

*You're the only one I have confided in,* Henry thought.

Gail took a deep breath and looked away roughly in the direction of where Henry knew the Alliance building was located. *I should probably get back. How and when do we do this?* she asked.

*We can meet at a farmhouse not too far from here. We'll be safe there.*

Gail nodded. *Give me your number.*

They exchanged numbers and another awkward glance, before Gail turned to leave.

What a strange conversation they'd had, without even exchanging a single word out loud. And what an unusual, intriguing woman Gail was.

Henry had never had the benefit of reading anyone's mind, especially not a woman's mind. He had no idea what went on in Maggie's head most of the time.

Was she this complex as well? As guided by emotion?

Perhaps, though deep inside he suspected Gail *was* different. Either way, it didn't matter. Considering their unique connection, they'd work well together.

Henry returned to his car and changed back into his human self, making sure as before that he wasn't overlooked. From there he drove off straight to the farmhouse he'd alluded to; his childhood home.

He'd send Gail the directions upon arriving and wait for her to drop in after work. That's when they'd begin.

# CHAPTER SIX

———◆———

When Gail got back to her desk, she was still reeling with conflicted emotions. The encounter with Henry Weston had left her confused.

He obviously sensed her much more keenly now; that's what had allowed them to communicate so easily. And she'd felt whatever he'd felt. The attraction, the pull they seemed to have between them. She'd been ecstatic at first, sharing a secret meeting in the woods, just the two of them.

But he'd rejected their shared desires - he'd rejected *her*. Like none of what they shared meant anything. He wanted a partner to start some kind of revolution. He didn't want anything more intimate than that.

And who was this Maggie he'd kept thinking about?

Gail dropped the still full lunchbox into a drawer underneath her desk and pulled up files on the Glasgow office - the same ones she'd consulted earlier in the day in an effort to find out more about Henry himself. *Maggie, Maggie, Maggie.*

It didn't take her long to find a dossier about a Margaret who worked in Henry's office. So that was her.

Gail squinted at the picture that accompanied the file. She was a fierce looking brunette, reasonably attractive, fit.

So they were an item? Henry and her? The thought made Gail ill.

It was not supposed to be this way. When you find your mate, that was supposed to be it. There wasn't supposed to be any hesitation, any doubt. You were supposed to just follow your instincts and pair up.

# SCOTTISH WEREBEAR: A PAINFUL DILEMMA

Only Henry didn't seem to want to do that. All because of this woman.

Gail bit her bottom lip and fought the tears stinging in her eyes. This had been only the third time she'd met him, but somehow he'd made a space for himself in her heart. She should have told him to go away, that she wanted nothing to do with his revolutionary plans if he didn't also accept her as his mate. All or nothing.

She hadn't said anything of the sort, of course. Because she couldn't face the thought of *what if.* What if he'd rejected her demand? What if she never saw him again?

No, as much as it hurt, she had to meet with him again. She would do as asked and help him with his new movement. It helped that she shared his ideologies, so working together shouldn't be too difficult.

But it would hurt, being around him without being able to act on her instincts.

And he *had* felt something too, dammit! She had felt his lust as if it were her own.

This was *not* how these things were supposed to go!

"Hello, Love," a familiar voice behind Gail made her feel even more queasy.

"Agent Dumbarton, how can I help?" Gail pressed her lips together as she turned to look him in the eye. Instead of Finch, why couldn't Blacke have taken Dumbarton along with him to London? At least that would have gotten him out of her hair.

"Oh, I can think of a few ways." He winked at her.

Ugh. The sight of him made the hairs on the back of her neck stand up. Who the hell did he think he was? This was the wrong time to get on her bad side.

"I don't appreciate your tone," Gail snapped.

"Oh, don't you?" Dumbarton leaned down, resting his huge palm on the desk beside her, blocking her in.

Everything down to his scent repulsed her. Gail felt her skin tingle, the first sign that her inner bear was readying for a fight. Blacke was fond of Dumbarton, after all, they shared a similar propensity for violence, so getting into a physical altercation with him would not go down well. But Gail was close to not caring anymore about what her boss thought.

If it came down to it, she would defend herself against this brute.

"Well, perhaps you can relay a message to the boss."

"Sure," Gail said.

*Breathe in, breathe out. Calm down.*

"You can tell him that the prototypes for Project Safeguard are ready for field testing."

Gail nodded and made a show of noting down Dumbarton's message.

"Anything else?" she barked.

"No, darling. That's all for now." Dumbarton grinned at her and retreated from her desk.

Gail continued to stare at him as he took a couple of steps back and finally left her office. That's when she breathed a sigh of relief. God, how much she hated that guy.

———◆———

It was shortly after five o'clock when Gail started packing up her things, ready to leave. She'd received the message with Henry's directions a few hours earlier and memorized them. He'd asked her to leave her phone behind at the office, just in case Blacke had installed some kind of tracking software.

It was a bit paranoid, that request, but then again, tracking his own staff seemed like something Blacke would be capable of.

As she left the building, bracing herself against the frosty air, her nerves kicked in. What if she wouldn't be able to do this? Stay professional when every fiber in her body tried its best to do the opposite?

Well, tough. If she couldn't cope, that would be his problem. He would have sensed how she felt and asked for her help anyway. And *he* was the one trying to deny nature. It was all on him.

She navigated through the narrow roads leading away from the Alliance HQ, but rather than head home, she drove in the opposite direction. Gail had no trouble finding her way. Not only had she studied the route carefully all afternoon, it seemed like her instincts were guiding her right to Henry's position.

Of course, they did, he was her mate after all. Not that he accepted that.

Gail wrapped her fingers tighter around the steering until her knuckles turned white. This was going to be difficult.

By the time she pulled into the long driveway leading to the farm Henry had described in his message, she felt like she could pinpoint his exact location on the compound. He was waiting for her inside, heading for the front door.

The door opened just as she expected it to; only it wasn't just Henry greeting her. There was an elderly lady with him as well.

Gail got out and nodded at Henry, who immediately introduced her.

"Gail McPherson. A colleague from the Alliance." Henry's deep baritone made Gail's heart skip a few beats.

Gail offered her hand to the woman, who just stood there, smiling subtly first at her, then at Henry.

"A colleague. Sure, son. Whatever you say." Finally, she

did shake Gail's hand. "Helen Weston."

Henry looked at her, one eyebrow raised. Clearly this introduction hadn't gone quite how he had wanted it to.

"Nice to meet you, Mrs. Weston," Gail mumbled.

"No need to be so formal, sweetheart. Just call me Helen."

Gail nodded, though couldn't quite bring herself to do as asked.

Meanwhile, Henry was restlessly shifting his weight from one foot to the other. "Let's begin, shall we?"

"Sure," Gail agreed and followed him inside the house.

Henry led the way up the stairs, past framed old photographs and other mementos. When he had instructed her to come here, Gail never expected to actually be invited into the house he'd grown up in.

She took it all in. There were some pictures of just Henry when he was a boy, some with a man who bore a significant resemblance to him - probably his dad. Then there were the inevitable, much more formal family portraits of the three of them including his mother.

All of the photographs were decades old.

Unfortunately, Henry's pace didn't allow Gail to study each one of them carefully; she only managed a cursory glance while walking up the stairs and down the corridor, arriving at last in what must be the study. Shelves of dusty books lined the room, a grouping of leather arm chairs in the corner. There was a desk as well, shoehorned in between boxes upon boxes of old papers.

It was messy, but Gail felt comfortable at once. It looked a lot like Dad's study did, or at least how it used to look back before his retirement.

"We can work here," Henry said.

Gail nodded and stole a glance at him. So handsome. So tempting... While she admired him, he barely even looked up or paid attention to her.

*Stop it,* she reprimanded herself. If he wasn't interested in her, why should she be? The best thing for both of them would be to just get on with the job they'd come here for. Do the work and go home.

Henry sighed deeply as he sat down in one of the padded wooden chairs surrounding the desk and rubbed his forehead. Was he struggling with this as well?

"I have a mate already," Henry spoke softly, but his words were ringing in Gail's ears nevertheless.

"I know," she responded.

"As awkward as it is, I don't know who to trust with this." He gestured around at the boxes.

A closer look revealed they had Alliance labels on them. Had he taken home old records? What for?

"I understand," Gail forced herself to reply. *How about your so-called mate? Can't you trust her with this instead?*

Henry shook his head. "It's complicated."

Gail sat down opposite him and rested her bag against one of the legs of the desk. It wasn't any of her business why he wasn't working on all this with Maggie. What did she care?

*Fine, whatever. Let's get to work.*

And work, they did. After that initial ice-breaker, it surprisingly became easier to stay on task too. They understood each other perfectly. They agreed on a great deal of things, and their skills and experience complemented each other well too.

Henry knew how to do field work; Gail knew how Blacke ran his office and had access to information Henry could have never obtained.

Before they knew it, they'd spent hours in that little room, discussing strategy, drawing up plans and studying some of the files Henry had obtained. Dinner, which his mom had lovingly prepared, had been their only interruption.

Suddenly, by late evening, they'd gone from a whole lot of wishful thinking regarding how things *should be* to having a workable plan on how to make it happen. The New Alliance was born.

It was already past midnight when they said their goodbyes. Despite the initial difficulties, Gail felt a lot more positive about what she had come here to do. If she couldn't have him as a mate, at least they'd become friends.

Gail drove home largely on autopilot.

As much as it pained her to admit it to herself, he was right to want to remain faithful to Maggie. Henry wasn't the sort of man to shy away from his commitments. He was honorable and faithful. If only he had been hers.

# CHAPTER SEVEN

———◆———

When Henry got home that night, Maggie was already asleep. He took care to make as little noise as possible getting ready for bed.

Today had been a giant leap in the right direction. With Gail's help, this new movement of theirs actually had a chance.

The one thing he couldn't get out of his head, though, was how she'd made him feel. He'd tried to let her down easy - a near impossible feat, considering he couldn't even look at her straight. The hurt he knew she felt at his rejection had just made things harder.

Now, as he stood beside the bed in their shared apartment, he couldn't look at Maggie straight either. Something felt wrong.

*It's because I'm lying to her. Hiding what I'm up to*, Henry tried to convince himself. That didn't seem right, though. More likely, he was guilty because he'd put himself in a position where he was going to spend a significant amount of time with another woman. One he found difficult to resist.

And what was worse, no matter how hard he'd fought it, he'd started to care for the other woman as well.

*She's just a colleague. We're only working together, nothing else.*

He'd tried repeating those words in his head all evening, and they still didn't ring quite true.

But what was he to do? If he wanted the New Alliance to be successful, he'd need the help. It wasn't easy to find someone who believed in the same things. He would have never even found out about Gail's ideologies if he hadn't

421

heard her voice in his head. Surely that meant that her involvement was somehow meant to be?

Henry carefully got into bed and closed his eyes but couldn't find rest. Images of Gail danced in front of his mind's eye, forcing him to open his eyes again to stare at the ceiling.

They'd had their ups and downs, Maggie and him. But never before had he felt so alone in her company.

———◆———

The next morning, Henry started to put one of his plans into action. He drafted in the whole Glasgow office. Everyone was to investigate certain high-risk individuals in an effort to identify anyone engaging in so-called *unacceptable behavior.*

They had identified so many potential suspects that he broke procedure and ordered his agents into the field individually rather than in pairs. His reasons for this were two-fold: he'd have the opportunity to sneak away to the farm without Maggie noticing, and his agents would be forced to observe rather than act if they found anything untoward.

It was one thing arresting someone when it was two-against-one, but to confront a riled up bear who might think his mate's safety was being threatened? Nobody on his team would be reckless enough to attempt it, not even Maggie.

*Blacke's orders,* Henry had said. *Forget about the Sons; we've handed them off to HQ. I expect results on this. Find me some rule-breakers and fast.*

As the office started to clear out, with all his agents leaving to start their individual assignments, he was left behind at his desk. It was shocking how easily everyone had accepted their orders. As if nobody saw the insanity in violating the privacy of their own people on such a large scale.

Henry listlessly stared at the papers on his desk; he was unable to focus on any words in particular, though. It was all just a blur.

He sat back and rubbed his eyes. Thanks to his late return from the farm, he'd not had much sleep. If there was one thing bears didn't like, it was a lack of sleep or food for that matter.

But this was not the time for rest. A strong and extra sweet cup of coffee later, Henry forced himself back to work. After handing off the field jobs to his team, it was down to him to contact all the shifter families with young children to inform them about the tracker project. It wasn't ideal, trying to gauge their reactions over the phone, but this was the only way he could do it by himself.

Then, by the afternoon, he'd make a quick call to Gail to update her with any progress made. In turn, she would give him the latest updates on what was happening at the HQ.

That's exactly how the day went, and the day after that. By the third day into this new routine, some of Henry's team, most notably Maggie, had gathered actionable intel.

They were starting to deliver Henry's so-called rule-breakers, just as he had ordered. File after file containing observations from his agents landed on his desk. It was down to him to decide follow-up action.

It was sickening. All these lives, which Blacke intended to ruin. Couples, even families, to be torn apart. And everyone except Henry was so enthusiastic about it too.

At the same time, his work on Project Safeguard was chugging along slowly. He'd made progress for Blacke - a lot of the families sounded positive. Fear was a strong motivator to throw one's privacy out the window. This was bad news for the New Alliance.

"Another one?" Henry asked, his heart heavy with dread as Maggie delivered yet another file.

"This one's the most promising one yet. The couple has been together for years." She grinned at him.

"And the man is human, you say?" Henry asked, scanning Maggie's report.

"Yep. I verified it myself."

"Good job," Henry mumbled while flipping the page to find some holiday snaps of the couple together.

"So, when do we go in?" Maggie asked.

"This is a delicate matter. We don't want to tip off the others, or they might try to run," Henry reasoned. Actually, he didn't want to take official action at all, just approach these people himself to drum up support for the New Alliance.

"Understood. So... When?"

"I'll discuss it with Headquarters. Perhaps they've drawn up some guidelines..."

Maggie squinted at him and pursed her lips. What was she thinking? How convenient it would be if he could just read her thoughts too.

"In the meantime, here are some more cases you can look into." Henry handed her a stack of new files. "Good work. Keep it up."

She didn't look pleased, but he couldn't afford to get into a lengthy conversation about it right now either. Henry picked up another pending file off his desk and pretended to read until she walked away.

He counted the reports his agents had turned in. Half a dozen already, with more to come as they completed their various assignments. He'd contact HQ today, but not to ask for Blacke's orders on the matter.

# SCOTTISH WEREBEAR: A PAINFUL DILEMMA

After visiting with these people, he'd have to let Gail know about their progress.

Once Maggie had left the premises again, he picked up the first file from his desk. The one she'd just delivered. *Most promising indeed...* These people would have the most to lose.

Henry would start with them, try to reason with the woman on her own first, then perhaps involve the human partner in discussions as well.

It took him the whole afternoon to track them down, but at last, he managed to locate the woman, Irene Finch, and take her aside for a quiet chat outside her office.

"What is it you want from me, exactly?" she asked while studying his ID.

"Well - I hope you don't mind me calling you Irene-" Henry began.

She shook her head.

"You know about what we do at the Alliance?"

"Yeah. You investigate threats against shifters."

"Right, well, let's say that in recent times the Alliance's focus has shifted - excuse the pun."

"I don't understand." Irene gave Henry back his credentials.

"You might want to sit down." Henry nodded at a park bench near where they were standing.

She reluctantly followed him and took a seat. That's when he told her the whole Alliance story, from beginning to end. About Blacke's new initiatives, the trackers, the concerns about secrecy.

By the end, Irene had turned white as a sheet.

"What do we do? Clive is my mate. I can't just-" She held her head in her hands. "Oh, God."

"It's okay. I don't agree with them either. A few of us are planning an initiative of our own."

"I'm listening."

And so Henry told her a better-rehearsed version of what he'd said to Matt that day. Going public was the only way forward. If he didn't already believe in his cause so strongly, he would have convinced himself. Luckily, Irene agreed.

She was in. And even better, she knew a whole bunch of couples not yet on the Alliance radar who were in a very similar situation. With her help, the New Alliance would grow significantly overnight.

They called it viral marketing; Henry had read up on it. When you tell your friends about something, and they tell their friends. Within a short time, the number of people involved would grow exponentially, just like a virus.

By the time he left Irene, Henry was feeling pumped. It would soon get dark, early as it always did in winter. But he wasn't ready to head back to the office. Instead, he informed Gail of his progress and then pulled out the next file from the stack his agents had turned in. Perhaps he'd be able to locate another potential recruit.

They had no time to lose. Sooner or later, Maggie would lose patience and insist that they start rounding people up. He could only protect these couples for so long.

———— ◆ ————

By the time Henry got home, Maggie was already sitting in her usual seat at the dinner table, waiting. It had been her turn to cook tonight; food was on the table.

"Where have you been?" she asked.

He waved away her question. "Oh, I was just talking to some of the families who are good candidates for Project Safeguard. Some needed a bit more convincing than what I could manage over the phone." He took off his coat and eagerly joined her. "This smells amazing."

Henry smiled at her, but she didn't reciprocate.

"Potatoes?" Maggie held up the dish in his direction.

"Thanks."

The food tasted good too. Running around all afternoon had made him hungry, so he didn't hesitate to load up his plate. As he started to eat, Maggie just observed him.

"So how many candidates have we got?" she asked finally.

He shrugged. "Most of my afternoon was spent just trying to convince one set of parents. Don't you miss the good old days, when our days were spent running after the bad guys?" Henry joked.

Maggie didn't crack even the smallest of smiles. "We're still doing that, running after bad guys, just more quietly."

"Right," Henry said. Spying on unsuspecting people who might have mistakenly fallen in love with the wrong person would have been a more accurate description.

"I feel like I hardly see you anymore, now that we're working apart every day," Maggie remarked.

Henry looked up, to find those sharp eyes of hers staring at him.

"Perhaps we can go away somewhere, just the two of us, this weekend?" she suggested.

Henry looked down at his plate again and loaded his fork with more meat.

"Actually, I was hoping to visit mom again. As you know, she's-"

"I know," Maggie interrupted him. "She's been having a hard time lately."

She picked up her half-full plate and put some of the potatoes back into the dish. Then she got up and carried it towards the kitchen.

"You're done?" Henry asked.

Maggie didn't respond.

Henry shrugged and continued eating. They'd had some version of this argument already the day before he'd driven up to Stirling to meet Gail. Why Maggie seemed so jealous of him spending time with his mother, he'd never understand. He never did understand what went on inside her head most of the time.

Once finished, he did his half of the work for the evening; tidying up the kitchen. Then, he wanted nothing more than to crash for the night.

Maggie was already asleep on her side of the bed, so he took care not to make too much noise.

As soon as he'd rested his head on the pillow, just a couple of little words turned his world up-side-down.

"Who's Gail?"

# CHAPTER EIGHT

———◆———

Ever since Blacke had returned from his short visit to London, Gail's days had become busier than ever. There was always someone to call, a memo to write, a parcel to courier.

At the same time, her nights were shorter than ever. When she wasn't coordinating with Henry over the phone, she spent a ridiculous amount of time fantasizing about him. It was painful, recalling the details of their few meetings, and yet she couldn't stop thinking about him.

This morning was no different. Gail had been drifting in and out of sleep for hours; her mind occupied with just one thing. Every time she'd closed her eyes, the same images had overwhelmed her. Henry, looking at her with the love and admiration she knew he'd be capable of, if only he'd accept that fate intended for them to be together.

If she let herself, the images would get more intimate, more intense.

*Oh, why not.* She'd never felt anything as exciting as what she experienced when she let her mind run wild with the fantasy of Henry Weston.

All the bears she knew had hard, strong bodies, but none of them had anything on Henry. The visions her imagination chose to feed her were beyond compare. He was perfect.

*Henry hovered over her for a moment, holding his weight up with those muscular arms of his. His eyes focused on her lips for a moment, then he dove down and tasted her.*

Gail sighed. It never took long for the fantasy to have an effect.

She reached down between her legs and felt that she was already wet.

*He lowered himself on top of her, slowly. His naked skin felt hot against her fingertips as she explored the contours of his upper arms and back. Gail reached around him and pulled him against her tighter.*

*Together, they made the perfect couple. Hard muscle against soft curves.*

Gail had never dated much. A true romantic, she'd held out for Mr. Right. The one upside to this relative inexperience was that she knew exactly how to take matters into her own hands. Literally.

She writhed against the sheets as her fingertips found those special, forbidden places that very few had found before. What else could she do? This was the best she could hope for. To finger herself to orgasm to the dream of Henry Weston.

There was no way she'd get over him. No way could she bring herself to consider another man.

Gail's moment of ecstasy was short-lived. Her alarm pierced the silence of her bedroom, jerking her back into reality. Damn.

Another day of rushing around the Alliance HQ, running various errands for Blacke, awaited. Despite the pleasure she'd just felt, the loss that overwhelmed her now, while dragging herself out of bed, cut deep. Would she ever experience anything like what she'd fantasized about?

Probably not.

As much as that knowledge hurt, a light still awaited Gail at the end of what was going to be a long, dark day. Her daily phone conversation with Henry. Despite everything, she couldn't wait to hear his voice.

# SCOTTISH WEREBEAR: A PAINFUL DILEMMA

———— ♦ ————

Today, Gail didn't need to wait too long to hear from Henry. By four, he'd sent her a message, giving her some very good news indeed. He'd confronted the first of a number of mixed couples his office had identified in response to Blacke's recent orders.

The woman, Irene Finch, had pledged her support.

Gail smiled and put her phone back into her pocket and picked up the pot of coffee.

"Darling, how about you pour me a cuppa as well?"

Gail closed her eyes and took a deep breath. Don't engage him. Don't encourage him.

"Agent Dumbarton. I'm sure you're capable enough to know your way around a coffee maker." Gail turned to walk off with her boss's mug of coffee. Blond, four sugars, she'd counted them carefully to avoid a repeat of her first week, when she accidentally had added too much.

"Come on! No need to be rude." Dumbarton blocked her way.

"I'm needed in my office," Gail said.

Ugh. What a repugnant man. She didn't have time for this. Gail stepped aside to dodge him to be on her way.

That's when Dumbarton changed position, cutting off her exit route.

"What's the rush, darling?" He grinned.

Her heart started to beat faster, and a thin layer of sweat formed over her entire body. This was unacceptable. His behavior-

Gail scanned the room. Where *was* everybody? Normally, there were at least half a dozen agents hanging around the coffee maker or the water cooler, depending on the season. Another two or three would be sitting at their desks doing actual work.

Today, everyone seemed to have vanished.

Wouldn't someone - anyone - walk in to diffuse this bind Dumbarton had gotten her into?

"Mr. Blacke likes his coffee hot. I don't think-"

"I like something else hot," Dumbarton whispered.

"This is inappropriate," Gail insisted.

"Come on; nobody's around. You don't have to pretend. I know you're well up for it; I can smell it on ya." Dumbarton leaned forward, his face only an inch away from hers and inhaled sharply.

Gail's fight or flight instinct was kicking in. He was bigger and much stronger than her; Dumbarton was another brown bear. If she fought him, he'd win. She'd have to be smarter than that...

So instead of charging forward, she retreated, hitting into the cabinet behind her. She put the mug down - Blacke would not be amused if Gail broke his monogrammed mug - and flung her arm around while diving off to the side as though she'd lost her balance.

She hit her hand into the coffee maker, causing it to crash to the floor beside them.

It made an almighty racket as the glass receptacle smashed into a million pieces. That, plus the flood of hot liquid spilling onto the floor was enough to distract Dumbarton.

"Oh, damn, I'm so clumsy," Gail said. "I'd better get Gerry to clean that up before someone gets hurt."

Dumbarton still stood there, dumbfounded at what had just occurred as she marched off. Gail just remembered to snatch Blacke's still steaming mug from the cabinet before fleeing out the door.

That was a close call.

She looked down at the coffee stains on her suede

pumps. Damnit. She really liked these shoes too. Gail rushed into Blacke's office, placing the mug on his desk and immediately retreated to her own desk, right outside. What a relief.

From now on, she'd have to be more vigilant and not allow herself to get cornered by that man again. This, along with all the other crap she'd had to deal with in this job would have been enough to make her quit, if it wasn't for her alternate agenda.

If the New Alliance movement was going to succeed, they needed an insider in Blacke's administration. There was no way she'd give up now that they were getting so close.

"McPherson."

Gail looked up to find Agent Finch standing in the doorway.

"Agent Finch. How can I help?"

He looked around the hallway once before entering her office.

"This is a bit delicate," he started.

Gail observed the man. They hadn't interacted much during her short time working here. The most they'd ever spoken was when she'd made the arrangements for him to travel with Blacke to London. He'd always come across like a quiet man, serious about his work, but without the violent streak some of the others in the office demonstrated.

"Yes?" Gail asked.

Finch gestured at her to come closer and again checked left and right, probably to make sure they weren't being overheard.

Gail got up and joined him outside, then closed the door. Bears had exceptional hearing, but there was no way Blacke would be able to hear them with this kind of distance and a closed door between them.

"Well handled, the matter with Dumbarton," Finch said.

Gail took a step backward, hitting into the door from behind. "You saw that?"

"Not the whole thing. I was about to intervene when you- Well, good job."

"Was that all you wanted to tell me?" Gail frowned. This was an awkward conversation to have. Some things were best left undiscussed.

"Actually, I do have this." Agent Finch handed her the dossier he'd been holding. "I trust you'll know what to do with this."

He looked back and forth again and walked off as if their conversation had never happened.

Weird guy. He seemed awfully paranoid for some reason.

Gail opened the file and read the first sheet. It was a surveillance recommendation that had come in from the Glasgow office.

Her throat went dry when she read the whole thing.

*Target Name: Helen Weston.*
*Requested Mode: Phone tap.*

The request had been signed by the most unlikely of people: Henry Weston himself.

Gail closed the file and rushed back inside to her desk. She opened her drawer and found some old reports he'd filed with HQ. The signature was similar enough to convince most people, but not Gail.

There was no way he'd sign anything like that, so who could have done it? The other agents in his office would have access to his signature, so any of them could have faked it. This was bad. Someone within Henry's team had gone rogue.

She had to notify him as soon as possible. Gail checked her watch. It was almost five o'clock. He usually called around six, so she still had a little time to gather more details. Finch had handed her the file, rather than Blacke himself. Did that mean he doubted its authenticity as well?

Had someone else seen it and actually acted on it before it ended up with her?

Gail powered up her computer and checked the inventory. If someone had tapped the phone at Helen Weston's home, they would have had to check out a transmitter. Currently, this was not the case.

"Gail?" Blacke's voice called out from his office.

Gail quickly closed the inventory file and switched off her monitor. "Yes, sir?"

"A word, before you leave."

Typical. There were always a few things Blacke would remember at the end of the day, delaying her journey home. Gail forced a smile as she entered his office.

"I had a thought regarding old man Campbell, downstairs. Note all this down."

Gail nodded and started writing.

"He has a daughter." Blacke folded his hands and sat back with a smug grin on his face. "If we manage to track her down, I wonder if we'll have more luck interrogating him..."

"Very good, Sir. Shall I notify the Edinburgh office?" Gail asked.

Blacke shook his head. "No, I think I'd prefer to have my own men handle this."

# CHAPTER NINE

---•---

Henry stared at the ceiling. Shit, had Maggie actually just said those words?

"Who's Gail?" she repeated herself.

This was bad.

"You mean Gail McPherson? Blacke's personal assistant," he responded, in as calm a voice as he could manage.

"Aha..." Maggie said.

Was that it? Was that all she wanted to know?

"Why do you ask?" Henry asked though he wasn't certain he wanted to know exactly. What on earth had he done to spark this question?

"Is there any particular reason why she would call you after hours?"

Call him? What was she talking about? Henry instinctively reached for the spot on the bedside table where he always kept his phone, but there was nothing there.

"You'd left it in your coat." Maggie tossed the mobile onto his side of the bed. It landed in the center of Henry's chest.

He had a quick look. Three missed calls, the earliest at six in the evening.

"She must have been responding to the message I left, about how to proceed with those couples. Like I told you this morning, remember?" Henry explained, his mind racing. Had Gail sent any messages as well? Had Maggie *read* them? He generally made sure to delete his conversations with Gail; had he accidentally left something behind for Maggie to find?

Hang on, why was he feeling guilty? He wasn't doing anything wrong. They were just working together, Gail and him. Why was he making excuses and behaving like he'd cheated somehow?

"I can't do this anymore," Maggie whispered.

Wait, what?!

Henry sat up straight and turned to face Maggie.

"You can't do *what* anymore? What do you think is going on here exactly?"

Maggie shrugged. "Ever since the other week, when you drove down to Gartcosh by yourself - if that's where you actually went… I feel like we might as well live on two different planets, you and I. And don't try to deny it. You're not the same person." Her tone was ambiguous. Henry couldn't make out if she was angry, sad, or just fishing for a reaction.

Henry wanted to protest but decided to hold out. Perhaps she was just venting her frustrations about his refusal to take her away for the weekend.

"I saw you look at her, when Blacke was at the office. I didn't think much of it at the time, but now things are falling into place."

"There's nothing going on between Gail and me."

"So you call her *Gail*. That's how well you know each other!" Maggie taunted.

Damn. He'd walked right into that one.

"We've been talking a lot about Project Safeguard lately. Yeah, I know her a little bit."

Maggie nodded but refused to make eye contact with him or even turn in his direction. She just remained as she was, on her back, staring straight at the ceiling.

Things weren't so uncertain anymore. She was definitely angry and trying to cover it up.

Henry rested his hand on her arm, only for her to shake it off.

"Just come right out with it. Beating around the bush doesn't suit you," Henry said.

That's when he got a reaction. She turned her head and shot him a deadly glare. Maggie was not amused at all.

"Fine. Have it your way. Have you been *fucking* Gail McPherson? Huh?" she didn't speak the words as much as spat them out and folded her arms. Her eyes were once more glued to the ceiling.

"No." Henry shook his head, then leaned over to get back into Maggie's line of sight. "No! Look at me. I haven't touched the woman. Like I said, we've just been working together."

"Working together. That's just great." Maggie let out a fake chuckle. "I wasn't born yesterday. Does Blacke know the two of you are *working together*? And I don't know her, but who the hell makes work calls at nine in the fucking evening? Nobody is that dedicated, not even Blacke's precious little personal assistant."

"Look, Maggie, darling..." Henry tried to touch her again, but she flinched like the first time.

"I don't want to hear it."

"And Tuesday night? When you came home who knows when? You were with her, weren't you?"

So far, Henry had been skirting around the truth but not actually lied about Gail. Of course, he hadn't done anything appropriate. Not that he hadn't wanted to with every cell in his body. It would be easier to deny it, but that wasn't his style.

"Yes. Although I went to the farm that day, I was near Stirling anyway, so I felt it wise to arrange for a meeting."

"At night?"

"In the evening. It ran late."

"I don't want to talk about this anymore," Maggie's voice sounded choked with anger. "I think it would be best if you left now."

"What? This is my home too!" Henry protested.

"Just believe me. It's best for both of us. Just leave." Maggie turned onto her side facing away from Henry.

He was generally a patient guy, at least he liked to think so. And fair, he was fair as well. And despite his attraction for Gail, he hadn't crossed the line with her. Maggie had no right to kick him out of the house!

At the same time, if he wanted to increase his chances of making things right with her, perhaps it would be better to do as he was told. He'd give her this little victory, with a view to picking up this conflict later, and winning the war, as it were.

He'd explain everything, demonstrate how much Maggie meant to him, and things would work themselves out.

Henry got out of bed, put on the same clothes he'd changed out of only a little while earlier, and threw a few random items into a backpack. He was going to leave, if that's what Maggie wanted. But not empty-handed.

Once the bag was full, and he'd retrieved his toothbrush and other necessities from the bathroom, he left. He didn't say goodbye or look back. That would have just made Maggie's anger flare back up again.

There was nowhere for him to go, except one place. It wouldn't be comfortable, but at least the holding cells were empty ever since he'd delivered those prisoners to HQ the previous week. Tonight, it would be just him in that building.

Things would look different come morning.

———◆———

Henry hadn't had a good night. Throughout, if there wasn't a strange rustle or creak somewhere in the building disturbing his sleep, there were those incessant dreams he couldn't get rid of. Gail.

It was infuriating.

*This.* This right here was the reason Maggie had thrown him out. And as much as he fought Gail's pull on him, he just couldn't shut it off completely.

And the worst part was, he still had no idea how to make things right with Maggie. It was all his own fault, wasn't it? There was no excuse, no justification that would pacify her. *The truth.*

The truth would piss her off in an entirely new way. They'd made progress, Gail and him, but they were far from ready to go public with their plan. She'd never be convinced right now, would she?

But it was all he had.

Henry got up at five, stretching his aching limbs on his way out of the holding cell he'd repurposed as a bedroom for the night. The hard cots the Alliance had provided were far from comfortable, especially for someone as tall as Henry.

Once at his desk, coffee in hand, he let his mind run through the various potential outcomes for Maggie and him. He had no other choice. Maggie needed to know the truth.

So he waited. And waited some more.

By eight, the first agents started to arrive. Some looked surprised to find Henry already at work, but nobody said anything.

Maggie was nowhere to be seen, though.

Finally, by nine-thirty, Henry had had enough. It was one thing to turn him out of his own home after accusing him of stuff he didn't actually do. But she had a job to do here. Not showing up for it was unprofessional and very unlike her. So he did what he would have, had any other team member not shown up for work; he called her. No answer.

That was it. If she wasn't going to come in on her own accord, he'd have to go to her.

———◆———

"Maggie, open up!" Henry called out through the letterbox of what had been their shared apartment for the past two years. He'd tried unlocking it, but Maggie must have put the latch on from the inside.

There was some movement inside but no response.

He knocked on the door again, harder this time.

No way would he just give up on this. Their relationship meant too much to him.

"I'll explain everything. Believe me, you will want to hear this," Henry pleaded.

He waited around a little longer, listening for Maggie's footsteps inside. Finally, he heard her approach.

The lock clicked, and the door opened just a crack.

"Not here. I don't want to discuss Alliance business out in the street," Henry said.

Maggie pressed her lips together in contempt and averted her gaze to the floor. Then she stepped aside, allowing Henry inside the house.

"Make it quick," Maggie said and folded her arms. Like the previous night, she didn't even look at him.

"I left last night to give you space. But I never did anything with that woman. Please believe me," Henry whispered.

Did she not know him at all? How could she think he'd be unfaithful?

"So why was she calling you at nine in the evening? And don't give me the same bullshit again. I can tell when you're lying," Maggie said.

"Then look at me. You'll see I'm telling the truth." Henry reached for her, guiding her chin up toward him.

"It wasn't Alliance business, not exactly. But we are working together."

Maggie cocked her head to the side, frowning. Her eyes were cold; he couldn't read them.

"You remember when we had dinner the other week. I was talking about some doubts I had..."

"What does that have to do with-"

"I'm getting to it. Just let me finish."

Maggie sighed, then looked away again. Somehow, not having her stare him down actually made it easier to explain the rest.

"For a while now, I've felt like we're heading in a dangerous direction, the Alliance is, I mean. Like our focus has shifted from our actual enemies towards members of our own community who have made certain lifestyle choices..."

"Secrecy is the only way we have to ensure our safety," Maggie argued.

"I'm not sure of that anymore. If we educate the human population- if we show them that they have nothing to fear from us..." Henry said.

"They'll hunt us down. We won't be fighting just a small group of humans, but millions of them!" Maggie took a step back and glared at him.

"People are better than that. They're only afraid of what they don't know. We just have to make sure that we're the ones talking to them, rather than the Sons!" Henry took a step forward, placing his hand on her arm.

Maggie shook her head, slowly at first, then more violently.

"No, I don't accept that. And I can't believe that someone who works in Blacke's very own office would believe that either."

"But she does. Gail does believe that. That's what we've been working on together. To figure out a way to educate people!" Henry said.

"I don't want to hear her name anymore."

"Okay..." Henry squeezed Maggie's arm. At least, she wasn't retreating anymore.

"And I can't accept these crazy ideas of yours." Maggie bit her bottom lip.

"They're not crazy. Just give it a chance, once we get support..."

"No. No way. I can't."

"Please, Mags. This is important to me," Henry pleaded.

She shook her head again. "No. This is it. You have to decide what's more important to you. This stupid plan or our relationship."

Henry couldn't believe his ears. He could understand that she had trouble seeing his side of things - she could be very stubborn after all. But to make him choose?

"I mean it, Henry. You pick. Me or *this*..." Maggie gestured at him. "This lunacy."

Henry took a deep breath. That was it. He wouldn't give up on Maggie. She was his mate.

So he had to bear another loss. To win the war.

# CHAPTER TEN

———◆———

Gail woke up early. But it wasn't the same old visions of Henry that had roused her from her sleep; it was something else. A nagging feeling in the pit of her stomach. Something was wrong, and she couldn't figure out what it was.

For hours, she tossed and turned, but that feeling never left her. Was she coming down with something? Or perhaps she was dreading going to work because of what had happened with Dumbarton yesterday?

The thought of him just made her angry, not anxious. She'd freed herself of him once; she'd do it again. No, something else was causing this.

Unfortunately, without knowing what it was, Gail couldn't do anything about it. So she followed her usual routine and went to work as if nothing had happened.

By the ten o'clock, she was a nervous wreck. No matter what she tried, she couldn't focus at all. What had started as an awkward sort of sensation in her stomach, had grown and evolved. Palpitations, cold sweats; it was as though she had a fever coming on, but with none of the usual symptoms of the season flu that had been going around.

Finally, she couldn't take it anymore and hid herself away in the ladies' room. The reflection looking back at her from the mirror didn't look like her usual self. Normally, she never had dark circles, but this morning she did. Her skin had turned from its normal warm olive to a sickly sort of yellow even foundation couldn't fix properly.

Gail was still staring at herself wondering what had

happened to her overnight when her mobile rang, scaring her half to death.

She fumbled with her handbag and retrieved it as quickly as she could. Henry. Her chest tightened, breaths quickened. That was it. Something was wrong with him!

"Hello?" she answered, her voice trembling noticeably.

"Gail. What I'm about to ask of you isn't fair, I know. But I have no other choice." Henry's voice sounded flat. Gail couldn't detect emotion in his tone at all.

"What's wrong? Something's happened; I could feel it all morning!" she blurted out.

"It's best not to dwell on things. The bottom line is, I can't work with you anymore."

Gail was speechless. That wasn't what she expected him to say at all.

"You don't want my help anymore?" she asked finally.

"No, no. Your help is more crucial than ever. I'm talking about my own involvement. I can't-" Henry took a deep breath. "The New Alliance must go on without me."

Gail turned her back against the wall and sank to the floor. This was it. The terrible black cloud that had been hanging over her. Henry was terminating their working relationship.

Why, though? There was only one reason that made sense. Somehow, Maggie must have found out about it and forced his hand.

"This was your project. Your idea. How will I continue on my own?" Gail whispered. *How will I survive on my own if I never see you again?*

Silent tears streamed down her face.

"It's not my choice. My duty is to my mate first."

So Maggie *was* the one who had inspired his sudden decision. Gail hated her with all her heart. How dare she interfere in the good work they were doing? The New

Alliance would ensure the safety of generations of shifters to come.

At the very least, someone had to stop Blacke before he put his latest ideas into practice. The man was trying to secure his position, and it would be near impossible to get rid of him once he succeeded.

"Your duty isn't to your people as well? Isn't that why you took a job with the Alliance in the first place?" Gail argued.

"I'm sorry. I can't do this anymore." With those last words, Henry hung up.

Gail dropped the phone into her lap and rested her head in her hands. She couldn't contain her despair anymore and started to sob, her whole body trembling as she released the heartache she felt.

It was like being cut in half. His duty was to his mate first, bah! That Maggie woman was only his mate in name. Their connection wasn't real, it couldn't be, not after everything Gail had felt in his presence.

He'd already discarded her as a lover from the moment they started working together, but as long as they kept in touch, there had been a glimmer of hope. One day he might see the truth for himself. One day he might understand that they were meant to be.

But now, this? After all she had done for him? The New Alliance wouldn't have been possible without her help; he'd said so himself. And she'd believed in the cause as much as he did. How dare he leave her alone in this! *How dare he!*

Gail wasn't sure how long she'd sat there, waiting for the flow of tears to stop. Blacke would be wondering where she was... Gail got herself up off the cold bathroom floor and looked in the mirror.

In one morning, she'd aged a decade.

# SCOTTISH WEREBEAR: A PAINFUL DILEMMA

This just wasn't right. Why couldn't things just be simple, like they were supposed to be? They were supposed to be partners, and now she was alone. Gail couldn't begin to think about how she'd handle things.

She bit her lip and took out a wet wipe from her handbag. If she had to go out there and face her boss, she couldn't do it with streaks of mascara on her cheeks.

It took her a while, but by the end, Gail had eliminated most of the evidence of her breakdown. Of course, she couldn't do much about the redness in her eyes or the puffiness...

She picked up her bag and left, keeping her eyes mostly on the polished wooden floor on the way to her office. Blacke never paid much attention to her, just barked orders through the intercom and expected her to quietly act on them. Hopefully, he wouldn't take note of her today either.

"Gail," Blacke's voice made her flinch as she sat down at her desk.

"Yes, Sir?" she answered, with as steady a voice as she could.

"In here, if you please."

*Oh, crap.* Had she done something wrong?

Gail pushed her chair back and got up again, her calves aching with every step.

Once inside, she folded her hands in front of her and kept her head down and gaze averted.

"Where have you been? I've been calling for you for the better part of an hour!" Blacke demanded. Damn, had she been hiding out for that long?

"I'm sorry, Sir. I was..." Gail sighed. She had nothing.

"If your work here is too demanding, do let me know. There are plenty of others who would jump at the opportunity to work here." Blacke pushed his chair back and folded his arms as he stared in her direction. He'd never looked at her directly for this long before.

"I understand, Sir. It's not that."

"Approach," Blacke ordered.

Gail did as asked.

"Closer."

She took another step towards Blacke's desk, trying her best to remain calm. He wasn't about to pull the same sort of crap she was getting from Dumbarton, was he?

"Are you coming down with something? Be honest," Blacke asked.

Gail finally did look up only to find Blacke frowning at her. He wasn't *concerned* about her wellbeing, was he? That wasn't the Adrian Blacke she had grown accustomed to. She shrugged, not sure how to answer.

"Well, I can't have you infecting anyone here. Not with all the important work we have going on. I think it would be best if you went home."

Blacke picked up a diagram of something or other from his desk and started to focus on that. The conversation was clearly over.

So he had no concern for her after all. He was more worried about coming catching a little cold himself if she stuck around.

If that's what he wanted, Gail wasn't about to argue. She quietly left his office, packed up her things and made a beeline for the exit. After everything that had happened this morning, she needed time to think more than anything. She needed to regroup.

———— ◆ ————

By the evening, Gail had received a number of emails from a generic Yahoo email address. They were unsigned, but she was pretty sure they could only be from Henry. His tone was concise, business-like. The entire thing read more like an Alliance field report than an email.

So this was it, the last time he'd communicate with her.

She fought the tears that tried to force their way out again and instead focused on the information detailed inside the emails. Despite getting out, Henry had compiled all the details she'd need to continue their work. There were names, scans of reports his agents had prepared about various shifters they suspected of illicit activities. A second set of files outlined families who had refused to participate in the tracker program.

Then there was something much more significant: an actual list of people Henry had already approached.

Gail pinched the bridge of her nose and read the list again. The first was Matthew Argyle, unsurprisingly. Along with his name, there was an address, a phone number, and a note in the form of a single word; *reluctant.*

There were a few more names, one of which stood out. Irene Finch. She was the one Henry had approached first. Gail remembered his message about it. Next to her name there was nothing of any use, just an exclamation mark.

The other names on the list did not seem familiar.

A muffled buzz startled Gail. Her phone. She picked up her handbag and looked for it. Maybe it was Henry, making sure she'd received the information.

If that were the case, she ought to not pick up. He couldn't have it both ways; handing the work to her and then continuing his involvement. It was either all or nothing.

The number on the screen wasn't Henry's, though. It was a landline, Glasgow area code.

"Hello?" Gail answered reluctantly.

"Oh. Is this Gail McPherson?" It was a woman, on the

other end.

"Yes, who is this?" Gail asked.

"Irene Finch. Agent Weston referred me to you. I want to help. Please let me know what I can do."

Gail sighed and rested her head on her free hand. So that explained the note by her name.

"Very well," Gail responded.

The woman's insistence didn't leave much room for arguments. And anyway, sitting at home feeling sorry for herself wasn't going to do Gail much good.

They agreed to meet that evening, in a quiet country pub just outside the city boundary. The timing wasn't ideal, but the movement had to live on.

When Gail arrived, she was surprised to find the place much fuller than she'd anticipated.

A woman who looked vaguely familiar approached her first.

"You're Gail? Irene. Pleasure to meet you."

Gail reluctantly shook her hand while scanning the room. Over a dozen people stood around the two as they met.

"I've taken the opportunity to invite a few like-minded folks I know." Irene gestured around the crowd. "Bears, humans, wolves; everyone's represented here. And we all feel that the world would be a better place if we all just work together."

Gail smiled. She hadn't wanted to come here tonight while her loss still felt so raw. But now, she was glad that she'd agreed.

# CHAPTER ELEVEN

The days following that last phone call to Gail had not been easy for Henry. He'd agreed to stop his involvement with the New Alliance at Maggie's insistence, but that didn't mean he had to be happy about it. In fact, it was like a part of him had died.

The New Alliance had been his idea, his brainchild. It wasn't so much that he wanted credit... He wouldn't be able to see it grow first hand or ensure its success. He couldn't do the one thing he had vowed to always do: work as hard as he could to keep his people safe.

In trying to make Maggie happy, he'd betrayed his conscience. And that had taken its toll.

What was worse, Maggie hadn't been particularly cheerful either. She'd grudgingly let him back into the house, but insisted he sleep in the living room. Every time he left the house for whatever reason, he could feel her suspicious stares boring holes in his back.

And the atmosphere around the office wasn't any better. Perhaps his mind was only playing tricks on him, but sometimes he could swear that his agents were suddenly a lot less eager to take orders from him than in the past.

His capitulation had lost him something significant.

But it was all for the best, to save his relationship with Maggie. She could only be angry with him for so long, right?

During another one of those long, bleak days at the Alliance base, Henry tried his best to stay positive. HQ had been busy, too busy to send an official order for Henry's people to go out and arrest the people they had identified as being involved with someone human. The only thing halfway relevant that he'd received was an unsigned memo - probably from Gail - specifically instructing every Alliance branch to not just investigate shifters fraternizing with humans, but also those who had chosen to mate outside their own shifter sub-species.

He put the paper down and scratched his chin. What was the point of this? Weren't they all on the same side? How did it matter whether someone got involved with a different shifter? That didn't violate the secrecy rules at all.

"Boss. HQ is on the line," one of his team members, agent Carlisle interrupted.

HQ. That meant Gail.

He wasn't ready for that.

"Take a message. I'm not in," Henry picked up his coat as well as the offending memo and stormed out.

What the hell was he doing? Was he actually running from the woman?

Pathetic.

He paused, but then followed through on his original plan and left the office. No matter how he felt about everything, he was pretty sure Maggie wouldn't take kindly to him chatting with Gail over the phone even if it was official business for a change. Of course, he couldn't avoid her forever, but for now, it was a necessary precaution.

Henry wasn't quite sure where he was going, so he just got into his car and drove off. After navigating the streets around the Alliance office aimlessly for a few minutes, he found himself heading towards the motorway. He only stayed on for a few miles before taking an exit.

His muscles were painfully tight, and he could feel himself get more riled up with every breath. He needed fresh air, space. Preferably without onlookers. He needed to be alone, in order to be himself.

Had Maggie done the same when she'd suspected him of cheating on her? Had she run off into the wild to let her animal side out?

For some reason, his instincts had brought him to Gartcosh, the small suburban settlement where Matthew Argyle lived. But Henry wasn't headed to his house. Instead, he bypassed the town and headed straight to the neighboring nature reserve.

Henry pulled into the first available parking space he could find near one of the entrances to the reserve. He didn't waste any time, grabbing his phone from the center console and almost jogging into the park. It was raining, and he was the only one crazy enough to go for a nature walk in this weather.

He was about to strip and hide his belonging in the undergrowth when his mobile rang. *God, now what?*

Henry half expected it to be Maggie checking up on where he was, but it wasn't her name on the screen. Gail.

Oh hell no.

He disconnected the call. It had been difficult enough to cut all ties with her last week. He would not get into a rematch with her.

Henry shoved his phone back into the pocket of his jeans and did what he had come here for: go for a run to blow off steam.

———◆———

By the time Henry got back to the office, he'd had three further missed calls from Gail. This was unacceptable. Didn't she realize she was jeopardizing everything? If he spoke to her and Maggie found out about it, she wouldn't take it lightly. What if she turned Gail into Blacke and his goons? The entire movement could go down because of stupid behavior like this.

Henry switched off his phone and removed the battery, stashing everything in his desk drawer. Now he could breathe easier.

The office was quiet, as it had been lately. People were out in the field for the most part. There was only one agent in the house; Maggie, who had eyed him from the moment he'd come in.

As soon as Henry sat down, the walls started to close in on him again. His little excursion had done him some good, but it hadn't been enough. The switchboard rang.

"Henry. There's a call for you," Maggie said. He analyzed her voice. She sounded gruff, but that was nothing unusual. It was unlikely to be Gail then, or he would have been able to detect jealousy in her tone.

"Who is it?" Henry asked.

"Your mother." Maggie pressed a few buttons, transferring the call to his desk.

"Hello?" Henry said.

"Son. I need you to come." His mother's voice was low and serious. She didn't sound like her usual, cheerful self. Something was wrong.

"What's happened, ma?" Henry's muscles tensed up again.

"Not over the phone. Just hurry."

The line went dead.

*What the hell?*

"What was it about?" Maggie asked. There was something in the way she said it that rubbed Henry the wrong way.

He didn't respond, just shook his head. If he engaged her or tried to explain, they'd have another argument. This wasn't the time.

# SCOTTISH WEREBEAR: A PAINFUL DILEMMA

He picked up his coat and rushed out of the building, straight to the Alliance van outside.

He didn't know how fast he drove, or what route he'd taken, but somehow, he reached the farm in record time. His mind had been racing the whole time. What could possibly have happened which she didn't want to tell him during the call? Whatever it was, it had to be bad.

Henry drove up the drive straight towards the front door and slammed his break, causing the van to skid as it came to a halt. Then he ran.

*Was she all right?* Ever since his dad... His mother was the only family he had left.

He stopped dead in his tracks when his mom opened the front door. She looked just fine. But... she wasn't alone.

Behind her stood two large, shadowy figures. *Shit.* Had Blacke found out what he had been up to and sent in two of his agents to come after his mother?

"What's going on here?" Henry demanded.

"Henry, son. You need to come inside and listen." His mother spoke calmly, which made Henry even more suspicious.

She averted her gaze and stepped aside. Only then did Henry recognize the two men. Matt Argyle and his brother, Jamie, who led the Edinburgh Alliance office.

"What are you two doing here?" Henry asked, uncertain whether they still posed a threat or not.

"I gave them the address," another voice spoke up from further inside the house. Gail.

He'd been had.

"I told you that was it. I can't get involved anymore-" Henry protested. He'd never expected her to fight dirty like this. To involve his own mother in a ruse to meet with him! Although he could now see her more clearly, he refused to look directly at her.

"You're going to want to hear this," his mom interrupted.

Henry shook his head. "No. I promised Maggie. I-"

"Oh, son. I know you're just trying to do right by her. Gail explained what happened already. But what's going on is more important than that."

Henry pressed his lips together and tried to get his anger under control. He did *not* like surprises. And this...

"Jamie, perhaps you'd like to explain."

"My mate, Alison. When I got back from work, she was nowhere to be found."

Henry frowned. *So?* What did that have to do with him?

"She's human," Gail explained. "Blacke had her brought in."

"Then your office must be involved. Someone must have tipped him off!" Henry speculated.

"No. My people are loyal to a fault."

"Alison is Lee Campbell's daughter," Gail said.

Lee Campbell. Henry knew the name but wasn't sure where from anymore.

"It was Jamie's team that captured Campbell with Alison's help. He's been in the dungeon in Stirling for almost a month now," Gail added.

"Your mate is the daughter of the highest ranking Sons member ever captured?" Henry blurted out. It had all come back to him now. No wonder the name had seemed significant somehow. He shook his head in disbelief. "Okay, well, that's unfortunate, but what did you expect?"

"How dare you," Jamie growled, his right hand going straight for Henry's throat.

"Guys! This isn't helpful," Matt interrupted them, positioning himself in the center of the two angry bears, forcing them apart again.

"The point is, we have the Edinburgh office on our side," Gail said. "The time is right to act. The dungeon is filling up fast, so Blacke's men are transporting Alison to a secondary holding place tonight. With the help of these guys," Gail nodded in Jamie and Matt's direction. "We can take her back without Blacke knowing what - or who - hit him. *If* we make sure we outnumber them."

"Your whole office is ready to oppose Blacke?" Henry asked. With bears being as secretive as they were, how could Jamie be so sure of their loyalties?

"They'll follow me over Blacke, that's for sure," Jamie said.

"So you seem to have everything worked out. What do you need me for?" Henry asked.

"That's very simple. We need you to do nothing," Gail said.

*What?!*

*If something goes wrong, and Blacke calls for your help to get Alison back, don't come running to his aid. Don't interfere until we have the chance to get away.* Gail's voice, no, Gail's entire being had entered his mind.

Henry was stunned into silence by her presence within him. During their short time apart, their connection had become even stronger than on previous occasions. He could even catch glimpses of her memories.

He could see the moment when he'd made that phone call last week. How she'd collapsed onto a cold tile floor and cried.

Henry could feel her heartbreak like it was his own.

Or was it, in fact, his own?

Henry cleared his throat. "I need a moment," he mumbled, and marched down the hall, into the kitchen, leaving the confused brothers and a fragile looking Gail behind.

He'd had this urge before, that deep, all consuming urge to protect Gail, to keep her safe and happy. And of course, he'd done the exact opposite. Henry sat down at the small table where they used to have breakfast when he was a child. This had been his safe place when he was younger.

"Son." His mom shuffled into the kitchen and rested her frail looking hands on the backrest of the chair opposite Henry. "I know you're just trying to do the right thing."

Henry looked up at her. "Whatever I do, I hurt someone."

"Listen to me." She sat down and folded her hands in her lap. "I know you've made a commitment to Maggie. And now you're just trying to stand by that."

Henry nodded. That's exactly what he was trying to do.

His mom got up and retrieved a sheet of paper that had been lying on the kitchen counter. She placed it on the table in front of Henry. "Perhaps it's time to admit you've made a mistake."

Henry's heart sank as he started to read.

*Surveillance Recommendation.*
*Target Name: Helen Weston*
*Surveillance Mode: Phone Tap.*

His signature was there at the bottom, but he sure as hell hadn't sanctioned this!

# CHAPTER TWELVE

———◆———

Gail made sure to keep her distance as she observed the conversation between Henry and his mother. She'd wanted to warn him, but just hadn't had the chance. For that, she was sorry.

She had to feel for Henry, whose mind was racing, running through the various possibilities of how that request had come into being. His thoughts kept circling back to the same conclusion: Maggie. She was the most likely culprit. And then he'd reject his conclusion and rethink.

This went on for a good ten minutes until Gail could no longer stand to watch him struggle within himself.

"It was her, you know," Gail said softly.

"How can you be sure?" Henry turned around, his features tense, determined.

"This is just a print-out, but with the help of one of Jamie's men in the Edinburgh office, we were able to hack into her computer and find the original document. It was right there on her work computer."

"What if someone just used her computer?" Henry slumped back in his chair again with his back towards Gail.

"I know your history makes it harder to accept this, but deep down you already know the truth."

*How could she do this? Sanction surveillance against my own mother, her future mother-in-law?* Henry's thoughts raged.

*Who knows what she was thinking? What's more important is for you to decide how to proceed now,* Gail responded.

He sighed and pushed the sheet away from him in disgust. *Was she successful? Did anyone act on this crap?*

*We swept the house top to bottom. It's clean. Looks like we intercepted it just in time,* Gail replied.

"Very well." Henry pushed his chair back and got up.

His eyes were colder than Gail had ever seen them before. There was nothing more dangerous than a bear who'd been forced into a corner.

He walked right past Gail and marched down the hallway towards where Matt and Jamie were waiting.

"What's the plan?" Henry asked.

Jamie nodded at Matt, then partly turned to include Gail in the conversation.

She'd felt bad about springing this on Henry, but a life was at stake. Alison's life. Blacke had picked her up so he'd have leverage over Campbell during future interrogations. He wouldn't think twice about hurting her - or worse - to get what he wanted.

Now that tempers had calmed, it didn't take long to come up with a plan.

Gail had marked the route on a map, and Henry recognized the road immediately. It ran straight through a dense forest. They didn't want to harm the agents, so they'd lay a trap. If everything went well, they'd get what they wanted without having to resort to too much violence.

———◆———

It was good having Henry back on their side. Gail couldn't help but steal glances at him as he lay beside her in the bushes overlooking the road they'd just blocked off.

Jamie and Matt were hiding just opposite them. And behind the blockade waited two of Jamie's team members; Aidan and Heidi. As he'd said, they didn't think twice about following Jamie into battle against Blacke.

# SCOTTISH WEREBEAR: A PAINFUL DILEMMA

They hadn't been waiting long when a black van approached, its lights bouncing off against the branches of the large tree they'd placed across the road. Breaks squealed as the vehicle came to a stop right in front of the obstacle. There was no way around; they'd made sure of that.

Beside Gail, Henry took a deep breath and put his eye to the scope of one of the rifles Jamie had provided for the job. It looked like a proper hunting rifle, but took tranquilizer darts instead of live rounds.

Across the road, an owl seemingly called out; the signal.

Henry pulled the trigger, and the agent nearer to him cursed and grabbed for his upper arm. At the same time, another, similar rifle went off, and its dart hit the other agent in the thigh. It took barely a second for the two men to sink to the ground.

They were on.

Gail pulled the balaclava down over her face and jumped across the shrubs they'd been hiding behind. Henry was right behind her.

First, they made sure the agent was knocked out, then they pulled the dart out of his arm and tied his hands with Alliance issue plastic ties they'd retrieved from his own tactical jacket. They would leave as little evidence behind as possible.

Jamie nodded at Gail as he located the keys to the van in the other agent's pocket. He and Matt hurried to the back of the truck and unlocked the door. The two other agents from Jamie's office lifted one of the agents off the street and back into the van.

They were going to hide it in the forest once they were done. It was in everyone's best interest if this ambush remained undiscovered for as long as possible.

Gail watched as everyone did their part. The New

Alliance's first act of rebellion.

A sense of pride filled her chest that almost made her forget the ache left behind by Henry's rejection of her. Almost.

She looked at him as he methodically searched the pockets of the agent he'd disabled. They'd confiscate their weapons, communications equipment and anything else that would help the New Alliance.

Their goal was to create a non-violent resistance against Blacke's Alliance, but once he got wind of what they were up to, things could very well escalate. They had to build up a stockpile of weapons. And plus, any gun taken away from these guys meant one gun less for Blacke to aim at their heads if the time came.

Meanwhile, Jamie emerged from the back of the truck, carrying the precious cargo they'd come here for. A red-haired woman, who seemed fast asleep despite all the activity that surrounded her.

"She's been drugged," Jamie whispered.

Gail nodded. "Take her to the farm; she'll be safe there."

The way Jamie looked at the woman in his arms made Gail's knees weak. She'd had her own concerns about Alison's family background, but what she observed now had taken all that away. They were mates. They were meant to be, and at least, Jamie knew it.

As he walked off into the dark forest, the others continued to sanitize the scene. The van was parked off the road and covered in fallen branches. They also dragged the tree back off the road. Then they packed up all their things and headed back to their individual vehicles.

Only Gail and Henry remained.

"Wow, that went well," Gail remarked.

He forced a smile. It was obvious how much he was

still struggling with everything.

"What are you going to do now?" Gail asked.

Henry shook his head. "I don't know. I can't tell her that I know about the surveillance request, or she'll turn us in."

Gail wasn't sure how to respond. She wasn't even sure how to act around Henry anymore.

This was too much. His earlier decision to abandon their work together had crushed her. He hadn't done it to hurt her, of course, but that didn't change things. It was difficult, being so close to each other while both their emotions ran so high.

Gail took a moment to breathe in the icy air and scanned the dark forest that surrounded them. Was that a noise? A rustle? Perhaps an animal out foraging...

No, there was something else out there, something dangerous. Gail could sense it clearly.

"I knew it. I knew he had come out here to see you!" It was Maggie. She was on Gail before the latter had time to react.

Gail's instincts kicked in, and she transformed instantly, but Gail was no match for the much stronger female brown bear.

"Maggie, relax!" Henry called out from the other side of the road. He was with them in less than a seconds.

But Maggie was far from calm. Her paws were on Gail's throat, ready to rip her open if necessary.

Gail tried to struggle free, but it was hopeless. She was stuck. *She's going to kill me.*

*No. I won't let her.* Henry stared at Gail for a moment, his eyes emitting a reassuring glow. The doubt he'd shown earlier, the conflicted emotions, all of that was gone now.

As desperate as her situation was, Gail trusted him. He'd intervene.

"You promised you'd stop this. Liar!" Maggie hissed at Henry.

"I had. I had given up everything I believed in for you. For us," Henry said.

Maggie snarled. "Bullshit! You couldn't wait to run off again. With *her.*"

Gail closed her eyes and focused on calm, deep breaths. Maggie's claw dug dangerously into her throat, near the jugular. One wrong move and she'd be done for.

"It wasn't like that."

"Good thing I had the sense to put a tracker on your phone, or I would have never known for sure!"

"This is between you and me, she has nothing to do with this," Henry growled.

Maggie didn't respond.

"All I've ever wanted was to make a difference. Why can't you see that? Why does everything have to turn into a fight with you?" Henry paced around the car as he spoke.

Gail felt Maggie's grip on her tighten.

"I won't accept that. I can't."

"Then deal with me. Leave her alone," Henry straightened himself and started to transform. Fur, claws, teeth all seemed to erupt at once. And his muscles... He stood at least eight feet tall, towering over Maggie and Gail.

Gail had seen plenty of metamorphoses before, including brown bears. But Henry... He was something else.

Maggie flinched at the sight of him, giving Gail the chance to slip out from underneath her grasp. She was free, but her heart was out for blood.

This was the woman who had stood between her and Henry. If she killed her now, she'd just be defending herself. And that problem would be solved forever.

Gail let out a vicious roar and pounced, this time, it was her having Maggie by the throat. She'd rip her to shreds. It would be so easy!

"Stop!" Henry shouted, giving Gail pause. *Don't do it. This is my problem to take care of.*

Gail grudgingly retreated, leaving Maggie lying on her back in the dirt.

Now, it was Henry's turn to attack. He restrained her but took care not to do much damage.

*Get the gun.* Henry stared at Gail.

He *had* changed. His eyes were no longer cold and impersonal but full of fire. His bear had recognized her at last. Now that this charade with Maggie was well and truly over, he could see the truth she had known from the first time they'd met.

Gail shifted back into her human self and reached for the rifle that had ended up on the ground between them in all the confusion.

*Do it.*

Gail didn't need to be told twice and shot a tranquilizer dart right into Maggie's shoulder.

Henry turned away from his former mate as her body went limp, and slowly her limbs and body became smooth and hairless again, and what had once been a fierce brown bear had turned into a woman again.

"What do we do with her?" Gail asked.

Henry stared down at Maggie's limp body with disdain. If he'd loved her at some point, Gail could no longer see any evidence of it. Ever the gentleman, he draped some of his torn clothes over her and picked her up.

"We'll work it out later. For now, she goes into the van."

Together, they returned to Henry's van which was parked on an overgrown track just off the road. He got a blanket out of the back and used it to wrap Maggie in, before placing her on top of one of the benches inside. Then he slammed the door shut and got into the front. Gail followed.

They both sat back and gazed out the window at the forest stretching out of them. All seemed peaceful again outside, as though nothing had happened.

"How ironic, that while I was hiding my work here from her, she had her own secrets."

Gail had nothing much to offer in way of support. She smiled bleakly and lifted her hand to squeeze his arm, then changed her mind. This wasn't the time for uninvited physical contact.

*No. It's okay,* Henry thought.

Gail looked up and found him already staring at her.

This was that look. The one that she'd only seen before in those illicit dreams she used to have of him. *You were right. I was wrong.*

Gail held her breath and did finally place her hand on Henry's arm, actually touching him for the first time. *You're mine. I am yours.*

*That's right.*

# CHAPTER THIRTEEN

———◆———

Henry couldn't explain how it had happened, but when Maggie had threatened to kill Gail, everything had fallen into place. The dilemma he'd struggled with ever since meeting Gail for the first time had cleared itself up. His feelings of guilt and misplaced loyalty towards Maggie had vanished.

He'd finally achieved complete clarity.

He and Maggie had lived together for two years, sure. But she was not his mate.

Gail was.

And while he'd been in denial, Gail had known it all along.

In trying to do the right thing and act honorably, he'd almost thrown away the best thing that had ever happened to him. He'd hurt her deeply, which he'd regret forever. In trying to not betray Maggie, he'd betrayed himself and everything he stood for as well. He was grateful to get a chance to make up for it.

Henry glanced at her from the corner of his eye as he started the van.

She had an exotic beauty about her. Her skin tone richer than most native shifters. And those eyes, nearly black, that's how dark they were.

Gail met his gaze. Fiery black, did that even make sense? Either way, the intensity with which she looked at him was enough to light a fire under his imagination. The things he could do to her. The possibilities were endless now.

He couldn't take her home. It didn't feel right, with all of Maggie's things littering the place.

The farm? That would be awkward, with his mom right there.

*My place isn't far from here.* Gail winked at him and looked straight ahead out the window again.

Henry put the van into gear and drove off, following Gail's directions.

"I'm sorry, you know. For everything," Henry said.

"It's okay. I know you'll make it up to me." Gail rested her hand on top of his.

Henry's chest tightened, his breaths grew shallower. If they didn't reach it soon, he'd have to pull over and act on his impulses right here in the van.

*Take the next left,* Gail directed him. *It's the house at the end of the road.*

Henry focused once more on the road. Just a little while longer.

Once he'd taken the turn, he could see the house from afar. It was quaint, simple. A brick built cottage, much smaller than most houses they'd passed by on the way.

He parked at the side of the road and got out as fast as he could. Gail was already two steps ahead. They raced each other to the front door. Henry caught her on the last step.

Gail giggled. "Keen, are we?"

"Tell you'd rather have it another way, and I'll tone it down," Henry whispered in her ear.

"No way."

Gail unlocked the door, and they stumbled inside. Henry wrapped his arm around Gail's waist, twirling her around to face him.

The door clicked shut behind them. They were alone.

This wasn't the first time they had been alone, but in a

way it was. They were different now - at least he was. This time, they were both on the same page. Henry's true self was no longer in hiding.

He stared into her eyes. The tension between them was electric. How close he had come to never feel this way? *This was it.*

Gail tiptoed to meet him, and Henry leaned down. Her arms wrapped around his neck, and his hands grabbed hold of her hips. They never looked away as their faces came ever closer.

He'd had no hope in hell to resist this woman if he'd ever given himself permission to really look at her before. Gail melted against him, their lips meeting in a kiss that set both their bodies on fire.

How would she like it? Fast, slow?

As their tongues explored one another for the very first time, their minds raced with thoughts competing with each other in intensity. How he wanted her, in any, or every way.

He couldn't keep his hands off her. Her body felt so unlike his own. Soft, pliable, feminine.

Meanwhile, her hands were on a journey of exploration of their own. Up his back, over his shoulder blades, down his sides.

Gail pulled back, leaving him wanting.

*No, don't stop!* He needed her lips back. They tasted sweeter than anything he'd ever known. Addictive, intoxicating.

Gail smiled naughtily, averting her gaze downwards. She tugged at his collar. *This coat, it's in the way. I want what's underneath.*

Henry shrugged it off, letting it fall onto the floor. Meanwhile, he tugged at the waistband of her jeans. *So are these.*

Gail bit her bottom lip. *Race?*

He'd never guessed she'd be in this much of a hurry, but he liked it. He rid himself of the remainder of his clothes, only stopping to watch her do the same.

More and more of her smooth, flawless skin came into view. He'd want a taste of all of that, eventually.

The scent of her arousal hit him more strongly now, without any barriers in the way. That's when he lost control. He was no longer the same man who had tried to make a rational choice to resist the temptation she offered. He wasn't capable.

This was where they were meant to be; what they were meant to do.

He grabbed her by the wrists and pressed her body up against the wall. Then he dove in, licking, sucking, and nibbling on the side of her neck, her shoulders. Even her earlobes weren't safe from his affections.

She writhed against him. It was as though her body was begging for more. More touches, more kisses, more admiration.

Henry paused for a moment, finding that she'd shut her eyes. She dealt with the sensory overwhelm differently than he did. She had given herself over to pleasure, to him.

He sank to his knees, kissing his way down her ample chest and stomach as he went. She tasted of sweet vanilla, the expensive kind. Exquisite.

She moaned when he reached his destination. His fingers caressed her folds, before following the same path with his lips and tongue. Delicious.

He spread her as best he could with his hands and lapped at her juices, which had started to flow. Her pleasure heightened to dizzying levels. She was ready. He'd make it happen.

Gail cried out his name as he slipped his finger inside

her wet slit.

He felt his entire body fill with a light so bright it overpowered everything. As Gail shivered underneath his continued manipulations, her pleasure peaked, spilling over from her being into his.

Henry closed his eyes and joined her on the wild ride of her orgasm. How keenly he could feel it. He could have never imagined this was possible.

She stirred in front of him. He looked up and found she was gesturing at him to get off the ground.

*My turn, lover.*

He might as well have been hypnotized. From now on, he'd never be able to refuse her anything.

As soon as he stood on his own two feet again, she took his hand and led him through the interior of the cottage until they reached her bedroom. She led him up to the bed and pushed him down onto his back. He went backward, and she followed, crawling on top of him.

Her hands found his hard cock, causing him to tremble.

*I want you.*

*I need you.*

*I can't wait.*

Henry wasn't sure who had formulated those demands, him or her, but it didn't matter.

She mounted him, and he found himself burrowed deep inside her. He knew this feeling. It was like a dream he'd had, which he'd forced himself to forget.

Gail's voice filled the room. Moans, cries. Like music to his ears.

She rode him hard. That first orgasm had done nothing to slow her down.

Amazing, how the reserved Gail he had first come to know had vanished, and been replaced by this free spirit that sought to free him as well now. He wasn't complaining, of course. He reveled in it.

After everything he'd done to her, he hardly deserved this. He didn't deserve her, but here she was.

His body became hot, from the inside out. It was no longer blood that flowed through his veins, but liquid fire. From the farthest points in his body, it all traveled in the same direction, towards his core. And there it pooled until he was so filled with heat, he thought he was going to explode.

Gail showed no exhaustion; instead, she sped up.

He couldn't take it anymore, bucking his hips upwards, into her. They were no longer two people, with differing opinions, opposing dreams.

Henry groaned as his body turned rigid.

They were one.

*We are one.*

Gail collapsed on top of him, shuddering, as tears streamed down her face.

*We are one at last.*

As soon as he caught his breath, he embraced her. Gail slipped off him, just far enough to straighten her body. After today, he'd never let her go.

"I love you," Henry said. Strange, saying that out loud. He'd never said those words before, not even to Maggie. And yet, after such a short time as mates, they felt appropriate now.

Gail sighed and rested her head on his shoulder. "I love you too."

They stayed like this for the rest of the night, dreaming, thinking, talking in silence.

For now, they were safe. But their peace wouldn't last long.

Soon, Maggie would wake up. They both agreed that

harming a fellow shifter, no matter what she'd done, would be unacceptable.

They'd have to let her go.

She would set Blacke and his men after them.

*We've got more people now. The New Alliance has grown significantly these past days.*

*Exponentially? Like a virus.* Henry smiled.

Gail ran her fingers over his lips. *Something like that.*

Perhaps it wouldn't be long then. They'd go into hiding until it was time to come out to the world.

*But we won't have anyone inside Blacke's office,* Henry suddenly realized.

*Oh, but I think we do.* Gail lifted herself and gave him a peck on the cheek.

That was that then. Their new plan. They'd be okay, as long as they stuck together.

# - THE END -

# Scottish Werebear

# A SECOND CHANCE

# CHAPTER ONE

———◆———

This was it, the moment of truth.

James folded his hands and concentrated on keep his breaths even and deep. He was a calm and balanced man normally, but today was different. It was the right thing to do, but he couldn't help worrying about what they would unleash.

Weeks of work would culminate in this one act of rebellion. By the end of tonight, the world would be a different place. They'd be free, or they'd be in more danger than ever before.

He looked around the van where his comrades - his brothers and sisters in revolution - sat. Each of the half dozen of them thoughtful, worried, excited. It was hard to pick just one emotion for tonight. They had worked so hard to make this happen, but there were no guarantees in life. It could all go horribly wrong.

"Five minutes," Henry Weston, their leader remarked, while checking his watch.

Beside him, Gail McPherson - James' former colleague - grabbed Henry's hand, and they shared one of those looks that seemed to speak a thousand words.

Henry cleared his throat, causing everyone else in the back of the van to look up at him.

"You all know this, but I feel it should be said out loud. We've achieved so much in an incredibly short time. Kyle, your internet campaign has made a bigger impact than I ever thought possible," Henry said.

Kyle nodded and looked down at his hands. In the short time James had known him, he'd quickly figured out that Kyle was even more socially awkward than most bears.

"Jamie and Aidan, you've managed to mobilize so many like-minded shifters through the network of contacts you'd built up. Today would not have been possible without your efforts."

The two senior members of the Edinburgh Alliance office exchanged a look and a nod.

James meanwhile rubbed his hands together. So many men and women in such a cramped space meant it was warm, yet his hands had remained cold and clammy.

"James." Henry looked right at him now.

James stopped his fidgeting and looked up again.

"James. The information and support you've provided from inside Adrian Blacke's office has been invaluable. We appreciate the risks you've taken."

James nodded at Henry, who nodded back and checked his watch again.

"The media will have collected outside. We've kept them waiting long enough. It is time."

Henry had barely completed his speech when Heidi, Aidan's mate, turned the handle on the back of the van and gave the door a strong push, causing it to fling open.

Some distance away, lights awaited. These weren't just ordinary streetlights; they were clustered much closer together. TV crews.

"This way," Gail called out.

The group of shifters changed direction and followed her lead, walking at first, then breaking into a sprint. They were going to meet the cameras from a more dramatic angle. As they got closer, the first reporters noticed them and started whispering amongst themselves.

The air was electric. Their campaign had managed to get everyone talking. But nobody knew exactly what was going to happen.

Until it did.

With ten feet to spare, Henry stopped and signaled the

rest of the group to do the same.

James stood just towards his left, his breaths short and quick. He felt his body get ready.

This was something they had never done before. It was forbidden. It was dangerous.

But, it was also necessary.

Henry took one step forward to face the media. "We are the New Alliance."

James closed his eyes as he listened to Henry speak. He thought of his reasons for doing this. Of his sister, Irene, who had first involved him to protect her family.

"You, and the whole world with you, will soon see things you may find hard to comprehend. Understand that we want above all a peaceful coexistence between our species. Do not fear us. Everything will be explained in time." Henry stepped back into line and nodded at Gail, who stood to his right.

The reporters started to whisper among themselves again.

James' skin started to burn and itch. His muscles tensed up. He wasn't just doing this for Irene. He was doing it for himself too. For what he'd given up many years ago.

"Now," Henry spoke in a whisper so low only a shifter could have heard it.

James let his innermost instincts loose. After the first sound of cloth, tearing, the humans that stood in front of them were stunned into silence.

One by one, the shifters transformed. Their group consisted mostly of bears, with a single wolf among them - Heidi.

James took a deep breath, loving the sting of the cold air in his lungs. This was his true nature. It was exhilarating to be able to show it to the world.

They stood proudly in front of the shocked reporters, who seemed frozen in place. Would they run? Would they scream?

Then the first one stirred, touching her earpiece and frowning, while still keeping James and the rest of the group firmly in her sights.

"I understand," the woman whispered. "Yes, it's the same thing here. Yes. I am ready."

She straightened herself and tried to shake off the fear James could smell on her. Then she turned her back on the shifters and faced her cameraman.

"Ladies and gentlemen, as you can see, the spectacle we are faced with here is much the same as on other prominent locations all over the country, as well as the rest of the world. In front of my eyes, these seemingly normal men and women managed to morph into animals. We do not know if they pose a threat, though they announced beforehand that they had no ill will toward us..."

Henry stepped ahead, causing the rest of the confused looking journalists to flinch back a bit.

"We are no threat to you. We simply wish to open a dialogue between your species and ours."

The woman who had been speaking into the camera slowly turned to face Henry. Her eyes were wide with fear.

One of the men behind her started to hyperventilate. "Holy... shit... it can... speak!"

James could hardly contain his concern. This was difficult for any regular human to understand. Would they choose to learn, or would they reject the chance for a peaceful resolution?

"Rachel Kinsey, Sky News," she introduced herself despite the tremble in her voice. "Would you be willing to answer a few questions?"

That was a good start, wasn't it?

"Of course. What would you like to know?" Henry responded.

James tried to listen to the reporter's questions and

Henry's answers, but his thoughts were a million miles away. They had actually done it.

After at least a thousand years, the secrecy rules had been broken. They had shown humankind that they weren't the only ones to walk this earth. What happened next was crucial.

James looked around at the other reporters, who were also reluctantly listening in to the interview that was going on just in front of them.

What if the old stories were right? Humans did seem very fearful of what they didn't understand. More so, because they'd ignored an important consideration. One which James had only come to realize now. Even though they spoke of peace and coexistence, they were predators.

A bunch of bears and a wolf.

It was no wonder these people had been scared half to death. Their fear wasn't illogical; it was simply instinct. James' group could tear these humans up in the blink of an eye if they wanted to.

For this reveal, what the New Alliance could have used were some nice cuddly, fluffy animals which humans would feel some sense of endearment towards. But in all their preparations and recruitment up to this point, they had come across only bears, wolves, and the odd fox. James had even heard of a lion and a tiger joining their ranks elsewhere.

Why were there no rabbit shifters?

In the distance, sirens blared. They seemed to be approaching fast. This was their cue.

Henry wrapped up the interview; they gathered up their shredded clothes and scattered as had been agreed in advance. James didn't look back and ran up the hill towards the castle; his agreed escape route.

The fences and barriers were easy for him to climb. Police cars came to a screeching halt further back, presumably where they'd left the reporters. But he wasn't worried. They wouldn't catch him. He ran across the courtyard and climbed the boundary wall. From there he made his way down the hill from the other side, leaving the castle and the cops behind.

Even if they'd just announced their presence to the world, he stuck to his old habits. He chose to stay in the shadows, avoiding any areas where he smelled a human presence. Still, James made good time. He reached his hiding place and quickly pulled out the change of clothes waiting for him. It was much easier to blend into city life if he shifted into his human form again.

So that's what he did. Within minutes, he looked like any other human out for an evening walk. James picked up the messenger bag that had contained his clothes and checked the side pocket. There they were. The keys.

He zipped up his coat and slung the bag around his shoulder. The bunch of keys was now safely in his pocket, though he held on to it tightly just in case.

The wind had picked up, so it took him a while to warm up again in his changed form. The brisk walk helped.

Another five minutes or so and he reached his getaway vehicle. Everything had gone exactly as planned. Still, as he turned the last corner, a strange sensation overwhelmed him. It felt like a presence, like someone had spotted him. But there was nobody around.

He was probably just being paranoid.

James shook off his concerns and pulled out the keys. He'd get in and drive without pause until he reached the New Alliance's hiding place. The city - any city - would be on high alert after the spectacle they had caused. Their faces were out there now. It would only be a matter of time before the authorities would know their identities as well.

Because of this, they had picked a remote location for

their hideaway.

The next step was to reconvene; the Edinburgh group would collect in person and communicate with the other factions that had formed all over the country. Together they would decide on their next move.

Tonight had gone reasonably well, but this was only the beginning.

# CHAPTER TWO

When Charlie reached home, she couldn't wait to get comfortable. She barely even acknowledged her roommate, Ella, as she made a beeline for her bedroom. Finally, after trading her sensible blouse and skirt combo for some warm pajamas and a pair of fluffy socks, she could breathe a sigh of relief.

"Hey you," Ella mumbled when Charlie joined her in the living room again.

"Hey." Charlie frowned as she noticed Ella watching the news. Ella never watched the news. "What's going on?"

Ella briefly glanced at Charlie as she joined her on the couch. "Don't tell me you forgot? It's all over the internet!"

"Well yeah, but don't tell me you believe that crap? *Tonight, your world will change for good.*" Charlie spoke in a dramatic voice. "Nonsense. It'll be a hoax; I'm telling you. They didn't believe it at the Herald either."

Charlie was about to get up again to get something to drink when the newsreader was cut off mid-sentence, and the screen flickered to reveal a red background with the words 'Breaking news' flashing on top.

*"We are interrupting your current program with breaking news..."*

"See!" Ella exclaimed, and picked up the remote to increase the volume. "No hoax!"

"For the past week, our country, along with the rest of the world, has been in the grips of what some have referred to as the most extensive social media campaign ever. A mysterious organization called the 'New Alliance' has promised us a grand reveal that will change our understanding of the world forever. What exactly this will entail, we do not know. But it better be big, or there is likely to be widespread disappointment. Over now to our reporters, who are on the ground in London, Paris, Berlin, even New York on location as communicated to us in advance by this so-called 'New Alliance' ..."

The screen flickered again to reveal a wind-blown man in a suit. "Thank you Shelley, this is Ben Thompson live from London. So far, we have not seen any activity yet."

The view panned to show more of the scenery. Westminster Abbey stood in the background with a busy road in front. Black cabs, as well as the occasional red double decker bus passed by the reporter, but nothing looked out of the ordinary.

"Try another channel," Charlie suggested.

Ella nodded and flipped across a few different channels. On each one of them, a flustered looking reporter stood in a different location around the country, braving the wintry conditions typical for mid-January. They paused on a local channel when they spied a familiar sight, the Royal Mile and a dramatically lit up Edinburgh Castle in the background.

"Wait," Charlie whispered.

She had been skeptical, sure. A healthy amount of suspicion was in her nature. That's what she thought would make her a good reporter one day. How she wished she was there, waiting for the New Alliance to show itself. But clearly, the news channels had taken the announcement seriously enough to disrupt their evening program and dispatch reporters out to various locations all over the world.

Part of her still wondered if it was a prank, even if she secretly hoped that it wasn't. With so many horrible things happening in the world lately; wars, natural disasters, terrible crimes. The prospect of change had seduced many. Even Charlie, with her level head and analytical thought process, hadn't been completely immune.

On the TV, the view changed. No longer was the camera pointed at the Castle, but instead, in the opposite direction. A group of people approached, though they were still too far away to be clearly visible.

Ella picked up a cushion and held it tightly against her chest. Charlie caught herself holding her breath.

Once they were close enough for their faces to be clearly visible, one of the men stepped ahead and started to speak. But Charlie couldn't focus on his words or his features. She was looking at someone just next to him. A familiar face.

Her heart raced, and she broke out into a cold sweat. A face she hadn't seen for years.

All those old memories came flooding back. She was the new girl in school, having only just moved to Stirling that year. The local kids were suspicious of her and kept their distance, at least at first. One made her feel welcome; the boy next door who also happened to be in her school, be it a year above her.

They'd bonded over concerns for the environment and discussions about politics which the other kids were least interested in. He had been an idealist, just like her.

And so they became friends, even if a part of her always knew she wanted to be much more than that. For a year, right up to his graduation, they spent almost every day together.

Suddenly, a certain anxiousness started to grow in her. He was graduating, she wouldn't, not for another year. He would go off to university, and she would be stuck here alone.

He said they'd keep in touch, but she was scared. She couldn't let him leave without following up on those secret desires that had been growing inside of her.

One summer evening, after the graduation ceremony, she mustered the courage. She told him.

He didn't speak, just looked into her eyes.

She stared back.

He closed his eyes. As did she.

They kissed completely on instinct. Thinking back, Charlie wasn't sure who had made the first move.

It was the best moment of her entire life.

The next day he was gone. He'd left her.

Charlie blinked a few times. Was it really him? He was a few years older now and sported a medium brown neatly kept beard. There was no doubt about it. His eyes were a dead giveaway.

Then, it happened. His features elongated and shifted around. His skin sprouted fur. Within a split second, the boy she'd once known was gone, and in his place stood a great big bear.

"Oh my God!" Ella yelled out next to her and grabbed Charlie's hand. "Are you seeing this? Tell me you're seeing this."

Charlie couldn't speak.

It was him.

James Finch.

She thought she'd never see him again. Wasn't sure if he was alive or dead even, and yet there he was. Despite the otherwise alien form, his eyes were still those same eyes she had known so well. Her best friend. The one who had broken her heart when he left.

The camera panned around and focused only on the slightly bigger bear, who was speaking again.

A talking bear. Charlie shook her head.

It should have shocked her much more, but her mind was still trying to process things. It was as though her chest had been torn open, and her heart ripped out. She ought to have been over the whole thing by now. They were kids back then.

But it hurt like it had happened yesterday.

"What's wrong?" Ella asked.

Charlie didn't respond.

"Why are you crying?" Ella said.

Charlie touched her fingertips against her face, and only now noticed tears had been streaming down her cheeks. She took a deep breath and dabbed at her eyes with her t-shirt.

"Nothing. I'm fine," she mumbled, suddenly angry that this guy could affect her still. He'd left. He hadn't wanted her. End of story.

"Bullshit. That was some freaky stuff we just saw, but that's no reason to cry!" Ella argued.

Charlie shot her a nasty look. "Leave it alone." This was ridiculous. She hadn't cried in years.

"Nuh-uh! You've got to tell me!"

Charlie closed her eyes and shook her head. "Fine. I recognized one of them."

"Oh?" Ella paused. "Oh..."

"Now please leave it." Charlie got up to grab a glass of water from the kitchen.

Ella followed hot on her heels.

"You're kidding. You know one of the New Alliance? That's like... wow. That's so amazing!"

"Yeah. Amazing." Charlie took a sip and brusquely put the glass back down on the counter. Then she just stood there, resting both her hands against the edge of the worktop and stared straight ahead at nothing.

She knew a member of the New Alliance. And he was right here in the city.

Charlie pressed her lips together. She *knew* one of them.

She looked over at Ella, who practically bounced up and down with excitement. "You know what. You're right. It is amazing."

Ella nodded enthusiastically.

"I'm gonna track him down," Charlie said. "I'm going to track him down and get an exclusive interview with him."

Ella clapped her hands and grinned. "Yes!"

"Maybe that'll teach old man Penderton to take me seriously."

"He should!" Ella cheered.

"Maybe then he'll have me work on some *real* stories, not bullshit cat treat recipes and home remedies for dandruff."

"Good on you!" Ella said. She smiled briefly, then bit her bottom lip. "Say... did you also notice how those guys were all pretty hot?"

Charlie frowned. James had always been a looker, even back in the day when they were awkward teenagers. And whereas the years had made her fill out rather in some unfortunate places, he had piled on muscle from what she could tell. The others, though?

She hadn't even noticed the others. "Mhmm?"

"Well, I was just wondering, if you know... If you track this guy down. And you get to know some of his friends..."

"Yeah?" Charlie asked.

"Well, perhaps you could introduce me. That's all." Ella smiled innocently.

Charlie rolled her eyes. "Whatever. I still have to find him, though."

"Yeah, don't you worry about that. The internet has information about everyone nowadays, and I might know someone who could help." Ella winked at her.

Now, Charlie smiled too. Ella was an avid gamer, and among her rather special group of friends and acquaintances, there was bound to be someone who could help track down James and the rest of the New Alliance. This could work.

Perhaps one day not too far in the future, she would

see him again in person. An exciting, though equally scary prospect. How would she face him?

She'd make a list of questions, stuff that people would be desperate to know more about. Just like a good reporter should.

Though she just had one question for him. *Why?*

Why leave like that?

After what she'd seen on TV, it was pretty obvious what his reasons would have been. But she still wanted to hear him say it in his own words. Why couldn't he just tell her then, rather than run?

Ella went back to the sofa and flipped around channels. Each of them, repeated images of different cities, where exactly the same thing had happened as in Edinburgh. Seemingly normal people had approached the waiting journalists and transformed themselves.

Charlie's suspicions had been proved wrong. The 'New Alliance' had done exactly as they'd advertised.

They'd changed the world.

# CHAPTER THREE

———◆———

It was well after midnight by the time James reached the remote farm far north of Edinburgh where they had agreed to gather. All had gone well.

He hadn't been followed; he knew this because the roads were so quiet, there was no way for anyone to do so without drawing attention to themselves.

When he pulled into the long driveway, he saw that there were some vehicles already parked up. Good. So the others had made it as well.

James unlocked the front door and stepped in. Muffled voices greeted him. They were all in the back of the house, no doubt discussing tonight's events.

"Hey," James greeted the first familiar faces. Heidi and Aidan, Henry and Gail; even Kyle was already here.

Jamie, the leader of the Edinburgh branch of the Alliance, was still missing.

"Good show, aye?" Kyle remarked, then focused once again on the TV flickering in the corner. Obviously, they had been watching the coverage.

"That's what I look like?" James mumbled to himself when they showed a still mid-shift. It was unnerving, seeing the transformation captured like this.

Of course, he'd seen other shifters transform, but it was always over so quickly, you couldn't see the process unfold. This right here was the naked truth. And it was quite ungainly.

"Strange, isn't it? We've been working toward this moment, and now it's over," Heidi remarked.

James looked over at her.

"Oh, it's far from over," Henry said. "Now, the real work begins."

James nodded in agreement and sat down on one of the empty chairs facing the television.

He watched in silence as the news channel showed images from various other locations.

The coverage from Paris took his breath away.

"I've never seen a lion before," Gail gasped, a few seats to his right.

The rest of the group mumbled in agreement.

They had done it. They had changed the world. But was it for the better?

Henry's phone rang; one of the other groups probably. He nodded at Kyle, who got to work immediately. He placed one of those flat conference phones in the center of the group and attached it to a laptop.

James meanwhile continued to watch TV.

"Ready," Kyle said at last.

Henry picked up the remote and dialed down the volume, and he pulled his chair closer to the conference phone.

"Hello? Are you there?"

"Eric from London, here."

"New York. Present."

"Paris."

"Berlin. The Amsterdam group have not yet reached their safe house, but we can speak on their behalf."

"Glasgow."

James' ears perked up hearing his sister's voice. Irene had made it.

"Very good," Henry said. "Let's begin."

Neither James nor the others in his group spoke much throughout the conference call, leaving Henry to do the talking. It was easier that way. They were all on the same page anyway.

They spoke of the human reporters' reactions. Shock, awe, fear. Though apparently in Amsterdam, one of the reporters turned out to be one of their own, who despite not having any previous interactions with the New Alliance had spontaneously decided to join in and shift himself.

They spoke of what to do next. How to demonstrate that they posed no threat to humans. How to educate them.

Kyle, of course, had already prepared the next steps to their internet campaign. An educational website that collected the history as well as important facts about the shifter world. He had even created a mobile game to get the younger generation interested.

All in all, the mood was positive. It seemed that James was the only one with questions. He decided to keep them to himself for now. He didn't want to dampen anyone's spirits.

So as the conference went on, he once again focused on the TV.

The coverage was getting repetitive; the same images kept scrolling past again and again. Until suddenly, the studio came into view.

James wished that the conference was already over, so he could increase the volume to hear what the news anchor was saying. The way she spoke, she was trying to remain professional, but her body language indicated she felt under threat somehow. Then the camera panned do the right and showed the last person in the world James expected to see on TV today.

"Guys. Turn up the TV," James stammered.

Henry shot him a disapproving look. "I'm sorry for my team member here. You were saying, Eric?"

"No, please just trust me on this. See!" James interrupted and pointed at the TV.

Everyone turned their head, and even Henry fell silent for a moment. He grabbed for the remote and increased the volume.

"I'm afraid we'll have to cut this discussion short," Henry said. "Switch on the BBC. You will all want to see this." He pressed the large button on the conference phone and cut off the discussion before anyone else had the chance to react.

"So, Mr. Blacke," the reporter said. "Please state your affiliation to these..."

"Shifters." Adrian Blacke stared into the camera grimly and folded his hands. "I am Adrian Blacke, leader of the shifter world."

"Well, I'll be..." Aidan blurted out.

"What the hell does he think he's doing?" Heidi complained.

"So does this mean you are one of..." The reporter's voice trailed off.

"Yes, I am a shifter. I'll spare you the theatrics. We have seen too much of that tonight already," Blacke responded.

"And you are a part of the New Alliance?"

Henry scoffed at the question.

"No," Blacke almost barked his response. "This so-called *New* Alliance is nothing but a group of troublemakers. I speak for the Alliance. The *real* Alliance. The one that has been around for generations."

"Troublemakers, sir?"

"That's right. They have gone against my orders simply for shock value, they..."

"Shit. This is bad," Gail said.

The group nodded.

"So you were not in favor of tonight's reveal?" The reporter asked, while nervously shuffling around her papers.

"Not at all. Of course, we wish to peacefully coexist with humankind as we have done for many years now.

You have nothing to fear. But this was not the way to do it."

"Oh, bullshit!" Aidan growled.

Behind them, the door swung open with a loud creak.

"Late to the party, I see. What did I miss?" Jamie spoke as he marched inside the room.

Nobody said a word, and James just pointed at the TV.

"What the hell is *he* doing on TV?" Jamie wondered aloud, as he pulled up a chair.

"What indeed," Henry said.

"If not like this, how would you have done it?" the reporter asked.

"Well. Firstly, I don't think the timing was right at all. There is enough going on in the world already without adding all this into the mix. There's the conflicts in the Middle East, famines in Africa..."

"What does he know about what's going on in the world? I can bet someone told him to mention these things," James snapped. In all the years he'd worked at Blacke's office, he hadn't known the man to give a hoot about current affairs of the human world. All he cared about was his own position. His power.

The reporter nodded. "But now that everything is out in the open. What if any next steps have you got in mind?"

Adrian Blacke looked up and stared directly into the camera. James felt like he was looking directly at him. "I'll have to manage the hand I have been dealt. Tomorrow I'll travel to Westminster to meet with your government officials. This is a serious matter, and a lot depends on how we manage the transition. In fact, I have already put certain projects in place to help put minds at ease. We are out in the open now. It is in everyone's best interest to ensure that both sides know exactly where they stand."

What projects? He can't possibly be talking about the tracker scheme? James felt his chest tighten with anger. He knew his old boss too well to ignore his words now. If Blacke made a place for himself in London, their efforts in creating the New Alliance and orchestrating tonight's announcement were as good as wasted.

"We can't let this happen." Henry stood up and looked around the room.

James glanced up at him, his expression equally resolute.

"No, we cannot."

"We need to get there before him," Henry said.

"We've been one step ahead of him since we organized ourselves," Gail said. "Let's not start lagging behind now."

"Call Eric. We have much to discuss." Henry gestured at Kyle to get the conference going again.

James got up and went straight for the door. He needed air, more than anything. He needed air, and he needed to think.

Henry would talk to Eric. That was probably wise. Rather than having everyone step into the limelight, it was best if the New Alliance put forth their own leader to take on Blacke in the capital. If those politicians had any sense, they'd see who the better partner would be.

Meanwhile, James had to think about what Blacke was most likely going to do next. He was the one out of the group who knew him the best. He was also probably the one Blacke had felt most betrayed by.

James left the house and broke into a jog. It had started to drizzle while they sat inside. It was pitch black outside. No street lights, no other houses anywhere around. James could see just fine, though. One of the advantages of being a bear.

He made his way into a nearby patch of trees and took a deep breath. He had shifted once tonight already, so he didn't feel much of an urge to do it again. But just the moist, cold air was enough to clear his head.

# SCOTTISH WEREBEAR: A SECOND CHANCE

Blacke only cared about himself. About securing his position and power. So that's what he was likely planning to do in London. He was going to try to make some friends in high places. He now wanted to be known not just as the leader of the Alliance, but the leader of the entire shifter world.

If that meant he had to hand over access to the shifter database he had been trying to build, then so be it.

He would push through his agenda on those infernal tracking devices, as well as the purity nonsense that had sparked the formation of the New Alliance. He would play on people's fears to legitimize his ideas on mixed families.

In the end, Blacke would push for a segregated shifter society, with him at the very top.

With this realization, James took another deep breath and rushed back to the house. If Henry hadn't already figured it out, he had to share his suspicions about what Blacke was planning to do.

# CHAPTER FOUR

The morning after the grand reveal, Charlie reached work at eight sharp. The office was already buzzing with activity, and although everyone looked excited, some of her colleagues did seem a bit worse for wear. It was obvious a lot of them had never gone home the previous day.

"I want to know everything, people!" her boss, a rotund grey-haired man named Harry Penderton shouted. "I don't care what you were working on yesterday; today is a brand new day. We need to know where these people came from, how they've been living in hiding for so many years without anyone noticing. We need backgrounds, research, expert commentary. Get to work. There will be no rest for anyone until we have the answers!"

Charlie couldn't suppress a smile as she approached the man. "Sir, I had an idea for a feature,"

"What? Oh, it's you, Charlotte." He adjusted his glasses and looked at her impatiently. "Well, what is it? We haven't got all day."

Just the way he spoke to her had put her off again. Nobody called her Charlotte anymore; not even her folks.

No. She wasn't going to show her hand just yet. "Well. There seems to be some conflict within their ranks. That man, Adrian Blacke said he represented the 'real' Alliance. And that the New Alliance were just troublemakers. It would be interesting to research that angle, don't you think?" Charlie suggested.

Penderton nodded. "Yes. Yes, indeed. Good thinking."

Charlie smiled again. Finally, he liked an idea of hers!

"Goodwin," Penderton called out across the busy office floor. A woman in her mid-thirties looked up from her laptop. "I want to know more about that guy, Adrian

Blacke and his Alliance and how the New Alliance fits in."

Charlie's heart sank. He didn't honestly just take her idea and give it to Diane Goodwin?

"But..."

"Yes?" Penderton frowned at her. "We need an experienced journalist on this story. You'll understand."

"So what am I meant to be doing?" Charlie spoke wearily.

"Culture. Human interest. How do they live; what do they eat? You get the drift."

Charlie sighed. Typical. Everyone else was working on the most exciting stories ever, and she would once again be reduced to writing columns about recipes and other inconsequential stuff.

She knew better than to argue, though. Penderton ran a tight ship. He didn't tolerate subordination.

So she would do as she was told, and at the same time go off on her own to get him a story that showed her worth. In this business, you had to show initiative to get ahead.

The only thing she needed was for Ella to call with something tangible...

Charlie looked around the office; her colleagues were scrambling. Those who weren't hunched over their computers researching this brand new phenomena were on the phone, asking anyone and everyone of their usual informants for information about these shape shifters.

They didn't even seem to know where to start.

The moment Ella's contacts would come up with something, Charlie would be miles ahead of the rest of the office. It was hard not to feel a little smug, at least on the inside.

"Boss, I've got a tip," Diane, called out from across the office.

Oh crap, Charlie groaned on the inside. All her

optimism had vanished in an instant.

Penderton joined her at her desk immediately. Charlie watched their discussion with bated breath. The story Diane was now working on had been *her* idea. How in the world had she already found something?

Their hushed voices made it impossible to overhear anything from Charlie's position, so she picked up her mug and approached the coffee maker in an effort to get closer. Of course, this meant she was forced to stand with her back toward them.

"Blacke, yes," Penderton mumbled.

"He will be..." Diane's voice went low again. "Perhaps I can intercept..."

"Good. Go ahead." Penderton said.

Charlie caught herself. She'd been standing here too long with her mug in hand already. Behind her, footsteps dispersed.

She turned and took a sip, before walking back to her desk. Penderton was long gone, while Diane was flitting around her cubicle, packing up her things. Damn. She must have found out something big for Penderton to let her out of the office at a time like this. If only Charlie knew where she was going.

Of course, she couldn't just ask. That would be way too obvious, and she wouldn't get a straight answer anyway.

Charlie sat down behind her desk and started on her own work instead, even if the speculations about Diane's discovery barely allowed her to focus. How did these shifters live? What did they eat? Did they even have their own separate culture, or had they integrated completely into human society?

Where to begin?

Charlie closed her eyes and was greeted with just one image. James.

She had known him so well before he left or so she

thought. He seemed like any other teenager at the time. Okay, actually that wasn't quite accurate. But then again, Charlie hadn't been an ordinary teenager either.

Charlie's parents both worked, so they'd mostly hung out together at her place or gone out to the park. But she'd met his parents, briefly, and although they were the sort of people who kept to themselves and didn't socialize much with the rest of the neighborhood, they hadn't seemed too unusual either.

If he was a shape shifter, that meant that his parents were too, right? It *was* hereditary, surely?

Charlie opened her eyes and started to take notes of everything she thought she knew about James and his family. There were precious few facts and a lot of conjecture.

Considering she had had no idea about his true nature until last night, she probably never knew him very well after all.

She sat back in her chair and looked over her list.

*Outdoorsy, fit, loner, massive sweet tooth, protective, quiet - except with her...*

And it went on. All this was just stuff she remembered about *him*, though. She couldn't simply assume that every one of them shared the same traits, could she?

Charlie flinched when her phone buzzed on top of her desk, the otherwise inconspicuous sound resonating and multiplying against the laminated wood. She checked the display. Ella.

*Hell yeah!*

She looked around to see if she might be overheard, then answered it as quickly as she could.

"Hey, what have you got?" Charlie said.

"Easy, tiger! How about a 'hello' first?" Ella teased on the other end.

"All right. Hello. Happy now?"

"Ask me how I am."

"Oh come on! You have no concept of the kind of day I've been having so far."

"It's only ten; how bad could it have been?" Ella quipped.

"Get to the point. You wouldn't be calling me unless you've got something, right? And you're making this as painful as possible, so whatever it is, it's good, yes?"

Ella chuckled. Charlie tightened her grip on the phone so much her knuckles turned white.

"Okay, I'll tell you. Remember Todd? Well, he managed to find out that a certain someone you know booked a flight into London early this morning."

Charlie let go of her phone, holding it tightly between her shoulder and side of her head instead and found a fresh page on her notepad. She scribbled down what Ella said as fast as she could. James. London. Early flight.

"Did he travel alone?" Charlie asked.

"Nope. Two others."

"Okay, that all?"

"They rented a car," Ella said. "I'll send you the details."

"Cool. I totally owe you!"

"We'll be even once you introduce me to those guys, yeah?"

"Okay, whatever." Charlie hung up and stared at her phone for a moment. This was it. Soon she'd have her chance to show these people what she was really made of.

"Charlotte," Penderton's voice brought her back to reality. "What's that you've got there?"

Charlie grabbed her notepad and held it up closer to her face; just out of view from where he stood.

"I've been working on what you said, boss. Researching their culture." Charlie looked up at him and forced a smile. The last thing she needed was to be grilled.

"Good. Found anything?"

Charlie remembered the list of supposed shapeshifter qualities she'd noted down based on her interactions with James. "They seem to be a lot like us, sir. Not very exciting."

Penderton nodded and scratched his chin. "Very well. Keep digging."

Charlie felt her grip on the pad tighten. She intended to keep digging, but couldn't do much about it while she sat here at this desk. Meanwhile, Diane was out and about making actual progress.

He was about to turn and walk off again when she spoke up again.

"I may have tracked down someone who knows more about their habits and traditions. Would it be okay for me to go interview them?"

Penderton raised an eyebrow. "You want to go into the field? As a junior reporter? This is highly irregular. If this-"

"Look, I don't know if this person is for real, and I don't want to waste anyone's time. I'm sure everyone else has more important things to work on..." Charlie smiled again, hoping to high hell it looked as innocent as she intended.

"Fine. But you come back with something, you hear?"

Her heart skipped a few beats. He had actually let her follow up on a fictional lead. This was major, and no doubt inspired only by necessity. The others *were* too busy to go on a wild goose chase after what he probably assumed was a nonsense tip anyway. Baby steps.

"Yes, sir. I will."

Charlie packed up her things just like Diane had done earlier. This was her chance to make an impression, and she wasn't going to waste it. If she hurried to the airport, she could catch one of the afternoon flights to London herself. And then...

Crap, would she need a passport? No, she wasn't leaving the country so any form of ID would do...

Her heart was racing now. This was a massive risk. Penderton had allowed her to leave, but that didn't mean she had a travel budget. Any expenses would come out of her own pocket.

Charlie grabbed her bag and took a deep breath before racing out of the office. She could feel her colleague's eyes on her as she left. She was the rookie. Her early departure would spark a lot of speculation and gossip.

Let them talk, Charlie thought when she reached the elevator. What do they know?

Instead of worrying about her reputation anymore, she checked her wallet. She had a twenty and some change. That was all. In the compartment behind her driving license and unused gym membership card awaited the one thing that would make her crazy plan possible. Charlie retrieved the carefully wrapped up little packet and peeled away the sticky tape that sealed it.

After making the final payment last year, she had promised herself not to use it unless it was absolutely necessary.

The blue and white logo greeted her like an old friend. Charlie checked her watch. There was no other way to get to London on time. She had to hurry. She had to find James.

She had no choice but to use her emergency credit card.

# CHAPTER FIVE

James looked out the window as they drove through Central London. Red double decker buses, black cabs, and famous landmarks greeted him.

He had never expected to be invited along on Henry's trip to London to meet with human government officials. In fact, he would have preferred for himself as well as the rest of his group to stay home as planned. They were courting danger; as they'd checked in for their flight, he was certain they'd get caught.

But Blacke was here too, doing the exact same thing, potentially with a head start. And James knew Blacke the best out of everyone in the New Alliance. He was the one most likely to predict his behavior.

So he'd agreed to make the trip. And so far, it seemed that the human authorities hadn't caught on to them yet.

The local New Alliance leader Eric had done his part and set up a meeting with his local Member of Parliament; he was a constituent after all. But that wouldn't be enough. Blacke would be planning to meet with someone much more important, and they had to somehow achieve the same.

As they drove along Whitehall, James just about managed to take a peek into Downing Street, where the Prime Minister's residence and office was. So this was it. The center of the human power structure.

It was a far cry from the comparatively modest and small Alliance HQ in Stirling where James had worked for years. Sure, the Stirling mansion was impressive, but it was just one building. These people had an entire borough dedicated to the government it seemed.

The security around this part of London was equally

impressive. Armed police guarded important streets and buildings. Did it always look like this? Or was it due to last night's big reveal that security had been stepped up? Were they perhaps on the lookout for James and the other occupants of this otherwise inconspicuous rental car?

James had never been to London before. Still, his mind refused to stop analyzing what he saw.

No doubt this was exactly the reason Henry had asked him to come along.

James glanced at his fellow passengers. Henry, Gail, and Eric looked determined. They were working towards one firm goal: get some kind of deal with the government in place before Blacke managed to do the same. Or at least minimize any damage Blacke was going to cause.

As they came up to Westminster, their expressions changed, except perhaps Eric's. He looked ahead with the same stoicism he had shown throughout. The others showed awe more than anything. James followed their line of sight.

Ahead stood Westminster Cathedral; a building he'd only seen before on TV. It was beautiful. As were the Houses of Parliament beyond. How many people came here, just like them, hoping to make a difference? How many had succeeded?

He preferred not to dwell on it. Instead, he pulled out some notes he'd made on the flight over. Blacke's likely talking points and strategy. They had to somehow find someone with enough influence to stop any of this from happening.

The last thing any of them wanted was for Blacke to trade his precious tracker program for the promise of power here. All they'd worked so hard to achieve would be wiped out if Blacke was successful. They wouldn't be free but just controlled by another master.

Eric pulled over into a nearby bus stop to let his

passengers out.

"Go on inside. I'll join you once I find a place to park," he said.

Henry shook his hand and stepped out onto the pavement, Gail opened her door and followed. James, meanwhile, got out from the roadside and joined his comrades once Eric had pulled away, but not before stealing a glance up in the opposite direction. Big Ben towered over them from the other side of the road. This was a very strange place. Very humbling.

The three of them didn't waste any more time. They had an appointment with a Conservative Member of Parliament. And hopefully that would be just the first step.

———◆———

The meeting with the MP had gone well. While Henry had done most of the talking at first, but when the time came to explain Blacke's background, James had taken over.

And the man himself, Oliver Teese, who had started off visibly reluctant to hear them out, had been won over. He was going to help them and take this up the chain. Not out of the goodness of his heart of course; James was certain he was just trying to gain points with more senior members of his party.

Clearly, Politics worked much in the same way everywhere, whether inside the Alliance or out of it.

Either way, the short meeting they'd had had paved the way for bigger, better things. But it wouldn't be until the next day before they had their meeting with the Home Secretary's aides, and then perhaps the woman herself.

"Good job," Henry said as they made their way towards the Central Lobby of the House of Commons. "We've made some real progress today."

James nodded. He still could hardly believe that the three of them had just been allowed inside to meet with someone, without much security at all. Sure, they had been searched, and passed through a metal detector on the way in. But considering their special abilities, that was hardly enough. A shifter even without weaponry posed much more of a risk than these humans seemed to realize.

All it took was one bad apple to ruin it for all of their kind. Surely that wasn't was Blacke was planning; he'd be way too keen to come to a diplomatic arrangement of some sort. But if it didn't work out... Was Blacke crazy enough to initiate an attack if things didn't go his way?

James wasn't sure.

And so he remained thoughtful and quiet, keeping his eyes on the floor, while Henry and Eric discussed the meeting in more detail beside him.

"Something wrong?" Gail, who had been similarly quiet, finally asked him.

James looked up at her. "Nothing. It's a lot to take in." He did have a nagging feeling that something significant was about to happen though. But it wasn't tangible enough to mention it to anyone, not even Gail - his former colleague from the Alliance HQ.

She nodded. "If all goes well tomorrow, we'll be well placed against Blacke."

He had to agree.

They walked on towards the exit when a figure caught his attention from the corner of his eye.

"James," a female voice called out to him. "James Finch."

He instantly froze. He knew this voice from a long time ago.

James turned around. There she was; a ghost from his past.

Charlotte McAllister blinked a few times, but maintained eye contact from the moment he'd noticed her. Those bright, intelligent eyes seemed to bore right into him, uncovering his deepest, most secret desires.

"Yes," he responded, more out of reflex than anything else.

It was unmistakably her, though there was something different that didn't match up with his old memories. Something in the way she looked at him had changed. Her eyes were colder, more guarded now than they used to be.

*Of course, you idiot. You shared a kiss and abandoned her. Of course she's going to be different now, so many years later.*

"Your presence here has been leaked to the media. They're all waiting outside," Charlotte nodded towards the main entrance halfway across the hall they currently found themselves in.

Henry cleared his throat and shot James a concerned look. "Friend of yours?"

He turned to face Charlotte and continued. "Anyway, we're not opposed to speaking with the media, but we prefer to do it on our terms. Now is not the time."

"Well, I can show you another way out, then you can avoid them." Charlotte smiled at Henry briefly, then continued to stare at James.

It had occurred to James that going public himself could have unforeseen consequences. But he'd had no way to predict a reunion with the one person from his past who could have changed his entire life. At the time, it seemed like the right thing to do. But as soon as he found out that his own sister had taken a human mate... He'd often worried that he'd made a huge mistake.

"Fancy seeing you here," James mumbled.

Charlotte frowned, then turned on her heel and started walking. "This way if you want to avoid the craziness outside."

Henry, Gail and Eric didn't waste time and left James behind scratching the back of his head. Was this a coincidence? He wasn't sure he believed in coincidences when it came to relationships.

He forced himself into motion and caught up with the rest of his group just as they entered a small corridor that veered left from the main hall. There they passed by the cloakroom and bathroom facilities, before ending up at a doorway to the outside world flanked by two guards who barely took notice of their departure.

Outside, the wind had picked up, but there was no sign of much activity - press or otherwise.

"Which way to the car?" Gail asked.

Eric took a moment to look around, before seemingly finding his bearings.

"Thank you very much, miss ..." Henry offered Charlotte his hand, who shook it without hesitation or fear.

"McAllister. Charlie McAllister," Charlotte said.

Clearly she knew who they were. But if the events of last night had made any sort of impression on her, she wasn't showing it.

"Yes, thanks," Gail said with a smile.

Eric had already wandered off to find the car, leaving just James to say goodbye to her.

Only... he didn't really want to.

He never expected to see her again, not after what had happened between them when they were only teenagers. Back then he had felt forced to leave her behind, but for what? Those uncertainties and concerns were the exact thing the New Alliance aimed to destroy.

Now, as he found himself once again looking into those endless blue eyes of hers, he wondered how things might have turned out, had he made a different choice back then.

"How about you guys go ahead," James mumbled.

Gail cocked her head to the side as she looked at him.

Henry frowned. "Are you sure?"

"I'll catch up with you at the house later," James added.

Henry opened his mouth to say something else, but didn't. Instead he exchanged a look with Gail and his expression softened.

The New Alliance counted a number of mated couples among its ranks, still the whole non-verbal communication trick they all seemed to know never ceased to amaze James.

"Very well. I'll hear from you. We have a lot to prepare for." Henry nodded at James and offered Gail his arm. They didn't look back as they walked off in the same direction as Eric, who had long since turned a corner and passed out of view.

"You don't want to go with your friends?" Charlotte asked.

Her tone was matter-of-fact, business-like, though he thought he could catch a hint of the dry humor he'd loved about her in the past.

"They'll be fine. We have a lot to talk about, you and I," he responded.

They were alone. He'd often wondered about what he might say if he ever met her again. Though right now, he couldn't remember any of the words he'd chosen for just this occasion.

"Do we?" Charlotte raised an eyebrow.

"How about we find somewhere quiet? Have lunch?" he suggested.

She looked back at the figures of Henry and Gail who had become smaller and smaller. "Why not? I have to admit I'm curious."

# CHAPTER SIX

———◆———

Charlie had taken the first available flight to London City. It was a risk, especially if it didn't work out. Penderton would be furious if she stayed away too long without anything to show for it, and worse, she'd have that credit card bill to worry about come next month.

But Charlie was confident about Ella's tip. It all made perfect sense. Assuming James and his people had no idea about Adrian Blacke's plan to talk to someone in government until his TV appearance, they would be scrambling to do the same thing. And that's exactly where Charlie would go to try to intercept them; Westminster. Luckily, she knew her way around the place a bit from previous visits.

*Can't become a serious journalist without ever having visited the seat of government,* as her Dad had said when they'd made the trip together a few years ago.

When she reached the public entrance to the House of Commons, she'd spotted her rival, Diane, waiting outside already. That's when her competitive juices had started to flow.

She wasn't about to watch her one chance at a big story fall to pieces because Diane-bloody-Goodwin got to these bear people first.

So she found another way inside the building and waited. It wasn't long before they appeared. A perfect coincidence? She could have so easily missed them, had she reached it only a few minutes later.

When she saw James enter the large hall with three others, her feet barely wanted to move. How would she face him? Then again, all that was in the past. They were kids back then. Surely she was over it?

So she forced herself into action and stopped them. And from the second she did, she couldn't take her eyes off James. The grainy images on TV hadn't done him justice. What she saw was far removed from the boy she'd known years ago; he had grown into so much more than that. And he kept looking at her too.

No matter how hard she tried to remain professional, her impulses were hellbent on trying to betray her.

When he sent the others away and asked to have lunch with her, she knew she shouldn't say yes. She'd lose herself if she spent too much time with him alone. But saying no wasn't an option either. Her heart hadn't permitted it.

And so she found herself sitting opposite him in a quaint little bistro, pretending to study the menu, without being able to focus on any of it.

She had to get herself under control somehow. This wasn't how a serious journalist was meant to behave!

"Are you ready to order?" The waitress looked disinterested, tapping her foot impatiently while making a show of holding up her notepad and pen in front of her.

"Roast beef on whole wheat and a latte," James said.

"All right. And for you?" the girl asked.

Charlie's mind was completely blank. She wasn't even hungry. "Uhh... Same thing please."

The waitress vanished immediately, leaving Charlie alone with James.

"Having second thoughts?" he asked. His voice sounded like he was grinning.

*Yes, definitely,* Charlie thought. Then she realized she was still staring at the menu and forced herself to put it down. She took a deep breath, but her heart refused to calm itself.

"I imagine you have questions," James remarked.

She stared at him again. Those brown eyes. She had missed them. She had missed him.

"You hurt me," Charlie blurted out, then immediately covered her mouth with her hand.

James averted his gaze. His expression had gone from cheerful to dead serious in an instant.

"I'm sorry, Charlotte."

The hairs on her arm stood up when he said her name.

"It's Charlie."

He looked up again. She knew it would be difficult to see him again, but this was excruciating.

She wanted to be angry with him, blame him for breaking her heart at the tender age of sixteen. But the moment he made eye contact with her, she just couldn't muster any anger.

"Charlie... I really am sorry. At the time I felt that I didn't have a choice," James whispered.

"Because of... the bear thing," Charlie said.

He nodded. "We have rules - *had* rules. Our kind has been keeping our existence a secret for centuries, perhaps even millennia."

"Until yesterday."

"That's right."

This was it. These were the sort of insights Penderton would salivate over. This conversation could put her name on the front page.

Charlie pressed her lips together. No matter what had happened between them, could she live with herself if she wrote all this up behind his back?

"Things have been difficult lately. There's this guy, who thinks of himself as the leader of our kind-"

"Adrian Blacke," Charlie said. This was wrong. She shouldn't push him for information without disclosing who she was first.

James sat back in his chair. "That's right. He's power hungry and dangerous. A lot of lives hung in the balance, and coming out publicly was the only way we saw to keep people safe."

This was major. If this Blacke fellow was as dangerous as James said he was, the world had a right to know. Especially if he was trying to make some kind of deal with the government! People needed to know who they were dealing with.

"Frankly, I never thought I'd see you again," James said.

Charlie felt the sting of tears in her eyes.

"But I'm glad that I have." He reached across the table for her hand.

When his index finger touched hers, it was like an electric current passed through the two of them. It took her breath away, and she flinched, pulling away her hand immediately.

This was too much. How was it even possible that after all these years he still had such a profound effect on her? How could she be so stupid, so juvenile Perhaps Penderton was right not to let her work on anything serious yet. She clearly wasn't professional enough.

"Charlie," James said.

His low voice sent shivers from the nape of her neck all the way down her spine. "Yes?"

"Have you ever wondered *what if?*"

That question, perhaps innocently posed, finally set off her anger. "Are you kidding me? The day after we kissed, I went looking for you. You were gone; your whole family was gone, leaving behind an empty house! I was sick over it. Don't even know how I managed to survive the next year on my own and graduate. I thought of nothing *but* what-ifs. If only I'd kept my feelings to myself. Perhaps we still would have been friends. I wouldn't have lost the one person in my life who meant the most to me!"

Charlie's eyes were filled with tears now. Tears of anger.

"I had no other choice. The moment I figured out you felt the same, I knew I wouldn't be able to stop myself if I stayed in touch. It would have put both of us, and my family, in an impossible situation."

Charlie shook her head.

Meanwhile, the waitress arrived with their order, causing a painful silence between them. Charlie turned away to disguise the fact that she was crying. She definitely wasn't hungry now. And the thought of coffee turned her stomach.

"Tell me, if you'd seen back then what you saw on TV last night, how would you have taken it?" James asked. His tone was flat, like he wasn't arguing, but had already admitted defeat.

Charlie picked up a stray piece of rucola off her plate and put it in her mouth. Its sharp, peppery taste seemed to ground her a little.

*Wait, what was his question?*

She stared at him again even though her vision had become blurry.

"I don't know. I don't even know what to think now." She really didn't. Seeing James again had shocked her to her core, so much so that the whole bear situation seemed comically surreal and far-fetched.

James nodded and looked down at his own sandwich.

"It's a lot to process. I thought leaving was my only option at the time. Now I'm not so sure." He pushed his plate away and rested his elbows on the table.

Charlie tried to process everything he'd said. If only she'd had the presence of mind to record it, like a real reporter. In all her confusion, she must have missed most of his words. *Dammit,* she'd forgotten all about that list of questions she'd carefully prepared in the plane earlier today as well!

"Charlie," he said, but she didn't react. "Charlie," he

spoke louder this time, causing her to flinch and focus on his eyes again. The tenderness and emotion she saw in them almost made her cry again.

"What if this is fate? What if we were meant to meet again after all this?"

Charlie frowned. She had never known him to be the sort of guy to believe in *fate*. And she wasn't sure she did either.

"What are you trying to say?" she asked.

"This is my chance to make it up to you. And then, who knows? Perhaps we could try again?" he asked. His eyes had widened now; he had gone from remorseful to excited and full of hope.

Charlie couldn't believe her ears, neither could she keep up with his strange, mixed signals. The wounds he'd left were still too fresh, despite the years that had passed in between. And when she'd decided to track him down, getting a second shot at a relationship with him had been the last thing on her mind. No, she was here to get a story. Perhaps some closure as well.

An apology and short explanation about how they were supposed to live in secret wouldn't do. It wasn't enough to rebuild what they'd lost.

James had been the only guy she'd ever allowed close to her, and it had backfired spectacularly. His disappearance had made her swear off love and go down a different path for herself. He was the reason she'd gone out on her own and made a career for herself.

Charlie shook her head. This wasn't how today was supposed to go.

"Think it over," James said, with a twinkle in his eye.

He pulled his plate closer again and picked up the sandwich.

*No way.* She didn't know quite how to respond.

And anyway, he wouldn't have said that if he knew why

she was actually here. This time, he wasn't the one with the secret, she was.

"You've got some guts," Charlie mumbled, as she watched him take a big bite of his lunch.

"You have no idea," he responded.

Behind them, some of the other customers started speaking up.

"Hey, someone, can you turn that up?" someone said.

"Yes, turn it up!" Another customer chimed in.

Charlie turned around to find a group of city people in suits, crowding around the counter to watch the TV on the wall.

The bored looking waitress picked up the remote and increased the volume enough so Charlie could hear.

"The latest development in the New Alliance reveal... Our reporter, Rachel Kinsey is in the field."

"Oh bloody hell," James mumbled. "It was only a matter of time before those people got involved."

Charlie turned to find him staring in the direction of the TV with a horrified expression on his face.

# CHAPTER SEVEN

Things had been going so well between the two of them, James thought. And then, just like last night, a single TV appearance changed everything.

As James watched the coverage of one reporter's visit to an anti-shifter protest in Glasgow, a sort of catharsis washed over him. This completed the list of players.

The New Alliance, as well as Adrian Blacke and his people, had always shared an enemy. The Sons of Domnall were getting in on the action.

The camera panned across hundreds of people who had gathered in Glasgow's city center. Some were carrying placards with slogans; others held up pictures of what James presumed were loved ones who had been captured or eliminated by the Alliance over the years. It was a scarily one-sided picture, which would no doubt sway public opinion against the New Alliance and the shifter world.

A middle-aged man with salt and pepper hair stepped up onto a makeshift podium and started addressing the crowd, as well as the camera. Underneath him on the screen appeared a white banner with a name that made James do a double-take. Victor Domnall, leader of the Sons of Domnall. In all the years the Alliance had fought against the Sons of Domnall, they had never seen or heard of an official leader. It seemed that the reveal had inspired everyone else to embrace transparency too.

"For too many years, we've struggled against these monsters in the shadows. For too many years, we have sacrificed our sons and daughters for the safety of the human race. It is time for our fight to enter the limelight. These *shifters-*" he spat out the word and made the quotation mark gesture with his fingers, "They talk of peace and harmony, but you've seen their claws. Their sharp teeth. They are not our friends. There is a reason ancient man hunted the predators of the animal kingdom to extinction in these parts. To keep our families safe. Just because these mutants have evolved some form of higher intelligence and the ability to disguise themselves as humans, does not change their true nature. In fact, it makes them all the more dangerous. They are beasts, meant to be conquered and tamed. We are The Sons, and our resistance serves you all."

James glanced at Charlie who sat across from him. She was intently watching the screen and didn't take notice of him. The rest of the customers in the cafe did the same. This man was bloody convincing; a brilliant orator. Just with those relatively few words, he might have swayed some of these people into supporting his cause.

The Sons of Domnall had always operated in secret, simply because most people probably wouldn't have believed in shifters unless they had seen one themselves. Now, this was no longer necessary. Except for those inevitable few who thought the reveal had been some kind of hoax or conspiracy, most people believed.

It wouldn't be difficult for the Sons to start recruiting new members. Not just those fringe elements of society who were suspicious of outsiders by nature, but regular, sensible people, who couldn't see past the predator exterior of the shifters.

The New Alliance had to step up their efforts to appeal to common people, or they would lose this battle before it had even begun.

This wasn't a holiday. He had accompanied Henry and Gail to London for serious work, not fun and games. Now, it was time to get back to it.

"I have to go," James said, while he fumbled with his wallet, leaving a few notes on the table to cover their lunch.

"What?" Charlie turned around.

"I have to get back to my people."

She looked at him in silence. Those bright blue eyes of hers could capture him just as they had done so many years ago. She finally nodded.

"Can I have your number?" she asked.

James smiled. "Only if I can have yours."

His heart meanwhile hammered away in his chest; as hard as he tried to cover it up, he couldn't ignore the danger they faced. The speech they'd just watched was a ticking time bomb. They couldn't afford for the Sons to gain momentum now while they were most vulnerable.

She scribbled her digits on a piece of paper. Meanwhile, he did the same.

"You'll get back okay?" James asked.

She hesitated for a moment and smiled awkwardly. "Yeah, no problem."

Her response gave him pause. "That didn't sound convincing."

"Yeah, no, it'll be fine." Charlie put the note with his phone number into her wallet, which she stuffed into the shoulder bag she'd been carrying.

"You don't live here in the city, do you?" James sat back and observed her.

She slowly shook her head.

"Do you have anywhere to stay?" he followed up his question.

She kept her gaze locked on the leftover sandwiches on the table between them and shook her head again.

James' protective instincts kicked in. He couldn't very well invite her along to Eric's place, but he could make sure that she was safe and comfortable.

He pulled out his wallet again and took out a few notes.

"Whoa, I don't want your money!" Charlie protested.

"Just find yourself a decent hotel somewhere at least!" James insisted.

She looked at the money and up into his eyes again. "I'll pay you back."

James smiled. "Sure. If that's what you want."

"Yes, that's what I want," Charlie spoke resolutely.

She finally accepted the money, her fingers brushing past his in the process. The first time they'd touched, the sensation had been intense. This time, it was even stronger.

James looked into her eyes and knew she felt it too.

Everything seemed to be falling apart around them, and yet his instincts told him to make her his. Of course, she hadn't forgiven him for what he'd done; for leaving her. He hadn't forgiven himself either.

James couldn't stop his mind from racing as they said their goodbyes. He wasn't sure how they'd ended up running into one another today, in what seemed to be a strange city for both of them. It had to be fate, as silly as that sounded.

She represented his one regret in life. He'd never even looked at another woman the way he was looking at her now.

They nodded at each other awkwardly and mumbled their goodbyes. Just as well they hadn't shaken hands or hugged; he wouldn't have been able to let her go.

This wasn't goodbye. He was certain he'd see Charlie again, and he wouldn't have to wait for ten years this time.

———◆———

"Henry," James greeted his leader as the latter opened the door to Eric's flat.

"James. We have a lot of work to do."

James nodded and stepped inside.

"You've seen the Sons protest?" James asked. The

flickering TV in the corner of the living room suggested his question was superfluous.

"He was good, wasn't he?" Gail, who sat on one of the sofas, asked. "I still can't believe we'd never heard of this guy..."

"Yes, he was. Their rhetoric has always been seductive. A certain proportion of the populace will identify with it." James took off his coat and pulled up a chair.

"You know what they say," Henry said. "Know your enemy."

Except for Henry, Gail, and Eric, there were a few new faces in their midst. Members of the London crew.

"So what's our next step?" Eric asked, looking at Henry expectantly.

"Our plan has been to educate from the start. We'll have to step it up if we want to avoid pushing people towards the Sons."

"They had names, pictures. Do we have a list of our own?" James asked. "I know we had some files over at Blacke's office of deaths and abductions which potentially linked back to the Sons, but they were far from complete."

Henry leaned forward and rested his chin on his hands. "The Glasgow office certainly did when I was in charge. I'm pretty sure the Edinburgh office had quite a collection too. I'll check in with Jamie." He sat up straight again and looked in Eric's direction.

"Can you reach out to anyone you might know in the London Alliance for this information? Perhaps someone who might be on the fence about whether to continue following Blacke? If the Sons ramp up their activities, it'll be bad for all of us anyway."

Eric nodded and got up to make the call.

James, meanwhile, pulled out his notes on Blacke and started to strategize. Education was definitely the only way forward. "How's our web campaign doing?" he asked.

"I'll get Kyle's report within the hour," Henry responded.

"And we might as well bring all this up tomorrow," James suggested. Whatever happened, they still *did* have a meeting with the Home Secretary's people in the morning.

"Actually, what we need the most," James thought aloud, "is a face. Someone with real skin in the game. Someone who has lost someone perhaps... Someone sympathetic."

James looked up at Henry, who returned his gaze. "Alison," both spoke together.

"Do you think she'll be up for it? She'd have to go public about her involvement with Jamie," James said.

Henry shrugged. "Only one way to find out."

"Why just her? How about the whole family? Jamie and especially his brother Matthew have quite a story to tell." Gail suggested from across the room.

James didn't know them too well, so he had no way of predicting if they'd be up for this. But the Brown child abduction case was well known in their circles. If they could somehow get Alison on record to speak about why she switched sides, and Matthew to share his experiences being kidnapped as a child and growing up in a strange environment without his brother and his parents... Perhaps they could even involve the parents as well!

That would make for an amazing story; one few people could simply brush away.

The truth was, there was heartache and loss on both sides, but the Sons had forced the shifter world to protect themselves by any means necessary. This was another reason why coming out into the open had been the only way forward. They had to stop the endless cycle of violence and hate somehow.

"That could work," James finally said. "We do need a way to legitimize our story, though. If we simply post it on our website, the Sons will brush it away as propaganda and lies."

"We need to do it through the mainstream media," Henry agreed.

"Meanwhile, what do we do about Blacke?" James asked, remembering the original problem that had brought them to London in the first place.

What followed were many more hours of intense discussion and brainstorming which left James exhausted. He - like most bears - wasn't used to this much talk.

They'd made progress, though. By the end of it, they had a list of talking points for the morning as well as a plan for making shifters seem more sympathetic. If it came down to it, they could even blame all the violence on Blacke. The conflict between the Sons and the Alliance had escalated under his watch after all.

It was one in the morning when James finally retired to the cramped room he shared with one of the London guys. Although exhausted, sleep didn't find him yet. Instead, he got out his phone and the piece of paper Charlie had given him. Her phone number.

He wanted to call her, or at least send her a message. It was too late, though. He'd only disturb her.

So instead he just stared at her handwriting. It had hardly changed in all those years.

When he closed her eyes, he could still catch her scent.

The man in the bed across the room started to snore, but James was still up. He had meant what he said to her. If she gave him the chance, he would do anything to fix things between them.

His whole reason for leaving her no longer existed. The secret was out.

Their chance meeting had been a sign. He was sure of it.

# CHAPTER EIGHT

———— ◆ ————

Ever since checking into her hotel, Charlie had felt restless. She had settled down on the bed and switched on the TV but couldn't focus on any of it.

What was she doing here?

Sure, she'd found James and spoken with him. She'd even managed to glean some insights into the current events and the reasons behind the New Alliance reveal. Perhaps that would be enough to pacify Penderton and guarantee she kept her job once she got back to the office. He'd let her out of the office to follow a lead, but she'd been gone an entire day already. By now, he'd be furious.

But she couldn't in good conscience report back on it behind James' back, could she?

Why not, actually? Why did she still have this sense of loyalty towards him when he had simply abandoned her a decade ago?

Just thinking about it made her sick. No matter how stupid and weak it made her feel, she couldn't betray him. The next time she saw him, she had to come clean.

Finally, after staring at the ceiling for an hour or so, her lids became heavy. She drifted off into a restless slumber. And even now, the memories of her lunch with James didn't leave her alone. She kept seeing him in her mind's eye. The way he looked at her. The way he spoke of second chances.

And finally, the way he'd left in a hurry after that weird man had appeared on TV.

"We'll meet again," she heard him say. "I'll find you. You're mine."

Those last words filled her with an overwhelming warmth. Yes. She wanted to be his. She wanted to kiss him again and so much more.

It had felt so good; that one kiss they shared ten years ago. If there was ever a moment in her life when everything was perfect, that had been it. She wanted to feel that way again. Excitement to the point of giddiness. Butterflies filling her stomach. And hope. Above all, she wanted to feel hopeful for the future again. That she wasn't meant to stumble through life alone, but that she'd have someone to share everything with.

When she awoke, all was dark around her. The alarm clock on the bedside table read 1:05.

What a dream.

Charlie stretched and turned onto her side. She picked up the phone that lay beside her pillow and stared at it for a moment. She wanted to call him so badly.

Earlier in the day, she'd been conflicted. His presence had reminded her of all those old feelings that still brewed in her. But she'd had trouble ignoring all the pain his disappearance had caused.

Now, after that dream... She just wanted him back.

Should she tell him she'd had a change of heart?

It was late, though. And perhaps this was just a moment of weakness, nothing more.

Charlie sighed deeply and pushed the phone under her pillow. This wasn't the time.

Still, she was awake already. There was no way she could fall asleep again.

So she switched on the light and grabbed her notepad and a pen. Work always provided a good distraction.

Rather than obsess about her feelings, she wrote down everything she'd learned about shifters. They had a dangerous enemy it seemed. The Sons of Domnall. The speech they'd seen at the cafe reminded Charlie of the kind of rhetoric you usually heard from nationalists. It was always *us vs. them*. The familiar vs. the *other*.

There was no doubt that it would appeal to people. She was biased, of course, because she knew James. Other people didn't have that luxury. They'd see teeth and fur and claws and let their most basic instincts take over.

If they wanted to prevent these people from gathering support, they had to show the world another side to the shifters. That there was more to them than their dangerous exterior. That they were human at heart.

Charlie noted down everything in a frenzy. This was exactly the kind of thing she normally did at the Herald. She was used to writing feel-good fluff. No matter how much she'd cursed her assignments in the past, they had taught her how to appeal to people's hearts.

If she had to come clean about her job, and why she'd come to London in the first place, she might as well offer her help. That way, she didn't have to keep secrets from James, and Penderton would be happy too. It was a win-win.

---

When Charlie awoke again, it was already morning. Light streamed in through the open curtains, bathing the whole room in a golden glow.

Beside her, pages upon pages of scribbled notes awaited. All this would help her talk to James about her work. She wasn't sure of his schedule today. With a bit of luck, they could have lunch again. Then she'd come clean and explain her plan to help their cause. Once that was done, perhaps she could get on an afternoon flight home so perhaps she could catch Penderton before he went home for the day and grovel her way back into work.

Charlie got up and immediately went in for a shower. Then she tossed her stuff into her messenger bag and made sure none of her belongings were left around the room. If he wanted to meet soon, she was ready to check out already.

Once everything was done, she sat down on the bed and took a deep breath before dialing his number. She let it ring, but there was no answer. The voice mail picked up after a while.

Fine. Perhaps he was busy. She hung up without leaving a message and tapped out a text instead.

*Call me when you see this - Charlie*

And then she waited.

Nothing. Was something wrong?

She tried calling again, but the same thing happened.

A growing sense of unease descended over her, which she tried to brush away as paranoia. Finally, she switched on the TV to provide some distraction.

The news coverage was mostly the same; repeats of the New Alliance reveal, the hate speech, Adrian Blacke's appearance. The only new thing Charlie saw was an appearance by some university professor who spoke about anthropological evidence of shifters in other cultures. He seemed flustered, as though he didn't want to be on TV at all.

An hour or so later, Charlie couldn't stand waiting around the room anymore. The endless repeats of the same news over and over grated at her. Plus, she'd missed the breakfast buffet and had started to get hungry.

So she picked up her things and made her way towards a quaint little cafe near the hotel. Despite being in a much larger city than what she was used to, this cafe didn't feel strange at all. She watched the world go by from her window seat.

People in suits, rushing to get to work while balancing takeaway cups of coffee and pastries or sandwiches in their hands. There was a bus stop outside, so it was only when one of those red double-decker buses arrived that Charlie could even tell she was in London and not Edinburgh.

A large latte, a danish pastry and a whole lot of people watching later, her phone rang, nearly causing her to jump out of her seat.

It wasn't James, though.

"Hello, Ella," Charlie answered.

"You sound disappointed! Were you expecting someone else to call?" Ella teased.

"Nevermind. I've not had much sleep," Charlie lied.

There was a pause.

"Anyway, I just wanted to check in to see how things were going..."

Charlie took a deep breath. It would be so much safer to keep everything locked up inside and not tell her anything. But somehow, that same paranoia, or whatever it was, had come back. She needed a release.

"I found him, yesterday," Charlie began.

"Oh! That's awesome! What did he say? Don't tell me that's why you haven't slept much?" Ella's voice had become shrill with excitement.

"We had lunch. That's all. But..." Charlie took a deep breath.

"But?"

"He said he wants to try again," Charlie said. It sounded surreal, hearing those words aloud again.

"Wow! Just like that?"

"Yeah... I don't know what to think. How can I trust him after what happened, you know?"

"Hmm, that's a tough one. I guess you gotta follow your heart on this," Ella said.

"And now today he's not picking up or returning my messages..." Charlie closed her eyes and rested her face in her hands. "I can't shake the feeling that something's wrong."

"I see. Well, perhaps he's just busy," Ella said; her uncertain tone didn't convince Charlie.

"And on top of that, he kept saying about how it was a sign that we bumped into each other..."

"That's... that's rather sweet, actually."

"Right. But it wasn't a coincidence at all, was it? I had tracked him down with your help." Charlie sighed and looked out the window again.

"True..."

"I still need to tell him what I do for a living."

"Oh, shit, Charlie! You had lunch with the guy and kept your job a secret? Don't tell me you wrote about him already!" Ella demanded.

"No, no, of course not! I would never-" Charlie didn't finish that sentence. She had planned to do exactly that; go in, talk to James - ideally record the conversation as evidence - and write an article that Penderton would *have* to put on the front page. Why hadn't she done it? Not out of the goodness of her heart, no. Simply because she wasn't over James, which was worse.

"So... are you going to tell him?" Ella asked finally.

Charlie nodded, though of course, Ella couldn't see it. "Yeah, that's what today was all about. I wanted to meet with him in person and come clean. But now I'm just scared that something has happened."

"Okay."

"What if I don't get that chance, Ella? What if-" Charlie's mind raced with paranoid scenarios that might have prevented James from taking her calls. "He could have been arrested. Or - did you see that strange protest on the news yesterday? What if some of those anti-shifter guys hurt him?"

"Charlie... Charlie!" Ella's tone was firm.

"Yes?"

"You've got to calm down. I'll ask my friend to look into it again. Perhaps we can figure out together what's going on. But give it a day, okay? Don't drive yourself crazy now. Perhaps he was just busy, and all of this will seem silly when he calls back later today."

"Yeah..." Charlie sighed again. She had lost it. Her mind as well as her composure. This was totally unlike her.

"Promise me you'll relax," Ella said.

"Okay. You're right."

"Now... Did you meet any of his friends? Were they hot?" Ella's eagerness made Charlie chuckle despite herself.

"You're impossible!"

"What? I haven't forgotten about our deal. I hope you haven't either, because I'll hold you to it." Ella laughed.

Charlie shook her head and smiled. "Fine! I'll tell you everything..."

# CHAPTER NINE

———◆———

The following morning, everyone was up early. James, Henry, and Gail had their appointment at the Home Secretary's office at nine. Meanwhile, Eric was going to meet with someone from the London branch of Adrian Blacke's Alliance. If they wanted to effectively counter the Sons, and get the public on their side, they had to work together.

James couldn't help feeling distracted, though. He hadn't heard from Charlie, and he couldn't wait to call her and perhaps agree to meet again later in the day. In the back of Eric's car, he kept peeking at his phone every so often. It was perhaps still a bit early; maybe she wasn't up yet. He should contact her later, after the meeting.

When he put his phone back in his pocket for the fourth time, he noticed Gail observing him.

Henry, who sat in the passenger seat, immediately turned and looked at him too.

"James, I didn't want to bring this up before the meeting, but perhaps it's best to get this over with."

James frowned. What was he talking about?

Henry and Gail exchanged a look.

"Your friend, Charlotte McAllister..." Gail spoke softly.

"What about her?" James asked.

"It was strange, how she just happened to be there yesterday to tip us off about the media waiting by the main entrance." Henry cleared his throat.

"A lucky coincidence," James said.

"Right. Well, I had Kyle do a bit of digging..." Henry said.

James felt his muscles tense up. Henry checked up on his woman? How dare he! He took a deep breath and remained silent, waiting for what more Henry would say. If he apologized, James still wouldn't be happy, but he'd keep quiet about it. Henry was the boss, after all.

"She's a reporter, James," Gail whispered. "It wasn't a coincidence."

James pressed his lips together and closed his eyes. That wasn't possible. He and Charlie had shared a connection. She couldn't possibly have tricked him, could she?

"He must have made a mistake," James spoke in a low growl.

Gail put her hand on his arm. "Kyle doesn't make mistakes."

James looked around the car. Eric kept his eyes firmly on the road ahead and stayed out of the whole thing. Gail looked at James with big, apologetic eyes. Henry... well, he was just Henry. He was neither apologetic nor sensitive.

"She's been with the Edinburgh Herald for two years now," Henry said.

James didn't know what to think. In between the hurt and anger Charlie had shown yesterday, he had still seen the girl he used to know back in the day. He had seen it in her eyes; she still had feelings for him, despite everything. Could she be that good an actress?

For the rest of the drive, the discussion was over, though James could still feel Gail's eyes on him every so often. But there was nothing more to discuss.

Henry and Gail had made their point. James had to accept it.

He thought of everything they'd talked about. He'd shared some details about their activities, their reasons for going public. Had those very same details already made their way into today's papers? The Edinburgh Herald was a local rag, but news had a way of spreading.

Had he shared anything crucial? He wasn't sure

anymore.

The car came to a halt in the same place it had done yesterday.

"I'll pick you guys up when I'm done with my meeting," Eric mumbled.

The three Scottish bears got out of the car in silence, and Eric drove off behind them. Then, James' pocket began to vibrate. He got his phone out. Charlie.

Henry and Gail exchanged a look, which he tried his best to ignore. He also ignored the call and put the phone back into his pocket.

"Let's go. We don't want to be late," James said.

Henry and Gail took the lead, and James followed. They passed through security and entered the building without incident. James was almost waiting for Charlie to show up again, intercepting them on their way to the Home Secretary's offices, but she was nowhere to be seen.

He wasn't sure how he'd react if he ran into her now. She'd lied to him by omission. She'd allowed him to think their reunion had been a coincidence. Still, he couldn't shake all those feelings he had towards her. It couldn't all have been an act from her side. Or was he so blinded by his own guilt and attraction that he just couldn't see the truth?

They were made to wait in a spacious wood paneled room, much nicer and more impressive than the one Eric's MP had received them in. The atmosphere was tense, and none of them spoke a word. Instead, James did his best to focus on the talking points they'd agreed on, while trying to forget about Charlie's deception.

About ten minutes later, the door behind them swung open, and the Home Secretary herself marched in, flanked by two armed guards. James was actually relieved to see the guards; finally, here was someone who had assessed the risks of meeting with three bear shifters and taken precautions.

"Morning," the Home Secretary said while scrutinizing each of the three visitors one by one. "What can I do for you?"

Despite the implied politeness of the question, James knew that what she really meant was for the shifters to justify their presence here. So after a short introduction by Henry, James took over.

"Madam Secretary, essentially, some of our kind have appointed themselves as a sort of shadow government. They've created laws, which are being enforced by an agency I am sure you wouldn't want to associate with your government. Many of our kind have been made to believe that this shadow government is the only legitimate authority in our world, and whatever happens in London is irrelevant to us."

"This authority you speak of is the Alliance, which your group has grown out of, I suppose?" The woman folded her hands and kept her steely gaze locked on James. Considering how petite she was in comparison to the huge wooden desk, as well as the shifters opposite her, the Home Secretary still commanded immense respect. She had the body language of an alpha.

"That's right. Adrian Blacke - the Alliance's leader - is used to ruling his people the way he sees fit. Secrecy helped him secure his position, of course, now that we've forced his hand, he's scrambling to remain relevant in a post-reveal world. We believe he will approach you, if he hasn't already."

The woman nodded, and somehow still managed to give nothing away. She wasn't about to show her hand and share whether or not she'd already been in contact with Blacke, James thought. Of course, she wouldn't. Knowledge is power.

"The point is, Blacke is used to ruling with complete

impunity. He has turned his own people against him - our organization and the support we've gained is evidence of that. Under his watch our struggle with a certain human element - who were aware of our secret before the reveal - has escalated as well," James explained.

"I see," she said.

"He will offer you access to certain schemes he's planning to put in place to further oppress our people. His offer will seem tempting, the perfect way to control a segment of the population you didn't even know existed previously."

"And what do you offer?" she asked.

"Peaceful coexistence. Most of our kind are friendly, law-abiding people, who are just trying to make ends meet. We only rebel when backed into a corner. We just want our freedom."

"And what of the recent claims made that shifters have been killing people all over the country?" the Home Secretary asked.

James swallowed hard. Everyone in this room had skeletons in their closet from their work with Adrian Blacke's Alliance. If it all came out, they might have to face the music.

"The Sons of Domnall have been hunting our kind for generations. We have dossiers and evidence to back this up, which we would be happy to share. As long as we kept our existence a secret, we were left to our own devices to defend ourselves. You, Madam Secretary have a problem on your hands now. Our reveal has also exposed a vast terrorist network operating right under your nose. And we can help you dismantle it through the proper channels."

Gail and Henry exchanged a quick look next to James.

The Home Secretary remained silent, as though she was thinking over everything James had told her.

"It's simple, really. What would you like this

government's - your - legacy to be? Freedom for all, or oppression and a potential genocide if the Sons of Domnall are left to run rampant?" James asked.

She nodded and pushed her chair back. "Alright. I have another appointment now, but I'd like to thank you for coming in today and sharing your concerns with me. Please leave your contact details with one of my aides so that my office may stay in touch to see all this to an acceptable conclusion."

James glanced at Gail and Henry, then back at the Home Secretary.

They all got up together, causing one of the guards to twitch slightly, though he didn't make a move. This was exactly the problem, James thought. The reveal had scared some people, and if they didn't handle the follow-up correctly, the Sons would be swamped with new recruits and supporters.

The Home Secretary nodded at each of the three bears individually and retreated through the same door, with both bodyguards at her side.

James breathed a sigh of relief.

"That went well," Gail remarked.

"I think so," James said.

"Let's wait, and see how it plays out first," Henry said. "We need to move forward with our media campaign as well. If public opinion sways our way, she'll have no choice but to work with us over Blacke or God forbid, the Sons."

Gail and James nodded. They needed to rally Jamie's family, and perhaps others who had seen tragedy at the hands of the Sons, or Blacke, or both, and quickly. And they needed a trustworthy reporter to cover the whole thing, ensuring that the story wasn't spun around to make them look bad.

James put his hand in his pocket instinctively. The only reporter he knew was Charlie. And she'd lied to him.

But did they have time to find someone else?

James followed Henry and Gail through the corridor, down the stairs and into the main lobby, where Charlie had found them yesterday. She was still nowhere to be seen. They left via the main door this time, only to be greeted by a large crowd of protesters.

There were hundreds of them. Some carried banners; some shouted slogans.

*Animals belong in the zoo.*

*No monsters in my neighborhood.*

*A bear is always armed.*

Along the front of the rally, a group of women stood in a line, each of them carrying a photograph of a different young man with the words *missing, presumed dead,* written underneath. James didn't dare look at any of them in case he recognized someone he'd seen in Blacke's dungeon.

The three bears kept their heads down as they passed by the crowd, hoping they wouldn't attract too much attention. The last thing they needed was to cause a scene.

"Call your friend," Henry said, as though he had read James' thoughts from before. "Figure out whose side she's on. Meanwhile, I'll call Jamie and Eric."

James nodded. Time was of the essence.

# CHAPTER TEN

It was almost noon when Charlie's phone rang again.

Her chat with Ella had helped somewhat to calm her down, as had the cup of Chamomile tea she'd ordered to counter her anxiety. But the sound of her phone had startled her all over again.

This time, it *was* James.

Relief washed over her as she answered.

"Hey, James!" she said.

"Charlie," he sounded curt, putting her on edge again.

"What's wrong?"

"Nothing. Why would anything be wrong?" he said.

Charlie's heart started to beat faster. "I don't know. You sound... Anyway, what's up?" she stammered.

"I need to see you," James said.

That was exactly what she wanted as well, but now she was certain. Something was definitely wrong. She could hear it in his voice, and she'd already felt it all morning. If this was just paranoia, she was about to lose her mind.

"Okay... Where?" she asked.

"Marble Arch. Half an hour?"

"Sure. I'll be th-" the line had gone dead before Charlie had had the chance to finish her sentence. Had he just hung up on her? What the hell was going on?

Charlie packed up her things, paid for the tea and headed straight for the tube station down the road from her hotel. Half an hour to get to Marble Arch should be more than enough time. Still, she caught herself impatiently tapping her fingers on her shoulder bag as she waited for the next train to arrive. Time moved at a crawl, and the otherwise reasonable four-minute wait for her train felt endless.

Finally, it arrived, and she got on. It was overcrowded, and she found herself stuck in the entrance area with no hope of getting a seat.

Still, she was glad to finally be making progress towards her destination. She had to get there on time and figure out what had happened with James to make him sound so tense. And of course, she had to clear the air between them. If she wanted a chance to move forward, there should be no more secrets.

A change and another crowded train later, she finally arrived at Marble Arch. Once Charlie made her way up to street level, she took a moment to find her bearings. It was impossible to miss the famous white landmark across the street.

There was no sign of James yet, so she waited. It was a clear winter's day, but the sun didn't do much to warm her. It had to be below freezing, and the coat that had kept her comfortable at the cafe had lost its efficacy. She hadn't even thought to keep a pair of gloves out.

"Charlie," a voice made her jump.

She turned, and there he was. James.

"Hi," she mumbled while rubbing her hands together and blowing into them in an attempt to warm up.

From one day to the next, his whole demeanor had changed. He'd gone from hot to icy cold.

"Tell me about your work at the Edinburgh Herald," he began.

Her heart sank, and her lower lip started to shake. So that's what this was. Just when she'd planned to tell him everything, he'd found out first. No wonder he was angry.

"That's exactly what I had wanted to talk to you about," she whispered.

His dark expression barely changed, and why would it? If she were in his position, any explanation she could offer now wouldn't convince her either.

"I should have told you yesterday," Charlie said while keeping her eyes fixed on the ground between them.

"I just need to know one thing," James began.

Charlie looked up but immediately averted her gaze again after making eye contact. As cold and angry as he sounded, he didn't look it. His eyes were filled with emotion, but there was no anger in them. He looked hurt more than anything else.

"What is it?" she asked.

"Did you submit anything yet?"

"What?" Charlie blurted out. "I would never! Sure, I used certain perks of the job to get out of the office and come here to see you. But I haven't reported back. In fact, after sabotaging my colleague's chances at a story by guiding you out the side entrance yesterday, I'm not even sure I still *have* a job."

Tears filled her eyes. How she regretted not telling him sooner. The more time she spent in his presence, or even thinking about him, the more she had started to wonder if perhaps they *could* give things a go again. It didn't make any sense, but now that everything hung in the balance, she knew exactly what she wanted. She wanted him back.

James sighed and looked around. "Walk with me," he said.

Charlie nodded and followed his lead. They walked across the small green patch around the Marble Arch in silence, crossed the road and entered Hyde Park.

"We have a proposal for you," James finally said.

*We?* So this was all business now? "Yeah?"

"You saw that protest on TV yesterday. We need to improve our image, so those *people* don't get the upper hand, you understand?"

Charlie didn't answer. This was exactly what she would have suggested, if only she'd had the chance to come clean about her work first.

# SCOTTISH WEREBEAR: A SECOND CHANCE

"There was another protest yesterday outside Westminster," James added. "Knowing how they operate, they will escalate as soon as they've got the numbers they need. We'll all be targeted. We've been fighting these people for years, so we know they're capable of violence."

Charlie balled her fists in her pockets. This was bad. When Charlie had seen their leader's speech, she'd compared them to nationalists. And although nationalists did at times inspire hate crimes, they mainly sought a political solution to their problems: stricter immigration laws; closing the borders.

But this wasn't an immigration issue. Shifters already lived among them, and they seemed to be native to this place. How do you resolve a conflict with a native minority? The only examples history could offer painted a bleak picture.

"You think they want to instigate a genocide? Why would people even go along with that?" Charlie stammered. The thought seemed so preposterous when spoken out loud; she wasn't sure she wanted to believe it. And yet...

"You tell me. What's the logical next step?" James asked.

If people were scared enough... Anything was possible.

Charlie felt her chest tighten, which made her lose her balance slightly. She grabbed for James' arm to steady herself. "Oh my God," she whispered.

The second she touched him, she felt it again. The jolt of energy. The butterflies. The overwhelming urge to forget herself and get him back. This wasn't helpful. *Focus, woman!*

She let go and made a beeline for the nearest bench, where she sat down and rested her head in her hands. This was too much.

Tears were once again flowing freely.

This was ridiculous. She hadn't cried in years and now, in the span of three days, this was the third time!

James sat down beside her. She hadn't looked up and thus she hadn't seen him, but somehow she felt his presence right next to her. It made her cry even harder. She should have told him from the start. Instead, she ruined their second chance from the start.

*It's okay... Please don't cry!*

Charlie looked up and found James looking at her. His eyes seemed more intense than usual, as though they were glowing slightly. Had he just said that out loud? Had she just imagined it?

*Please. I can't stand to see you cry.*

There it was again! It wasn't like her to have such an active imagination.

*How come I can hear you?* Charlie thought.

The voice didn't respond. Instead, James took her hand in both of his. He was so warm; his touch sent shivers down her spine.

"I didn't mean to lie to you," Charlie said while looking down at her hand in between his. They were huge. Strong, and yet infinitely gentle.

How small she felt next to him. This was quite a feat; ever since she'd started to fill out a bit in college, she'd never had much cause to feel small or even vulnerable.

"I know," James said. "I know that you wanted to tell me."

How did he know?

*I can feel it,* the voice in her head said.

This whole thing, it was so unreal. Was she actually out here with him? Or would she wake up any moment now and find that it was all just a dream?

*How is this possible?*

Charlie looked up at him. His eyes had changed again. Gone was the pain she'd seen before. It had been replaced with the same tenderness and hope she'd seen yesterday.

This man was going to drive her crazy with his mood swings.

"We may have shown ourselves to the world now, but there's still a lot you need to know about our kind," he said.

"I've got time," Charlie whispered.

Neither of them broke eye contact. The air between them seemed to be heavy with tension.

"Well," James started. "When a man meets a woman... and they really like each other." He winked at her.

"Don't tell me you're going to talk about birds and bees next," Charlie remarked.

"There she is, my old friend Charlie McAllister. She's back!" James joked.

Charlie scoffed but couldn't suppress a smile.

"So I was saying. When a couple *really* like each other, they connect on a deeper level."

James' tone was serious again. No matter how strange it sounded, he was no longer joking.

"And then they hear voices?" Charlie asked.

"They can communicate by thought, yes."

Charlie shook her head. If she hadn't just experienced it, she would have never believed it.

"You're a weird lot; you know that?" she said.

James shrugged. "There are a lot of upsides. If you can deal with crazy paranoid humans hunting you."

"Such as?"

"Well, couples have no secrets. They're faithful for life. When a shifter finds their true mate, they become whole together."

"But I'm not a shifter," Charlie remarked.

"I know. And that's why I left back then. Under the old rules, we were only supposed to pair up within our species. But I've since learned that it works the same even if one partner is human."

"Wait, are you trying to tell me that simply because I kissed a shifter when I was seventeen, I basically ruined any hope of ever having a relationship with anyone else? And if we hadn't run into one another now, I would have remained single forever?" Charlie asked.

"Uhh..." James looked away sheepishly. "If it helps, there's been no one else in my life either."

Charlie sat back on the bench and looked across the open views of the park ahead of them. "That's so weird."

James put his arm around her, causing her to close her eyes involuntarily. Who could have guessed that today would turn out this way? Sure, she'd hoped it would, but when he confronted her about her work, she had lost all hope.

"James Finch?" a voice interrupted them. A man approached. His hair was cropped short, and he was wearing a black leather biker jacket, jeans, and heavy black boots.

Charlie could feel James tense up beside her. Although there was nothing obviously wrong yet, she sensed the danger his instincts had alerted him to. This telepathic communication thing really did work.

"Who wants to know?" James asked.

"Victor Domnall sends his regards," the man said.

*Knife!* Within a split second, James pushed her down the bench and flung himself at the stranger in a blur of claws and fur. That's when the darkness claimed Charlie.

# CHAPTER ELEVEN

———— ◆ ————

By the time James got Charlie back to Eric's place, everyone was on high alert. She was still out, so he laid her down on his bed before joining the rest of the crew in the living area.

Everyone sat around, lost in thought, but Henry was furious.

"How could this happen?" he demanded. "Were you followed?"

James thought back to earlier that day. He'd been upset after finding out about Charlie's job. Had he let his guard down? It was possible.

"I'm not sure. I sure as hell didn't see anyone," James said. Then again, he had been so focused on Charlie, he hadn't even seen the guy videoing the whole thing on his phone.

"And did you *have* to charge at him the way you did? It's all over Facebook now!" Henry paced back and forth.

"He tried to attack my mate with a knife. What would you have done?" James felt himself get angry all over again. Of all people, Henry should understand. He would stop at nothing to defend Gail.

"Oh. She's your *mate* now, is she?" Henry barked.

James stood tall and faced his leader, staring him down with only inches between them. "Yes, she is. What are you going to do about it?"

"Now, now. Let's all relax," Gail spoke up from the sofa. "We can't change what happened. And if Charlotte is James' mate, so be it. The freedom to pair up with whoever you like is one of the fundamental reasons the New Alliance came into existence."

Henry backed down and joined Gail, though his

expression still betrayed his displeasure. James retreated as well. Henry was right, though. This was bad. The Sons could spin this any way they wanted.

"We need to do some damage control before this hits the evening news," Gail said. "Sure, the police arrested the attacker and let James go, so that's a good sign. But that in itself might not be convincing enough."

James nodded, as did Henry and Eric, who had so far stayed out of the whole conversation.

"Once she wakes up... And if she indeed is your mate," Henry's skeptical tone grated at James, but he decided to let it go for now. "Perhaps she can help us."

James shook his head. "No way. They've seen her face now and already tried to attack her once. I'm not going to let you make a bigger target out of her."

Henry glared at James. "What choice do we have? We need friends in the media now more than ever. We already agreed on that."

"Yeah, we agreed. But things have changed," James growled.

"Bull-" Henry started, but then glanced over at Gail and stopped talking.

"Guys, if you'll allow me to say something," Gail took over. "She works for a morning newspaper, yes? We need to fix this now, today. If she knows someone else who can help..."

"Wait, you said it's all over Facebook. Can't Kyle help somehow? Hack in and remove the video?" James suggested.

"I'll ask... But we still have to manage the fallout; we need a plan," Henry said.

James nodded. As much as he hated to admit it, Henry was right.

"He knew my name. How did he know my name?" James wondered aloud.

Gail shrugged. "Maybe they have their own computer guy. Your face has been all over the news since we came out. With the right know-how, I'm sure it's not that hard to find out someone's identity. Kyle probably could have done it."

She made sense, but James still felt there was something more to it. In his years working for Blacke, his intuition hadn't failed him even once. He hardly dared to consider the consequences if somehow the Sons had gained support within law enforcement. If that were the case, then everyone in this room would have to look over their shoulders from now on.

"Talk to her," Henry repeated himself. "We need to sort this out as soon as possible."

James wanted to argue for Charlie's safety again but didn't get the chance.

"No need," a female voice interrupted their conversation.

James closed his eyes as she approached. Her presence overwhelmed him now, so strong was their connection; their attraction. No matter what happened, what she'd kept from him before, it was impossible to ignore or fight her pull. They belonged together, for better or for worse.

"I'm in. Just tell me what you need me to do," Charlie spoke directly to Henry now.

———◆———

When Charlie woke up, she barely remembered the confusing events at the park. She blinked a few times in an attempt to let her eyes adjust to the darkness of the strange room she found herself in. Slowly, outlines of furniture came into view. She was in a single bed, still fully dressed. The side of her head was tender, as though she'd been bruised somehow. Across from her bed, stood another one with a desk and chair in between underneath the window. Where was she?

She closed her eyes again and inhaled deeply. James had been here. His scent lingered on the pillow, which reassured her. She was safe.

After laying there, finding her bearings for another minute or two, she got up to investigate the rest of the house. She opened the door and heard voices coming from down the hall. One she recognized as James, the other, she wasn't sure. They were arguing.

As she walked along the hallway, the cold of the tiles underfoot alerted her to the fact that she wasn't wearing her shoes anymore. Still, she didn't just march into what she presumed was the living room. No, she stayed back a bit and listened. Something about a video on Facebook. They needed help to manage the fallout from it.

This tied in perfectly with the idea she'd had at night. She could help these guys swing public opinion their way. She could help appeal to people's hearts to convince them the shifters weren't the bad guys here.

"Talk to her. We need to sort this out as soon as possible," one of the men - the one she'd heard arguing with James before - said.

That was her cue.

"No need. I'm in," Charlie spoke as she stepped into the room that contained about a half dozen shifters, mostly men. All eyes were on her all of a sudden. "Just tell me what you need me to do."

She glanced over at James, who was staring at her as well now. She could feel him so keenly now; it was unnerving. If this was what it meant to be part of a couple, she had to wonder how these people got any work done whatsoever.

Charlie closed her eyes and took a deep breath, and she sat down on the couch beside James, taking his hand. *It'll be fine. Let me help.*

"Very well," the man across from them said. Charlie recognized him as the one who had been there with James at the House of Commons the day before. "Take a look at this."

He got up and handed her a phone; on it was a video of what had happened at the park. Her memories had been sketchy, but even so, the video wasn't much better. Everything had happened so fast that the camera had had trouble capturing it all. Within a couple of minutes, it was over.

"This sort of reminds me of those ambiguous bigfoot or yeti videos - no offense," Charlie spoke. "It's not very clear."

"None taken," the woman who'd been with James yesterday as well spoke with a subtle smile playing on her lips.

*That's Gail, and the man next to her is Henry. They're a couple,* Charlie heard James' voice in her head. Very convenient indeed, being able to communicate like this without anyone else knowing.

"Here's the deal. I work at a paper up in Edinburgh, but I'm not high up or anything. If you want to influence how this is perceived, I'm going to have to convince my boss to help us."

"Is he trustworthy?" Henry asked.

"If we offer him an exclusive of some sort, I don't see how he could refuse."

Henry and Gail nodded, as did most of the other people she'd never met before.

"Very well, so here's the deal," Henry started. He explained the back story of Matthew Brown's childhood kidnapping many years ago by a rogue Sons member, and how he'd only recently been reunited with his family. He spoke of Jamie, a member of the Edinburgh Alliance, who had paired up with a prominent Sons member's daughter who had switched sides. All of these people would be willing to face the media to make their case against the Sons of Domnall.

Charlie noticed her bag leaning against the side of one of the sofas and got her notepad out. She wrote down everything Henry told her, as well as her own ideas for how to best present the story. By the end of it, she'd filled three A4 sized pages.

"This all sounds promising. My boss will salivate over it; I can guarantee it," she said. "If that's all, I should make the call."

James squeezed her hand. *Are you sure you want to do this?*

Charlie smiled briefly. *Anything, as long as it helps keep you guys safe.*

So it was agreed. Charlie got up, grabbed her phone and notepad and retreated to the bedroom she'd just woken up in. Penderton would give her an earful, at least at first. But this was necessary. James had charged at the guy at the park without hesitation, and in the process potentially ruined the shifters' image. The least she could do was call up Penderton. What was he going to do? Yell? Fire her? Once he heard her story, he *had* to come around.

She dialed his number with trembling fingers and waited. The phone rang once, twice...

"McAllister, what a surprise!" His tone was heavy with sarcasm. "I thought you'd vanished permanently."

"Sir, please hear me out. That lead I told you about the other day? It panned out. I managed to track them down, and I'm on the inside with the New Alliance."

"Wait... what? You were supposed to talk to someone who *knew* them! Instead, you fall off the radar for two days. Who knows if these people are who they say they are. And if you're talking to the actual New Alliance, I need an experienced reporter on the story, not you!" he argued.

The experienced reporter rant again. Charlie took a

deep breath to maintain her cool.

"Sir, if you could please log on to Facebook. See the trending topics. At the top, there's a video which I'm sure will prove that I'm telling the truth."

Penderton didn't say a word; there was only rustling on the other end of the line. Then she could hear the beginning of the video when the stranger called out James' name. Penderton let out a slow whistle, presumably when Charlie came into view.

"Okay, McAllister. I'm listening," he finally said.

Charlie felt a rush of excitement as she picked up her notepad. This was her chance!

She went through the whole story Henry had told her. About the disappearance of little Matthew Brown, the desertion of Alison Campbell from the Sons of Domnall, as well as her role in the capture of her father.

Penderton barely said a word, though she could hear him scribbling it all down at his end as well.

Charlie ended on the most important point of all: that if he wanted exclusive access to these prominent New Alliance members, he had to figure out a way to spin this video in their favor, and do it fast. The exclusive interviews and other content would keep flowing, as long as Penderton guaranteed it made the New Alliance look good. It was mutually beneficial cooperation they were after, and they wouldn't approach any other media outlets as long as Penderton and the Edinburgh Herald remained their allies.

"Understood. I'll get things moving immediately," Penderton said. "And... McAllister, good work." Charlie forgot to breathe as she heard these words.

Finally. The recognition she deserved.

# CHAPTER TWELVE

———— ◆ ————

Once she'd finished her call with Penderton, Charlie breathed a big sigh of relief. No matter the twists or turns in this story, she had achieved what she'd set out to do. And in the end, she didn't even need to deceive anyone either.

She lay the phone down on the bed and stared at its black screen for a moment. Penderton was on it, and knowing how he worked, he'd get some kind of strategy together quickly.

Only now did Charlie realize how exhausted she still was. The events at the park had taken a toll on her. The bruise on her head throbbed. She hadn't even checked herself out in the mirror yet; who knew how bad it looked?

The door opened behind her, and it seemed the atmosphere of the room instantly changed. She didn't even need to turn to see who it was, because she already knew. James.

He rested his hands on her shoulders and started to massage her.

*You're tired. You should rest.*

Charlie closed her eyes. His touch was magic.

*I promised to help, so that's what I need to do.* She put her hand on his. It didn't make sense, how much she wanted him. How absolutely desperate she was for his affection now. Gone were the doubts and anger she'd felt when they had lunch together. Even the memories of the heartache he'd caused had faded.

She'd never felt this way, except perhaps during that one moment they'd shared so long ago.

Funny, she'd never even believed in true love or any of that stuff. Some people - Ella most notably - were quick to call her a cynic, but Charlie considered herself a realist.

Not anymore.

She believed now.

Charlie turned to face James and found that his eyes were that same funny color again like at the park. They definitely *were* glowing now.

*You're the most beautiful woman I've ever seen.*

Charlie pressed her lips together and averted her gaze. Nobody had ever told her that.

*You're not so bad yourself,* she thought, as she looked up at him again. Bloody hell, he was gorgeous.

"Why are all shifters so handsome?" she wondered aloud.

James chuckled. "They're not. Shifters all look the same. Humans are beautiful in their diversity."

Charlie frowned. She'd never thought of it like that.

James sat down in front of her on the bed and raised his hand to her cheek.

*I want to kiss you again.*

He leaned forward, his face neared hers until their lips were just a fraction of an inch apart.

His scent intoxicated her, making her feel faint. She reached out for his upper arm to steady herself.

Then, the intrusive ring of her phone made her flinch. James pulled back and held it up to her. "I guess that's your boss?"

Yep, it was Penderton all right.

Charlie sighed. "The man isn't known for his timing."

James smiled and let his gaze linger on her lips. "You'd better get it before he changes his mind about helping us."

"True," Charlie said and raised the phone to her ear. "Mr. Penderton."

"McAllister, here's what we will do: I've made a few calls and set up a press conference for four o'clock. All the major news outlets are sending someone."

Charlie checked her watch. Not much time to go on. She had known he was well connected, but even so, everything was happening very quickly indeed.

"Okay, and then?" Charlie picked up a pen, readying herself to take notes.

"Start the press conference by playing the video. It's already out there, and you can't deny it. All you can do now is attempt to control the narrative. Point out the threat posed by the attacker. How this is typical of the kind of persecution shifters have had to endure at the hands of the Sons of Domnall. Get some photos up of victims already claimed by the struggle. Focus on the protective nature of shifters, how they'd sacrifice themselves to keep their loved ones happy. Make the public love them."

"Wait... you mean for *me* to attend the press conference?" Charlie dropped her pen in disbelief.

"Why, yes of course! If they speak for themselves, it'll be less convincing. Plus, you're in the video, so you might as well own it. Once you've said your piece, let one of the New Alliance take over and confirm the message. The people have nothing to fear unless they attack first."

James took Charlie's hand and squeezed it gently.

*It's too dangerous. Let someone else handle it,* his voice urged.

She shook her head. Penderton was right. And she was already in the video anyway.

"I understand." *I have to, James. I have to do this.* She picked up the pen again.

"That's step one. Step two; talkshow appearances for those people you mentioned. The brothers who have only recently been reunited and the rest of their family. The public will lap up their story. They'll do the morning show circuit; regional as well as national. We'll keep hammering the viewing public with their story until *everyone* knows it by heart. We want to get people talking about it at work, at school, everywhere. This will take some time to set up, of course, in the meanwhile, have them call me, and I'll see to it that they receive some media training. At the same time, we'll get missing persons spots on the reality crime shows. Those features will subconsciously teach the public that a lot of shifters have been harmed by the Sons; that shifters are the victims here."

"Okay..." Charlie struggled to write fast enough. In truth, her mind was somewhere else already. Penderton meant for her to be the New Alliance's spokesperson. She'd never been on TV, though, of course, her journalism degree had covered the basics of every type of media, so she'd done some role playing. But that was a few years ago now...

"McAllister. Are you listening?" Penderton demanded.

"I'm sorry. I was just thinking."

"You'll be fine. Get to the Grosvenor by three-thirty."

"Wait, the conference is at the Grosvenor?" *How on earth did he swing that?*

"The manager owes me a favor. Don't worry about that. Just get there, understood?"

"Yes, Sir."

"Good," Penderton said, and the line went dead.

Charlie couldn't believe what had just happened.

"Oh my God," she stammered, as she put her phone down on the bed between James and her. She looked up at him and found that he was already staring at her. The concern in his eyes was clear as day. But at least he didn't argue for her to change her mind anymore. She'd made her choice, so he would accept it.

She glanced down at her notes again. Press conference. Talk shows. Her head swam.

"I'll go tell Henry the plan. And that Jamie, Alison and Matthew are to contact your boss." James suggested. *We'll pick up where we left off after the conference.* He winked at her, making her smile despite herself. He got up and left her to prepare.

Charlie blinked a few times to get the notes back into focus again.

They didn't have much time, and she needed to know exactly what she was going to say. The last thing they needed was a newbie journalist fumbling over her words. That would ruin any chance they had to get the public on their side.

But most of all, she needed a paracetamol. Luckily she always had some in her bag. *Did shifters take medicines like humans did?* She'd make sure to ask James later.

———◆———

When Charlie arrived in the marble-clad lobby of the Grosvenor hotel with James, Henry, and Gail, they were greeted by the last person she expected to see.

"McAllister. So it's true," Diane Goodwin said.

The two rivals eyed each other suspiciously.

"Diane." Of course. She'd been in town chasing the same story already, so it was obvious Penderton would rope her in to help set up the event.

"The stage is ready," Diane nodded in the direction of one of the conference rooms. "People will start to arrive soon. We'll play the video, I'll introduce everyone, and then you take over."

Charlie swallowed hard. "Yeah. That's fine."

James placed his hand on her shoulder, which did help in giving her some strength. Of course, Diane noticed the gesture instantly as well and rolled her eyes.

"If you need make-up, someone's waiting for you behind the stage," she said.

Charlie waited as Henry and Gail made their way to the conference room already.

Diane leaned forward a bit, perhaps hoping to stay out of James' earshot - an impossibility, as long as they were in the same room.

"One of these days, you'll have to let me know how you managed all this," Diane said.

Charlie shrugged. "Just lucky, I guess."

"Yeah..." Diane glanced at James and back at Charlie. "Well, you best get yourself ready. I'm going to make sure everyone finds their way inside."

James placed his arm around Charlie's shoulder, and they both walked into the conference room. Bloody hell. Was she really going to sit up there in just a short while? In front of the stage stood at least fifty empty chairs. Surely they weren't expecting *that* many reporters? Not at such short notice?

Charlie inhaled sharply and breathed out slowly, like how they'd taught her during her course. *Relax. It'll be fine.*

She sat down behind the stage and closed her eyes while the makeup artist Diane had arranged got to work. There wasn't much to be done. Just bare minimum touch-ups so she would come across well on TV.

*You can do this,* James encouraged her.

She smiled. Normally if someone said something like that to her, she might have brushed it away as just politeness. But with James she didn't just hear his words but felt his true intentions and feelings as well. He meant it.

With her hair and makeup done, Charlie got up and started to pace around while rehearsing her speech in her head. Walking always did help calm her down. As did the breathing exercises from her course. But most of all, it was James' support that kept her from freaking out.

Before she knew it, it was time. She signaled at Henry and Gail to join her; obviously, James had never left her side. The four of them climbed up onto the stage and took their seats. The formerly empty chairs in front of the podium had mostly filled up. The turnout was amazing.

Charlie squeezed James' hand underneath the table and scanned the crowd. This was major.

All the big networks seemed to be represented here. Charlie thought she recognized some of the faces in the crowd.

The lights turned on, and Diane marched up on stage, carrying a microphone.

"Esteemed members of the press, welcome! And thank you so much for joining us today." Diane spoke with so much ease, it was impossible for Charlie to suppress the sting of jealousy. She closed her eyes as Diane introduced them and the topic for the press conference. Breathe in sharply, exhale slowly... Breathe in, breathe out...

She opened her eyes just in time to catch the video on the large screen beside them in her peripheral vision.

*You can do this,* James encouraged her.

The video finished, and Charlie's heartbeat surged in a crescendo of nerves and determination as she adjusted the microphone in front of her. "Thank you, Diane." Charlie nodded in her colleague's direction. "Hello everyone, and welcome. I want you to know that I am one of you." Charlie took a deep breath and channeled all her energy into remembering her lines. "But I have been lucky to get to know the members of the New Alliance over the last few days. I have learned of the challenges they've faced. And the great love and companionship they're capable of." Charlie's voice grew more steady with each word. "Today, an unfortunate incident happened, which you've just seen in the video. We were publicly attacked, for no reason other than James being different."

Every sentence Charlie spoke was interrupted by camera flashes, but she kept on going just like she'd rehearsed.

"Today was different, in the sense that the incident was captured on camera for all to see. But these sort of hate crimes have been happening for years. The organization led by Victor Domnall has been targeting shifters since before they made their presence known to the world. You'd be hard pressed to find a shifter who doesn't know of someone hurt or lost in this struggle."

Charlie glanced over at James, who seemed to not even notice all the cameras and eager faces in front of them; he only had eyes for her. "Yet they haven't lost hope. They haven't lost the faith that if given the chance, humanity will accept and perhaps even embrace them. They're not after a fight; they just want to get by like the rest of us."

Charlie smiled briefly. James was right. Everything was going to be fine. As she continued through the rest of her part of the conference, her confidence kept growing. She might never have set out to become the New Alliance's spokesperson, but now that she had started on this path, it felt right. This way she could do her bit to help them. Their faces were already out there. They were already targets unless they could get the public on their side. This was the right way forward - the only way forward.

# CHAPTER THIRTEEN

James had hardly been able to take his eyes off Charlie throughout the conference. He'd been confident that she'd do well, even when she felt doubtful herself. But in the end, she blew him away along with the rest of the crowd.

When Henry took over and introduced himself as leader of the New Alliance for the audience questions segment of the conference, James grabbed Charlie's hand again. Although he wanted nothing more than to just look at her some more, he now kept an eye on the audience instead.

Their body language, combined with the sort of questions being asked gave him a reading of the mood in the room. These reporters acted very different than the ones they'd first revealed themselves to. Gone was the shock, the fear.

Perhaps it was because there were so many of them faced with only three shifters this time? Or it was a sign that their efforts to educate were starting to make an impact.

Charlie, of course, had been very sympathetic, whereas Henry wasn't really. He remained professional and kept a certain distance between himself and the audience. And that was fine; he was their leader, after all. That is why they'd agreed that for particularly sensitive questions, Gail would be the one to answer.

The questions lasted for another half hour. Most of them aimed at Henry, Gail, and even Charlie. Though a few to do directly with the attack were for James himself. Still, he couldn't wait to get out of there.

The moment everything was over, and the four of them got up and off the stage, James' focus had completely shifted. *Charlie.* She glanced over at him, a subtle smile playing on her lips. She knew exactly what was going on in his head.

"Eric will have recorded the live coverage. Let's go back and review it," Gail suggested.

James took Charlie's hand. How small and delicate her fingers were. He would never tire of how her presence made him feel. And to think how close they came to being forced apart again. This deep connection, the one shifters and their true mates shared had helped them overcome it all.

"Actually, I hope you don't mind if we catch up with you tomorrow. Charlie has been through a lot today; a bit of rest would do her good," James said.

*You don't mind, do you?* he thought.

*Couldn't have said it better myself,* she replied.

Gail and Henry exchanged a look.

"Fine. I suppose there's nothing more to be done today anyway," Henry said.

*Where's your hotel?* James asked.

Charlie squeezed his hand. *I thought you said I should rest.*

*Of course... eventually.*

As if on cue, Charlie's phone rang.

*Penderton,* she thought. She excused herself and walked off to the other end of the stage to answer.

"I think it went quite well," Gail said.

James nodded. "Couldn't have gone better."

Their small talk was interrupted by Charlie's colleague, who had taken the stage to introduce them at the start of the conference.

"Hello, I'm Diane. Nice to meet all of you," she smiled politely but hesitated before finally offering her hand.

"Good work, Diane," Henry said.

"Thanks..." she glanced back at the dark stage. Was she nervous?

Now that James had had a taste of what it was like to read someone's mind, he wished that talent extended to more than just one person. Unfortunately, that wasn't how it worked.

"You might want to take the back exit if you want to avoid the crowd..." Diane suggested.

Henry nodded and placed his arm on Gail's shoulder. James watched as the two of them followed Diane out of the conference room. Funny, how fate worked. James had always felt they were a rather odd match.

His idle observations were interrupted by Charlie, who returned with her phone still in her hand. The moment she got close, James' entire being seemed to respond. His bear was raring to break free and take what was his.

"That was Penderton," she explained.

"I know," James responded. "What did he say?"

"He was watching. Thought it went very well."

"That it did. You were amazing," James said.

Charlie grinned at him. "You're just biased."

"That may be. Doesn't make it less true." James smiled back at her.

Those full lips. How he yearned to feel them against his again. They'd been interrupted before, but he wouldn't let that happen this time.

Charlie had been the first and only girl to ever catch his eye. The years they'd spent apart had done nothing to change that. If anything, she was even more beautiful, more desirable now.

*Stop thinking like that, or I'll give in to temptation right here, and we might have a shifter sex scandal on our hands,* Charlie teased.

She was still the same old Charlie, with whom nothing was off limits. James knew she was only half joking, though. He felt her desire as though it were his own.

*So let's get out of here.*

# SCOTTISH WEREBEAR: A SECOND CHANCE

He grabbed her hand and took the lead. Out the same double doors which Diane had shown Henry and Gail out from only minutes earlier. Diane's perfume hung in the air, making it easy for James to follow her route. They rushed outside, avoiding the reporters who would have lingered around the main lobby still.

James put his arm around Charlie's shoulder. In good old British fashion, the weather had turned during the two hours they'd spent inside for the conference. An icy cold drizzle was falling now as clouds shrouded the city, obscuring much of the skyline.

"Where to, madam spokesperson?" James joked.

Charlie took out her phone for directions. "This way," she said, pointing up at the road ahead.

He wrapped his arm tighter around her, aiming to protect her from the elements as best he could and off they went.

\*\*\*

Charlie wasn't sure what exactly had happened through most of the press conference. Equally, she had no idea how she'd found her way back to her hotel.

But here they were.

She looked at James, who was taking off his coat and hanging it over a chair to dry. Charlie followed his example.

Was this actually happening? The culmination of all those forbidden teenage fantasies was finally coming true?

Her sensible side should have doubts. She should wonder about why she could trust him to stay now after he'd just left the last time. She should equally worry about whether they were even compatible at all. Different species, different backgrounds. She should be concerned about what this meant for the future. Did this mean they could never have a family? Who knew how compatible their biology would be?

But her head wasn't doing much thinking right now; her heart was. And that was convinced that somehow, everything was going to be all right.

James stepped up to her, cupping her face in his hands. She didn't want to wait anymore. This time, nobody and nothing could interrupt them.

She tiptoed to get closer to his level and wrapped her arms around his neck. His scent filled her nostrils. Like a classy aftershave, only better. The anticipation threatened to overwhelm.

Charlie closed her eyes and felt herself become weightless in his arms.

Finally, their lips touched, releasing a decade of tension and frustrations. So soft, his lips were. So gentle.

He tasted even better than she remembered.

Words couldn't describe the feeling of the tips of their tongues dancing around each other. Butterflies? Certainly not. Fireworks? Not even close.

It was as though her whole body was on fire, and the only thing to soothe the burn was him. His kisses, his touch.

Charlie opened her eyes and was instantly mesmerized by the raging inferno in his.

James carried her over to the bed and laid her down gently on her back. She refused to let go of him, forcing him to climb on top of her.

Their hands, now hungry to catch up on lost time, roamed the other's bodies. Discovering, familiarizing, conquering whatever was in reach. She tore at his shirt, which finally gave way at the seams. Meanwhile, he took her blouse in his teeth and ripped all the buttons right off it in one swift tug.

There she lay on her back, exposed. How different their bodies were. Soft curves against hard muscle. Charlie thought again about what he'd said. How shifters were all the same and humans were more beautiful because they were different. It made sense the other way around too.

The body that rested on top of her was uniquely beautiful; a human lover would have been different. Not so strong, so tall, definitely not that muscular. This was a level of perfection you didn't normally find out in the real world.

He dove down and tasted her skin. Nibbling, sucking and licking at her cleavage; leaving sweet pleasure wherever his mouth went.

She couldn't do much more except enjoy herself. She was helplessly at his mercy.

With one hand, he rid her of her bra, giving him even more exposed skin to play with.

Charlie grabbed for his hair, tugging at it playfully at first. But when his lips found her nipple, she lost almost all control.

The rougher she touched him, the more turned on he seemed to get. Still, he took care not to hurt her. Their levels of strength were so vastly different, and yet he knew exactly how to touch her right.

After teasing her nipples, one after the other, he slid down further and sucked on her belly button and nibbled on the skin surrounding it. Charlie wouldn't have expected it to earlier, but even that felt good.

Then, he raised himself off her and looked into her eyes.

"I want to go down on you," he said in a low growl.

It wasn't a question but a demand. Not that Charlie had the self-control or desire to say no anyway.

She bit her lip and looked him over top to bottom. The look in his eyes gave her chills, but in a good way. And that flawless body, was all that really hers to enjoy now?

He was still wearing his jeans, but she'd make sure that wouldn't be the case for long. In the meantime, though, she wiggled out of her skirt and finally her tights and panties.

James didn't waste any time. The moment she was fully nude, he spread her legs apart and dove right in for his first taste of her.

Charlie moaned and clawed at the sheets, so intense was the pleasure he dished out. She closed her eyes, as he licked her deeply, then took her clit in between his lips. He repeated that same move again and again, edging her further towards ecstasy each time.

How was it that he knew exactly what to do? She couldn't have told him this. She had no way of knowing how good this would feel.

And yet...

He pushed his tongue into her again, causing her to buck up her hips at him. She had precious little control over herself.

"Oh God!" she cried out.

She had nothing to compare this to, except the occasional illicit dreams she'd had of him over the years. Was it always this good? Something told her that it wasn't; what they shared right now was something special, which most people would never experience.

He got up on one elbow while licking at her clit again. Charlie writhed against the sheets with pleasure. Then he touched her, running the tip of his finger along her folds, and made her cry out all over again.

He inserted one, then two fingers, all the while continuing to lick at her most sensitive spot. *More! Deeper!*

Charlie was done for. As he circled his finger over her G-spot, she lost the last shred of control. Her orgasm overwhelmed her before she had a chance to realize what was happening. She cried out his name, her whole body quivering with the aftershocks of her release.

Then, just like that, his two fingers were gone, as was

his mouth.

Charlie opened her eyes to beg him for more, when she caught a glimpse of him casting off his jeans. Before she could say a word, he was back on top of her, filling the void his fingers had left with his cock.

*Bloody hell,* Charlie thought. *How are you so good at this?*

James didn't respond, just looked down at her. From her eyes, his gaze traveled downward to her lips. Charlie wrapped her arms around him and drew him closer.

His rhythm sped up; the slow, careful first movements made way for more urgent, feverish thrusts. It wasn't just her on the brink of pleasure anymore. He was right there with her.

She wrapped her legs around his waist and closed her eyes again.

The strange thing was, she could still see him above her. And she could feel his pleasure, as he did hers.

Faster and faster he thrust into her. Charlie dug her nails into his back, which only seemed to encourage him further.

She started to moan, louder and louder. He pressed his lips against her, muffling her cries. Charlie was on the brink again, when he slipped his hands between the mattress and her back and lifted her up against him. He didn't miss a single beat; going faster, harder, deeper, while she clung on to him, unable and unwilling to let go.

She first felt it in her lower abdomen; a certain tension, which grew until it seemed to fill her chest too. His final push was like a pin prick to a balloon. As his cock pulsated and twitched inside of her, all that pleasure was released, causing it to travel through her whole body. From her abdomen out, reaching even the tips of her fingers, and the soles of her feet. She could keenly feel every nerve, every inch of her skin, as her body celebrated their union.

They stayed like that for minutes, perhaps hours,

Charlie couldn't tell anymore. Their bodies entwined and connected, as one.

Charlie blinked a few times until his face came into focus again. There was nothing to say, nothing more to be done. His eyes seemed to smile at her, and she smiled back.

They had come a long way since that first, awkward kiss ten years ago.

Now she knew they were meant to be. There was no turning back, no chance of changing their minds.

Everything was going to be all right.

James had always been the one for her. The one she loved, even when she thought he didn't love her back. And even though he hadn't said it yet, she knew she'd been wrong.

He'd always loved her too.

# EPILOGUE

---•---

"Welcome back," the Home Secretary spoke as she entered the room, flanked by two armed guards.

Charlie took a deep breath and got up to greet her along with the rest of them; James, Henry, and Gail.

"Please, take a seat," the woman said as she sat down behind her large mahogany desk. "We have a lot to discuss."

Charlie opened a fresh page in her notepad and started to write. This was her first big job covering a New Alliance story for Penderton, and she wasn't going to miss a thing.

"Thank you for meeting us again," Henry said.

His forced tone amused Charlie, who had learned in the time she'd known him that pleasantries were not part of his usual vocabulary. This was all Gail, working behind the scenes.

"Firstly, we're working on drawing up some amendments to existing legislation which will include shifters at an equal footing with humans. Any rights and duties enjoyed by the citizens of this country will extend equally to your people." The Home Secretary folded her hands and looked directly at each of her visitors. "Of course, this process will take some time, so I ask for your patience in letting the government follow its usual processes."

"Of course," Henry said. "We are pleased to hear of these positive developments."

Charlie scribbled it all down, along with a note to get her colleague Diane to find out which exact laws were going to be amended, and what the implications would be.

Governance and politics were her specialty after all.

"Next, Victor Domnall is still in the wind. Ever since that press conference of yours-" The woman put on some reading glasses and adjusted them until they sat on the tip of her nose. "Scotland Yard has been picking up a lot of chatter, but they don't seem ready to act yet. The winds are changing, and the effects are starting to be felt."

Charlie smiled subtly. She could feel James smiling beside her too, which still amazed her. Ever since their first night together - and of course, every other night since then - she'd been able to sense him so much more clearly. She could almost see him if he was nearby, without looking at him. She could feel his presence and hear his thoughts through walls now.

"As long as they're still out there, they pose a threat," Henry said.

Charlie flinched and started to write again. *Focus!*

"Agreed. They've gone unchecked for too long. Sure, you've had your own initiative in place against them, but that's no longer an option."

Henry leaned forward as though he wanted to argue but must have changed his mind at the last moment. He remained quiet for now.

"If your goal is to coexist in human society, it's imperative that you follow human laws. We don't tolerate vigilantism. A crime is a crime, no matter who commits it, or who the victim is." The Home Secretary stared Henry straight in the face now. She wasn't messing around.

Charlie was secretly glad she was only here to observe.

"If our people are in danger, something must be done, though. We must have some recourse," Henry said. His voice, as well as his body language, were tense now.

"I'm coming to that. But first I want your assurance that your people aren't going to go off and take things into their own hands anymore. We can't accept such behavior as part of a civilized society. We don't go around kidnapping and hurting those who disagree with us."

The Home Secretary's tone, combined with those glasses balancing on her nose reminded Charlie of their old headmistress back home.

*She looks an awful lot like Mrs. Bunnings,* Charlie thought.

*Stop it. You're going to make me laugh,* James responded.

Charlie kept her head down and continued to take notes of the back and forth between Henry and the Home Secretary. In the end, Henry conceded, but his agreement was dependent on the safety of his people.

Charlie wondered how the others would take this. In the past weeks, she'd heard the story of Matthew Brown's abduction so many times she could recite it by heart. But that wasn't the only tragedy orchestrated by the Sons of Domnall. In Jamie's crew in Edinburgh, there was a guy named Aidan McMillan, whose parents had been killed by the Sons. In every city, every New Alliance splinter group, there were people who had been affected in this struggle. So much pain and heartache would be difficult to overcome.

"That's fair. We will set up an initiative to ensure shifters can live freely, and safely, within our borders." The Home Secretary picked up a dossier from her desk and handed it to Henry, who opened it. "Here is a proposal put together by various agencies. There will be a joint task force. Part human, part shifter. It'll be run independently but work closely with local law enforcement, even Interpol. This task force will follow the normal protocols as far as they're relevant and report directly to me."

Charlie looked at Henry to gauge his reaction. He was impossible to read. Gail, however, seemed pleasantly surprised as she grabbed Henry's arm.

*That's good, isn't it?* Charlie thought.

James agreed; she could feel it.

"And this task force will be well financed and given all opportunities to track down these people, yes? Including surveillance, access to whatever databases you have, intercepting communications..." Henry said.

The Home Secretary took off her glasses and placed them on the table in front of her.

"Subject to using the proper procedures. Nothing without a court order. I won't tolerate anyone cutting corners or trampling all over the rights and liberties of innocent people, just because someone has a hunch."

"I see." Henry's tone was guarded. Charlie couldn't make out if he was happy about the proposal or not.

An awkward silence filled the room.

"As a sign of good faith, I'm prepared to share something with you. But all this is off the record." The Home Secretary looked directly at Charlie now. "If this ends up in the papers tomorrow, the deal is off the table, you understand?"

Charlie put her pen down on the pad and held her hands up. "Off the record. No problem."

"The attacker that was taken in during the incident at Hyde Park. We offered him a deal, but only if he was willing to talk. It turns out he was able to track you down with the help of an old friend of yours."

Charlie frowned. Who could she be referring to?

"It turns out your former leader, Adrian Blacke, hates your movement so much he was willing to make a deal with the enemy. It seems he had an axe to grind with you personally, Mr. Finch," the Home Secretary's voice sounded almost triumphant. "We have him in custody. Considering what we found at his mansion in Stirling, it won't be difficult to keep him locked up for a long time."

"No way," Charlie whispered. She looked across at the others and saw they were equally shocked. The mention of Stirling, her home town, sparked her curiosity, though.

Whatever they found there, she had to know. She would ask James about it later.

"This has been verified?" Henry asked.

"I'm afraid so." The Home Secretary cleared her throat. "I understand that we may find things there which will connect some of your people to what Blacke has been up to. Different times, shall we say. We're willing to overlook some of it, as long as everyone understands that those days are over."

Henry leaned back in his chair.

"This is a lot to take in, I understand. If you need time to think about it, that's fine," the woman said.

Charlie waited with bated breath. What would Henry say to all this? How would the New Alliance proceed?

"No need," Henry finally spoke up. "Your proposal for a joint task force is acceptable. My priorities lie with keeping my people safe. That's what our entire movement has been about from the beginning. We still have a long way to go before everyone accepts us for what we are."

Henry took a deep breath. "Now that Blacke is no longer a threat, we'll have to focus on Victor Domnall and his people. He will have gathered quite a bit of support, and although there may not be much activity right now, I've had the misfortune of dealing with his people for too long. As long as they're out there, they're planning something."

Charlie breathed a sigh of relief. This was the right way forward; she was certain of it.

"In that case, my people will be in touch when the groundwork has been laid. We'll arrange for an office and put forward a shortlist of human candidates. Please prepare a list of your own. They'll have to undergo some training to make sure they're aware of our laws and procedures."

"Of course," Henry said.

"Then we are all in agreement." The Home Secretary pushed her chair back, nodded at everyone present, and finally shook Henry's hand to symbolically seal the deal.

Charlie's head was spinning now. This was huge, though of course, she couldn't report on the entire last part of the conversation, but still.

She looked over at James, only to find his eyes already on her.

*How about that, eh?* Charlie thought.

He smiled. *We won. The New Alliance has won.*

She smiled back at him. It certainly did seem so.

Sure, they hadn't quite won everyone over yet. And the Sons of Domnall were still out there. But with shifter equality making its way into existing legislation, and this joint task force...

This was the way forward, and the future was bright.

# - THE END -

# Sugar & Spice

## A SCOTTISH WEREBEAR XMAS

# FATE: LILY & KYLE'S STORY

---◆---

On the morning of the 24th of December, all was quiet at the Alliance office.

Everyone else had plans for the holidays, but Kyle didn't. He'd visited his folks in Manchester about a month ago, and even they had Christmas plans that didn't include him, so he was just going to stay back at the office and catch up on some much-needed systems maintenance. It was the perfect time for it, without having anyone there to interrupt him.

It didn't bother him. He'd never really gotten along with his parents. His last visit to Manchester had been difficult. All they seemed to be concerned with was trying set him up with the girl next door, in whom he had no interest.

*You're not getting any younger. Why not settle down with a nice girl?*

That's why he'd cut his visit short and spent the night at a hotel, instead of their house. *And what a night it had turned out to be...*

He shook off the memories that threatened to flood him. This wasn't the time. He wasn't about to waste precious minutes reliving a one-night stand with a stranger in a hotel, no matter how amazing it had been. There was work to be done, and Kyle was keen to get started.

He'd stayed the night upstairs in one of the rooms above the office, rather than at home with too many distractions. That's how he envisioned the rest of his holiday – work without having to deal with other people, enjoy a bit of take-out, then retreat to the room upstairs for a bit of rest and repeat the cycle all over again the next day.

By the time everyone returned in the new year, he had wanted to have all the computers upgraded and secured with new software that would allow them to better cover their tracks online.

It was important for an organization like the Alliance to keep their activities a secret and not just from enemies like the Sons of Domnall, who seemed to have a lot more technical know-how than one would expect from a group of militant skinheads. It would be an even bigger disaster — for everyone — if the authorities found out about the Alliance and the Sons alike.

While the Sons had been tracking down and capturing shifters for centuries, the fight between the two sides had intensified in recent years after the formation of the Alliance had allowed the shifters to push back. So far both sides had been careful not to involve any outsiders in their activities, and the Alliance, at least, was set on keeping it that way.

Shifters were accustomed to living in secret, driven by the certainty that coming out as a different species would have the entire human world - and not just the Sons - up in arms against them. People feared what was different. What could be more different than those who could change into wild animals at will?

That was why data security was so important to Kyle. He was the one person in the Alliance's Edinburgh branch who knew better than anyone how vulnerable modern technology really was. The others didn't understand.

Kyle started with Jamie's system, adding more memory so it would be able to handle the extra software, and then he ran diagnostics on it to make sure it hadn't already been compromised. He had barely finished that when the door unlocked with a click and a creak.

He looked up to find Aidan standing in – or rather, filling – the doorway.

"What are you doing here?" Kyle asked.

"What kind of a greeting is that, mate? Good morning to you, too," Aidan remarked.

"Yeah... morning." Kyle ran his hand through his hair and stared at the unexpected intruder. "So, what *are* you doing here?"

"We were just leaving for Skye. And in the interest of Christmas cheer and all that, we couldn't fathom the idea of you staying behind working through the holidays."

Kyle squinted. As if catching up on much-needed upgrades was a bad thing. "Okay. And?"

"Why don't you join us?" Aidan asked, an expectant grin appearing on his face.

"But... I've got all these things to do." Kyle pointed at all the components littering his desk. Although he now presented it as work, he'd looked forward to the alone time as well.

"Oh, they won't go anywhere, will they?" Aidan asked.

"I suppose not, but I can't very well do this with everyone here. I'd just be disturbing you guys," Kyle tried to justify himself, but he quickly realized there was no way to explain this to a guy like Aidan. No way of telling him that staying back and working on some machinery was actually *fun* without sounding like a pathetic recluse.

"I promise whenever you want to do this, we'll stay out of your way. Besides, a smart guy like you won't take the entire week just to fix computers, will you? This is just a couple of days of work for you, right?" Aidan smiled again. He knew he'd already won.

Kyle realized that Aidan was just buttering him up, but he had to agree to some extent. This wouldn't keep him occupied throughout the holidays. He was probably going to finish within a few days and spend the rest of the time playing video games. He'd rather looked forward to it.

"Right. And Abbott's on-board?" Kyle tried one last approach.

"You don't believe me, go ask him. He's waiting in the car with everyone else."

"Okay. I suppose there's no harm." Kyle brushed some non-existent dust off his jeans and made a half-hearted attempt to organize the various tools and things he'd laid out for his work today. He had to admit defeat, Aidan had won the argument.

"Why don't you go pack," Aidan urged.

"If you say so. All right, then." Kyle looked around the room for a moment, as if it would somehow help him come up with a reason to refuse after all. Then he went upstairs to the bedrooms where a fully packed bag was already waiting for him on his bed. In his eagerness to get started on the work, he'd never even emptied his luggage. Almost as though he wasn't meant to stay here today.

Within moments, he'd picked up the rest of his things, stuffed them on top of the bag and joined Aidan downstairs again.

"Ready?" Aidan gestured at him to follow him outside.

Kyle took one final look around and sighed deeply. *Goodbye, computers...* His folks had always tried to teach him that there were times to do what you wanted yourself, and times where you had to go along with what other people said, out of politeness and to make *them* happy. He had to admit grudgingly that this was one of those times.

He could only hope that he wouldn't end up regretting this later.

# BONUS STORY: SUGAR & SPICE

Lily's flight was uneventful, even relaxing, but she still felt restless. She was traveling to the Isle of Skye to spend Christmas with her best friend, Clarice. This ought to be something to look forward to, but things didn't seem all that simple.

Only months earlier, Clarice had made the same journey. What was supposed to be just a two-week working vacation to finish her book had turned into an abrupt and permanent relocation. Lily had only seen her friend briefly when she came back to London to pack up her things and vacate her apartment, and that meeting hadn't answered any of Lily's questions.

Clarice had fallen for the farmer, Derek, and he'd invited her to stay with him. That was a weak explanation, especially for Clarice. How could you even fall in love with someone in such a short time? Sure, Clarice's messy break-up with Alan earlier in the year had left her wounded, but she was no pushover. In all the years Lily had known Clarice, she had shown herself to be an intelligent woman who made decisions with her mind before her heart.

How could a formerly independent city dweller like Clarice suddenly decide to up and move to the middle of nowhere in Scotland? And for what? To become a farmer's wife? There wasn't even any cell phone reception up there. Had she been brainwashed in a moment of weakness?

Lily rushed through the small airport terminal to pick up her bags and then she marched straight to the car rental desk where she'd pre-booked a car. She had to find out what was going on. Just in case a rescue was in order, Lily had rented a bigger car that would fit all of Clarice's stuff in the back.

There was no time to waste, so Lily didn't allow herself

to take even a coffee break at the airport before moving on to the lot where the large van-shaped Peugeot awaited her. After turning on the in-dash GPS system, she started the car and was off. A long drive lay ahead, and Lily was set on reaching her destination before dark.

How do you deal with someone who's been brainwashed, she wondered. Lily had no idea but for her friends' sake, she intended to figure it out.

Every time Lily had spoken to Clarice these past couple of months it had seemed like for everything she'd said, there were hundreds of words left unspoken. It was those secrets that had made Lily all the more suspicious.

They never used to keep secrets from each other. Clarice was the one person Lily could have come to with anything.

Like a month ago when Lily, in a momentary lapse of judgment, had gone home with a nameless stranger she'd met in her hotel lobby during a business trip. She would have told Clarice about that night, but nobody else. She would have even admitted to her that, rather than feeling embarrassed about the rash decision to climb into bed with someone she'd only just met, she'd quite enjoyed herself. She might have even allowed herself to voice that oh so dangerous *what if. What if she hadn't left early that morning?*

But that was the kind of friendship they used to have. Now, everything had changed. Lily hadn't told Clarice about that one night stand because it didn't feel right to discuss that kind of thing during a rushed phone call. All because a man had come between them.

As Lily drove on, following the robotic directions of the GPS system through the city and finally into the countryside north of Edinburgh, she kept thinking back to the good old days.

# BONUS STORY: SUGAR & SPICE

Lily had first met Clarice years ago when they'd joined the same local gym in their neighborhood in London. Both were swayed by the slick brochure and the even slicker personal trainer who sold them an annual pass. It was early January, and they'd made the same New Year's resolution to get in shape, once and for all.

Their stint at the gym didn't last long. They only made it through the first two spinning classes before throwing in the towel and taking their weekly meetings to a local restaurant instead. Lily and Clarice enjoyed the same sort of things; romantic comedies, which Clarice would obsessively analyze in her efforts to make it as a romance writer, and fine dining. They bonded over girl talk about their current significant others.

Boyfriends came and went - more so for Lily than for Clarice, whose love life had always been a bit more conservative - but their friendship had endured. Until now.

*What if she had asked for the stranger's phone number after their night together? He'd seemed interested enough. Perhaps then she wouldn't have to worry about Clarice's new relationship as much as one of her own.*

Lily realized that her thoughts weren't helping anyone and turned on the stereo instead, to drown out the ugly voices in her head. That's how she drove the rest of the way, making only one pit stop for coffee and a sandwich roughly halfway.

By the time Lily made it over the bridge and onto the Isle of Skye, it was nearing three o'clock. She would have to hurry if she wanted to make it to her destination by sundown.

The route leading her to the farm was as Clarice had described: she passed through a tiny village and then nothing but fields until she started to worry that she had gone wrong somewhere. She hit a dark wooded patch that finally did lead to McMillan Farm just as foretold.

When she pulled into the driveway and first saw the house, Lily could almost see the attraction of living here. It was a beautiful place. Mysterious, more so under the setting sun, and the old building added a certain historic charm to the surrounding countryside.

Lily's optimism was short-lived thanks to the bitterly cold winds that threatened to infiltrate her to her core as soon as she opened the car door. It was bloody freezing. If this were normal, then she couldn't imagine spending an entire winter here.

She opened the trunk of her car to get her luggage out when a voice made her pause.

"Lily, you made it!" Clarice shouted, waving excitedly when Lily turned to greet her friend.

"Of course. I wouldn't miss the chance to spend the holidays with you for anything in the world." Lily stretched out her arms and gave her friend a warm, if bittersweet, hug.

Nothing in Clarice's smile suggested she was anything but pleased to see Lily. She looked well, with a healthy glow on her cheeks.

"Nice place," Lily remarked, allowing herself to look around for a moment.

Soon after, she focused on Clarice's face again, though. There was something different about her. Had she changed her hair? Had she lost weight? Lily couldn't put her finger on what it was. Perhaps it was just the weirdness of seeing her after such a long time.

"Thanks, yes, it's great. I can't wait to show you around. Here, let me get your things."

"Watch it, it's heavy," Lily argued, while Clarice tried to pick up the suitcase.

That's when Lily first saw a large man's silhouette in the

doorway of the farmhouse. As big as the entrance was, the man managed to fill it almost entirely. *Was that...?*

"Derek, darling. Give us a hand? This is my friend, Lily," Clarice invited the man over, and he lumbered down the steps towards the two women.

"Hi," he said, stretching out one of his huge hands in Lily's direction.

So this was Derek, Clarice's new lover. *Jesus.*

Lily reluctantly accepted the handshake, and smiled at the man briefly, then stared back in Clarice's direction, eyebrows raised, while Derek lifted the heavy suitcase and effortlessly carried it into the house. *Holy hell, what a catch.*

Clarice let out a little giggle. "I know. That's pretty much how I reacted when I first saw him."

"What the-!? Honestly, would it have hurt you to give me a little warning?" Lily asked.

"Would it have helped?" Clarice winked at her. "Let's go in."

Lily shook her head and followed Clarice into her new home.

Funny, after all the hours in the car, speculating about what she might find here, Clarice's new reality was still unexpected. Lily observed her from the corner of her eye as she almost sashayed into the entrance hall. She couldn't blame her.

Lily took her time looking around while following both of them. As desolate as the location of the farm was, the decor of the main house was surprisingly cozy and inviting. It didn't seem to lack anything and the warmth inside starkly contrasted with the bitter cold from which they'd just come.

"I've prepared your room down the hall from ours," Clarice said, walking behind Derek through the living area into a hallway to the back of the house. Lily followed almost reluctantly. There was so much to take in, so much to see. She could hardly drag herself away from the beautifully decorated tree in the living room.

"Here's the bathroom." Clarice pointed to her right. "Here we are," she said, gesturing to the door opposite, "and here you are."

They paused in front of a large wooden doorway further toward the back of the building. Derek had already placed the luggage inside and quickly excused himself, edging past the two women in the hallway and back to the front of the house.

"Wow. This is beautiful!" Lily mumbled as she stepped inside the room.

A rustic wooden bed stood proudly in the center, with a huge wardrobe lining one of the walls and a cozy arm chair and book rack filling the far corner of the room.

"I do hope you'll be comfortable in here," Clarice said.

"Will I ever! It's like I've walked onto a photo shoot for Good Housekeeping."

Clarice let out a chuckle and sat down on the bed. Lily joined her, suddenly finding herself lost for words.

"This is going to sound weird..." Lily began. "But I had a hard time working out why you'd just drop everything to move here. I'm starting to figure it out now, though."

"Ha, you thought I'd lost my mind, admit it!" Clarice teased, and then her tone turned more serious. "The thing is, when you just know that something feels right, why fight it?"

Lily stared down at her feet. She had to admit she felt rather silly now. "Well, what would you have thought if you were in my shoes?"

"The same as you, probably. That's why I was keen to have you over, even if it's just for a few days." Clarice squeezed Lily's arm. "How about we have a nice cup of tea? There's cake also."

"Brilliant. I'll take a few minutes to get organized here and join you in... the living room?" Lily asked while getting up from the bouncy mattress.

"Sure." Clarice smiled at her friend once more, and then she was out the door.

Lily rubbed her eyes and let herself fall back against the pillows. She'd been so tense throughout the drive here, and for what? Clarice seemed genuinely happy with Derek. Lily had seen women who were trapped in relationships with controlling men, but Clarice didn't show any of the indicators that she didn't truly want to be where she was. But why had Clarice acted so weird when she was in London? Perhaps she'd just missed Derek. They were newly in love after all.

The bed was so comfortable, Lily scarcely wanted to get up again. It was perfect actually, save for one detail — she'd be sleeping in it alone. Her mind wandered back to that single night of perfection and the stranger responsible for it. *Stop it! Just because Clarice got a new man doesn't mean you need one, too!*

Lily was exhausted from the flight and then the long drive, but mostly from all the days spent worrying leading up to today, yet her thoughts wouldn't shut up. She still had a niggling suspicion that Clarice wasn't telling her everything there was to say about her relationship with Derek, but perhaps they'd have some time alone to have a proper heart-to-heart like they used to.

Every muscle in Lily's body objected when she forced herself back upright. Tea would be just the thing to cure her current state. She quickly changed into something a little more comfortable and hid her still messy suitcase inside the huge wardrobe. Unpacking could wait.

———◆———

Luckily Aidan had had the foresight to rent a van rather than a car, so the five of them comfortably fit inside and still had room to spare for their luggage. Kyle sat all the way at the back on his own, ahead of him sat the two women: their colleague Heidi and Alison, whom Kyle didn't know very well. That left the passenger seat for Jamie Abbott, the man in charge of the Edinburgh Alliance task force, while Aidan sat behind the wheel.

The drive was quiet for the most part and yet Kyle knew the others were probably chatting their way to glory, covertly. They were mated couples; that much was obvious. Even though everyone had been very discreet, Kyle wasn't stupid, he just didn't care much for gossip, so he hadn't made a big deal out of any of it.

All mated couples could communicate telepathically and Kyle's parents certainly could and often used that skill to their advantage. There was no reason why the two couples he shared the car with wouldn't be doing the same thing right now.

He didn't mind, just as he didn't mind sitting all the way at the back on his own. He kept himself entertained by watching the scenery whiz by, or keeping an eye on the Alliance security system using his smartphone.

Kyle wasn't much of a conversationalist, at least not unless the topic was something he was really passionate about, like technology, or even science fiction. Considering most bears – both brown bears or black like himself - were way more outdoorsy than he was, he didn't often find a lot in common with his peers.

But that didn't matter. Kyle hadn't joined the Alliance

to make friends or socialize. He was there to work for the greater good, to apply his knowledge of computers and other tech to the struggle shifters faced nowadays.

The silly thing was, the reason he was sitting in this van full of colleagues wasn't work-related at all. They were heading up north to celebrate Christmas with Aidan's brother, of all things. The longer he thought about it, the less he knew what he was doing here.

He rested his head against the cold window and kept staring at the dreary views outside. The wind and rain-lashed pine forest made way for barren cliffs rising from the surrounding soggy grasslands. It looked cold and inhospitable. He was thankful to be in a warm car instead of out there, but it was still a very far cry from the cozy mess of wires and computer screens he'd left behind in Edinburgh.

Hours later, and under cover of total darkness, the car finally pulled into a driveway leading up to an old farmhouse. The brightly lit windows greeting them looked a lot more inviting than the countryside they'd had to conquer on the way.

While everyone else eagerly got out, Kyle took an extra moment to double check that his bag was securely packed, so he was the last to approach the house.

That's when he saw her.

Everything made sense all of a sudden. Why he hadn't unpacked his bag at the office, why Aidan had invited him at the last possible moment. Everything had lined up perfectly to get him to come here and meet her. Or rather, to meet her again.

His inner bear kicked and screamed, desperate to take over - something that was very rare for him. Kyle took a deep breath and was pleased to note that she'd recognized him, too. A neon sign couldn't have been more obvious to him than the scent of her elevated hormone levels hanging in the air. Then, of course, there was the look of utter shock on her face...

"Hi. My name is Kyle," he said, all too aware that their night together had ended without either of them formally introducing themselves.

"Lily," she whispered.

Even her name was pretty.

———◆———

The tea had gone down well, as had the girl talk Lily and Clarice's discussion had evolved into. Derek was taking care of whatever one does on a farm, allowing the two friends some much-needed privacy. Things were starting to feel more normal, right up to the point that a horn outside alerted them to the arrival of more guests.

"That'll be Derek's brother, Aidan," Clarice explained while rushing towards the front door. "And a few of his friends from Edinburgh. I'd better welcome them."

Lily got up and observed their arrival from the safety of the front steps. The freezing winds had gotten worse since Lily's arrival earlier that afternoon, so she was grateful to be able to wait where she was. No way was she going to venture all the way out behind Clarice.

Her heart started to beat faster as a man as huge and built as Derek unfolded himself from the driver's seat of the van parked beside hers. That was Aidan, probably. Shortly after, a blond woman joined him from the back seat. Next came another couple featuring an equally big man and woman with fiery red hair.

What were the odds that every guy to arrive here was that tall and broad? Lily had never been to Scotland before today. Was it all that Highland Warrior heritage? Or had she accidentally found herself at the annual Nightclub Bouncer Christmas mixer?

"Welcome, Aidan, everyone!" Clarice marched ahead, shaking hands and introducing herself to her new guests as Lily continued to look on. "Why don't you come in and we'll sort out who is going to sleep where later?"

It was unlike Clarice, to be hosting a bunch of guests like this, half of whom were strangers, but she seemed in her element. If all of this wasn't enough to process, the last person to exit the vehicle nearly caused Lily to faint.

She couldn't be sure at first; it was dark outside, after all, but when he finally turned in her direction, overnight bag in hand, she was totally certain. The black-haired athletic man staring up at her was *the guy*. Her stranger, whom she'd spent only a single night with about a month ago.

Lily couldn't breathe. He'd had a hint of an accent, but she hadn't thought about it too much at the time because their physical connection had been too distracting. It made sense that he was Scottish.

Frozen in place, she couldn't get a word out when Clarice introduced her to all the others. Aidan, Heidi, Jamie and Alison.

She only had eyes for one of the guests...

"Hi. I'm Kyle," he introduced himself at last.

She swallowed hard when he took her hand and shook it. The glimmer in his eyes suggested he'd recognized her, too, but he wasn't about to advertise their history to his companions. It was like his fingers were on fire, and she had to force herself not to snatch her hand away instantly.

"Can I get anyone something? Tea? Something a bit stronger?" Clarice asked, then turned to stare at Lily suspiciously.

"Tea would be great," the red-haired woman said.

"Yeah, for me too, please," the other female guest agreed. "No sugar."

All of them entered the house, leaving their luggage behind in the hall.

"Okay, great. Lily, mind giving me a hand?" Clarice insisted.

Although her feet seemed to want to grow roots, Lily reluctantly followed Clarice into the kitchen, while the guests' chatter moved into the lounge.

"What the hell was that?" Clarice asked, squinting as she scrutinized Lily's face.

"Uhh..." Lily knew the game was up. There was no way she could brush this aside and pretend it had never happened. Still, she turned to fill up the kettle.

"Oh no, you can't hold out on me now!" Clarice grabbed Lily's arm, forcing her to turn around again.

"Remember I mentioned going away for work some time back?"

"Manchester. I remember."

Lily took a deep breath. Whatever. Better out than in. "I met a guy at my hotel. Things happened. I never thought I'd see him again, so I left before he even woke up the next morning."

Clarice let out a chuckle. "Oh my - and of all the people to tag along with Derek's brother today..."

"Honestly, what are the bloody chances of that?" Lily complained.

"Maybe it's fate, eh?" Clarice playfully prodded Lily in the arm with her elbow, then took the kettle from her and put on the tea.

"Hmm, I'm not sure I believe in that kind of thing."

"You'll be surprised what you start to believe when you find the right person," Clarice teased.

"I don't even know if I like him like that!" Lily

exclaimed, but caught herself and lowered her volume by the end of her outburst.

"Jeez. You should have seen the way you looked at him. And he at you, I should add!"

"Still, I'd appreciate it if you didn't mention this to anyone!" Lily insisted.

"Of course. My lips are sealed but if I were you, I wouldn't count on being able to keep this a secret if you can't force your eyes back into their sockets while he's around."

"What should I do?" Lily wondered out loud. "If this were one of your novels, what would you have me do?"

"Depends. What do *you* want?"

"I don't know," Lily whispered.

"Don't do anything until you figure that out."

It was sensible advice, but it didn't help Lily with how to face Kyle, who was perhaps dealing with a similar dilemma while waiting in the living room. Still, she couldn't very well hide in the kitchen all night, so when the tea was made, and more cake was laid out on a platter, Lily had no choice but to follow Clarice inside.

She avoided eye contact as much as she could with Kyle, who seemed to be playing it cool as well, at least at first. In fact, in front of everyone else, he was the quietest of the lot. He hadn't been much of a conversationalist during their short encounter either, although it had been far from quiet.

Everyone had been sitting around, getting acquainted for the better part of an hour when Kyle's resolve seemed to wear thin. Lily tried not to look, but every time she did glance in his direction, she found his deep black eyes staring in her direction. It was unnerving.

*Stop staring!* She thought.

*Why* ? A strange voice seemed to answer.

She looked up at him in surprise, but he didn't waver. Two black eyes continued to pierce through her defenses.

*I don't even know you, not really* .

Lily couldn't explain how she knew, but she was absolutely certain he could hear her. There was something in the way he looked at her, a familiarity that she couldn't explain. They'd met as complete strangers, didn't even learn each other's names until about an hour ago. But somehow, that didn't matter, at least to him. There was a reason they hadn't been able to resist temptation that night in Manchester.

*How about we remedy that tonight?* A glimmer of a smile appeared on his lips as his suggestion entered her mind.

Why not? Why not give in tonight as well and get the chance to see where this might lead?

Lily took a deep breath and glanced around the room, only to find Clarice winking at her. It didn't matter that they'd grown apart a little bit ever since she'd moved away, her best friend could still tell when something was going on. Lily smiled back at her nervously, then looked back at Kyle again. *Okay.*

---

Despite the loudest of company, Kyle stayed quiet all evening. As did Lily.

They were surrounded by people, but they might as well have been alone. While everyone else discussed everything ranging from the weather to the traffic on the way, Kyle and Lily were in their own little bubble together. Sitting at opposite ends of the room, ten feet apart, and yet they were able to communicate with ease.

The telepathic connection Kyle had only heard spoken

of had felt odd at first, but they soon got comfortable. It was so easy! No wonder all the mated couples he knew used this trick all the time.

He wasn't much of a talker, never had been, but he *was* a thinker. There was always something going on in his head. Lily seemed to have a similarly active imagination though one thought kept recurring: *how come I can hear you?*

The answer was complicated, so Kyle decided to keep his thoughts simple. He wondered how Derek had overcome the gap between what humans accept to be true, and reality. Lily had no idea what Kyle and the others really were. Would she be able to deal with the truth?

Kyle knew the others had kept a low profile because a mixed relationship was not generally accepted by the Alliance, or other shifter groups for that matter. His own parents probably wouldn't approve. But from the second he saw her again, he knew there was no way he could let her go. That had been a mistake, and he wouldn't make it twice.

For better or for worse, they had to cross this bridge sooner rather than later.

*Tonight. Tonight you'll learn everything there is to learn about me.* Kyle thought.

Lily smiled at him.

She looked so sweet, innocent almost. She had no idea what was in store for her. He only hoped she would be able to adjust.

Once dinner was over, and everyone was getting ready to retreat to their various bedrooms, Lily and Kyle decided to play it cool and wait. Heidi and Aidan were the first to leave the group and head to the holiday cottage Derek had prepared for them. Alison and Jamie, who had the other cottage, followed soon after.

Then Lily announced she was planning to sleep early and left.

Derek took a quick moment to show Kyle to his room, which was just down the hall from Lily's, and returned to the kitchen almost straight away, leaving the two of them alone with just a wall in between.

He could sense Lily's presence, despite being in different rooms. He felt irresistibly drawn to her. The feeling was mutual, because shortly after Derek had gone, there was a careful knock on his door.

"Hello?" Lily entered.

"You have questions," Kyle said.

She nodded, then looked away, a smile playing on her lips. "I'm not sure I have the patience to ask them, though."

Kyle wasn't sure he had the patience for more conversation either.

"Say, how about we talk in my room?" Lily stole a glance at the single bed in the center of the room.

Kyle didn't need the ability to read her mind to know what she was thinking. He put down the bag in his hands and followed her.

Indeed, her room was a lot more comfortable, featuring a large double bed as well. Just what they needed.

"You're not like other guys," Lily observed.

Kyle shook his head. She was sharp; he had to give her that. His movements largely on auto-pilot, he approached her and cupped her face in his hands.

She was cute, even if he hated the term normally. Those large green eyes and dimples in her cheeks made her smile look all the more radiant. He couldn't hold back any longer and dove in for a taste of those plump lips of hers.

Sweet. Just like last time.

As lean and athletic as he was, she was luxuriously soft

and feminine. There was nothing at all he would change about her. She was the yin to his yang. The human to his animal, even if that aspect of him was normally quite subdued.

He could shift right this second, and it would be effortless. Normally it wasn't all that easy for Kyle. Unlike the others, he felt much more in tune with his human side most of the time. His current state of mind was refreshing, so full of energy and strength.

His heart was pumping so hard he could feel the blood rush through his entire body. Right now, with her, he felt invincible.

"Why didn't I feel this way the first time around?" Lily wondered aloud between kisses.

Kyle had nothing to say. Perhaps because they'd been drinking? Perhaps the time hadn't been right. Her half-open hungry eyes suggested she wasn't too concerned about getting all the answers.

"Why did you leave in the morning?" Kyle asked instead.

"I don't know." Lily melted into his arms.

"Please don't do that again." The thought of losing her after tonight hurt more intensely than any physical injury ever could. He wouldn't be able to accept it, or survive it.

"I don't know how I know, but I won't. Ever." Lily blinked a few times as if she was confused at her own response. Then she focused on his eyes and her demeanor changed again. Her eyes, previously a bright green, had darkened with need.

His own reflection betrayed a similar heightened state of arousal. They couldn't resist each other anymore. They couldn't hold back.

He started first, tugging at her knitted sweater, almost tearing it off her. Meanwhile, her hands traveled straight to where it mattered most: the zip of his jeans.

Within seconds, they were naked. Despite the freezing conditions outside, the two of them were red hot. Kyle paced around her for a couple of seconds, with her tracking his every move. Like two animals, raring for a fight.

But violence wasn't what they were after.

Her eyes and her posture challenged him. He didn't know why, but something in her spoke to him to assert himself. He made the first move.

Kyle grabbed her hips, pulled her against him and took her into his arms again. Her skin was soft as silk; he couldn't imagine ever growing tired of touching her.

Full breasts crowned with pink nipples. He needed a taste, and he knew from the last time that she loved that kind of affection, so he didn't hold back.

Meanwhile, her hand sought to explore the much harsher and more angular contours of his body; a muscular back, buff chest and defined abs. He wasn't as tall as the brown bears they'd spent time with earlier, but he wasn't any less built. Such was the advantage of being a bear. There was no such thing as an unfit one, even if said bear preferred computers over more active or outdoorsy pursuits.

She moaned loudly when he ran his tongue over the very tip of her hard nipple. The rawness in her voice gave him shivers. It also made him ever more impatient to move on to the main course.

He let go of her, but before she had the chance to protest, fell to his knees in front of her and kissed her folds. He loved how the soft curls of her mound brushed against his face, and the sweet taste of her nectar tickled his tongue.

Her moans turned to groans. He felt her legs tremble,

so he held her steady.

She had other ideas though, and she stumbled back a couple of steps away from him and fell onto the bed.

He followed, like a predator undeterred by his prey's retreat. It wasn't much of a chase, considering she lay spread-eagle in front of him, surrendering completely.

Fine, if she wanted it like that...

*I do!* Her thoughts confirmed what he already knew.

She reached out for him, guiding his thick, pulsating manhood exactly where she needed it the most.

She'd been eager the first time around, but this time, their union was even more intense, like an itch that hadn't been scratched in months. Indeed, it had been too long since their first night together. He hoped that he'd never have to wait as long for her again.

He entered her, and her fingernails drew blood on his back.

The pain just aroused him further, so he plunged into her deeply, relishing the tight grip of her sheath.

She was so beyond control; she could barely keep her eyes open. If he kept staring at her expressions, he wouldn't be able to keep it together either. He pulled away and with one swift move turned her over by hooking his arm under her knee.

The two lush curves of her behind looked delicious enough to bite into. But he didn't give in to that particular temptation, instead mounted her again, groaning with pleasure when he was welcomed back inside her slick pussy.

"Oh God!" she all but screamed into her pillow.

"You like that, do you?"

"Shit, just...just don't stop!"

He didn't.

Every time he buried himself deep inside her, she

ground her hips up against him. But he wasn't fully satisfied yet. While leaning on one hand, he slipped the other one underneath her and kept her steady as he sped up.

Helplessly restrained, Lily could do nothing but moan with each of his strokes, and shudder at the sudden emptiness she must have felt when he withdrew almost all the way. She didn't struggle against his firm hold on her. Instead, she wrapped her arms around his, unwilling to let go of whatever part of him was within her reach.

"Faster," she begged, almost inaudibly.

He didn't need to hear that again and did as asked. Pressed up against him, this beautiful woman, this goddess, was writhing in pleasure. Kyle wasn't much of a ladies' man, but right at this moment, he knew exactly how to handle himself and his partner.

Her hair smelled so sweet he couldn't resist it. He buried his face in it and let the scent overwhelm his senses. Her skin was so soft, he nibbled and sucked on her neck until in his enthusiasm he left behind marks. She was delicious all over.

He could hardly breathe, but couldn't stand the idea of stopping either. She reached the precipice of her release first, covering her mouth with one of her hands as she let out a moan-turned-scream. Her body seemed intent on keeping him inside of her, twitching and pulsating around his cock, while the rest of her muscles turned utterly limp.

That was it, all he needed. He felt his hot seed burn its way through him and into her and lost control of his own body. They both sank into the mattress, a hot sweaty mess of limbs and tussled sheets.

It was beautiful, and a little bit dirty.

He slipped off her a few seconds later and turned onto his back for a breather.

# BONUS STORY: SUGAR & SPICE

It took her a little longer to find the will to move, but then she nestled into him, tucked into the space he'd left between his arm and torso.

"You really aren't like other guys," Lily sighed as she rested her head against his shoulder.

"I'm not," Kyle confirmed. He didn't know how he would explain it to her in words, so he closed his eyes and concentrated on creating the perfect image for her. With his mind, he captured the exact moment between man and bear. The shift.

She flinched and pushed herself back against his naked torso, broadening the space between them.

"That's not possible!" she mumbled.

"I know it's a lot to take in," Kyle said. She had to be okay with this, right? It wasn't possible that she was his mate and yet would be unable to accept his true nature?

"More than you know." Lily leaned up on her elbows and stared straight ahead. "When I was little, my grandmother used to tell me these stories. Of course, we didn't take her seriously."

Kyle sat up next to her while she filled her as well as his mind with images of her own. He took her hand, and the visions they shared became even clearer. Her grandmother had been different as well.

Through Lily's veins ran not bear blood, but another species altogether. Her late grandma was a fox shifter who upon meeting her mate - Lily's grandpa - had turned her back on her own kind and instead chosen a human life. She'd told Lily and her cousins stories which sounded like fairy tales at the time.

Her stories told of fox people who lived in secret exactly like bears did. They'd been hunted almost to extinction by wealthy landowners and aristocrats who'd enjoyed killing the foxes for sport. Those that were left either made sure to keep to themselves, never shifting in places where they might be discovered by trigger-happy humans, or they suppressed their animal selves like Lily's grandmother had done, and adopted human ways as their own.

"I never knew about fox shifters," Kyle remarked. "But it certainly explains a lot."

"Does it?" Lily still looked frazzled.

"Yeah. Our intense connection, and the fact that we're able to communicate so well already. It must be because you're part shifter!"

"I guess that does make sense."

Lily took a deep breath and let herself fall back into his waiting arms. "I never thought today would end quite like this."

"Me neither."

"So...the others, are they like you?" Lily asked.

"Close enough, yeah," Kyle confirmed.

"That does explain a lot as well."

Kyle glanced over at her, then couldn't suppress a smile. "You're really cute when you're confused."

"That's funny." Lily crossed her arms and glared at him. Seems she couldn't stay mad at him for long, though, because a smile quickly broke through her lips as well. "I guess at least now I know grandma wasn't crazy after all."

"That's a good silver lining."

"Right?" She picked up his arm and tucked it across her chest tighter. "And I also know I'm hopelessly stuck."

"Oh?"

"There's no way I'm going back to my old life of boredom and loneliness now that I've had another taste of super-hot shifter sex." Her tone had changed, gone was the seriousness that had washed over her just now, replaced by her usual much more playful self.

"Again, I don't see the downside," Kyle remarked.

"So how is Edinburgh at this time of year?" she asked.

"I imagine it's pretty much like London, except wetter."

"I should have known. Oh well... I guess a change would be nice, as well as timely."

"Is that what you want to do? Move to Edinburgh?"

Lily shrugged, then turned onto her side and smiled at him. "I've heard it's a nice enough place. Is it?"

"I suppose so."

"So it's settled then."

"I think I love you," Kyle whispered. He'd never been the emotional type, and tended to get uneasy when hearing other people utter these words to each other, but right now it felt completely right.

Lily stared at him for a second, then smiled again. "I love you too."

# ACCEPTANCE: HEIDI'S STORY.

———◆———

"So how does this work exactly?" Heidi asked, looking up from her partially packed suitcase.

Aidan zipped up his own bag and glanced up at her. "How do you mean?"

"Well, Christmas. What's going to happen?"

"You guys don't celebrate Christmas?" Aidan exclaimed.

"Don't sound so shocked! It's much weirder that you people actually *do* celebrate it. I always thought it was a human thing." Heidi folded her arms and cocked her head to the side. Although they'd been together for a couple of months now, bears often still seemed like a mystery to her.

"Well, it is and knowing Derek, the entire thing will have been Clarice's idea, not his. But if you ignore the religious aspect for a moment, what's not to like? You come together and enjoy some good food, exchange gifts, etc."

"Gifts? You never said anything about gifts before, and now I don't have anything to give!" Heidi's confusion about the entire affair instantly turned to panic.

Aidan let out a chuckle. "Relax, sweetheart. That's just what people generally do. You're not expected to give anyone anything."

Heidi wasn't convinced. Perhaps he was just trying to make her feel better. "Are you sure?"

"Really. It'll be fine." He reached out to her, caressing her cheek with the back of his hand. The amusement at her outburst was still written all over his face. "Look. We're just spending a few days at the farm where I grew up. I promise it'll be fun."

Heidi smiled. "I *am* rather curious to see that."

"You'll love it. It's really quiet, perfect to go for a bit of a run, even hunt some small game if you want."

It sounded idyllic, almost like home. It had been just over two months since she'd left the wolf settlement in Rannoch Forest to come work for the Alliance in Edinburgh. Previously she'd loved nothing more than to go out and lose herself in the woods, but that just wasn't possible in the city. Even Aidan's favorite escape, Holyrood Park, wasn't much of a stand-in for the vast countryside to which she was accustomed.

There were two reasons she'd fought the urge to run off somewhere quieter. The Alliance's work to protect all shifters against the illustrious Sons of Domnall was too important to leave behind, and of course, there was Aidan. They were mates – despite their differences – and inseparable. The work they did together was even more important to him than it was to her.

"All right then. But if someone mentions gifts, I'll say you told me not to get anything," Heidi warned him.

Aidan laughed again. "Deal. So, don't you wolves celebrate any holidays?"

"Of course we do!" Heidi said. "Midwinter is a big one."

"So what do you do for Midwinter?"

"It's a time for new beginnings, so a lot of couples have their mating ceremony at Midwinter. All able-bodied pack members take part in the Midwinter Games; it's how the new hierarchy is decided. To keep things fair they divide the pack into two groups, youth and adult. The grown-up winner of the games can choose to challenge the alpha to take his spot if he wants to, although that hasn't happened in a long time," she explained.

Heidi was a little sad about missing the games this year, and every year to come. Her interspecies relationship with Aidan had made a return to Rannoch unlikely, if not impossible. Before setting off, she'd had a few hunches about who might win this year's games, and would have liked to see the outcome for herself.

"Did you ever take part?"

"What, in the Midwinter Games?" Heidi looked down at her hands. "Only males can compete."

"Oh." Aidan ran his hand through his hair. "That's too bad, I guess they don't want to risk losing to a girl, huh?"

"Probably." She looked back up at him, his brown eyes full of warmth. Although he couldn't relate to the gender inequality that was prevalent in wolf society, she was grateful that he'd always been tactful about it.

"So tell me what kind of things they do during the games?" Aidan grabbed her arm and pulled her close to him while he sat down on the bed.

Heidi didn't resist, and sat down on his lap while telling him about the different challenges. Combat, tracking, hunting... All the while, his touch warmed her to her core, making her feel just a little bit less wistful about being so far away from it all.

"You know we have something like that, a competition, but it takes place in the spring or summer," Aidan remarked when she was finished.

"Oh yeah? I had no idea."

"Ever heard of the Highland Games? It's not quite as varied as your games though, mainly about physical strength."

"You're joking – I thought that was a human thing, too?" Heidi turned and scrutinized Aidan's face, looking for any sign that he was just pulling her leg.

"That's just what we want everyone to think." Aidan

grinned. "Anyone can enter, humans included, but I'm sure you can guess which species tends to win..."

"No kidding."

"How about I take you next year?" Aidan said, running his fingers through Heidi's hair.

"That would be nice." She closed her eyes, enjoying his continuing affections.

"But first I'm taking you to Skye to celebrate Christmas with my little brother and his human." Aidan leaned in for a kiss that sent shivers down Heidi's spine.

"Indeed," she whispered against his lips.

"Let's go then."

They shared another kiss, then Heidi got up off Aidan's lap and collected the remainder of her things. They still had to swing by Jamie Abbott's place, who would join them along with his very own human mate, Alison.

What a strange bunch they would be – three bears, two humans, and a wolf – celebrating what was essentially a human holiday. It was a funny coincidence that this little group had formed in which every couple had gone against the grain, necessitating a certain amount of discretion and secrecy.

Traditionally, bears mate with bears, wolves with wolves, and humans don't even get into it. If anyone else found out about the lot of them, there'd be hell to pay.


A long drive later, Heidi found herself at Aidan's childhood home. It was every bit as idyllic as it had sounded. The little woodland around the farm was practically calling out to her, but this wasn't the time to run off.

Instead they were invited inside and pampered by Clarice, the human Aidan's brother Derek had paired up with. Tea, cake, cookies, everything was laid out for them. Two months at the Alliance had helped Heidi acclimate to the sweet tooth bears seemed to have, though she couldn't quite keep up with any of them. She stuck to her unsweetened tea and some nuts as a snack, leaving the confections aside.

Heidi had found a surprising amount of common ground with Jamie's mate, Alison, whose background was even more different than her own. The two women had started chatting in the car, and it seemed like the beginnings of a friendship were starting to develop.

Heidi had left her family when her father had sent her to work with the Alliance, and now everything back home was probably just how she left it. If she wanted to, Heidi could go back for a visit any time she liked. Her own feelings were the only thing standing in her way. She hadn't found the courage to tell them about Aidan and as such had avoided contact.

Alison, meanwhile, had lost her whole family permanently and irreparably. She was the daughter of the enemy, essentially. He'd sent her in to pose as an informant for the Alliance, to covertly gather information for the Sons of Domnall. That was when she'd found herself intensely drawn to Jamie and switched sides, directly resulting in the capture of her father and brother, who were still being held by the Alliance Council.

There was no going back for Alison. This handful of unlikely people was the closest thing to family she would have now. Heidi admired the woman and the strength and resolve she had shown, despite having her world turned upside down this past month.

The same pretty much applied to Aidan and his brother, Derek, whose parents had died in a car crash so many years ago. They never even got to say goodbye.

Perhaps Heidi ought to suck it up and call her parents. At least she still had that option, even though the prospect filled her with dread.

Through the laughter and conversation, Heidi noticed Aidan staring at her.

*All okay?* She heard his voice in her head.

She shot a quick smile in his direction. *I'll be right back.*

Heidi removed her phone from her pocket, but upon switching it on immediately realized she had no network.

*There's a phone in the entrance hall,* Aidan suggested.

Although she'd have preferred to go outside for a bit more privacy, she took a deep breath and decided to make do with what she had before she lost her nerve altogether. She closed the door behind her and flexed her fists a couple of times. *You can do this! What's the worst that'll happen?*

Heidi dialed the number and waited, her heart beating in her throat.

"Hello?" her mother answered the phone like she usually did. It was a bit of a relief. Heidi had wanted to speak to her rather than her dad anyway.

"Hi... Mom?" Heidi tried her best to disguise the tremble in her voice.

"Heidi, darling! It's been so long since we've heard from you? Where have you been? Are you all right? Your father kept saying she's old enough to know what she's doing, but I've been so worried!"

"Yeah, all fine. I just wanted to say hello. We're all celebrating Christmas together." Heidi said.

"Christmas? Isn't that a human thing?" The question made Heidi smile — it was just what she'd asked Aidan earlier.

"Apparently not. Well... How is everything back home?

Are you and Dad okay?" Heidi asked.

"We're just fine, don't you worry, sweetie."

"I have something to tell you, but I don't know if you should tell Dad, all right?" Heidi knew she was stalling, but she was scared of what the reaction might be. Still, it was inevitable. Her mother would know what to do with the information, whether it was something to pass along to Dad or not. Either way, Heidi simply couldn't take the secrecy anymore.

"What's that?"

Heidi took a deep breath, counted to three, and went for it. "I've found my mate."

"Oh, honey, that's wonderful! Who is he? Which pack is he from? When do we get to meet him?"

She closed her eyes. Her throat felt like it was closing up, but there was no turning back now.

"He's... He's not from any *pack.*"

"Oh?"

"It's a guy from work. A bear."

The line fell silent. For a painful five – or perhaps ten – seconds, Heidi could hear nothing at all. "Hello?" she asked, wondering if the call had gotten disconnected.

"Oh, darling... That's... well, that's unexpected, to say the least."

"What's unexpected?" Heidi heard her dad's voice further away from the receiver. *Oh, crap.*

"It's Heidi," her mother explained. "Heidi, will you give me a second?"

"Sure," Heidi said, but her mom hadn't waited for her answer. Muffled voices were going back and forth in the background. She'd probably covered the receiver with her hand.

This was a disaster. She hadn't even had the chance to

explain properly before her dad got involved in the conversation. Then again, what was there to explain?

She and Aidan were mates; their feelings had told them as much from the first time they saw each other. There was no questioning it, no fighting the pull they felt toward each other. Surely her parents would understand that?

"Heidi," her dad's voice said on the other end.

"Yes, Dad?"

"Do you realize what this means?"

"Umm... I have some idea," Heidi said.

"Your mother and I had hoped you'd pair up with the next alpha, once I step down."

"I understand. But..." She had nothing. There was nothing she could say that would help right now.

Her dad took a deep breath on the other end.

Heidi rested her head in her free hand. They were disappointed, of course they were.

"Please be frank. Are you happy?" he asked at last.

"I am... but..."

"We've never told you this, but when your mother and I got together, it wasn't what our parents had in mind either. They had picked out a different mate for her."

"Really?"

"Her father was alpha at the time, and he'd picked his successor. Everything was set, and there was no convincing him. But we felt it. We felt the connection."

"Yes! I feel it too – with him, I mean," Heidi agreed.

"There was only one thing I could do to make things right. I had to prove my worth to her father. Do you know how I did that?" he asked.

"The games?"

"That's right. I trained for months and months, and won the games that year. That's when he finally accepted my claim on your mother."

Heidi remained quiet. She'd never known how her parents had gotten together, but she always assumed that everyone had simply agreed to their match without any conflict or difficulty. It was a lot to take in. It seemed her parents weren't quite the people she thought they were.

"Heidi, darling," her mother spoke into the receiver.

"Yes, Mom?"

"You know we love you, right?" she asked.

"Me too..."

"Things are a little difficult right now, but when things calm down, we'd rather like to meet him."

"Sure. Just let me know." Heidi's lip started to shake and her eyes glazed over. As terrified as she'd been about telling them, the conversation had gone surprisingly well.

"Please stay in touch, darling. We'll visit when we can." Her mom's voice cracked slightly on the other end. Or was that just some distortion in the line?

"Okay."

"How do they say it? Merry Christmas?"

"Yeah. Merry Christmas, Mom." Tears ran down Heidi's face as she looked at the now suddenly very quiet receiver in her hand. She'd been putting this off for so long, and for what?

Almost instantly, the door behind Heidi opened, and Aidan appeared. They didn't need words to discuss what had just happened. He simply took her into his arms and held her tight. Everything would be all right.

They remained there, silent, for at least ten minutes.

"Let's go back in. Have some dinner," Aidan said.

Heidi swallowed the rest of her emotions and looked up at him. It was nice to be so completely understood by another person. She'd never had even a fraction of that until meeting Aidan. Her entire life she'd been a bit of an outsider, which was unusual for a wolf, considering they're pack animals.

"Okay, I'm ready," Heidi said.

———◆———

Heidi and Aidan stuck around in the main farmhouse for as long as it seemed polite to, but finally, at nine, they made their excuses and retreated to the holiday cottage that had been prepared for them. But Heidi wasn't in any mood to rest just yet.

"What?" Aidan asked when he noticed Heidi's stares.

"You're not *that* tired, are you?" she asked while watching him organize his luggage.

"I did drive all the way, you know," he teased.

"Yeah, but... Don't you feel all stiff? Like you need to stretch your limbs?" Heidi cocked her head to the side.

"I see where you're going with this." Aidan walked up to her and cupped her face with his hands. "You've seen the house I grew up in already, but how about I show you my special place?"

"You have a special place?" Heidi asked.

"Sure. Doesn't everyone?" Aidan smiled down at her.

"Sounds great."

"Now, it's quite a distance away so we'll have to run. You up for that?"

"Always."

Before Heidi could say anything else, Aidan was already out the door. They started off slow, tiptoeing around the garden and driveway in an attempt not to make too much noise, but as soon as they were past the main gate, they broke into a jog.

Moments later, Aidan paused behind one of the bigger trees and started to undress. "We should be safe to change here."

Heidi followed his example and folded both their things and hid them neatly beneath some fallen leaves. The air was icy cold against her skin.

Aidan transformed first, so quickly that any casual observer would not have believed their eyes. In a fraction of a second, the naked man with the brown hair and chiseled abs had turned into a huge brown bear.

Heidi focused, though she didn't really need to. The cold spurred her on to change equally quickly. As soon as her greyish-brown fur sprouted all over her body, she felt better. The cold could no longer harm her.

Aidan looked back only once, then started to run east.

It was a dark, starless night. The only light source, the full moon, was partially obscured by thick clouds. Still, Heidi could see just fine and expertly negotiated the uneven ground between the trees.

As tempting as it was to let loose, she made sure to stay behind Aidan. He was fast for a bear, but wolves were faster.

The trees thinned and finally made way for open heathland. It had a sort of desolate beauty, this island. There wasn't much cover, which Heidi only found unnerving until she realized that there wasn't a soul anywhere within sight.

They continued to run across the vast countryside, further and further, until they made it to a tall cliff at the edge of the island. Far down below, the waves battered against the rock, creating a deafening and yet very relaxing noise.

Heidi had grown up on the mainland. The settlement at Rannoch was safely tucked away in a dense forest. The only water around belonged to a big loch nearby, but it was quite far away from the sea.

Aidan sat down beside her as she stared down into the

black depths of the sea.

It was mesmerizing.

*Beautiful, isn't it?* Aidan thought.

Heidi nodded in agreement. From the corner of her eye, a pulsating light attracted her attention.

*What's that?*

*A lighthouse.*

Heidi squinted to get a clearer picture of it, but it was too far away. Humans were amazing in their own way. These waters were so treacherous many lives would have been lost trying to navigate them. But rather than give up and let nature have its way, they'd build stronger ships and bigger lighthouses in order to conquer their environment.

*It's a beautiful place,* Heidi thought.

Aidan shuffled closer to her until she could feel the warmth of his fur against hers. *That's not all.*

*No?*

Aidan got up and nodded at her to follow. Off to the right, he made his way through a gap in the cliffs and started to climb.

Down they went, this time with her following him a bit more carefully. She might be a faster runner, but bears were way better climbers.

Finally they made it to a ledge about halfway down the cliff.

*Here.*

Heidi stepped ahead of Aidan and noticed the dark entrance in the rock. A cave.

She entered first, drawn in by the familiar scent permeating the place. This was Aidan's special place.

Inside waited a few old blankets and other assorted things he must have carried here years ago. It was cozy, of course it was.

*I always thought one day when I'm old enough I might come here and hibernate one winter. Just like they used to do in the old days.*

Heidi had to chuckle. Only bears could embrace a totally human concept like Christmas, while idealizing old fashioned ideas like hibernating.

*That's not funny!*

Heidi turned and grinned at Aidan. *It is a little.*

*Oh you wolves, you'll never understand.*

*Did you ever think you'll bring a girl here to hibernate with you?* Heidi teased.

Aidan got up on his hind legs and let out a low growl.

Heidi immediately got the signal and started to circle him just like her instinct told her to. The hair on the back of her neck stood to attention involuntarily.

*Bring a girl here? Yes, that crossed my mind. But not to hibernate, exactly!*

As soon as Aidan had fully formulated that thought, he lashed out. His paw hit Heidi on her flank and she rolled over onto one of the blankets. It was surprisingly soft.

A split second later, Aidan was beside her, holding her down.

They transformed back into their human forms instantly.

Although it was freezing outside, the inside of the cave wasn't so bad. Aidan grabbed the corner of the blanket Heidi had landed on top of and wrapped it safely around her naked body.

She giggled uncontrollably when he nuzzled the side of her neck and kissed her in that most sensitive, most ticklish spot below her ear.

*I'm sorry, I'm sorry! It's a lovely place you've got here!* Heidi tried to appease him.

"Damn right, it's lovely," Aidan whispered.

# BONUS STORY: SUGAR & SPICE

She wrapped her arms around his neck and sighed deeply when she felt his body heat melt into her entire body. Despite feeling hesitant about the whole Christmas holiday idea, she was glad that she'd agreed to come. She wouldn't have wanted to miss this place — this moment, right now — for the world.

They shared kiss after kiss, each one deeper and more passionate than the last.

Together, their bodies heated the cave and each other even further.

Heidi climbed on top of Aidan, straddling him as he steadied her. This was the view of him that she loved the most. He was on his back, but far from helpless.

She leaned down, kissing and licking her way across his chest while he wrapped his arms around her again. He was hard for her, and impatient.

Aidan reached down between them and teased her with his fingers, just for a moment, until she lost her patience as well. She lifted herself and allowed him to enter her.

There was nothing she wanted more, nothing that could make this moment more perfect than it already was. They'd learned a lot about each other since they'd been together, but seeing his childhood home and now this place had been huge. Maybe one day she could return the favor.

For now, though, all she had to offer was her body and mind.

She thought of the sea below, of the roaring waves crashing into the rocks beneath the cave. Water, as dangerous as it was, had a strange erotic quality to it.

Her visions of the sea mingled with glimpses of her past encounters with Aidan. How their bodies felt, crashing and mingling together, much like those same waves.

Aidan joined in, fantasizing and feeding her images of how she looked to him. Her strawberry blond locks flying wildly when she rode him. The deep pink tint her lips took on after too many shared kisses. Her feminine curves, which he so admired.

Heidi closed her eyes for better focus and just hung on while Aidan took her from underneath. It wasn't long before she felt the tension in her lower abdomen grow.

He felt the same, she could feel it in her entire being.

They were on fire, their shared pleasure coursing through their veins.

*I want to see you,* someone thought. Heidi wasn't sure if it was her own thought or his. Maybe both of theirs.

They opened their eyes at the same time, staring into each other's souls as they moved rhythmically towards a mutual release. Her orgasm washed over her like the water she'd admired earlier, as did his, causing them to nearly drown.

Heidi collapsed into his arms, still, until they both caught their breath again. She wasn't sure just how long they'd stayed in that cave, safely tucked into those soft blankets that had survived years just to make tonight possible.

By the time they got up and changed back into their animal selves for the return journey, the outside world had changed along with them. The previously deep black rocks were speckled with white. Soft white flakes were still falling from the sky.

They climbed up the rocks back to the plateau on top of the cliff and ran back, catching snowflakes in their mouths on the way. Heidi sprinted for a few minutes, feeling the last bit of stiffness from the long car journey earlier leave her body.

She waited for Aidan by the tree where they'd hidden

their things. He showed up just minutes later.

*That was amazing,* Heidi thought.

*I'm glad I got to share that with you.* Aidan transformed into his human form and picked up the clothes from underneath the snow-dusted pile of leaves. "Here."

Heidi underwent the same metamorphosis and gladly accepted her things. The snow had taken away the wind chill, but it was still quite cold. They hurriedly put their clothes back on and sneaked back through the woods and onto the driveway of McMillan Farm, where they rushed towards the cottage they were staying in.

As if nothing had ever happened.

But something had.

And Heidi was glad for it, too.

# MIRACLE: CLARICE & DEREK'S STORY

———◆———

Clarice Adler had been living at McMillan Farm for over two months already. Although she was over the moon to have found and fallen for Derek, she did look forward to a bit of a change come the holiday season. Christmas was going to be her chance to have a house full of guests, including her best friend, Lily.

Her lifestyle had changed drastically ever since she'd decided to stay with Derek. Back in London, she would have thought nothing of living on ready-meals or take-out day after day. That was no longer an option now, but she didn't miss it. Living the good life at the farm had been an eye-opening experience.

That wasn't to say that the transition had been easy for Clarice. Before coming to the farm, she'd never cooked anything more complicated than eggs or baked beans on toast, but with Derek's encouragement and help, she'd soon learned the basics.

Christmas was going to be a test and a potential triumph. She wanted to handle it herself, taking only the minimum amount of input from Derek, and prove to herself more than anyone that she could roast a turkey and have it turn out edible too.

The days leading up to the big one weren't smooth sailing, though. She'd written and re-written the menu plan multiple times. She'd read all the relevant books, even studied handwritten notes left behind by Derek's late mother, and discussed things with him ad nauseam as well. With all the preparations came a strange case of tinnitus; a rustle or noise would overwhelm her sometimes for a few seconds at a time. Stress, probably.

Derek supported her efforts, even if he had shown some trepidation at the idea of a big Christmas celebration. But he'd agreed, and she could feel that he genuinely wanted her to have her perfect holiday. He'd even baked a big Christmas pudding already, weeks in advance, so that it had time to sit and mature.

Yet every time she and Derek had agreed on something, there was still a little niggle or doubt that she couldn't ignore. Something felt wrong. It felt like, despite the best of plans, she wouldn't be able to manage, as though something or someone was out to sabotage her efforts. It was around the 23rd that the funny noise in her head took on a slightly different quality; no longer indistinct, every so often Clarice thought she could hear someone call out to her, whispering her name.

But how could that be? It wasn't Derek, for sure; he sounded different when he was in her head.

Still, the preparations were ongoing and she was making good progress. The tree had already been put up, decorated to perfection using some of the ornaments Clarice had found in the things left behind by Derek's parents. Everything was right on schedule. But there was still something tugging at her.

What could it be?

On the morning of the 24th, before the guests were meant to arrive, she started preparing the side dishes. The oven in their kitchen was big enough to fit the turkey as well as a tray of potatoes and vegetables all at once, so it was just a matter of timing everything to be ready at the same time. No big deal, right?

Clarice peeled more potatoes than she'd ever had to peel before. Then came the carrots, parsnips, and other winter vegetables. By the end, she could do nothing more than slump down on one of the wooden chairs in the kitchen and rest her tired hands. She was right on schedule, and yet...

*Clariiiice*, that same whisper she'd heard before entered her mind again.

When she tried to shake it off and get back on task, the sight of the freshly cleaned vegetables made her nauseous.

Clarice closed her eyes and covered her face with her hands, but the earthy smell of raw potato on her fingers just made things worse.

*Clariiiice!*

The voice seemed to get clearer and more distinct every time she heard it.

The room started to spin, faster and faster. In the end, she could do nothing but run to the nearest bathroom. Of all the times to catch the stomach flu, did it have to be now, on the morning of Christmas Eve? She still had so much to do!

She took a deep breath and washed her face, noting that she felt much better already. That was weird, right? When you have the stomach flu, you don't just feel okay like that.

She studied her face in the mirror, noting that there was something different about her reflection, but she couldn't figure out what exactly. The healthy blush on her cheeks also suggested that whatever was ailing her wasn't the flu.

A little twitch in her stomach distracted her from her mirror image, and the voice seemed to have come back as well. *God, don't make it start all over again!*

Clarice rested her hand on her lower abdomen and immediately the funny feeling passed and her mind became quiet again. *Odd.*

Derek was out doing his daily chores around the farm and Clarice didn't want to bother him, so she headed back to the kitchen for a well-earned cup of tea. Perhaps it would settle her stomach.

She cleared all the prepped food away, though the smell had stopped bothering her, and put on the kettle. Despite her earlier discomfort, she couldn't resist a quick bite to eat while waiting. This was really very strange.

Steaming mug in hand, she left the kitchen and settled down in one of the armchairs facing the Christmas tree. That's when she noticed it had started to shed, badly. The previously lush and green needles were thinning so much that some of the branches had started to look much like the tall trees surrounding the farm: barren.

That pile of dried up needles underneath the tree was threatening the perfection Clarice was aiming for. She sighed, put her tea back down and cleared up the mess, which seemed never-ending, with new needles falling where old ones had just been picked up. It was hopeless.

By the time she gave up, her tea was lukewarm. *Bloody brilliant, can't I catch a break?*

"Darling, a moment?" Derek stuck his head around the door.

She took a big sip. *Ugh.* Clarice put her mug down again and followed Derek into the entrance hall.

"The first arrival is here," he said, nodding at the front door. "I guess it's your friend from London."

Only then did Clarice hear the car creep over the gravel in front of the house. *No rest for the wicked...*

"Are you all right?" Derek asked, studying her face.

"Yeah. Fine." Clarice took a deep breath and headed outside into the cold, leaving Derek in the doorway. "Lily, you made it!"

———————◆———————

On the eve of the big day, Derek was struggling to maintain the obligatory festive mood.

When Clarice had first brought up the idea of organizing a big Christmas party, inviting family as well as friends, Derek McMillan hadn't really liked the idea. He loved his farm as it was: quiet, peaceful, with only the occasional guest staying in one of the cottages. His brother Aidan's occasional visits had been enough of a distraction from his daily routine to keep him happy.

But the sparkle in Clarice's eyes when she told him about all her plans for the perfect holidays had swayed him. She was so intent on having a picture-postcard Christmas during her first winter at the farm, he couldn't bring himself to refuse it.

Christmas was a painful time for Derek, and for Aidan as well. Some of their favorite childhood memories involved a roaring fire, homemade cookies and Christmas pudding, enjoyed by the elaborately decorated tree. But a large part of those cherished memories was missing forever; their parents had died in a car accident when Derek was only a teenager.

Ever since that dark day so many years ago, Derek and Aidan had stopped celebrating their favorite holiday.

Until now.

Derek had kept his concerns to himself while he watched Clarice sort through the old Christmas decorations hidden away in the attic of McMillan Farm. She'd selected a set of old-fashioned painted wood ornaments to go with the green and red glass baubles. Funny how a few boxes of decorations and a pine tree could completely transform the living room.

He'd even baked a Christmas pudding and helped her pick the recipe for the roast she was planning to make on the big day. It was Clarice's first attempt at cooking for more than just the two of them.

The guest list had started simple: Aidan and his mate, Heidi, whom Derek had only briefly met a couple of months earlier, and Clarice's best friend from London, Lily. Their cousin Elise and her mate Jack had been invited as well but declined because of earlier commitments.

Five people in total, that was quite manageable.

From there, though, things had gotten out of hand. Before setting off from Edinburgh, Aidan had suggested they invite his colleague from the Alliance, Jamie, along with his human mate Alison. That made seven.

Now, when Aidan phoned up to let Derek know he was on the way, it turned out he'd invited yet another guest! Aidan and Jamie's colleague Kyle had tagged along at the last minute. Derek was happy enough to indulge Clarice and let her have her party, but this wasn't what he'd signed up for.

Not only would the farm be overrun with bears and their various non-traditional mates, there were also going to be two loose cannons to deal with: Kyle, whose loyalties were as yet unknown, and Lily, who under no circumstance could find out about the shifters' real nature.

Derek valued the opportunity to shift at will and go for a run through the nearby wilderness whenever the urge arose, but with so many people around - human as well as shifter - there wouldn't be any point. Wherever he could go, he'd be sure to run into someone or other. And so, his mood had soured significantly.

Lily was the first to arrive, and despite Derek's grumpiness, he had to admit she seemed nice enough. He left the two friends to themselves for the rest of the afternoon, instead making sure that everything was ready for the remaining guests.

The two holiday cottages at McMillan farm each had a cozy little living area with open plan kitchen, and a bedroom with a king-sized bed. That took care of the two couples they were expecting. Where to put Kyle, the fifth wheel, though? There was another bedroom in the house, of course, but it was far from appropriate – Derek's childhood room.

He hadn't spent much time in there, especially not lately. Over the years - ever since he'd started to use the master bedroom himself - his old room had turned into more of a dumping ground than anything else. The bed was still there, but unfortunately so were boxes of random things that had been thoughtlessly discarded.

Of all the things he wanted to do today, reorganizing and sorting through old crap wasn't one of them, but Aidan hadn't left him much of a choice.

Derek pulled himself together and started piling boxes and other random things together, carrying them up to the attic. It took multiple trips until the bed underneath even became visible. Every trip up the flight of stairs leading to the attic was like another journey into the past.

Old items of furniture that no longer had a place downstairs stood around gathering dust. He hadn't been up here in so long he'd forgotten about a lot of it. There was even an old crib standing in the corner, no doubt the one he and Aidan had both slept in as babies. Derek recognized it from old photographs. Their dad had built it himself, but by now it had seen better days.

Derek wasn't sure why, but seeing it there, abandoned in the corner, paint flaking off the sides, made him feel funny. Like it deserved a better fate.

# BONUS STORY: SUGAR & SPICE

All of this stuff actually... Perhaps he ought to take a few days, after all the guests left, to sort through these things to make sure they were even worth keeping. Perhaps it was time to take some stuff out of storage and put it back to use.

But now wasn't the right moment to consider any of that. Derek dusted himself off, and made the final trip down, shutting the hatch to the attic behind him for the time being.

The room wasn't perfect, but it had to do. He laid out some fresh linens and bedding and declared it ready. If the guy, Kyle, didn't like it, he could sleep in the damn barn for all Derek cared.

It was getting late, and dusk had already set in by the time Derek was done. Lily and Clarice were still in the living room, chatting like they had years to catch up on, so he went out to tend to the animals. He finished his evening routine in a rush when another car rolled into the drive.

*Aidan and company,* Derek grudgingly thought. He should probably go out there to say hello, but decided instead to head out on his own for a bit of alone time in the woods. He'd see them all soon enough...

By the time Derek returned to McMillan farm, it was getting close to dinner time. Feeding a bunch of hungry shifters, especially bears, wasn't an easy task if one wasn't used to that kind of thing. No way could he leave Clarice to her own devices for this.

He went inside and said a quick hello to all the guests, who had made themselves at home in the lounge. Aidan had even lit the fireplace already, making the place look a whole lot like it used to, so many years ago when they were still kids.

Derek had to admit that it was nice, coming back to a house full of people for a change. Their cheer was infectious.

"Glad you could make it," Derek said while giving Aidan a quick hug.

"Any time." Aidan responded, then turned to face the decorated tree in the corner, his arm still around Derek's shoulder. "It's nice seeing all this stuff again, don't you think? Mom would be pleased it's still in use."

Derek had to admit Aidan was right. Their folks been gone a long time, but in a way parts of them would always be around. He caught a glimpse of Clarice leaving the room to heat up dinner.

Aidan let go of him and joined Heidi on the sofa.

They'd both found someone to share their lives with. That, too, would have pleased their parents. It was time to leave the painful past behind and look ahead.

———◆———

It was hours before Clarice got another chance to sit and relax. The voice that had been plaguing her all morning never really got totally quiet but was drowned out by the conversation of the guests descending upon McMillan Farm for the holidays.

But by the time she was in the kitchen on her own, filling the dishwasher with the empty remnants of dinner, her thoughts returned to the weird bout of sickness as well as everything else that had been going on.

*Clariiice! Soon!* The strange voice seemed to whisper.

What could it be? Had this been one of her novels, the sudden nausea would trigger suspicion.

*Wait, how long had it been since her last period?*

Clarice's heart raced as she tried to remember. It had been a while, for sure, but in all her planning for the holidays she'd completely lost track.

# BONUS STORY: SUGAR & SPICE

*But that's not possible, is it?*

She used to be on the pill but hadn't seen the need since Derek was pretty sure nothing could happen. She was human; he was a bear. They wouldn't be compatible enough to be able to have a baby. And yet...

Clarice sunk down onto one of the chairs and rested her elbows on the wooden table. Was this actually happening?

She wasn't sure how to feel about it and didn't get the chance to make up her mind.

"Sweetheart?" Derek opened the door and gave her a concerned look. "I know I've been asking this all day but are you okay? I was just walking by and could hear your heart beating much faster than normal."

Clarice didn't know what to say. *I don't know!*

He came up to her, resting one of his hands on her shoulder. She closed her eyes and tried to collect herself again.

*I think perhaps I might be pregnant...*

"You what?" Derek blurted out.

His eyes were wide open, mouth agape. *Shit. We're not ready, are we? I never even thought this was possible!*

"Are you sure?" Derek asked, and kneeled down on the floor beside her.

Clarice covered her face with her hands. "No. I'm not sure of anything right now."

He paused for a moment, then placed his hand on her stomach. "It's not possible," he whispered.

*And yet...* Clarice looked up again. Derek's brown eyes seemed to have turned a few shades darker.

"I never thought..." He took a deep breath and pressed his lips together.

Oh God, they were so totally not ready for this.

"I never expected I'd ever become a father." Derek looked helpless, his eyes moistening slightly.

"I'm sorry, I feel like I should have been more prepared," Clarice whispered.

He shook his head. "No. Don't."

She bit her lip. What were they going to do?

"This is nothing short of a miracle." He reached out to her, wrapping his arms tightly around her. His embrace filled her with warmth.

Clarice had been so distracted by all that had happened that she hadn't listened to her gut. She was scared. So was he, but more than that she felt a different emotion spill over from him into her. Derek, more than anything, was ecstatic.

Silent tears ran down his cheeks before falling onto her shoulder. "You'll make a great mom," Derek mumbled.

It was too intense, too much. Clarice couldn't help herself and started to cry as well.

"So will you. A great dad, I mean," she said, her voice cracking as she spoke.

Somewhere deep inside of her something else demanded attention. The mysterious voice was back.

*Soon. I'm coming!*

"Did you hear that?" Derek asked, pulling back and looking her in the face.

Although she wanted to remain serious, she simply couldn't. It started as a smile, quickly turned into a giggle and then a laugh.

"Oh my God, I've been losing my mind hearing this voice! It never occurred to me that you'd be able to hear it too," Clarice blurted out.

Derek wiped his face and eyes with the back of his hand and smiled back at her.

"That's her. Our daughter," he said.

"How do you know?" Clarice asked. "Is this normal?"

"It only happens with some couples; when the bond is particularly strong, they can hear the baby before it's born. Unfortunately not after, though."

"So she won't be able to simply tell us if she's hungry, huh?"

"Sadly, no. The connection is lost after birth."

"Wow. So much to learn," Clarice said.

"Yeah. We'll figure it out."

"I hope so." Clarice rested her forehead on his shoulder and closed her eyes. *Should we tell people?*

Derek got up, took Clarice by the hand and then gathered her up in his arms in one swift move. No matter how often he did it, she'd never grow tired of this.

"We'll get an appointment to see the doctor after the holidays and see how it goes. It's still early days, isn't it?"

Clarice wrapped her arms around his neck and rested her face in the crook of his neck. It had been a long and emotional day and tomorrow would perhaps be even longer, but his scent was stirring up something inside her that she couldn't ignore.

"How about we get some rest. I'll tidy up the rest of the kitchen in the morning before you get up," Derek suggested.

Clarice just smiled and held on tightly as he carried her through the now empty living room and hallway. She hoped he wasn't all that serious about resting just yet. She needed him more than ever right now.

Just before he carried her into their bedroom, she noted the two muffled voices filtering through the adjoining door; Lily's room. Clearly she'd had made up her mind on what to do about Kyle.

*You've got to be joking!* Derek thought, causing Clarice to chuckle.

*They already knew each other. It's a long story.*

Derek shook his head and walked over to the bed, laying her down gently against the pillows. He'd always been an attentive lover, but tonight he was even more so.

He undressed her slowly, savoring the view as he exposed more of her with each item of clothing removed. He lit up her skin with gentle kisses, worshiping her body even more so than normal. When he slipped his hand between her legs, she couldn't suppress a soft moan. Hopefully, they were too busy to hear her next door. But it wasn't just Lily and Kyle who were potentially listening in! What about the young life growing inside of her?

"You don't think she'll mind, do you?" Clarice whispered.

"I think as long as you're happy, she'll be happy," Derek responded.

That made sense, or at least, it was close enough to what Clarice wanted to believe. She relaxed again and focused only on Derek's fingers – how they traced her folds, caressing her, teasing her until she no longer cared about who heard what.

By the time he spread her legs wide, and kissed her most intimate lips, she had reached a different plane of existence. There was no room next door, no potential audience. There was only Derek, his tongue, and her pleasure.

She wanted to repay the favor, take him into her mouth and please him as he was pleasing her, but he wouldn't hear of it. Stubbornly he remained down there between her thighs: licking, tasting, tickling her.

Clarice's mind fogged over. All she was able to do was hang on tightly to the sheets beneath her and enjoy the ride.

Just before reaching the edge of her orgasm, Derek

pulled away and guided his thick cock into her slick entrance. She twitched and spasmed, eager for him to fill her completely. He was equally swept up in emotions as well as lust.

She reached out for him, her fingernails leaving marks on his muscular chest. He didn't mind. If anything, it seemed to encourage him to move faster, plunge into her deeper.

Above her, his face; the face she dreamed of when she went to sleep at night. The one who could set her alight just with his presence. She'd never felt so strongly for anyone, yet it was almost impossible to remember the time before him.

He was her everything, as she was his.

She closed her eyes for the final push, the final sprint towards their mutual goal.

Their minds felt even more connected now than before, if that was even possible.

He loved her more than himself; she could feel it in her heart.

As did she.

Her release was sudden and explosive, taking her breath away.

When he shuddered to a halt buried deep inside her and filled her with his seed, she felt a lone tear escape from the corner of her eye. She'd never considered that there could be anything better than the love they already shared. But now she knew that wasn't true.

In a few months, fingers crossed, there would be a third party to their relationship. A child. Half his, half hers.

She couldn't wait.

———◆———

On Christmas morning, Derek and Clarice got up early. So much to do, so little time. Although Clarice had insisted that she wanted to handle it all herself, Derek still followed her into the kitchen just in case.

He watched her go through the routine they had carefully planned out earlier; stuffing the turkey, putting it in the oven, starting the side dishes. She was relatively new to cooking, but she looked confident and in control. Most of all, she looked happy.

Within half an hour, their guests appeared one by one. Lily came in first and poured herself that all-important first cup of coffee. She joined Derek around the table in the center of the spacious kitchen. Kyle came in just minutes later.

Although Derek wasn't one to get involved in other people's private affairs, he couldn't help but notice how different they were with each other this morning. Clarice hadn't gotten around to telling him the whole story about how they knew each other, but Derek could tell they were even more familiar now.

He could only speculate about whether she knew about Kyle's true nature – and therefore, everyone else's.

*That's between the two of them,* Clarice's thought entered his mind.

He had to agree. There was no way either of them should get involved. Kyle always seemed like a sensible guy. He'd handle it if he hadn't already.

*Isn't it weird that nobody here has paired up with someone of their own species?* Clarice thought.

It was weird indeed, perhaps a sign that the old rules no longer worked in today's world. Derek didn't know how many bears were left in Scotland, but humans and even wolves greatly outnumbered them, that much he was certain of. And apparently they weren't so different after all, considering Clarice's current condition.

If they could breed, were there any limits to what they could do together? Perhaps in time, they'd see the other couples follow in their footsteps and have kids of their own.

These were the things Derek thought about while Clarice whizzed around the kitchen, cleaning, chopping and prepping things just as planned.

As soon as the rest of them came in, he took care of everyone's breakfast and got them out of her hair and into the living room. While everyone ate in silence, Derek was tempted to share the happy news with his brother against his own advice. He resisted, though.

What if something went wrong? It would only be more painful if everyone already knew about it. No, they should stick to the plan and wait at least until after they had the chance to consult a physician.

So they chatted about this and that, exchanged some gifts and even went out for a bit, giving Clarice some space to set everything up for lunch just the way she wanted. She'd evicted everyone, including Derek. Only Lily was allowed to stay back to offer a helping hand.

Most of the shifters took the opportunity to stretch their legs with a quick run through the woods. It had snowed overnight, leaving the surrounding countryside covered in a blanket of white. They wouldn't have been able to risk it elsewhere, but since the island was only sparsely populated, they didn't worry about leaving paw prints in the snow.

By the time they all got back, the room had been transformed. A perfectly set table awaited them, featuring the finest china and antique cutlery that had been in Derek and Aidan's family for generations.

Lily came in carrying a huge tray of roasted potatoes, followed by Clarice, who carried the turkey. The feast was ready and it was perfect.

Derek kept stealing glances across the table after everyone had seated themselves. Clarice looked happy, accomplished. Despite initial hiccups, everything had fallen into place. After so many years, McMillan Farm was hosting a Christmas meal.

They'd previously decided not to exchange gifts - shopping on the island was difficult at the best of times, and especially in winters when treacherous weather could strike at any time. But yesterday's news was the best surprise gift Derek could have ever asked for.

Every time he looked at her, he could feel the additional presence of their child. He'd been taken with her beauty from the first moment he'd seen her, two months ago, when she'd visited the farm as a tourist. But now, after everything, she took his breath away even more.

*We're going to be parents,* Derek thought.

Clarice looked at her plate and blushed. *I know. It's crazy.*

*I know I said to keep it under wraps, but I just want to shout it from the rooftop.*

*Me, too.*

Aidan had stood up to carve the turkey, but Derek gestured at him to sit back down. Clarice got up and joined Derek by his side.

"Just a moment, we'll get to eat soon enough." Derek took Clarice's hand and squeezed it gently. This was their moment, to hell with caution. "But first, an announcement..."

# ABOUT THE AUTHOR

---◆---

**Dear Reader,**

Thanks for reading the complete Scottish Werebears series. Although this is my debut series, I'm not new to writing in general. In fact, my mom still tells me to this day about how I would make up stories, and attempt to record them in my clumsy, shaky handwriting from the moment I learned to read and write. From there I went on to write fan fiction and other stuff meant for my own eyes only.

I've always enjoyed stories of the paranormal. Vampires, shape shifters, witches and magic, all featured in the books I loved the most, even when I was still growing up. But it wasn't until much later that I got into romance. One of the first writers (a self-published author just like me!) I came across was Tina Folsom, via her Scanguards Vampire series. I was hooked. From there I went on to read more paranormal romance until I found a new favorite kind of hero: bear shifters, like the kind written by Milly Taiden, Zoe Chant, and T.S. Joyce. What I love about bears is how they can be all strong and independent, a bit reclusive, and almost grumpy, but they always end up having a heart of gold (plus they tend to know their food, and we all know that a man who can cook is doubly sexy). All that (except for the shifting into a powerful bear) almost exactly describes the sort of man I ended up falling for and marrying in real life, so it's no surprise that this is what I started my publishing career with.

# LORELEI MOONE

**To find out more, check:**

LoreleiMoone.com (And why not sign up for the newsletter to be the first to find out about new releases.)

You can also get in touch with me via Facebook (search for Lorelei Moone), or email at info@loreleimoone.com

x Lorelei

CPSIA information can be obtained
at www.ICGtesting.com
Printed in the USA
BVHW041410131020
590916BV00010B/355